The
Shipyard Girls

Nancy Reve... ...writer and journalist under another name, and has worked for all the national newspapers, providing them with hard-hitting news stories and in-depth features. She has also worked for just about every woman's magazine in the country, writing amazing and inspirational true-life stories. Nancy has recently relocated back to her hometown of Sunderland, Tyne and Wear, with her husband, Paul, and their English bull mastiff, Rosie. They live just a short walk away from the beautiful, award-winning beaches of Roker and Seaburn, within a mile of where *The Shipyard Girls* series is set. The subject is close to Nancy's heart as she comes from a long line of shipbuilders, who were well known in the area.

The Shipyard Girls

Nancy Revell

arrow books

Arrow Books
20 Vauxhall Bridge Road
London SW1V 2SA

Arrow Books is part of the Penguin Random House group of companies
whose addresses can be found at global.penguinrandomhouse.com

Penguin
Random House
UK

Copyright © Nancy Revell 2016

Nancy Revell has asserted her right to be identified
as the author of this Work in accordance with
the Copyright, Designs and Patents Act 1988.

First published in Great Britain by Arrow Books in 2016

www.penguin.co.uk

A CIP catalogue record for this book is available from the British Library

ISBN 9781784754631 (paperback)
ISBN 9781473536746 (eBook)

Typeset in 10.75/13.5 pt
in India by Thomson Digital Pvt Ltd, Noida Delhi

Printed and bound in Great Britain by Clays Ltd, Elcograf S.p.A.

MIX
Paper from
responsible sources
FSC
www.fsc.org FSC® C018179

Penguin Random House is committed to a
sustainable future for our business, our readers
and our planet. This book is made from Forest
Stewardship Council® certified paper.

To my Mum and Dad, Audrey and Syd Walton.

Acknowledgements

A tribute must be made to the amazing women who worked in the shipyards during World War Two, whose strength and resilience, and the invaluable part they played in the building and repairing of ships has never been formally recognised or commended.

For help with the research, I would like to thank former female shipyard worker, Joan Tate, and her daughter, local historian Pam Tate, retired shipyard worker, John Bedingfield and his son Peter, author and historian Jack Curtis, journalist Sarah Stoner from the *Sunderland Echo*, the Sunderland Antiquarian Society, Sunderland Maritime Heritage, and Royal Navy historian, Jock Gardner.

A special thank you has to go to my mum, who has given me so much help and inspiration for the book in so many different ways – and who has always encouraged me to follow my dreams; to my dad for instilling in me a love and loyalty for the town in which I was born and brought up; and my sister, Jane, for her love, care and encouragement, and for sharing with me her and her husband Sion's three lovely children, Ivor, Matilda and Flynn.

I would also like to thank my agent Diana Beaumont for her belief in me as a writer, and the lovely team at Arrow, who are a continuing joy to work with.

And, finally, I could not have written this book had it not been for my husband, Paul Simmonds, who not only upped sticks and moved 267 miles from his hometown of Oxford to my hometown of Sunderland so that I could write *The Shipyard Girls* – but, for asking the question which started it all off, '*Did women work in the shipyards?*'

'Oh, 'tis love, 'tis love, that makes
the world go round!'

The Duchess in *Alice's Adventures
in Wonderland*, Lewis Carroll

The
Shipyard Girls

Chapter One

Sunderland

'Mr Hitler is *not* going to get in the way of my favourite little girl's birthday celebrations!'

Agnes Elliot's theatrical tone of voice and exaggerated facial expressions triggered an eruption of giggles from her two-year-old granddaughter.

Agnes had just placed the little girl's birthday cake in the black lead cooking range, and was feeling rather pleased with herself as she'd managed to make the cake from real eggs and milk. There was even a jar of her own home-made plum jam and half a teacup of icing sugar waiting on the side to make it into a proper Victoria sponge.

'Oh, and look at this.' Agnes pointed at the replica birthday cake her beloved grandchild was drawing on the back of an old washing powder box. 'Our very own Vincent Van Gogh.'

Agnes stood for a moment, looking down at this little girl happily drawing away, her legs stretched out on the threadbare floor rug, before her attention was diverted by the sound of footsteps hurrying down the tiled hallway.

'Ah, but he's not a patch on our Lucille,' Agnes's daughter Polly declared, announcing her arrival and bustling into the kitchen.

'Auntieee,' Lucille squealed with excitement.

1

'Look at you! What a bonny birthday girl you are.' Polly bent down to pick up her niece and gave her a big cuddle.

'You managed to get away on time then?' Agnes asked as she went into the back scullery to fetch some plates and cups and saucers.

'Yes, you know Mrs Hoggart, nothing's ever a bother.' Polly was balancing Lucille on one hip, whilst picking up her niece's crayons and artwork from the floor. 'Besides, it wasn't as if we were rushed off our feet. Dead as a door-nail more like. Who wants to have tea and cake sat looking out at a load of barbed wire? You can't even see the beach, never mind the sea. To be honest, I can't see the cafe stay-ing open for much longer – I think it might be time for me to get another job.'

Polly searched her mother's face for a reaction, but didn't see one since Agnes was only half listening. Her mission at this moment was to make this the best birthday possible, given the times they were now living in.

As Polly sat down at the large wooden kitchen table, balancing Lucille on her knee, she smiled. She had to hand it to her mum: she really was the master of make-do-and-mend, with a real knack for turning the ordinary into something special. Today she'd outdone herself with a candle lit in an old jam jar and some colourful wild flowers arranged in a milk jug. She'd even dug out some Christmas decorations and paper chains and hung them around the kitchen.

'Happy birthday, sweetheart,' Polly whispered into Lucille's ear. 'Let it be a happy, *and safe*, year for you.'

'About ten minutes for the cake,' Agnes declared, put-ting her best pink and copper lustre crockery from the town's famous Garrison Pottery on the table. 'Hopefully Bel will be back by then.'

The words were barely out of Agnes's mouth when a soft voice could be heard singing, 'Happy birthday to you, happy birthday to you, happy birthday, dear Lucille . . .' Bel's perfectly pitched rendition resounded down the hallway and through into the heart of the house, causing Lucille to cry out with glee that her mummy was home.

'Perfect timing,' Agnes said, smiling at her daughter-in-law, who was more like a real daughter than simply a daughter through marriage.

Isabelle, whom they had all called Bel for as long as they could remember, had been more or less a constant presence in the Elliot home since she'd been knee-high, owing to a mum who'd spent more time in the pub than at home, and no father worth mentioning. Bel and Agnes's son Teddy had only ever had eyes for each other, even as children, so it had been no surprise when they'd declared their intention to marry each other when they were just sixteen. Agnes had persuaded them to wait until they were both eighteen, and exactly nine months after they tied the knot Lucille had been born. But the little girl had so far been denied a brother or sister, as Teddy and his twin brother Joe had signed up within days of war being declared.

As Agnes's mind drifted to her two boys, she felt the heavy pull of worry in the bottom of her stomach and she had to consciously push away all thoughts of her sons, at least for the next hour. This lunchtime party was going to be fun. And frivolous. They were all going to have at least one hour off from this wretched war.

'I was just telling Lucille that Mr Hitler is not going to stop our favourite little girl having the best second birthday party ever,' Agnes told Polly and Bel as she pulled open the drawer of her kitchen dresser to retrieve the cutlery.

The two women both looked at Lucille and, like a comedy duo act, dramatically rolled their eyes to the ceiling, making the birthday girl chuckle.

'I saw that,' Agnes said in mock anger, without looking round. 'I have eyes in the back of my head, as you both know.'

'Ma, it's like you're waging your own personal war against the Nazis in this very kitchen,' Polly laughed, although she and Bel both secretly admired Agnes's stubborn determination to win at least a culinary war against the Germans. It never ceased to amaze them that, by hook or by crook, Agnes always managed to put food – and tasty food at that – on the table in spite of rationing.

'Oh Agnes, this looks lovely.' Bel stared at the mountain of ham sandwiches and the plate of oatmeal biscuits on the table. Her mother-in-law had even managed to get hold of an orange, which she had carefully peeled and cut into segments for them all to share.

'Now, let me just take a quick peek at that cake and see if it's rising.' Agnes grabbed hold of her oven gloves and bent down to inch open the heavy oven door. 'I don't want to let too much cold air in, just in case,' she muttered to herself as she squinted to see through the tiny crack of the partially opened stove door. But at that exact moment, the mournful wail of the air raid siren suddenly started up, sounding out across the town, and infiltrating the Elliot household and their joyful little party.

All three women looked at each other, shocked. This was the middle of the day.

Hitler's Luftwaffe had only ever visited their town at night. So far every single air raid warning had been during darkness. Indeed, it had only been these past few weeks that the physical reality of Hitler's malevolence had shown itself to the town. The first bombs had been dropped eight weeks before, killing two horses and obliterating a barn in

4

the nearby fishing village of Whitburn. The second attack had damaged the town's railway bridge and one of the shipyards, and the third had left a deep crater in the town's east end, just a few streets away from the Elliots' home.

So far there had not been any human casualties.

'No. Not today, of all days.' Agnes flung open the oven door and pulled out her half-baked cake. The middle of the piping-hot sponge immediately sank to form a crater. This was one battle the Germans were going to win in Agnes's small kitchen.

Polly snatched up their boxed-up gas masks from various corners of the room and, clocking the hesitation in her mum's demeanour, shouted, 'Come on, Ma!'

Agnes was clearly loath to leave her lovely – and hard-earned – birthday party.

'Damnation!' Agnes tossed her apron aside and followed the two young women and toddler out the front door.

As they hurried out, Polly grabbed her niece's favourite raggedy soft toy off the floor. 'Here you are, Lu,' Polly tried her hardest to smile and appear casual, 'your favourite bunny.'

She was determined that this little girl would not be left scarred for life by the sound of sirens and the explosions of bombs. The very least she could do as her aunty was try to pretend it was all a lark, a bit of excitement and fun, and not a terrifying run for their lives.

As they hurried down the street and towards the nearest air raid shelter, Lucille jiggled about like a baby monkey, legs tightly wrapped round Bel's thin frame.

'Do you want me to take her?' Polly asked.

'No, I can manage,' Bel said breathlessly.

Polly could tell there was no point in arguing, as she could see a pale-faced Lucille was not going to be peeled away from the safety of her mum's arms.

As the women joined the throng of people heading to the nearest underground sanctuary, not for one second did Polly or Agnes take their eyes off Bel and Lucille. Teddy had made his mum and sister promise to guard his wife and precious baby girl with their lives, although it was something both women would have done without even consciously thinking about it.

When Polly, Agnes, Bel and a wide-eyed Lucille arrived at the shelter underneath the old church, which also doubled up as a community centre during the week, they were immediately ushered down the steep stone steps and into the large, windowless crypt. Candles had been lit and there was a smattering of toys brought down from the nursery cupboard for the children to play with. Those who had arrived before them were busy putting up the black fold-up chairs for the more elderly members of this impromptu congregation to sit on.

Within minutes of arriving, Agnes was rallying the other children together and explaining to them that they were going to have a party to celebrate Lucille's birthday.

'There's not going to be any food or presents,' Agnes explained to the curious little faces listening to this dishevelled older woman with smudges of flour still on her face, 'but there's going to be plenty of games.'

Over the next hour Agnes, Polly, Bel and a few of the other mums helped to organise marble competitions, card games, pin the tail on the donkey, and even musical chairs, thanks to an old wind-up gramophone and a few scratched records which had been left there.

As Bel watched her mother-in-law organise this most unconventional of birthday parties, she counted her blessings that she'd fallen in love with a man whose family had taken her in as if she were their own.

When Teddy had signed up to go to war and asked her to go and live with Agnes and Polly, she hadn't fought his wishes. She hadn't wanted to be left alone with a new baby, worried sick about whether the man who meant the whole world to her would come back from this hateful war alive.

'I know you and Lucille will be in safe hands there. They'll look after you both until I get back,' he had told her as he'd packed up their few belongings to take to the house he'd been born and grown up in. And Bel had had no doubt that they would. Agnes had been more of a mum to her than her own mother, so it had been just like going back home, or rather going back to a home she wished she'd grown up in.

Bel was snapped back to the present by the sound of a series of distant explosions. The party fell silent as they felt the soft thud of each aftershock resound underneath. A while later, when the single monotonous sound of the all-clear siren could be heard, they breathed a collective sigh of relief and all emerged bleary-eyed from their self-imposed prison.

As Agnes, Polly and Bel, with Lucille holding both her mum's and her aunty's hands, walked quietly back home, they knew the German air force had succeeded in leaving its imprint on their hometown. Just like the Luftwaffe's ominous-looking emblem of a giant eagle carrying a large black swastika like a dangling piece of dead prey, its aeroplanes had released a succession of bombs from their metal talons over the skies of Sunderland. Although their own home had escaped unscathed, several four-thousand-pound bullet-shaped hulks of metal and explosive had succeeded in tearing up dozens of homes, as well as damaging gas and water mains on the other side of the River Wear.

For the first time since war had been declared, the town had suffered fatalities. An air raid warden had been killed, and the bodies of a family of three were discovered buried under the bricks of their kitchen.

7

The Battle of Britain was now well and truly under way, with one of Hitler's primary targets being the world-famous shipyards in Sunderland, County Durham, on the north-east coast of England.

The trio of women tried to lighten the mood as they walked back over the threshold of their home, but like Agnes's sunken cake, it was nigh on impossible to lift their spirits. The worry they all felt for the future, and, most importantly, for the future of this innocent little two-year-old in their care, hung heavily on them all.

Chapter Two

Two days later Polly handed in her notice and worked her last shift at the little cafeteria only a stone's throw away from the beach in Seaburn, which was just a few miles up the coastal road from Sunderland. Before the war, and especially at this time of year, the promenade across the road from Mrs Hoggart's tea shop would have been teeming with families enjoying a day out, the air filled with the smell of fish and chips and the screams and shouts of hundreds of children enjoying the nearby funfair.

But today, like just about every day since Hitler and his thugs had stomped into Poland in September the year before, the resort was more like a ghost town, with just a few locals taking a teatime stroll.

'You'll be missed, hinny,' Mrs Hoggart told her, giving her a big bear hug, but Polly could see that there was a part of her kindly boss which was also relieved. Polly hadn't been exaggerating when she'd told her mum that the cafe had been deathly quiet. The beautiful sandy stretch of beach directly in front of the tea shop was covered in landmines and was no longer visible through the barbed wire barriers that now formed an important part of the coastal defence. The small cafeteria had been far from a hive of activity for some time now, and Polly knew that Mrs Hoggart couldn't really afford to keep her on, but had done so through the goodness of her heart, knowing

Polly and her family would really struggle if she was out of work. Polly hated feeling like a charity case, so had been keeping a sharp eye out for any other job vacancies.

When she'd heard that the shipyards were taking on women she couldn't believe it. She had been thrilled to pieces, and had immediately made a beeline for the labour exchange in town to apply for a position – any position – in any of the town's nine yards. Because this wasn't just about getting another job for Polly – it was a dream come true. A dream she'd never thought could become a reality.

Polly had taken her letter of employment to show Mrs Hoggart, partly as a means of explaining why she was leaving her job so quickly, but also because she simply wanted to share her exciting news with someone else. News which, until today, she had more or less kept to herself.

At the top of the sheet of paper the words 'J. L. Thompson & Sons – Shipbuilders – Ship repairer, North Sands Yard, Sunderland' were embossed in big, bold, black lettering, then typed underneath came the words which Polly knew were going to change her life for ever: 'This is to certify that Pollyanna Harriet Elliot (employee number 111) is due to commence employment as a shipyard welder on 19 August 1940.'

'So, yer ganna be working in the yards? And a welder at that?' Mrs Hoggart hadn't able to keep the surprise out of her voice when she'd read the letter and seen where Polly was off to. 'Hard work but good pay.' Mrs Hoggart had tried to sound upbeat, but what she'd really wanted to say to Polly was that she thought she was as mad as a hatter, and that the yards were no place for a woman. But she hadn't wanted to upset Polly, especially as she seemed so overjoyed about her new job, so had simply said, 'Following in the family tradition then, pet?'

Polly had nodded with undisguised glee.

Mrs Hoggart knew that Polly, like so many others in the town, came from a long line of shipbuilders. Polly's brothers were riveters, the so-called 'kings of the shipyard', who worked in squads bolting together the great big metal sheets which created the shell of the ship. Her dad, who had died when she was just a baby, had been a plater – a hard job which involved cutting, burning and preparing the sheets of steel – and her granddad had been a boilermaker.

In fact, the family's employment in the shipyards dated back to the early 1800s, before the advent of steam and oil, when ships had been constructed out of wood and sail, and had transported coal and coke all around the world.

Polly had always been incredibly proud of her family history and her hometown, which was revered for its skill in building ships – a skill which had given Sunderland the title of 'Biggest Shipbuilding Town in the World'.

But Polly had also felt like an outsider. Because of her gender, she had always known she would never be a part of the rich tapestry which made up the fabric of the shipbuilding industry.

Until now. Until the start of this second world war.

As a general rule, shipyard workers weren't conscripted because their skills were needed to build and repair merchant vessels and warships, but many, like her brothers Teddy and Joe, had still downed tools and signed up. As a result, there were no longer enough men left in the town to keep the shipbuilding industry going. Their jobs now *had* to be done by the women – whether people liked it or not.

After leaving Mrs Hoggart's cafe, Polly nipped into the butcher's on Sea Road, and taking a shortcut back into town down one of the residential streets, she slowed her pace when she saw for herself the destruction caused by Thursday's lunchtime air attack. Her heart felt heavy

11

as she stared at a space where there had once been two houses. Homes.

Now all that remained was a pile of rubble.

'Bloody Jerry.' An old man spat out the words with venom as he shuffled past.

As Polly continued on her way, she saw yet more scenes of desolation, more homes brought to their knees. There had been twenty bombs dropped in this area on the outskirts of the town, all within a matter of minutes, and it showed.

'God forgive them,' she heard a woman, dressed from head to toe in black and making the sign of the cross, mutter as she pushed a pram across the road, away from another scene of carnage.

Polly stopped and looked at the dozens of smashed-up roof tiles that littered the carcass of what had once been a couple of new semi-detached, bay-windowed properties. Through the dust and debris she could just about make out the odd piece of furniture. Spindly wooden legs sticking out from plaster and brick. A flutter of fabric waving in the breeze like a forlorn flag. But it was the sight of a half-buried rag doll that made Polly catch her breath.

The big, round cloth face and outstretched yellow pigtails facing up to the sky was an image of the fate which could easily have befallen any of the adults or children living there.

Thank goodness it wasn't our street, Polly thought somewhat guiltily. She would never have wished this on anyone, but the thought this could have been her house, with the people she loved more than anything else in it, made her heart ache.

She turned away from the scene of devastation and the lingering smell of soot, burning wood and foul water that had poured out of the gutted buildings and still pervaded the air. It was not the noxious odours, though, that Polly carried with her while she walked home, but a great sense of purpose.

The four lives which had been so cruelly snatched away just forty-eight hours previously had made Polly's heart weep with sorrow, but it had also fired every part of her with an even greater resolution to do everything she possibly could to help rid the world of this evil which was sweeping across Europe, killing and contaminating everything it came across.

'If I can't fight alongside our Teddy and Joe,' Polly had sounded off to Bel when she'd told her about her job, 'then I'm jolly well going to step into their boots and do their jobs while they're away fighting and risking their lives to save ours.'

Bel had sighed and said, 'Oh, Pol. You've never been one to do owt by halves.'

There was only one slight blight on the horizon for Polly, which was causing her to feel a wave of apprehension as she walked home. It wasn't the prospect of starting a new job – and one of the toughest jobs in the shipyards at that – but the fact that she hadn't, as yet, told her mum.

Agnes was going to be furious.

And as she was due to start work on Monday at 7.30 a.m. sharp, Polly couldn't put off telling her any longer.

She knew her mum well enough to predict exactly how she was going to react and what she would say, for underneath her mother's soft exterior was an iron core, and if she perceived there to be any threat to her nearest and dearest, there would be another war on. And there was no doubt that seen through Agnes's eyes, the town's shipyards would most certainly be viewed as a threat to her daughter.

As Polly passed the Hudson Road School, which she had gone to as a child, and which was now closed for the holidays, she braced herself to turn into Tatham Street.

Passing the fruit and vegetable shop, which was just closing up for the day, and the Tatham pub, which was just opening, Polly crossed the road and walked towards her front door, steeling herself for the inevitable battle that was about to take place.

Chapter Three

As Polly approached her home she was greeted by a familiar sight. Agnes was washing the front doorstep. It was her mother's daily ritual. Polly had often wondered if this was her mum's way of telling the outside world that if the front of her house was nipping clean, then the inside was too.

'Hi, Ma,' Polly said, forcing an air of gaiety. 'Shall I put the kettle on for a nice cuppa?'

Agnes hauled herself up, putting her hand on the base of her back and stretching her spine into a gentle arch. 'That'll be nice. I'm parched.'

Agnes looked at her daughter and immediately noticed the folded-up letter in her hand. She knew there hadn't been any post today and felt her body bristle. Something was up and it wasn't good. That much she knew.

Seeing her mother's gaze drop to the letter of employment in her hand, Polly stuffed it back into her pocket, and out of the other produced a few slices of tripe wrapped in newspaper and tied with string. It was Polly's peace offering in advance.

'Look what I got from the butcher's on the way home – some tripe.'

Agnes cast a wary eye at her daughter as she dried her hands on her pinafore and made her way into the house. Agnes loved her tripe fried with onions; it was one of her favourite meals, which was just as well as it was also one of the cheapest bits of offal you could buy. But Agnes wasn't fooled. She knew her daughter better than she knew herself.

As Polly went into the kitchen and busied herself filling the kettle and putting it on the hot stove, Agnes sat down on a kitchen chair, back bolt upright. She waited, then, when the tea was made and a cup placed in front of her, she finally demanded, 'What is it? Spit it out,' her face now serious, her dark brown eyes piercing her daughter's greeny-blue ones. Eyes identical to Polly's father's.

'Ma, it's nothing to worry about,' Polly said, taking a deep breath and preparing herself for the fireworks about to explode in their little kitchen. 'Actually, it's good news. I've got myself a new job.' She tried to make her voice sound as light and carefree as possible, but didn't quite succeed.

A foreboding silence followed as Agnes carefully poured some of her tea into her saucer, raised the dish to her mouth and gently blew on the small brown lake of liquid to cool it down. Polly had rarely seen her mum drink her tea from an actual cup.

'*Where?*' Agnes said, her face like thunder.

'I've been taken on as a welder at Thompson's,' Polly blurted out. She tried to smile but it came out more of a grimace.

Agnes's face had now clouded over completely. She slammed her saucer back down on the kitchen table, tea splashing over the edges and on to the wooden tabletop.

'You're what?' she said, trying to keep a lid on her boiling fury.

'They're taking half a dozen women on to be welders,' Polly said. 'And I've been chosen.'

'Well, they're just going to have to unchoose you.' Agnes was incensed. 'No daughter of mine is going to work in the yards.' Her voice was getting louder, and they both automatically turned to look at Lucille as she started to stir from her later-than-normal afternoon nap in her cot by the side of the range. 'It might have escaped your notice, but the bombs they've been dropping these past few weeks have been targeting our shipyards. One hit the Deptford yard just the other day – in broad daylight – when everyone was there. Working.' Agnes spat out her words.

As if for protection from her mother's onslaught, Polly went to pick up her little niece, who had pulled herself to her feet and was beckoning for a cuddle with outstretched arms poking through the cot's railings.

'Yes, but no one was hurt, were they?' Polly shot back. 'They only managed to damage the engine works there.' She picked up Lucille, who immediately wrapped herself around her aunty like a little koala bear, nestling her sleepy face into Polly's neck.

'Only by chance and bad luck on their part!' Agnes's voice was starting to reach fever pitch. 'I cannot believe you,' she added incredulously. Agnes was so angry she could hardly get her words out.

'But Ma, the yards aren't the only places the Germans are trying to bomb,' Polly tried to reassure her. 'They're not too keen on the collieries we have here either.'

'Yes, but you're not going to work down the mines, are you?' Agnes snapped back.

'Ma, there's more chance of us being bombed here in our own home after what I've seen today walking back. They've hit more houses than anything else. I'm probably better off in the yards, the rate they're going.'

Agnes knew there was truth in her daughter's words, as the homes of the townsfolk stood more or less side by side with most of the town's industry.

'That might be the case now, but practice makes perfect,' Agnes argued back, 'and Jerry's aim is going to get better as time goes on.' But she knew her daughter well enough to know she wasn't going to back down. Polly had been a determined child and had grown into an even more determined woman, and like so many of the town's brave men, her daughter also desperately wanted to be a part of the war effort.

As if reading her thoughts, Polly said angrily, 'I mightn't be able to fight in the trenches, but I'm *damn* well going to do whatever I can here.'

'I'm your mother,' Agnes said, taking a deep breath, 'and I say you *can't* go to work at the yards.'

It was worth a try, but Agnes was far from surprised by her daughter's outraged response.

'You can't stop me, Ma,' Polly shouted back, causing Lucille to jerk her sleepy head up. Their mother–daughter argument had reached the *no you can't, yes I can* stage, but they both knew the very fact Polly was now an adult trumped Agnes's rights as a mother. 'Ma, it's all arranged. I start Monday morning.'

Agnes sucked in breath at the immediacy of her daughter's new job, but she still wasn't quite ready to capitulate. She gave one last throw of the dice. 'But Pol, welding's a man's job,' she implored. 'Working in the *shipyards* is a *man's* job.'

'Oh, how many times have I heard that one?' Polly said, exasperated, as she balanced Lucille on her hip and opened the larder door with her free hand to try to find some powdered milk. 'Ma, there's no more men here to do the "men's" jobs – it's up to us women now.'

At that moment Bel, still looking smart in her conductress uniform despite a nine-hour shift, came in through the front door, which had been left open. She'd just finished a relentless day working the Sunderland to Durham bus route and she couldn't wait to see her darling daughter. It pained her every day to leave her little girl at home, but they needed the money. She knew she was lucky in that she couldn't want for anyone better than Agnes to look after Lucille, but it didn't make leaving her all day any easier either.

As she walked down the hallway she caught the tail end of the ongoing argument and braced herself. When Polly and Agnes were at loggerheads it was like the battle of the Titans.

As soon as Agnes caught sight of Bel coming into the kitchen, she demanded, 'Did you know about this?'

Bel gave a quick sidelong glance at Polly before being distracted by her daughter's beautiful little face and breaking into a big smile. Every day Lucille seemed to look more like her handsome daddy. Or was it that the more time passed, the more Bel looked for those similarities to keep the memories of the man she loved as close to her as possible?

'Know about what?' Bel asked in all innocence, pulling a funny face to make Lucille gurgle with laughter.

'Polly's new job at Thompson's,' Agnes said, trying to soften the tone of her voice for the sake of her granddaughter, who was now giggling and revelling in her mum's return.

'No, I didn't,' Bel said, faking wide-eyed surprise wonderfully.

Not for the first time, Polly was in awe at her sister-in-law's hidden talent for acting. Polly had told her numerous times, 'You're wasted on the buses. You should be on the stage.'

With her corn-coloured curly hair and heart-shaped face, Bel also had the looks to be a budding starlet, but the nearest any of them had ever been to the stage was at the Regal, where they'd watched an occasional film or, more recently, newsreels of the latest war updates.

As Polly handed Lucille over to Bel, she whispered 'Thank you' in Bel's ear. It would have added oil to the fire had Agnes learnt that she was the last to know about her daughter's new job. Polly could easily foresee the apocalyptic outburst which would have inevitably followed had Bel let on she knew about the new job, with accusations of 'Am I really the last to know?' and a sarcastic 'Who am I? Ah, I'm only your mother' erupting from her mum.

Bel had always had Polly's back, even as kids when they were growing up on this very street. They'd both been small children when Polly had first brought Bel back home after finding her crying and hungry and shut out of her own house. Bel had gradually become a part of the Elliot household as she was frequently left home alone by her mother, who'd often disappear, sometimes for days on end, on what Agnes referred to as 'benders'.

Bel had never forgotten how Polly had rescued her that day, and as a result she was fervently loyal to her. She'd always stick up for Polly if she got into any scraps and had told her on numerous occasions, 'I'll always be by your side, Pol.' And she always was.

Today was no exception, although she'd have to play it canny and make Agnes feel she was really on her side if she were to bring her much-loved surrogate mum back down off the ceiling and stop that fiery Irish temperament of hers running out of control.

'Not only has our Pol just gone and signed up for a job down the yards, but as a welder, of all things,' Agnes said, gasping with disbelief.

'Really?' Bel said, faking yet more surprise.

'Yes, the very yards that are that madman's prime target. Is it not bad enough me two boys are out there fighting in some remote desert on the other side of the world, without me daughter sticking herself slap bang in the middle of one of the most dangerous places in the whole of the country?' Agnes's latent Irish accent was surfacing from deep within, as it always did when she was either angry, excited or had drunk a rare glass of stout.

'If everyone thought like that, Ma, then we all might as well start practising our German now,' Polly snapped, 'because that's the language we'll be speaking if we don't get the ships out to help win this war.'

'She's right, Agnes,' Bel quickly intercepted, knowing if she didn't defuse the situation now it was likely to get out of hand. 'The yards are desperate for workers. Most of the welders and riveters, like Teddy and Joe, have gone, or are just about to go. Someone has to step into their shoes. And besides,' she added calmly, 'you're always telling us: "You can do anything you want – just because you're a woman, it doesn't mean you're any less than a man."'

Agnes's mind scrabbled around for a convincing argument, but Bel was right. She'd always told Polly and Bel that they were as good as the next person – and the next man. She had become a victim of her own successful indoctrination.

And now that Bel was here and gently arguing Polly's case, the wind went out of her sails and Agnes slumped back in her chair.

It was true: when word had gone round that they were allowing the town's women to fill the positions in the shipyards left vacant by the menfolk, her first reaction had been, 'It's about time.' She'd never understood why they'd had women working in the shipyards in the First World War – some of those women had even been commended personally by King George V when he'd visited Laing's yard – but had then dropped them like a ton of bricks as soon as the war had ended. But, the mother inside of her argued, that was different. This was her daughter. And this was a different war.

The shipyards that lined the River Wear were renowned for their excellence, as well as their closely knit production sites, and it was exactly for these reasons that they had become one of the main targets for Hitler's bombers. Because of this the whole town now lived under a dark and threatening cloud, constantly vigilant for the distant drone of the Luftwaffe's planes.

Agnes knew she wasn't going to win this argument. Wild horses wouldn't stop her Pol from starting this job. 'How any daughter of mine has ended up so pig-headed is beyond me,' she said, defeated but adamant she would have the final word.

Polly and Bel exchanged a look of relief. They had won. Agnes had capitulated.

The two girls drifted out into the backyard and unpegged the laundry and bedlinen Agnes had put out on the line earlier on in the day, and which was now bone dry.

Agnes stayed at the kitchen table, sipping at her saucer of tea and getting lost in thought.

Polly's determination to work in the yards shouldn't have surprised her. She should really have seen it coming. She'd always loved to hear about her older brothers' day when they came back from working in Doxford's shipyard. And when she was little she was forever begging her mum to take her down to the docks to see the latest launch. Her favourites were those made from Bartram's further down the river on the south dock, as it was the only yard in the whole country that launched directly into the sea, which made it far more unpredictable and risky as the waters could be turbulent and cause the ship to keel over if the tugboats guiding it out didn't do their job properly.

Polly had never been a great one for dollies or playing house. Not like Bel, who had loved nothing more than to sit in the kitchen and watch Agnes cook and then go off and pretend to be 'mummy', and feed and clothe any of the little baby dolls Polly had discarded through lack of interest. Polly had always been a bit of a tomboy. It probably hadn't helped that she'd been brought up with two very loud and energetic brothers – and twins at that. But Agnes thought Polly's boyish tendencies were more likely due to the fact that she'd been trying to compensate for not having a dad, just like Bel had been trying to make up for not having much of a mum by pretending to be one herself.

As her mind wandered once again to her darling Harry, Agnes got up and walked into her bedroom. She opened the top drawer of her bedside table and took out her husband's medal. Her Harry had been taken from her too soon, during the final weeks of the First World War in 1918, and now Agnes lived in constant fear that the same fate would befall not only her boys, but her daughter also.

Polly had just been a baby and the twins two and a half when Harry was declared 'missing presumed dead', but Agnes had tried to keep his memory alive, not just for her own sake, but for the sake of her two boys, and for her little girl who had never even got to meet her own father.

And she'd done a good job – perhaps too good, as Polly had hero-worshipped the dad she'd never known, especially when she'd learnt he had given his life for King and country. She'd demanded her mum tell her in exact detail everything about her dad: how they'd met, got married, had children; what he looked like; what his job had been before he'd left for war. Everything.

The one thing Agnes could never answer was where Harry had died. His body had never been found, and so there was no grave to visit.

The only physical reminder Agnes had been left with was a medal to commend her husband's sacrifice and his bravery, the Military Medal for 'acts of gallantry and devotion to duty under fire'. It was a medal Agnes cherished like the Crown jewels themselves. Even more so. If Agnes had been offered a swap, it wouldn't have mattered how poor they were, there would never have been any doubt: the medal would have won over every time.

Agnes's reverie was broken by the sound of clattering pots and pans and Polly's voice shouting out, 'Ma, I'm going to get the tripe on now. Where've you hidden the onions?' Her daughter sounded more relaxed now she'd dropped her bombshell and come out of it relatively unscathed.

'Where they always are,' Agnes shouted back. 'Open yer eyes.' She couldn't be angry with Polly for long, or sad for that matter. There was too much of that about these days. 'And put some tatties on the boil while you're at it,' she said, walking back into the hub of the kitchen.

Chapter Four

As Rosie Thornton climbed the three storeys up to her small bedsit at the top of the big red-brick Victorian terrace, half-way up the second flight she met Mrs Townsend, one of the more elderly residents, carefully making her way up to the next landing. The old woman's gnarled arthritic hands grasped the staircase banister and used it to pull her aged body up the steps one by one.

'Hello, Mrs T,' Rosie said, carefully taking the pensioner's arm.

'Ah, is that my Rose?' The old lady half turned to look at the young woman who was gently helping her up the final few steps to her floor. Her eyesight was so bad, blighted by cataracts, she now relied heavily on her hearing, which was as sharp as a pin. She recognised Rosie's confident tone, which had only a hint of a north-east accent.

'Yes, Mrs T, it is. How are you today?'

Every time Rosie came across Mrs T going up or down the steep staircase, she wondered why the landlord wouldn't give her accommodation on the bottom floor. It really was beyond her. She was amazed the old woman left her room at all.

'You off gallivanting tonight?' the old woman asked as she took a breath after finally making it to the top step.

Rosie smiled. The old woman might be half blind and barely able to walk, but she didn't miss a trick.

'Yes, Mrs T. But I don't think you could class it as *gallivanting*. I'm off to see my sister and her children over in Shields.'

Rosie hated lying, but she didn't have an option. Mrs T didn't know that she didn't have a sister, or any other family there for that matter. But it was better than her knowing the truth.

Also, by saying she was going over to South Shields, which was a good hour's bus journey away, it would explain her late-night return if Mrs T was still awake. And it was more than likely she would be. Rosie couldn't remember ever seeing the old woman's door shut. It didn't matter how quietly Rosie would tiptoe back up the worn carpeted stairs late at night, she was sure she always heard her.

'Well, I wouldn't blame you if you were out *gallivanting*,' the old woman chuckled. 'Believe you me, I used to when I was a young 'un. I'd foxtrot until I dropped,' she said, laughing to herself and hobbling her way over to her front door.

As Rosie said goodbye to Mrs Townsend and continued up the next flight to her own room, she felt sad that she couldn't get to know her neighbour better. She could tell Mrs T had been a live wire in her day and she was interested in her life and the times she'd lived in. She bet herself Mrs T had some tales to tell. But those stories would have to go untold because Rosie had to be careful. She wouldn't allow herself to become too friendly with anyone in her building.

Rosie had stayed here longer than normal, but she just couldn't face moving again. Her usual tenancy in the rooms she rented was six months. She'd already gone over that now. And it was showing: Mrs T knew she went out most nights and was curious.

She always tried to avoid being friendly with anyone else living in her building, preferring complete anonymity if at all possible. That was the way she liked it. She didn't want to get any more acquainted with her neighbours beyond the odd 'Hello' and a polite 'How are you?'

She climbed the last few remaining steps up to her room, giving a weary sigh as she thought of the evening ahead. She may have just completed a shift of overtime, but her work today was still only half done. When Rosie turned the key and stepped into her own living quarters, she was hit by a sudden feeling of loneliness. You didn't have to be Mrs T's age to feel isolated and on your own.

'Stop feeling sorry for yourself, Rosie Thornton,' she said out loud to the sparsely furnished room. 'Get some tea down you and get going,' she mumbled. She put a kettle on her little two-ring gas hob and cut herself a few slices of bread to make a sandwich. As she opened up a tin of corned beef, she realised just how hungry she was after a day's work. But her working day was far from over. She needed money, and so she needed to work. In fact, Rosie needed a lot of money, more than any other young, free and single woman living on her own in a cheap bedsit in the poor part of town.

After she'd drunk her tea and eaten her sandwich, Rosie stood up and, like most nights of the week, took off her daytime work clothes, gave them a good shake and carefully folded them up, before going over to the basin and giving herself a good washdown. She quickly towelled herself dry and then opened up the large mahogany wardrobe, which was far too big for the amount of clothes she actually owned. She reached up to the rail and took out the garments she needed for her evening job.

The clothes she was now having to change into were very different from the ones she wore during daylight hours. Her baggy overalls were replaced by a tightly fitted black skirt cut just a fraction below the knee, her cotton work shirt exchanged for a clinging low-cut blouse.

Rosie dabbed the tip of her eyeliner on to her tongue before she carefully drew a line up the backs of her legs to give the illusion she was wearing a pair of silk stockings. As she did so her mind started to wander. She could almost hear her little sister's voice asking, 'Why are you doing that, Wosie?' Her baby sister, Charlotte, had never quite mastered her R's when she was small and although she now had, her big sister had remained 'Wosie'.

Rosie wondered what Charlotte was up to now.

'Hopefully in bed and reading a book,' she said, again aloud to her empty room. Rosie reprimanded herself. She really must stop talking to herself. Anyone hearing her would think she was daft in the head.

She looked at her small collection of theatrical make-up – pots of white face paint, powder, and red face crayons she had bought from a second-hand shop – and she wished more than anything she could use it on Charlotte for the purpose for which it had been made, as dressing-up-for-fun make-up.

Instead she used the creamy white face paint sparingly as a pale foundation, covered it with a light layer of powder and dabbed the red clown paint on her cheeks in place of rouge, and on her lips instead of lipstick. She then got her black eye pencil, the same one she'd just used to draw on her make-believe stockings, and carefully created dark, defined, arched eyebrows in the shape of those sported by Hollywood sirens Carole Lombard and Betty Grable. She then opened up a little square cardboard box of mascara. With a tiny wetted brush she gently created a paste before applying it to her long eyelashes. Rosie was very frugal with how much she used, as some of the other girls at work were now having to resort to burnt cork. Real make-up had become a rarity due to the increasing amount of items being rationed, and had she not needed it for work, Rosie would have happily gone without.

Again Charlotte's voice came into Rosie's head and sounded in her mind as clear as if her little sis were right next to her. 'Let's play pretend,' she heard her saying.

It was her sister's most repeated request. Charlotte had a wonderful imagination. She never really needed toys, just someone else who would 'play pretend' with her. And despite the seven-year age gap, Rosie had always enjoyed their fantasy games too. The pair of them would go into secret worlds, making up stories of magical lands full of talking animals and wicked witches, which, of course, they would slay with their imaginary weaponry. Either that or they'd try to concoct perfume from mashed-up flowers and leaves, or make dens from old sheets and blankets.

But when Rosie's mind wandered to images of their mum shouting for them to come in for tea, and she remembered the lovely smells which had always seemed to be drifting out of their kitchen, she had to stop herself. This wasn't the time or the place to think about her mother or father. They would have to stay in their special compartment, shelved in the deep recesses of her memory, for the time being. Rosie only allowed herself to look in there on special occasions.

Come on. Get a move on, Rosie, she told herself, only this time the words were voiced silently.

Rosie freed her thick, naturally blonde hair from the confines of the headscarf she wore for work, brushing it out and expertly pinning sections back to create a coiffure of rolls and waves that swept away from her face. Looking at herself in her small compact, which she treasured as one of the few precious belongings she had of her mother's,

Rosie was satisfied with her speedy transformation. Her mask was now in place.

She forced her tired feet into a pair of popular Mary Jane-style shoes with their dainty ankle straps and higher than normal heels, and stepped across to fetch her full-length grey mackintosh coat which was hanging on the back of the door.

Rosie was just about to leave when she hesitated, turned around and walked back over to her bed. Bending down, she pulled out a box from underneath its metal frame. She sat back on the mattress, took the top off the box and carefully picked out a neatly folded letter from underneath a small pile of wage slips and pound notes.

A flicker of emotion broke through her newly created mask, a mixture of both joy and sadness as she sat and read. The letter, like all those she received from her little sister, had been read and reread many times over.

Dear Rosie,

How are you? I'm using the fountain pen you sent me for my birthday to write this letter. Do you like it? I love it and all the girls are very envious. You always send me the best presents. The ones they get from their parents are really boring or old-fashioned. I think they all wish they had an older sister like you too.

Term is just about to end and everyone is getting excited about the summer holidays. Even the younger girls aren't so weepy at night because they know it's only a few weeks before they go back home.

I can't wait to go to Mr and Mrs Rainer's because then I know it won't be long before you come and visit.

You seem so far away – you ARE so far away.

There's lots to tell you. The most exciting news is that I have learnt to swim. It was really scary at first. We were all

*in the swimming pool freezing and shaking. Then our PE
teacher Mr Evans gave us all little green cans with a handle
on each end and said, 'Pick up your feet, girls, and kick.' I
started kicking my legs out, making a right splash and then I
was floating forward!*

*Now I don't need the cans and can do breaststroke.
Mr Evans says I'm a natural and next week we're going to
learn front crawl and backstroke.*

*Anyway, in answer to your questions in your last letter:
Yes, my favourite subjects are still French and art.*

*And, yes, I'm 'eating well'. All the girls here moan
awfully about the food, but I don't mind it. I'm always hungry, and always manage to get seconds. The dinner ladies
say that I must have hollow legs as I eat so much and yet I
still 'haven't a pickin' on me' (their words). I say I take after
my older sister. Remember how Mum used to despair at how
we were both always hungry and she'd tell us off if we ate
anything before our meals?*

*Anyway, don't worry, no one is bullying me, and yes, I'm
behaving myself and haven't been in any trouble. I'm being
as 'good as gold' (your words). And yes, I have a nice friend.
She is a new girl and her name is Marjorie. She's from New-
castle. She knows Sunderland. I told her I did go to Newcas-
tle once but I was very young and cannot remember it very
well. She has something called asthma which makes her short
of breath and she wheezes a lot during the night so the other
girls are always moaning at her.*

*Matron has just shouted 'Lights out!' so I will send this to
you tomorrow.*

*I wonder how long it will take to get to you? I hope this war
ends soon as last time it took weeks for your letter to get to me.*

I love you oodles (my new word).

Charlotte x

PS I will write and tell you about sports day. Marjorie and I are doing the three-legged race together. I hope it doesn't rain.

Reading her sister's words always buoyed Rosie up. It made what she was about to go and do bearable. Worth it. To know her sister was well and happy and was getting a good education was all Rosie wanted.

She knew Charlotte would be enjoying her summer break with their parents' elderly friends, Mr and Mrs Rainer, who would undoubtedly be spoiling her rotten. They had never been able to have any of their own children and so lavished all their unspent love and care on Charlotte.

Rosie shuddered when she thought of what would happen to Charlotte if she couldn't afford to keep her at her state-funded boarding school.

She would never forget the words of the welfare worker who had come to see their neighbours after their mum and dad had been knocked over and killed by a hit-and-run driver. 'They've no other family then?' she'd asked the neighbours.

Rosie had been sat at the top of the stairs, secretly listening to the harsh-sounding social worker.

Charlotte, who had only just turned eight, had been asleep in their kindly neighbours' spare room. She had fallen into an exhausted slumber after crying more or less non-stop after being told that her mummy and daddy had died. It had been of no consolation to her, or to Rosie, that the two most loved and most important people in their lives had 'gone to heaven'. 'But I want them *here*. Not in heaven!' Charlotte had raged.

Rosie had also been filled with an incredible anger, followed by the deepest hurt and sorrow she had ever felt in her whole life.

But when the initial shock of losing both her parents had started to sink in, she'd begun to become aware that this was not the end of her and Charlotte's tragedy. In fact, it was just the start. And it was then that Rosie's survival instinct had kicked in.

She had heard the old couple, who had taken them into their home only as a temporary measure, quietly asking the woman social worker, 'What's going to happen to the children?'

And that was when her decimated world had crumbled even more. Her mind had raced. They had no grandparents, nor any other family. Certainly none they knew about, or none who had ever visited them at the home they'd lived in all their lives in Whitburn.

It was only when she heard the butch-looking child welfare worker again asking if they had any relatives, here or in any other part of the country, that a deep feeling of dread had overwhelmed Rosie. She was about to turn sixteen and knew enough of the world to understand what happened to children when they were orphaned.

Although Rosie had never felt poor, as she and her sister had always had shoes on their feet and food in their bellies, their parents had not been rich, or even really comfortably off. Rosie knew instantly where she and Charlotte would be sent by the woman from the welfare – the infamous children's home run by the Poor Sisters of Nazareth in Sunderland. It was called Nazareth House and took in orphaned babies and children, as well as youngsters who were deemed uncontrollable or had been accused of petty crimes.

A few years previously, the mother of one of her school friends had suddenly become unwell and died. The girl's father had been killed in the First World War and so she'd been sent to live with the nuns in town.

About a year later Rosie had seen her old friend, but had hardly recognised her. She had the look of a dog that was regularly thrashed, her eyes barely able to connect with

Rosie's, and when Rosie did manage to stop her and say hello, her once vibrant eyes had looked dead. There was no life left in them. And certainly no joy.

Rosie had been shocked to see bruising on her friend's skinny arms, and when she'd watched her walk away she had even seen welts on her legs.

When she'd told her mum about the girl, Rosie had asked, puzzled, 'I thought nuns were meant to be kind, like Jesus was?'

'Mmm.' Her mum had taken her time in answering her daughter's query. 'Sometimes people are not always what they appear to be. Sometimes a person is meant to be a certain way and they aren't.'

It was the first time Rosie had seen a snippet of another world. A crueller world, very unlike the one she had been brought up in.

And so, sitting at the top of the stairs, and realising that the social worker was going to send them to the same place which had changed her friend and taken the life out of her, Rosie had been resolute: she and her little sister would never spend even one night under the nuns' roof.

It had taken some doing, but she had succeeded in keeping them both out of harm's way. But it had come at a cost.

Taking a deep breath, Rosie folded up the letter, placed it back in the box, and returned it to its hiding place under the bed.

She stood up straight, putting on her coat and buttoning it up so it covered every inch of her brash ensemble, before quietly leaving her room, shutting and locking the door, and tiptoeing as quietly as she could back down the staircase.

As she did so she was hit by the smell of suppers being cooked, the cry of a child and a sudden burst of laughter. She yearned to be on the other side of the doors she passed, with a loved one, or sitting round a table for a family meal. But that seemed not to be the kind of life she was destined to live. The cards Rosie had been dealt early on in life had left her with a poor hand, but like a professional poker player she had become a master of making a bad hand work for her. She was adaptable if nothing else, and had become a great illusionist – as well as a convincing liar.

Rosie made her way along Grange Terrace, heading out of town. She walked to save the money she would have spent if she had taken a bus, which was tempting as she lived practically next door to the main bus depot in Park Lane. Within ten minutes she'd gone from the fume-filled streets of the town centre to the plush suburb of Ashbrooke, with its wide, tree-lined avenues of grand Victorian townhouses. Even the colourful names of the streets – The Esplanade, The Oaks, The Elms – spelt out the area's affluence.

Rosie walked along one of the main streets, the houses of which overlooked the prestigious cricket club, before turning down one of the side streets. She then hesitated and looked about her to see if there was anyone around. The street was quiet. No one was there. Rosie then quickly slipped down a cobbled back lane where the rear entrances of the three-storey houses of the street called West Lawn could be accessed.

Shining out of one of the ground-floor rear windows of the third house down was a small, discreet but nevertheless distinctive red light.

Chapter Five

Rosie lifted the small brass knocker on the back door and rapped it three times. She saw the glint of light escape through the little spyhole, before the door was unbolted and opened, letting out a warm gust of smoky air mixed with the smells of a variety of different perfumes and the tinkling sound of a piano being played.

As she stepped into the hallway, it was like being transported from a world of black and white into one of Technicolor, like the film *The Wizard of Oz* she had taken Charlotte to see, when the main character Dorothy enters the land of the Munchkins and begins her journey down the Yellow Brick Road. Rosie only wished that, as it had been for Dorothy, this peculiar world she had just entered, and which she visited every other evening, was actually only a dream. But it wasn't.

Rosie took a big breath and pasted a smile on her face. 'Hello, George,' she chirped as she saw one of the regulars.

'Hello, Rosie. You look as gorgeous as ever this evening,' said the man in a smart blue three-piece suit as he handed his overcoat, fedora and leather gloves in to the little makeshift cloakroom, attended by a pretty young girl.

George was a First World War veteran who was as much a friend as he was a client. He had a large scar which ran from his temple, skirted past his ear and ended at his jawline, as well as a slight limp that he refused to acknowledge with the use of a cane.

'Rosie. *Enchanté*. Lovely to see you, my dear. Come through – we've got a gentleman here who is very keen to meet you.' The voice which beckoned Rosie through to one of the high-ceilinged reception rooms belonged to a small, slightly plump older woman with a blaze of ginger hair, which was piled high on to her head in a slightly chaotic bun. Loose wisps of hair framed her ageing but attractive face. Her voluptuous shape was wrapped in a meringue-shaped dress consisting of layers of red taffeta, corseted in at the waist with a plunging neckline to show off her ample bosom. The extravagant evening gown trailed lightly on the carpet underfoot and rustled as she walked. This may have been 1940, but looking at this wonderfully attired woman, anyone would think they were still inhabiting the grandeur and opulence of the Victorian era.

Rosie knew the woman as Lily, although she doubted that was her real name, just as she knew the French accent was also most certainly not authentic. But no one here cared whether Lily was from Paris or Portsmouth. This place was for men who wanted to escape reality, even if it was just for a few hours, and if they had to pay for it, then so be it. Rosie knew that most of the men who came through the door saw the services she and the other women gave as either a reward for surviving battle, or a refuge from the threat of imminent death.

Of course, they came for pleasures of the flesh, but many of them also came to drink, smoke and sing, and for the chatter and the laughter. And Lily made sure that was exactly what they got. There was never a sad face here within the confines of this house of ill repute, or rather this bordello, as Lily preferred to call her establishment. Lily often repeated her motto, 'All they want is a little love, a little laughter.' And if she caught any of her girls looking gloomy or down in the mouth they were ushered into the back kitchen and told to 'buck up' or shown the door.

Rosie was one of Lily's favourite girls as she always had a smile on her face from first walking through the door till when she left. And Lily was no fool: she could see that there were plenty of nights when Rosie was tired or worn out, but she always managed to disguise it well, or at least well enough for her clients not to notice.

Lily gently took Rosie's arm and ushered her into the front room, which was filled with a handful of men and women chatting and smoking and looking as though they were just having a quick drink before heading off to the theatre.

'Ah, Mr Jones, your escort for this evening has arrived. Meet Rosie, who is looking as radiant as ever this evening.' Lily always made sure she gave her girls lots of compliments.

An older man in an admiral's uniform, who was sitting quietly on his own, pushed himself out of a creaking leather armchair and stood up to shake Rosie's hand and introduce himself.

Rosie thought he looked kindly, if not a little sad. Sometimes the men who came here didn't always want a night of passion, but just to relax and enjoy some female company and conversation. Rosie hoped this might be the case for this evening's client, but somehow doubted it.

The man asked Rosie if she'd like a drink, and when she declined he politely suggested they should 'perhaps retire upstairs'. Like a true gentleman, he took her arm and guided her towards the wide staircase, and the mismatched pair slowly made their way up to the first floor before disappearing into one of the half-dozen rooms which lined the thickly carpeted landing.

Later on that evening as Rosie was preparing to leave, Lily beckoned her into the kitchen. 'Do you want a cuppa before you go, Rosie?' she asked as she put the big cast-iron kettle on to the stove. 'Or do you fancy something a bit stronger?'

'I'll just have a quick cuppa, thanks, Lily. I've got work tomorrow, so best keep a straight head.'

The two women chatted about the bombings which had started, and seemed to be getting more and more frequent across the whole of the country, as well as in their own town.

'I heard your old home and some of the other fisher-men's cottages were the first to take a beating from the Luftwaffe,' Lily said.

'I know, but no one was hurt, from what I can gather.'

It was clear Rosie wanted to change the subject – she hated talking about her past to anyone. Lily was about the only person who knew a little about her childhood, her parents' sudden death, and the reason she came here to work every other night. She had confided in Lily one evening over a large glass of port that had gone straight to her head and lowered her defences. It had felt good to confide in another person about her life, and as Lily was herself a businesswoman and had a good head for figures, she had listened carefully when Rosie had told her how she'd managed to juggle the money she earned at the yard and what she earned at Lily's to pay the fees for Charlotte's boarding school.

Although Lily had no children of her own – none that Rosie knew about anyway – she had been interested in hearing about the state boarding school Charlotte went to, where the actual education was free, it was just the board and lodgings which had to be paid for.

'There would have been no way I could have afforded it if I'd had to fork out for both,' Rosie had told her, 'and luckily there was enough money left in Mum and Dad's will to pay for the entire first year straight off.' She'd admitted, 'The school still think that's where the money for Charlotte's fees comes from, and I've done nothing to make them think differently.'

She had, however, told a little white lie when she had said to the school's headmistress that she worked as a secretary at the yard – and not as a welder. Just like she hadn't mentioned that her dad had also been a welder who had worked at the local colliery just up the road from where they lived in Whitburn.

'You have a good head on your shoulders,' Lily had told her. 'Anytime you want to come into business with me, just say and we can talk.'

Rosie hadn't wanted to say that her work at Lily's was just meant to be temporary until she found another way of funding Charlotte's education, so she'd just smiled.

Sometimes Rosie regretted Lily knowing her background, as she hated anyone knowing anything about her, but she knew it wouldn't go any further. Lily could be very verbose but she didn't tittle-tattle about her girls' personal lives.

Sensing their chat about Rosie's old home had touched a raw nerve, Lily changed the subject. 'Well, you just be careful in that shipyard of yours. It's that they're after destroying. I don't want anything happening to my favourite girl,' she said with a serious face, counting out Rosie's earnings for the evening.

Rosie smiled. Lily called all her girls her 'favourites', but she knew Lily had a soft spot for her and, more than anything, liked her because she never caused her any grief. Rosie was also a good listener, and Lily loved to reminisce about her time in Paris and any news she heard from her old friend who was still over there.

'There's a roaring trade over the Channel,' Lily told her. 'The soldiers are actually queuing up outside many of the Parisian bordellos.'

Both women were astute enough to know why. The climate of these unpredictable times was very much to enjoy every hour of every day – if you could. Rosie certainly wouldn't judge the men who used establishments like Lily's. She'd never been one to judge, just as she hoped others would not judge her.

'And it's not just the Parisians who are enjoying a boom in business,' Lily continued, 'but over here too, especially in London.'

There had already been a number of occasions when Rosie had come to work to hear Lily complaining that she'd lost another girl to 'the bright lights'. It appeared an increasing number of young women were going to work in the capital's red-light district. Some were staying there for the duration, and some would just go there to work on the weekend before heading back home to their normal jobs, and their families. There was no doubt that there was decent money to be made, and even though many goods were now being rationed, you could still get most things on the black market if you had the readies.

'They call the girls down there the Piccadilly Commandos,' Lily informed Rosie. 'They work in an area of the city called Soho. It's the red-light capital of London. Well, of the whole country really.'

As Rosie got up to leave, Lily couldn't resist telling her just one more piece of salacious gossip she'd heard from her Parisian madam. 'In some of the more upmarket establishments, they're starting to put a blue light above the door instead of a red one,' she said, almost whispering it to Rosie as if it were a great secret. 'It's to show the punters that the house is primarily for those higher up the ranks, or for the upper gentry,' she explained, before adding, 'I was actually thinking of doing the same here and replacing the red light in the back window with a blue one. What do you think?'

Despite her tiredness and her eagerness to get home, Rosie had to chuckle. 'Oh, Lily, if you do that, you won't get any punters. Everyone'll think it's a cop shop, not a knocking shop.'

Both women burst out laughing.

'Ah, Rosie, I do believe you might be right,' Lily hooted. 'And that's the last thing we want here – any boys in blue turning up. Having said that, it's not unheard of to have some of the local constabulary here on the odd occasion.'

Both women were still chuckling as Lily opened the front door and Rosie stepped back into the cold, dark night.

'You take care on your way home,' Lily told her before shutting the door and returning to the last of her guests.

Chapter Six

Rosie stood in the darkness and opened her handbag, feeling around for her little electric torch. Without it she would only be able to see a few feet in front of her as these streets, like all others in the country's towns and cities, were blacked out. No lights were even allowed to shine out from any windows. The Ministry of Information had repeatedly told the general population, through broadcasts and newspaper announcements, that if the streets were lit up, enemy aircraft would easily be able to find their targets by identifying the town's shape. Now cars had hoods over their lights to direct their beam to the ground, and buses were sprayed grey, with half their windows painted blue. But plunging a nation into such darkness had its problems, and there had been a number of pedestrians knocked over and killed crossing the road. White lines had been painted around the edge of vehicles so that people could actually see them, and the government had even gone as far as to advise anyone out at night to wear light colours to help them remain as visible as possible.

'You should be wearing white,' Mrs T had nagged Rosie on more than one occasion when she'd seen her slip out in the early evening.

'Oh, white's not my colour,' Rosie had joked back. 'Besides, it's a nightmare to keep clean.'

In reality, though, the last thing Rosie wanted was to be seen. Her little electric torch, which was permitted providing it was used sparingly, did the job of allowing her to see where she was going, but at the same time allowed her to remain as invisible as possible. Besides, Rosie liked the dark, not just for its ability to keep her movements a secret from prying eyes, but because on a clear night she could see all the stars in the sky. She would often just stand after a night at Lily's and look up into the inky darkness embedded with its glittering diamonds. She'd allow herself to be transported back to her childhood home, where she'd often lain in her bunk bed, with Charlotte sleeping underneath, and looked out of their bedroom window and up at the night sky, listening to the rhythmic sound of the waves gently lapping against the nearby rocks.

When Rosie got back to her bedsit, she grimaced when the wooden floorboards squeaked as she made her way up the first flight of steps. On reaching the second landing, she breathed a sigh of relief to see Mrs T's door was, as usual, ajar, but her light was out.

At the third floor she quietly opened her own door and gently shut and locked it behind her. She sat down in front of her dressing table and removed her garish make-up. With her mask removed she wiped all thoughts of her evening's work out of her mind. She hung her work outfit up in her oversized wardrobe, pulled on her nightie and climbed into bed.

She was exhausted.

Within minutes of laying her head on the pillow, Rosie was dead to the world. That night, though, her dreams were muddled. Charlotte was swimming in a large lake, laughing and shouting at her big sister to come in. She could see the outline of her mother from behind as she picked winkles from the granite-grey rocks jutting through the sand. And she saw her father's masked face showing her how to weld on a little table in their yard just a stone's throw from the beach.

But it was the appearance of a cruel face from the past which caused Rosie to wake in the morning feeling unsettled. The image of the familiar face from her old life stayed with her as she climbed out of bed and changed into her overalls, pulled on her boots and wrapped her hair up in a headscarf.

As she forced herself to eat some toast and marmite, washed down with a cup of tea, she pushed back the images her sleep had conjured up. There was no time to dwell on dreams which didn't make sense, or faces from the past she wanted to forget. She had to get to work.

Rosie hurried out of her room and down the stairs. She focused her mind on the challenges of this new day. Like most of her fellow workers she loved and hated the shipyards in equal measure. They were a hard taskmaster, and the work itself was gruelling and could be hazardous, but the yards had also provided her with work when she'd desperately needed a job, and there was no denying they were an exciting and vibrant place to be – full of life, noise and chatter. Rosie may have been an outsider in many ways in this life, but in the yards she was part of a massive team, and every time she saw a ship launch she never failed to feel a deep sense of pride that she had been a part of its making.

Today would be particularly different and challenging for her as this week her new batch of trainees were all women. The yards were normally only inhabited by metal and men. These new women who were coming into the yard to work were another sign of the times. This, at least, was one of the positive changes the war had brought about. Women throughout the country were finally being allowed to edge nearer to an equality which had been terribly out of kilter for too long, by being permitted to work in environments which were normally the domain of the menfolk. Rosie was determined to play her part in helping the half-dozen women she would start teaching this morning to be a success, and to forge a permanent place in the shipyards, both now and after the end of this damnable war.

Chapter Seven

Monday, 19 August

Agnes had lain awake most of the night, her head full of too many thoughts and feelings to be able to sleep. She'd realised from the moment her daughter had told her about her new job that she didn't have a cat in hell's chance of preventing her from working in the shipyards. But that didn't stop her from being worried sick. She had managed to let off some steam yesterday evening when her next-door neighbour Beryl had asked if she could borrow some tea, something Beryl had silently wished she'd done without as Agnes had promptly poured out her woes.

'As if it isn't bad enough that me two sons are thousands of miles away fighting in a land I didn't even know existed, now my daughter's cock-a-hoop at getting a job at the one place that madman's determined to obliterate,' Agnes had ranted. 'She's going to be like a sitting duck. Bang in the middle of what has already been the target of every single bomb dropped on the town already. I used to feel as proud as punch of the shipyards,' she'd vented, barely drawing breath, 'chuffed to pieces that our yards were a thorn in that Nazi's backside. But *now*,' Agnes had reached her crescendo, 'the yards have become a great big thorn in *my* backside.'

A tired Beryl had vigorously nodded her agreement. All the men in her large family also had jobs in the shipyards.

Both their families had helped build the warships, and a great many of the merchant vessels which had kept the country from starvation in the so-called 'war to end all wars'. Beryl had seen the worry and fear in her friend's face and knew them only too well. She had a husband and three sons at war, but even before they'd all joined up, Beryl had lived with the long-standing worry that the men she loved could be injured or killed at work. It was certainly far from uncommon. Both women knew of just about all the tragic accidents, many fatal, which had happened at the yards over the years.

After Agnes had worn herself – and Beryl – out, they'd said their goodnights and Agnes had forced herself to go to bed, where her mind had drifted back to what had seemed like a different lifetime, when Polly and the twins were just young children and would come trooping in for their supper like miniature musketeers, all breathless and rosy-cheeked from playing out. Polly in particular had never failed to arrive back home looking as if she'd been dragged through a hedge backwards, always demanding her mum look at some grazed knee or bloodied cut, like it was a war wound she was proud of.

As the morning light started to filter through the blackout curtains, Agnes recalled how she had told all three of her children on countless occasions when they were growing up, 'You can't be soft in this life.' As a single parent, with no man in the house, and barely two pennies to rub together, she'd needed to be tough.

In hindsight, Agnes thought that perhaps she might have been too hard on all of her children, especially Polly, whom she had treated more like a son than a daughter.

'It's your own fault,' Agnes reprimanded herself as she lay there looking at the large spots of mould in the corners of her bedroom ceiling. 'You were so obsessed with making sure she could look after herself, it's no wonder she wants to do a man's job.

'Well, you can't start wrapping her up in cotton wool now,' she argued with herself, as she gave up on sleep and padded through to the kitchen, taking care not to wake the rest of the house, especially little Lucille. Once she was up, no one would get any shut-eye.

As she started slicing up her home-made bread to make up the day's sandwiches, Agnes remembered how her greatest fear as a woman on her own had been that there would be no one to look after her children should anything happen to her. Her own parents were dead, and she had lost touch with her older brothers and sisters, most of whom were still over in Ireland.

Now that her children were all grown up, that fear had been replaced by an even worse dread: that something would happen to them over which she had no control. The Nazis or the shipyards were both easily capable of maiming or, worse still, killing her cherished bairns.

Agnes's worries of doom and gloom were broken by Polly's cheery 'Morning, Ma' as she walked into the kitchen and gave her mum a quick cuddle, before putting the kettle on to the stove to make a pot of tea. Spotting the mammoth sandwiches her mum was making, Polly laughed, 'Oh my goodness, Ma, I don't think I'll be able to get my mouth round them, they're that big.'

Polly too had barely slept a wink, but it was a mixture of excitement and nerves which had kept her awake most of the night.

A few moments later Bel, carrying a bleary-eyed Lucille, traipsed into the kitchen. She also did a double take at Agnes's oversized doorstep sandwiches.

'No sandwiches for me today, thanks, Agnes. I think I'll go to the canteen for a change.'

Polly took Lucille out of her sister-in-law's arms. 'Morning, little bundle of gorgeousness,' she said, giving her a big kiss on her cheek and popping her into her high chair.

Lucille watched wide-eyed as the women who adored her worked in unison to get the breakfast ready. Polly made a large pot of tea, and placed it out of Lucille's reach in the middle of the table to brew. Agnes stirred up a pan of oats to make a smooth porridge, while Bel fetched the jug of milk and a small bowl of sugar out of the larder.

As they all sat down to eat, Agnes told them sternly, 'Get plenty down you. Both of you. But you especially, Pol. Heaven knows you're going to need it today.' Agnes mightn't have been happy about her daughter's new job, but she was damned if she was going to let her go to work without a hearty breakfast and a filling lunch to keep her going.

'By the looks of those sandwiches, I'll have eaten enough to sink the *Titanic* by the afternoon,' Polly said, making Bel splutter on her tea.

After they'd all eaten their breakfast and the bowls and cups and saucers had been washed up and put away, Polly grabbed her boxed-up gas mask and her holdall bag, and slung them both over her shoulder.

'Right, I'm off now,' she announced. 'I can't be late on my first day.'

'Have you got your packed lunch?' Agnes demanded, following her daughter down the long hallway to the front door.

'Yes, Ma,' Polly said, turning and giving her mum a hug. For the first time Polly saw her mother's age. She seemed smaller and a little vulnerable. 'Don't worry, I'm going to be just fine,' she said, hurrying out the front door and on to the pavement.

'And remember, you're—' Agnes began to say.

'—as good as the next person!' Polly shouted back.

Chapter Eight

Polly made her way down to the quayside, joining the teeming mass of flat caps which from afar resembled a huge colony of worker ants, all moving in the direction of the numerous shipyards lining the River Wear. It was just after seven in the morning, but the east end was already alive, echoing with the sound of hobnailed boots on cobbled streets, and full of the hubbub of chatter and the smell of cigarette smoke. Polly felt invigorated and was hit by an overwhelming sense of purpose and belonging.

By the time she dropped down on to Low Street, which hugged the south side of the river's edge, she was jostling shoulder to shoulder with a crowd of fellow workers all headed towards the ferry that would take them across the breadth of the Wear to Thompson's at North Sands, which, as the name suggested, was on the north side of the river.

The ferry was already half full with dozens of workers either chatting to their fellow travellers or quietly gazing out to sea. As she paid the halfpenny fare to the ferryman who stood on the top of the stone steps leading down to the gently bobbing steamer, Polly noticed a few workers quickly slip behind him unnoticed.

As the *W. F. Vint*, her name painted in big black letters on the bow, moved slowly away from the dock, Polly felt adrenaline start to pump around her body, like the swell of the water beneath. She leant against the iron railing which ran around the side of the overcrowded, oval-shaped vessel and lifted her face skyward to feel the cool sea breeze gently blowing away the last vestiges of sleep still clinging to her.

The ferry picked up speed, and she looked back at the receding stretch of the quayside and saw the fishermen mending their crab pots and preparing their nets ready for their next haul. A group of four young children ran out of the big harbourmaster's house and started to play tag, breaking off to wave at the ferry and the other assortment of ships, minesweepers, tugboats and steamers bobbing on the water.

Five minutes later the ferry's live cargo disembarked on to the north dock. Polly was pulled along the two-hundred-yard stretch by the growing wave of bodies heading towards the imposing iron gates of her new place of employment. At the side of the wide gated entrance to the shipyard stood the timekeeper's office. While Polly stood in line, she watched each worker shout out their own unique identification number to the little man whose wizened face poked out of the counter. Each worker was given a whitewashed piece of card known as a 'board', on to which was scrawled their number and start time. It was just a few minutes before seven thirty and Polly knew from her brothers, when they'd worked at the yards, that if you were even just a few minutes over the start of your shift, you'd have time docked off your wages.

'One one one,' Polly shouted out when she reached the timekeeper, trying to sound as confident and as loud as the men who had preceded her in the queue. The old man's deadpan face flickered with a rare show of interest, before he scribbled on her board in pencil, handed it back to her and shouted, 'Next!'

Within seconds of walking through the gateway of the shipyard, Polly was greeted by a piercing wolf whistle followed by a 'Hey, bonny lass! What's a girl like yer deein' in a place like this?'

As there were no other women around her, Polly could only presume the comment was directed at her. It didn't matter that she was in the midst of a throng of other workers crowding into the expansive yard, Polly felt as if she had a spotlight pointing on her, following her every step. As she looked to see who the harsh, heavily accented voice belonged to, she saw a small gaggle of men, all easily old enough to be the father she'd never had. But their behaviour was far from paternal. Polly felt as though every inch of her body was being inspected as she walked to the offices on the far side of the yard. She had never felt so clumsy, uncomfortable or self-conscious walking just a few hundred yards.

However, the shipyard leeches weren't the only ones to have noticed Polly. 'Put a sock in it, yer load of old has-beens!' a woman's voice blared over to the gang of gawkers.

Polly turned round to find the slightly scary voice belonged to a very pretty blonde, who looked much younger than she sounded, probably only about a year or so older than Polly herself.

'Don't take any notice of them,' the woman said in a much gentler voice. 'They're full of hot air.' The woman with the Jekyll-and-Hyde voice introduced herself to Polly with an outstretched hand. 'Hi, I'm Rosie. I'm one of the welding instructors here.'

'Oh, what a coincidence. I'm starting today – as a trainee welder,' Polly said, shaking her hand.

Rosie smiled. She'd guessed as much, had been keeping an eye out for what she called her 'new recruits', the half-dozen women who'd been mad enough to sign up to do this punishing job. She'd spotted Polly a mile off – eyes agog, staring around her as she walked through the towering metal gates. It was the familiar look of a new-comer. A shipyard virgin.

As Polly walked with Rosie over to the prefabricated building with the sign 'Welders' Office' hanging above its door, the yard's starting hooter sounded out the beginning of the working day and Polly could feel the buzz of activity around her notch up a gear. Dodging the other men heading straight for their particular work areas, the two women arrived at the small single-storey office building, which had been constructed with a mixture of steel and aluminium panels.

Inside they saw an old man sitting behind a desk, and two women standing to the side looking like fish out of water.

'Trainees?' Rosie asked them both.

Both women nodded.

'Hello, I'm Hannah,' the younger of the two introduced herself. She was very small and softly spoken, with thick, dark hair which had been cut short. Polly picked up a hint of an accent which wasn't British, but which she couldn't quite put her finger on.

'And I'm Gloria,' the other, older woman said, with more volume and confidence, and with a dialect that showed she was Sunderland born and bred. Polly was surprised that a woman who looked around the same age as her mum would be here, starting a new trade – and as a welder at that.

Just then the door opened and two other women trooped in, one after the other.

'Ah, and the rest of my new flock,' Rosie said. 'Come on over here and let's get you all signed in and then kitted out.' She pointed to Frank, the old man behind the desk, who was now looking at the women with wide-eyed wonder.

'It's not every day yer see the gentler sex here in the yards,' he cackled. 'Apart from you, of course, Rosie,' he added with a mischievous twinkle in his ageing, pale blue eyes. 'Yer a true rose, fer sure,' he chuckled. 'Lovely, but with a load of spiky thorns to contend with,' Frank laughed, before breaking out into a hacking cough.

Rosie liked Frank, but felt sad for him too. He had worked in the shipyards all his life, and would die here too. His cough wasn't due to smoking, like so many of the men who worked here with their roll-up cigarettes hanging out of their mouths. Frank's bad chest was down to the fumes he'd inhaled for the six decades he'd spent hunched over smouldering steel. Rosie was glad the yard's manager, Jack Crawford, had made sure he'd been given a job to see him through his dotage after it was clear he wasn't up to welding any more.

As Polly stood in line behind the other women, she was pleased to see that most of them looked as nervous as she felt. All except one, an uncommonly tall and well-built woman who appeared totally unperturbed by her surroundings.

'Martha Perkins,' the woman announced to Frank, who was clearly struggling not to show his shock at the mountain of 'gentler sex' which stood before him.

All five women stood in line and, in turn, gave their full names, dates of birth, and their last employer, if they'd had one. Each piece of information was written down in the appropriate columns in a big Employees Book.

Polly tried her hardest to hear what each woman had been doing before signing up for this job, but the noise outside seemed to be getting louder by the second and she struggled to hear even what they were called.

Then, all of a sudden, the door was flung open and a young girl came flying into the office. 'Sooo sorry I'm late,' she gushed, not sounding the least bit sincere. 'I got completely lost and ended up in the boiler room on the other side of the yard!'

Rosie scowled at the woman, reminding Polly of her Jekyll-and-Hyde voice. Polly made a mental note not to get on the bad side of her new teacher.

Rosie pointed to the desk. Frank, suppressing a smile, asked, 'Name?'

'Dorothy, but everyone calls me Dot,' the girl said, breathlessly.

'Dorothy . . .' Frank said as he scrawled in his spider-like writing. 'And does Dorothy have a surname?' he asked, now all official.

'Williams,' Dorothy replied, forcing a smile and looking around at the other women.

Dorothy gave her date of birth, which Polly quickly calculated made her seventeen. Her previous job had been as a shop assistant at Binns, the town's main department store. Polly wondered why Dorothy was swapping drapery for machines and metal.

'Thanks, Frank,' Rosie said, before guiding the newcomers out of the door and into the supply building next door. 'Right now, let's get you all into your new gear.'

The women stood and stared at the wooden shelves full of piles of denim overalls, shirts, boots and protective gloves. Martha was the first to walk over and start riffling through the assortment of sizes.

Polly didn't think she had ever seen such an incredibly hulky woman before. Martha's hands alone were bigger than most men's, and she probably had more muscle on her than the rest of them put together.

'She'll be lucky to find something that fits her,' Dorothy whispered to Polly as they followed Martha's lead and started picking out appropriately sized clothing. Polly shot her new workmate an icy look and moved away. Polly had known a few 'Dots' at school and couldn't abide any kind of bitchiness.

'Come on, we haven't got all day.' Rosie hurried them along.

Ten minutes later the six women stood looking ever so uncomfortable in their new but ill-fitting overalls. All of them apart from Martha had had to roll up their sleeves and their trouser legs, and had used leather belts to try to hoick up their oversized overalls to make them a better fit. Their new footwear was a pair of ankle-high black leather lace-up boots.

For the first time in her life Polly was actually glad she had what her brothers had always teasingly called 'great big plates of meat'. Her feet were far from petite, and she'd always struggled to find nice shoes to fit her, but today they were just about perfectly sized.

Rosie laughed, 'Welcome to the shipyards. It's a man's world here, with man-sized clothes. But,' she added helpfully, 'if you're handy with a needle and thread and want to tailor your new work gear to fit better, feel free. These elegant garments are going to be your new second skin from now on, so it might be a good idea to make them as comfy as possible. Besides,' she said, 'you'll be forfeiting a small amount out of your weekly wages until you've paid for them.'

Polly heard Dorothy gasp in disbelief.

Rosie pointed them to a row of lockers along the back wall where they could keep their belongings, and explained to them the whereabouts of the women's lavatory.

Apart from being a little swamped, Polly felt quite at home in her new clothing.

'I don't think we'll be making it into *Vogue* anytime soon,' Dorothy chirped up, pulling her belt tighter to accentuate her voluptuous hips even more.

Martha stared at Dorothy as if she'd just spoken another language, while Hannah and the other young woman, Mary, let out a quiet chuckle.

'With this job you won't have the energy left to even read a copy of *Vogue*, never mind be in it,' Rosie said with a straight face before taking them out into the yard.

Like a female Pied Piper she led them all over to an area of the vast concrete yard not far from the edge of the quayside, where there was a long wooden bench with half a dozen box-like welding machines by the side and a smattering of goggles and large metal welding masks on top.

'Help yourself,' Rosie instructed them all, pulling on a pair of long leather gloves that went up to her elbows.

As Polly picked up her new heavy headgear with a small rectangular window in the middle, she felt a ripple of nervousness run through her body.

'This is going to be your new best friend,' Rosie told her new recruits in all seriousness. 'You two are going to become as close as the sheets of metal you'll be welding together.'

Polly's face was a picture of earnestness as she soaked up every word, every instruction Rosie uttered.

'This ugly metal mask is going to be the sole protector of your eyes, face and neck,' Rosie continued, glaring at Dorothy as she started fiddling with one of the buttons on her overalls. 'It's going to protect you from flash burns and sparks of metal, which can leave you permanently scarred, and also from the heat of the metal, which can give you the worst sunburn ever. You'll blister and scar, and it'll hurt like hell.' Rosie's voice went up an octave in order to get Dorothy's full attention. 'The little rectangular window,' she said, pointing to the tinted glass box jutting out of her own mask, 'is covered with a filter that will stop you being blinded by the weld's ultraviolet light.'

Polly listened intently as Rosie explained that the helmet also prevented something called 'arc eye', which happened when the cornea of the eye became inflamed.

'Not to put you off this job before you've even begun, but this is one of the most painful conditions known to man – and woman,' Rosie warned. 'And I speak from experience. It feels like your eyes are never going to stop watering, like you have a thousand glass splinters stabbing into your eyeballs. It's complete and utter agony. It'll come on in the middle of the night, make you feel you've got the fever from hell, and your head is about to explode with the worst headache ever. And,' she added, 'if you weld for long enough without protection you will actually burn the retina of the eye – and if this happens, you'll be using a white cane for the rest of your life.'

Polly didn't think she'd ever dare lift the mask off her face, just in case.

As Rosie moved on to the workings of the welding machine, which produced the electricity to enable them to arc-weld, Polly felt overwhelmed with information.

And she wasn't the only one. 'I feel I back in the school,' Hannah nervously whispered in broken English to Polly.

'I know,' Polly agreed, thinking that Hannah looked young enough to still be at school.

While Rosie continued to talk to the women about their equipment, Polly felt slightly in awe of this woman who knew so much, and was so confident and skilled. But more than anything she was just glad their teacher was a woman, and not one of the aged Lotharios she'd encountered earlier on.

'The indicators on your welding machines show the voltage. The higher the voltage, the more intense the heat.' Rosie tried to make it as simple as possible. 'But now for the exciting stuff,' she said, taking a long black lead connected to the welding machine, and picking up what looked like a metal alligator's jaw. 'This is called a stinger, which attaches on to the end of the lead, and is used to grip the metal rod.'

She switched on her welding machine, which buzzed to life, and then pulled down her helmet. The women followed suit.

'Take two pieces of this scrap iron,' she said, shouting above the drillers that had just started up nearby, 'put them close together, then place your rod on to the metal plates.'

As Rosie did so, a small explosion of sparks flared up like a brilliant white firework. A shock of excitement rushed through the circle of women. Their eyes were glued to Rosie's hands as she steadily moved the rod from left to right. It looked as though fire was flowing from the tip of the rod, creating a pool of metal which moved like a slow, placid stream.

'And then there is one,' she declared. The completed weld had fused the two pieces of metal together in a straight line, leaving a dainty feathered pattern.

Polly thought how easy Rosie made it look.

'Like sewing a patchwork quilt,' Dorothy said.

'Yes, exactly,' Rosie agreed. 'It's like sewing up a seam but with molten metal instead of cotton. Right, your turn now,' she said to the women, switching off her machine and laying down the rod and stinger on the workbench.

'How exciting,' Dorothy exclaimed.

'And no talking. Just concentrating,' Rosie said, making it quite clear who this last instruction was aimed at.

The next two hours seemed to pass in two minutes as they all practised their welds – with varying degrees of success.

As the morning wore on, the noise in the yards seemed to get more and more intense and Polly could tell Rosie was beginning to struggle to be heard above the banging, clashing and clattering that seemed to be enveloping them all.

At the stroke of midday, a bellowing klaxon horn sounded out. Immediately a cloak of calm and quietness descended across the yard. Polly had never imagined there could be so much noise, and within a matter of seconds, such quiet.

'Lunchtime,' Rosie declared.

Polly and the other women, faces now smudged with streaks of sweat, soot and dirt, followed Rosie over to a resting area where they were to eat their packed lunches. Martha plonked herself down on the ground, sitting cross-legged, while the other women sat on some nearby wooden pallets.

Rosie took a walk over to the canteen to grab herself a thick-crusted meat pie, but came back to eat it so as to keep an eye on her fledgling welders.

As Polly started to chomp on her mum's doorstep Spam sandwiches, she didn't think she'd felt so hungry in her entire life. Or so exhausted. She was relieved she wasn't the only one to feel so drained when Gloria announced to them all, 'Well, I don't know about you lot, but I'm knackered.'

'I am too,' perked up Dorothy. 'And we've still got the rest of the afternoon to make it through.'

Polly felt like telling her if she didn't chatter on so much she might conserve some energy, but then decided that was a bit unfair. Dorothy looked as shattered as Polly felt. She also noticed her hands were shaking involuntarily.

Everyone agreed they were jiggered. Even Martha, who looked as though she had the strength of a Trojan, nodded her head up and down and started to massage her right arm.

A silence fell over their small group as they all munched on their lunches. Polly looked around the rest of the yard, glad to let her eyes relax and enjoy the break from the intensity of staring at a sheet of scorching metal. She watched as small huddles of men sat quietly chatting and eating their food, the occasional blast of raucous laughter breaking through the relative calm. A little raggedy tea boy busied around the workers, balancing a long metal pole on his shoulder with tea flasks jangling against each other ready for a refill.

Polly marvelled at the mammoth ships moored by the riverside. Some were on the slipways getting ready to head back out to sea, another, not far from where they were sitting, was in the dry dock, half built and looking like the iron-ribbed skeleton of a massive Moby Dick just waiting to be fleshed out and brought to life.

As she sat enjoying the feel of the sea breeze on her face, her attention was suddenly drawn to a large, flat-bottomed wooden boat bobbing gently by the side of the dock. A couple of men wearing dungarees were pulling on thick ropes slung around what looked like a huge pulley. It was as if they were trying to land some gigantic fish from the depths of the river. Enthralled, Polly watched as they pulled and pulled, eager to see what they were trying to reel in.

Finally she saw the glint of an enormous round metal helmet breaking through the surface, water pouring around its three small portholes. What looked like a giant's body, encased in a thick green canvas body suit, slowly appeared from the depths of the river.

Helped by the ropes which were attached to the suit through metal rings, the giant slowly climbed up the iron rungs of the ladder at the side of the boat. It was like seeing a deep-sea monster comic book character come to life in front of her very own eyes.

By now Polly wasn't the only one to have spotted this strange apparition being hauled out of the river. 'Wow,' Dorothy exclaimed.

'Blimey,' said Gloria.

'*Bože*,' said Hannah in a language none of them recognised.

Martha and Mary didn't say anything but both looked totally agog.

'That's Tommy Watts,' Rosie explained. 'One of the deep-sea divers employed by the River Wear Commissioners. It's the diver's job to repair and do just about anything underwater that needs to be done to a ship, in the port, or anywhere along the river. At the moment we've got a team here to help with the repairs. It saves time and money if the ship can stay in the water rather than be brought into the dry dock.'

The women watched, entranced.

As soon as Tommy's big steel-capped boots thudded on to the boat's decking, the tug-of-war workers immediately started to unscrew nuts and bolts around the bottom of his copper helmet, which was attached to a metal corselet covering his shoulders and the top part of his body. As they carefully unscrewed the helmet and lifted it off, Polly was mesmerised to see Tommy's pale, angular face appear. She didn't think she had ever seen such a serious but also such a bold and handsome face in her life.

The other women lost interest and started to chat amongst themselves, but Polly couldn't tear her attention away from Tommy as she watched him speaking to the workers unhooking ropes, as well as a thick rubber tube, from his diving suit.

Then, all of a sudden, as if sensing he was being watched, Tommy turned his head around and looked up to the quayside. When his eyes fell on Polly, it was his turn to stare. His piercing hazel eyes looked straight back at her. He too seemed unable to drag his gaze away.

For what seemed an age, but was only really a matter of seconds, they both remained motionless, staring into each other's eyes, captivated by one another.

Suddenly feeling embarrassed, Polly looked away, but she felt his stare linger. A feeling of awkwardness overcame her and she self-consciously dusted crumbs from her overalls, relieved to hear the horn blaring out, signalling the end of their lunch break.

'You're going to be making beads this afternoon,' Rosie told them. 'And I don't mean the kind you wear round your neck, Dorothy.'

They all giggled in unison. Dorothy blushed, but was obviously delighted at being singled out.

The women clustered around Rosie as she showed them how drops of molten metal could be used to bind the sheets together. When the women tried it themselves there was much hilarity.

'They're meant to look like cable stitching,' Rosie told Martha, who was struggling with the more delicate side of welding. 'Or a miniature twisted rope,' she said, looking over Gloria's shoulder and noting how precise her welding was. Rosie reckoned she was the oldest person she had ever taught, and she was surprised at how quickly Gloria was picking up her new skill.

As Rosie moved round the table, she saw Mary was doing well, but looked as though her mind were a million miles away. Hannah, on the other hand, was struggling. Her hands were trembling and her beads were more like misshapen blobs.

'Keep going.' Rosie tried to be encouraging. 'It takes a while. Welding's not something you can learn overnight.'

Hannah forced a smile but her delicate face was white as a sheet, despite the heat from her rod. Polly's face, on the other hand, was pure determination. That girl's going to make a decent bead, even if she has to will it to happen, Rosie mused.

By 2 p.m. Polly felt as if it should be finishing time. Tonight she knew she would sleep like a log.

'My welds were better this morning,' she told Rosie, rattled. 'It doesn't make sense.'

Rosie took hold of her rod. 'Here, let me show you. You're holding it too far away from the metal.'

Rosie moved from woman to woman, taking care not to feel as though she was hovering over them and making them feel nervous. Every now and again she would show them a better technique, or give them a few words of praise.

By the time the klaxon went for the end of the shift at half past five Rosie had to suppress a chuckle as she saw the look of total and utter relief wash over the dirt-smeared faces of her new recruits. She had quite an eclectic mix of women to teach, and, without a doubt, had her work cut out.

She knew at least one of them wouldn't last the week. For the entire time she'd been doing this job, she'd not once had every single trainee stay the course. Rosie secretly made a wager with herself that it would be either the young, foreign girl Hannah, who reminded her of a tiny little bird, ready to flutter off at the slightest sound or threat (why on earth this girl with the strange accent wanted to work in the shipyards was beyond her. She was quite clearly not cut out for any kind of manual labour, let alone something as physically taxing as welding. The poor thing had struggled from the moment she'd first turned on her machine), or it would be Dorothy. She was strong enough to do the job, but was quite obviously a fly-by-night. Fickle, with the attention span of a goldfish, looking about the yard at any given opportunity, or desperately trying to be the centre of attention.

The Hercules-like woman Martha, on the other hand, was the complete opposite. There were no two ways about it – she was born to work in the yards. She hadn't spoken more than a few words the entire day, but Rosie knew there was nothing wrong with her hearing, speech or sight, and that she understood everything that was happening around her.

The other three women, Rosie thought, had potential. Gloria may have been getting on a bit, but was what she would call 'hardy'. Mary looked as though she could be a natural, and the pretty girl called Polly was stronger than she looked, and what she lacked in muscle, she made up for with enthusiasm.

'Leave all your equipment here,' Rosie told them, 'and get yourselves home.'

The women turned off their machines and took off their heavy masks, squinting as their eyes became accustomed to normal daylight.

Rosie knew exactly what every muscle in their bodies would feel like tonight when they fell into their beds. And she knew tomorrow would be the real killer, when they'd force their aching limbs back to work.

As they gathered up their belongings and turned to leave, Rosie added, with a smile, 'Oh . . . and come back tomorrow.'

Polly and the other women walked out of the yard, stopping at the timekeeper's booth to clock off and hand in their pieces of white board, barely saying a word. Their heads were as wrung out as their bodies.

By the time Polly boarded the ferry back to the south side she realised the other five women had all dispersed. She couldn't see any on the ferry, so she guessed they must live on the north side of town, or preferred to use the bus or tram to get home.

After reaching the south dock, the hundred or so workers who had been squashed on to the ferry poured off. Polly's weary legs retraced her steps from that morning, walking back up Low Street and along Borough Road. Once again she was with a crowd of other workers, although the flow was now much slower than in the morning and not as noisy.

Polly could see quite a few of the men filtering off into the local pubs dotted along her route home. She doubted she'd have the strength to pick up a pint, never mind drink one. Her arms felt like dead weights, her legs like jelly, her back ached, her ears were still ringing from the constant onslaught of noise they'd been subjected to, and her sight was fuzzy and speckled with the after-effects of seeing sparks of burning metal all day, albeit through filtered glass. Polly said a silent prayer that she hadn't the onset of the dreaded arc eye. It sounded beyond hideous, but worse still, it would prevent her from going back to the yard tomorrow, and despite the exhaustion, the aches and pains, and a headache taking root at the back of her eyes, nothing was going to stop her returning to her new place of work the following day.

Chapter Nine

When Polly arrived back home, she was greeted by the noisy chatter, laughter and cries of half a dozen children. She hadn't been the only person to start a new venture today: Agnes had also decided to 'do her bit' for the war effort, and, as of eight o'clock that morning, had transformed their home into a makeshift crèche. The government had stuck up posters emblazoned with the plea: 'If *you* can't go to the factory, help the neighbour who *can*', and Agnes had taken the call for help quite literally to heart.

'You're back.' Agnes raised her voice to be heard above the commotion. She stepped over a few of the little children playing contentedly with their wooden dolls and drawing on scraps of paper to give her daughter a big hug. 'Look at the state of you. You look like you've been down the mines – never mind in the yards,' Agnes laughed as she tried to wipe off some of the grime on her pretty daughter's face.

Polly picked up Lucille from her cot and followed her mum out to their small backyard. The few weeds sprouting up through the concrete slabs and up the stone wall didn't afford the area the title of a garden. With one arm slung round the large laundry basket doing a balancing act on her hip, Agnes unpegged the rows of towelling nappies, sheets and clothing fluttering in the gentle breeze. She was also taking in washing for some of the local businesses to bring in a little extra cash.

'Well, then? What was it like?' she asked eagerly.

As Polly started to tell her mum all about her day, the smell of a delicious rabbit, black pudding and dumpling stew pervaded the air, reminding her of just how hungry she was. Polly was saved the energy it would take to tell her mum all of the day's trial and tribulations by a loud knock on the front door that heralded the arrival of the first mums who'd come to pick up their little ones after work.

Not long after that Bel arrived back home, looking bushed after her day on the buses. She made a beeline for Lucille, who was loving all the hustle and bustle and attention. Next came their neighbours, Sheila and Jimmy, and their young son, Jimmy Junior, who had been out at the crack of dawn to catch them their rabbit supper. They were followed by Beryl and her two teenage girls, Audrey and Iris. They'd all been invited round for a special dinner to celebrate Polly's first day as a 'Wearside welder', as Agnes had taken to calling her.

Somehow they all managed to squeeze around the kitchen table, and for the next few hours there was much chatter, laughter and appreciative sounds made by them all over their scrumptious supper.

After they'd all finished eating, Agnes looked over at the clock on the mantelpiece and announced, 'It's time.'

Bel switched on the wireless and they all huddled round the little radio for their daily evening ritual, the BBC Home Service news report on the war.

When Polly finally fell into bed that evening her mind was buzzing with the events of the day: her new workmates, Rosie, the images of the huge half-built ships and the forest of overhanging cranes which dominated the skyline. She could even still hear the cacophony of sounds created by the shipbuilders at work.

But it was the image of the deep-sea diver Tommy being pulled up from the water which kept swimming to the forefront of her mind. His serious, slightly brooding face, short, coarsely cropped fair hair and his tall, thickset, muscular body were enough to catch any woman's breath, but it was the moment he'd looked over at her and they'd caught each other's eye that kept going round and round in her head.

It was as though she had been drawn into a trance from which she couldn't, didn't want to, break free. As they had looked into each other's eyes, she had felt a sudden spark of electricity course through her body, a spark that she intuitively knew he too had experienced.

Tommy's fearless face stayed with Polly right up to the moment her eyes closed and she fell into a deep sleep.

Chapter Ten

In a small, dirty bedsit Raymond Gallagher stubbed out his last Woodbine cigarette, crushed the empty packet in his fist and tossed it into his overflowing wastebasket. He then carefully counted out a small pile of coins and a few banknotes and put them into his trouser pocket, along with a new packet of smokes and his chrome Ronson pocket lighter. He pulled himself to his feet using the headboard of the bed, grabbed his intricately carved walking stick and picked up a small leather bag containing his few worldly possessions. He then walked out of the room, leaving the door swinging open.

The man behind the reception desk of the hostel barely looked up from his newspaper as Raymond left the building.

Despite his apparent disability and sporadic bursts of coughing, Raymond moved fast for someone with a walking aid. Another couple of minutes and he was on the main stretch of road heading for the city centre.

Durham itself was a mass of narrow, winding cobbled streets and was celebrated for its eleventh-century Norman cathedral and ancient castle, which had been built near the banks of the River Wear. So far the medieval city had escaped the ravages of war, but Raymond didn't bat an eyelid at the surrounding beauty or architectural magnificence: he'd just spent five years behind its prison walls and couldn't wait to see the back of the place.

The only reason he'd got out of jail before the end of his sentence and been given what was called a 'ticket of leave' had been due to the outbreak of war and his alleged 'good behaviour', which had amounted to him keeping his head down and his mouth shut.

When he saw the number 66 single-decker bus, its destination stated on the front board, idling ready for the off in the city's small depot, he grunted a greeting to the elderly male driver before tucking his ornate walking stick under his arm and using the side rail to haul his tall, skinny frame on to the bus's platform. He shuffled along the narrow aisle and passed the other seated passengers, before finding himself a place at the back by the window.

A few moments later a pretty female conductress, who he thought looked more like she'd just stepped off the silver screen than on to a bus, climbed on board and started to collect fares.

'Ah, the joys of war,' he mumbled to himself. This was the first time he'd ever seen a female conductor working on the buses.

Soon the young woman, clutching a long ticket rack close to her body, her leather money belt slung across her shoulder, reached Raymond, who had been watching her every move.

'Good morning, sir. Where would you like to go today?'

'Ah, now there's a question, my lovely. Anywhere yer'd like to take me,' answered Raymond, leering at the woman, whose tightly fitted navy-blue uniform with its peaked cap only made her look more attractive. When he was met by a blank silent stare, he laughed. 'Ah, dinnit take offence, pet. Only an old man having a bit of fun. I'm off to Sunderland. How much is that ganna cost, number . . . two five six five?' Raymond asked, his shifty eyes reading the bus company identification badge she was wearing, then wandering down to her bust that was straining ever so slightly against the confines of her tweed jacket.

Bel noticed him looking at her chest and a feeling of revulsion passed over her. It was not the first time a man had looked at her womanliness, but this shabbily dressed man had a sinister aura about him, and Bel instinctively felt herself stiffen.

'Sixpence, please,' she said in the coolest and most officious voice she could muster, her eyes drawn to the man's unusual wooden walking stick with the rounded head of the handle carved into the shape of a ram's head. Bel thought there was something quite menacing about it, like its owner.

She took the man's fare and gave him his ticket, trying her hardest not to touch his bony, veined hand. She felt his stare follow her and undress her as she turned away and walked back to the front of the bus.

Raymond smirked to himself. He got a great deal of satisfaction from making women feel uncomfortable, and was hit by another burst of appreciation for this war, which not only had led to his early release, but also had liberated women from the confines of their kitchens and made them more accessible to men like himself.

But what gave Raymond an even greater feeling of euphoria was that his plan, like this bus journey, was just about to get going. And, by God, was he going to enjoy every minute of it.

Raymond would have slept, or at least snoozed, the thirteen miles of his journey had his excitement not kept him awake, as well as his need to keep his wits about him. When he finally saw the massive Meccano-like green metal Wearmouth Bridge, arching over the river and joining the north and south sides of the town, Raymond sat up straight in his seat, the familiarity of his surroundings giving him a jolt of energy.

He had arrived. It had taken for ever, and not just this bumpy, stop-start bus journey. He had waited a long time to come back to his hometown and reclaim what was rightfully his.

Getting off the bus when it stopped after crossing the bridge at Monkwearmouth railway station, his sturdy wooden stick aiding his way, Raymond walked a route he knew well, along Dame Dorothy Street, passing the historic St Peter's Church on his right. After a few minutes he dropped down on to a narrow lane that took him to North Sands, the birthplace of the town's shipbuilding industry and now home to Cyril Thompson's yard. Soon his ears were resonating with the sound of the hammering and clanging of steel, and his vision was filled, not only with the great metal and concrete landscape of the shipyards, but also with the coal drops, timber stores and engineering works which lined the winding hem of the Wear. He looked at the narrow, bending river, filled with every boat imaginable, the necks of mammoth cranes straining over its waters, and barrage balloons floating above like gigantic fish in the sky. This was a part of life the war hadn't changed. The industry that lay on either side of the river was still very much the beating heart of the town, and the Wear itself the thick, pulsating artery that divided the town in two.

Raymond moved to an area where he could see but not be in obvious sight of those workers leaving the yard at the end of their shift. He waited patiently, taking in the smell, sight and sounds of a place he knew only too well. When the hooter finally sounded out, signalling the end of another working day, Raymond's eyes furtively searched the mass of people spilling out of the gates.

75

Finally he spotted who he was looking for. He congratulated himself on his eagle eyes, as he could easily have missed his prey. It had only been the thick strand of blonde hair escaping from her patterned headscarf which had caught his attention.

As he scrutinised the young woman hurrying out of the gates, haversack and gas mask slung over her shoulder, he knew for certain it was her. It was Rosie. She had grown up in the past five years, and more than ever she was the spit of her mother – his sister Eloise.

He took care to keep his distance. There was no way he wanted her to notice him. Not yet, anyway. He struggled to keep up with her fast, athletic pace, but he did it, despite his lungs feeling as though they were on fire, and suppressing bouts of coughing.

It must have taken half an hour to walk back along Dame Dorothy Street, back across the Wearmouth Bridge and through the town centre, past the museum with its celebrated Winter Gardens, until finally he was able to catch his breath when Rosie arrived at her destination. Raymond presumed this was where she was living now. It had been hard to keep track of her whereabouts as she was always on the move.

As he waited from his hiding place on the corner of the adjacent building, he had time to open a new pack of cigarettes and celebrate with a smoke.

Half an hour later he watched as Rosie walked out the front door of the building. Yet again, he struggled to keep up with her pace, but this time, thankfully, she wasn't walking so quickly. And he could see why: she was now wearing heeled shoes in place of her working boots. He cursed as he lost sight of her for a moment before she reappeared on the other side of the road. He slowed his pace as the streets started to become wider, and quieter, and he realised they were heading into the posh part of town.

He was torn between making sure he didn't lose sight of Rosie and worrying that he'd get too near and she'd see him.

He saw her turn a corner and walk up one of the side streets. If he had left it a second later he would have missed her. As it was, he just managed to catch a glimpse of her as she looked over her shoulder. For a second he thought that she had seen him, but thankfully she hadn't.

As he walked down the narrow alleyway she'd gone down, he spotted her disappearing into a doorway at the back of one of the large red-brick turn-of-the-century townhouses. But it wasn't any old doorway, for shining through the net curtains in the ground-floor window was a red light.

Raymond's thin lips slowly broke into a smile. A horrible, sly, eerie smile, which exposed his nicotine-stained yellow stumps of teeth.

This was better than anything he could have wished for.

Chapter Eleven

'I *can* do it!' had been Polly's silent mantra all week. She wasn't at all convinced she could actually do this job at first, but she managed somehow to brainwash herself with her repeated internal chant driving her on.

Welding was much harder than it looked, and it sapped every ounce of energy Polly possessed. Every evening she dragged herself off to bed as soon as she had eaten her supper and listened to the BBC Home news at nine o'clock. A few times she actually fell asleep while it was on, something she'd never done before.

Agnes, thankfully, understood her daughter's need to simply eat and sleep. 'I've watched your granda, your da and your two brothers come home after a day's work in the yards, and that's all they've wanted to do. Eat. Then sleep.'

Polly knew her mum hated the thought of her working in the shipyards, but it meant the world to her that she had her support.

'Thanks, Ma,' she said.

'What for? I haven't done anything.' Agnes never found it easy to accept any kind of thanks or compliment.

'For not giving me any more grief. And for understanding,' Polly told her. 'I couldn't do this on my own.'

One evening Polly caused an uproar at the kitchen table when she admitted, 'Eee, you know, I can see why a man needs a wife. I'd love a wife.'

Agnes and Bel hooted with laughter at Polly's outrageousness, but it was true. There was no way Polly had the strength to cook herself a meal every night, as well as do any chores or housework that needed to be done – never mind have a family to care for as well. She was just so thankful that every night Agnes somehow served up a hearty man-sized meal – some kind of offal or meat, vegetables and potatoes or dumplings.

'Are you forging your ration book, Agnes?' Bel joked one teatime after seeing another stew keeping warm on top of the range.

'No, but I'm not averse to a little bribery,' Agnes joked back.

They all knew Agnes was talking about Dennis the local shopkeeper, who owned the store on the corner of their street. He had managed to dodge conscription due to some bogus but convincing ailment, and had spent the first year of the war lording it over all and sundry who came in for their groceries, especially the women.

'Everyone but his wife knows he's playing away from home,' Bel had told them, 'with not just one, but a few of the women who live round the doors.'

'Heavens knows who would want to touch him with a bargepole,' Agnes had said with a look of revulsion on her face.

'Well, I don't think it's his body they're after,' Bel had exclaimed, before confiding, 'I heard on the grapevine that it can be a bit of a swap shop there – some rashers of bacon, or a few eggs to get his hands on some nice big melons, as it were.'

The kitchen had exploded with shrieks of laughter from Bel and Polly and mock outrage from Agnes. Even Lucille had started clapping excitedly.

Bel loved entertaining and had a tendency to embroider a story, but it was just for the trusted ears of her adopted family. She got plenty of her material from all the gossip she heard or saw working on the buses, and she loved nothing more than enthralling her mother- and sister-in-law with her little bits of scandalmongering.

Agnes was glad they were still able to make light of the strange life they had been thrown into this past year, but underneath it all her own feelings were very much in conflict. On the one hand, it pained her to see her daughter leave for the yards every day. She was worried sick that something terrible would happen to her. Her friend's husband, a plater, had died tragically when a gigantic sheet of metal had fallen on him, leaving his wife on her own to bring up nine children, the youngest just a babe in arms. But on the other hand, Agnes understood her daughter's determination – no, her need – to succeed and be able to do this job, and she felt incredibly proud of her, and of her true grit. She's her father's daughter for sure, Agnes had thought on more than one occasion that week.

It reassured Agnes to think her Harry was somewhere watching over Polly and the twins, proud as punch at seeing all three of his children doing everything they could to overcome a regime which was so utterly abominable and malignant. Still, every evening Agnes couldn't help but breathe a huge sigh of relief when she heard her daughter walk through the front door and shout out, 'Hi, Ma, I'm home!'

'She's got that wonderful confidence only the young have that nothing bad will happen to them,' Agnes said during one of her morning chats with Beryl over the wall in her backyard.

'I know,' Beryl agreed. 'They think they'll live for ever.'

Both women were each other's sounding board. They needed each other more than they realised to get their anxieties out into the open, and these past few weeks they were getting increasingly concerned as neither of them had heard from their boys.

'It's a wonder we've not gone grey,' Beryl joked.

'But we have!' Agnes roared. Both women were only in their early forties, but their once-shiny chestnut-brown hair was gradually being overtaken by a mass of grey and white streaks.

This morning Agnes felt the tiniest bit of relief. It was Friday, which meant a weekend's rest from worrying. As she stood at her front door, with Lucille in her arms, both of them waving goodbye to Polly and Bel as they left for their respective jobs, Agnes's mind wandered to the day ahead. She took Lucille and went back into the kitchen to have one last cuppa before the neighbours' children were dropped off. Her day would be filled with the demands of half a dozen boys and girls, all thankfully still young enough to know nothing of the fear and the uncertainty of the world outside their little playgroup.

Chapter Twelve

'Well done, all of you. You've made it to the last day of your first week. That's no mean achievement,' Rosie announced encouragingly to her group of trainees as they gathered around the workbench.

Polly felt her chest almost puff out with pride.

'And it's payday,' Dorothy chipped in.

Polly couldn't help but see the irony that, out of them all, it was Dorothy who needed the money the least. She'd learnt, through Dorothy's incessant chatter, that she lived in a nice house near Backhouse Park, which everyone knew was where those with a bit of money lived. Polly wasn't always the best judge of character, but she knew enough to know the other women weren't doing this job purely for King and country and would be more than aware that it was payday.

'But,' Rosie said, 'that doesn't mean you can slack off. We've got nine hours ahead of us, and still a lot to learn, especially as next week we'll be working with the platers, and I want you to show them you're all up to scratch.'

Polly immediately felt a burst of energy. Her competitive button had been pressed and she was determined not to let the side down.

When the horn announced it was their lunch break, Polly couldn't wait to get her iron mask off and feel the cool sea breeze on her face. It was unusually hot today and the combined heat from the weather and their welding was making her drip sweat.

As the five women chatted and ate, every now and again they'd break off and hold their faces to the sun and momentarily close their eyes. Every day they'd all sat together outside in the fresh air, with the seagulls squawking above them, all munching hungrily on their various packed lunches.

Polly was sure she wasn't the only one to envy the food Martha brought with her each day. If she wasn't feasting on sandwiches slathered in butter and stuffed with big hunks of cheese and ham, she was tucking into delicious-looking pork pies, or Scotch eggs the size of fists. 'That looks nice,' Dorothy had exclaimed more than a few times, but Martha never said much. A big smile would spread across her rosy, round face and then she would carry on eating.

Over the past week the women had fallen into what was becoming their routine chatter, which more often than not centred on which part of their body was particularly stiff or achy, with even Martha, the group's workhorse, pointing out the areas of her solid physique which were giving her gip. A few times they'd quietly discussed what was doing the rounds on the burgeoning black market: the docks were a good source for the movement of illicit goods. Dorothy had been over the moon the other day as she'd managed to get hold of some hairpins.

'What do you think happened to Mary this week?' Gloria asked the group as they settled into their usual places on the wooden pallets, with Martha cross-legged next to them on the ground.

Gloria and Mary both lived on the Ford estate, which had been built just a few years previously to replace some of the town's slums. The two women had got on well, but Mary had been a no-show since Wednesday.

'I'm not sure,' Polly said.

'I heard she hated leaving her little baby at home,' Dorothy butted in. They all knew that Mary had a baby girl just over a year old whom she had told them all about. It had been obvious by the way she talked that she not only totally adored the child, but also desperately missed her. 'Apparently she couldn't bear to be parted from the wee thing – but more than that,' Dorothy added conspiratorially, 'she didn't like to leave her at home with her dragon of a mother-in-law, who, by all accounts, doesn't have a maternal bone in her body.'

'Well, I know when my two were babies I'd have hated leaving them, even if it was with someone I liked,' Gloria sympathised, 'especially if there was an air raid and you weren't there.'

They all agreed, with Martha nodding solemnly.

Polly thought of poor Bel. She knew she felt the same about Lucille and how much it pained her to be parted from her during the day for that very reason.

'How old are your two now?' Dorothy asked Gloria.

Over the past week they'd all found out that Dorothy liked to ask questions as much as she enjoyed talking. Every time their masks were pushed up off their faces for a quick breather, they'd hear her voice, making some comic quip, or asking Rosie a question. Sometimes Polly thought that Rosie made them all weld that bit longer just to shut her up for a few moments.

'Nineteen and twenty – eighteen months between the two of them,' Gloria said. 'Both in the navy, somewhere in the Atlantic Ocean . . .' she added, her voice trailing off as she became lost in thought.

No one said anything, but everyone knew that the Atlantic was one of the most dangerous battlefields to be on as it was being waged on three levels – below, on and above the water. The Luftwaffe and the Kriegsmarine, the

German navy, were pretty formidable forces in the air and on the sea, but it was the silent U-boats underneath the water which were presently causing the most death and destruction.

Gloria's husband, Vinnie, was also ex-navy, and worked in the town's rope factory, but Gloria never seemed particularly keen to chat about him. Her boys, Bobby and Gordon, however, were a different matter, and when she'd mentioned them, Polly had caught a look of maternal love crossing her face, followed by a shadow of worry. It was a familiar look that she had seen many times from her own mother. However, Polly also felt that there was something else adding to Gloria's anxieties, other than the safety of her sons.

Seeing Gloria's change in mood, Dorothy quickly asked, 'So then, what are you all doing tonight with your hard-earned wages?'

'Well,' Hannah said with a cheeky smile on her impish face, 'I think I go see *Swan Lake* at the Empire, with drinks during interval . . . and four-course meal after in poshest hotel in town,' she added dreamily in her stilted English.

Gloria jeered, 'You wish! The poshest nosh you'll get round here at the moment is fish and chips. It's about the only thing they've not rationed.'

'And the nearest *Swan Lake* you'll see will be watching the ducks in the Winter Gardens,' Dorothy joined in the banter.

Everyone chuckled, with Martha letting out a loud guffaw.

Loving their make-believe conversation, Dorothy carried on, 'I think I'll dress up to the nines and then go out and paint the town red, drink gin, and dance all night until it's light again.'

'All right, daydreamers, let's get back to it,' Rosie announced, catching the tail end of their imaginary Saturday night.

Most days Polly had seen Rosie head over to the yard's canteen for her lunch, something none of the women yet felt brave enough to do. Dorothy had started to tentatively suggest they should all venture there for their lunch, but the rest of the women had agreed that the prospect of walking into the big cafeteria full to the brim of workers was just too daunting at the moment.

Today, as she watched the steady stream of men filter out of the cafeteria's doors ready for another afternoon of hard graft, Polly tried to find a woman in the mass of men. Rosie had told them that there were about ten thousand men working in the town's shipyards, and about seven hundred women employees, but that had only been since war broke out.

A lot of the women were operating cranes, and doing labouring jobs, and some, like themselves, were doing the more dangerous jobs like welding and riveting. As yet Polly hadn't seen any women at Thompson's working as riveters, but having observed the men here doing the job, it was hard graft. The rivet guns themselves weighed a ton and resembled mini canons, which, just like the real thing, had a ferocious kickback. Polly reckoned you'd need muscles of pure iron to work with them all day long.

'Promise me we'll go next week?' Dorothy had implored.

They'd all agreed, just to shut her up.

'It's a bit – what is the word? Overwhelming? – all these men, isn't it?' Hannah had sidled up to Polly earlier on in the week and confided to her.

'I know,' Polly had agreed. She didn't like to show it, but she really felt for Hannah. If Polly felt intimidated, then heaven knew what Hannah was going through. She must be feeling as if she were being thrown into the lions' den on a daily basis. Indeed, no one had said anything, but it was evident by the look on everyone's faces each morning when Hannah arrived at half seven on the dot, holdall in one hand, gas mask in the other, that they were all more than a little surprised that she'd turned up for another day's work.

As the women all got up and cleared away the remnants of their lunch, Rosie explained that this afternoon she wanted them to try welding in a different position.

'You won't always be welding on a flat surface. Look at that ship in dry dock,' she said, pointing to the immense black metal beast beached in the fitting-out quay. 'Just say something needs welding on the hull: you will have to do what is called an overhead weld from one of the platforms you can see by the side.'

All five women stared in wonder at the massive coal transporter. They'd seen the three-hundred-foot-long collier every day, but it was still awe-inspiring.

'If you're welding overhead,' Rosie continued, 'you've got to work and move fast or the liquid metal will end up on your face shield rather than in the joint. But the most important thing to remember is to make sure you are well protected. If you're going to get burnt, this will be when it happens.'

All five pairs of hands went to the scarves around their necks to check they were covering every inch of skin and that there was no exposed flesh a dripping bit of metal could brand. Their overalls had already become dotted with pinpoint burns, and they'd all got used to jumping every time a spark managed to bite them when they were least expecting it.

As Rosie continued to talk, a familiar shape caught the corner of Polly's vision. It was the man in the monster outfit,

Tommy, the deep-sea diver. Most days Polly had seen him either being gently lowered into the river, or slowly climbing up the metal ladder by the side of the divers' pontoon.

Polly had soaked up every morsel and titbit she'd heard about Tommy and the other divers – about their incredible copper twelve-bolt helmets, their alien-looking rubberised canvas suits, and how their greatest fear was something called 'the bends'.

'If a diver comes up too quickly then he can get a kind of decompression sickness because the body forms bubbles of gas which can cause death,' Rosie had told her trainees one day when she'd noticed how fascinated they all were with the divers they had nicknamed 'the monster men'.

This week the dock divers were working flat out to fix a broken propeller on a warship, moored by the side of the river. If it couldn't be fixed underwater, they'd have to bring it into the dry dock and that would take up valuable time and manpower. It was cheaper and quicker to do it underwater.

Polly saw Tommy, who was holding his huge helmet in front of him, standing by the quayside chatting to one of the linesmen. This past week they had caught each other's eye quite a few times, but every time they'd done so, Polly had immediately looked away, embarrassed. Today, however, when Tommy turned and looked straight at her with his deep, serious eyes, Polly didn't look away. She knew she should, that she shouldn't go around staring at men she didn't know, but she just couldn't tear her gaze away from him. His look seemed to bore into her very heart and it was hypnotising.

The two of them were a good few hundred yards apart, but Polly felt that they were right next to each other, that she could have touched his square jaw and firm mouth. It was as if there was no one else about, just the two of them.

As if their eyes, their very beings, had become locked together.

Polly and Tommy continued to look at each other – both transfixed. Then, at exactly the same moment, a tentative smile spread across both their faces, and, for the first time, they acknowledged each other.

'Hello, anybody at home?'

Polly heard Rosie's voice and the spell was broken. She swung her gaze back to her instructor.

'Sorry, I was just . . .' She tried desperately to find an excuse for her inattention.

The other women's faces were grinning.

'I think Cupid's arrow's just struck,' Dorothy said, and they all chuckled, apart from Martha, who looked a little puzzled.

'Come on – back to it. I want to see fantastic vertical welds before you all leave today,' Rosie said, trying hard to keep a straight face.

An hour later they had all had a molten shower rain down on them.

'Do you think it would be easier just to dangle us upside down by our feet? If I do much more of this I'll have arms like Popeye,' Dorothy said in total desperation, giving her arms a rest from being held up high for so long.

Finally at five thirty sharp, Rosie shouted out the words they had all been desperate to hear all day. 'Time to go home,' she said loudly.

The women didn't need telling twice. Five sets of machines got switched off almost simultaneously and five masks were immediately pushed up off their hot and sweaty faces.

'Hurrah!' Dorothy shouted out.

'I'll second that,' Gloria added. She looked shattered.

Polly surveyed the rest of their little group. Hannah seemed on the verge of collapse, and even Martha's huge bulk was sagging with tiredness.

'Do you know where you get your wages from?' Rosie asked the women.

'I do,' Gloria said.

The others didn't look so sure.

'Come on, follow me,' Gloria commanded, and like a mother hen with her four chicks, they all trooped after her as she marched with more vigour than she felt across the yard and over to a wooden outbuilding with the sign 'Wages Office' hanging above its door.

As they joined the queue that was rapidly forming outside, Polly spotted a smartly dressed man coming out of the office. She could tell he must be important, not just because of his expensive three-piece wool suit, but because all the men fell silent and parted to let him out. As he started walking away and the Red Sea of cloth flat caps flowed back together, the man's head jerked around to where the women were waiting.

'Gloria!' he exclaimed.

All four women stared at their workmate and back at the suited man.

'Jack, how are you?' Gloria asked. She sounded her normal self but her face had flushed red.

'What are you doing here?' the man called Jack asked, surprised.

As the two started chatting, the women turned politely away but continued to earwig in on their conversation. Gloria, who was pushing her brown curly hair away from her face a little nervously, told Jack that she was 'learning a new trade' and the two talked for a short while about their spouses and children. They mirrored each other's responses, saying how well their families were and how everything was just fine and dandy.

Polly wondered how the two of them knew each other. Gloria was most definitely working class, and Jack was obviously monied, although, judging by his weathered skin and hard vowel sounds, he'd not been born into riches.

By the time Jack and Gloria had reached the 'nice to see you' stage of their brief chat and said their goodbyes, the women had almost got to the front of the queue, and although the five of them were beginning to feel that they had known each other for a lot longer than a week, none of them, not even Dorothy, felt it appropriate to enquire as to who this Jack was. And, more intriguingly, how the two of them knew each other.

Chapter Thirteen

As Polly squeezed herself on to the ferry along with a horde of other shipbuilders, her mind drifted over the past week. Each day she'd felt her body toughening up. Her muscles seemed to be getting harder and more taut, although her wrists felt weak and lame. The last few days they'd been practising a lot of 'weaving', which was a more intricate welding technique achieved by a lot of wrist action.

The heat from the burning metal had also taken some getting used to, compounded by the fact her heavy helmet caused her face to burn up and drip with sweat. The tight leather band that kept her protector firmly fixed on to her head also made her temples sore to the touch by the end of the day, but it was better than risking it slipping and either getting burnt or waking up at night with the dreaded arc eye.

Polly felt as though they had all been learning to weld for a lot longer than they had in reality, which was probably because they'd been taught so intensively. They had learnt just about every welding technique there was to be taught – overhead, horizontal, flat, vertical; even one-handed welding, as Rosie had informed them there would be times when they would have to use one hand to cling to a ladder or a beam while welding with the other.

She had also told them in no uncertain terms, 'This isn't like doing an apprenticeship before the war. Time now is of the essence and I need you all to be competent welders – and quickly. The Germans are sinking Allied ships as fast as they're being built, so these ships,' she'd said, arching her gloved arm to take in the numerous vessels sitting in the dry docks, waiting on the slipways and moored by the river's edge, 'need to be back in action as soon as humanly possible. And you're going to help make that happen. But I have to warn you, there are going to be times when you hate me, and you're going to hate the yards too with a passion. But it's going to be worth it. Trust me.'

There had been times this week already when Polly had felt so frustrated learning her new craft, with its constant sputtering and hissing sounds, that she *had* hated it, but then halfway through the week something had clicked, and she'd started to enjoy it.

At first her 'beads', the drops of molten metal used to bind the sheets of steel together, had looked like the outline of some irregular mountain range – some big, some small – but gradually they had become more ordered, more uniform. A few times she had felt the thrill of what Rosie had described to them as 'the rhythm of welding'. It was the best feeling – almost cathartic.

Hannah had made a comment the other day that she thought welding was an art, and as they had all practised and repractised their welds, creating waterfalls of glitter-like sparkles, Polly had understood what she'd meant.

It hadn't been until today, though, that Polly had started to feel less bewildered, not just by her new trade, but also by her new working environment. It had taken time for her to make some sort of sense of the chaos into which she and the other women had been plunged on that first day. But she was getting there. Her observations of the past five days and the bits and pieces of information she'd gleaned had slowly been slotted together and had started to form the outline of a complex jigsaw puzzle. She was finally beginning to understand how these massive, awe-inspiring ships were born from this noise and confusion. Through her novice eyes, she was starting to realise just how regimented and structured the whole shipbuilding process was, and how this mass of ordinary human beings was producing the most incredible giants of ships. It was as though a mist had lifted, and Polly had started to comprehend not just her own trade, but how it was integrated with the various stages of building a ship.

Her mind was awash with a mixture of thoughts and emotions, and the feeling that she had just started a great adventure, which was a little scary, but also quite thrilling.

But if she was honest with herself, there was also something else buoying Polly up through the tiredness she now felt having reached the end of her first gruelling week – and it had nothing to do with welding or shipbuilding. As the waters lapped against the sides of the ferry while it crossed the river, Polly felt, rising in her, a sense of growing exhilaration as she recalled seeing Tommy that afternoon. They hadn't yet spoken a word to each other, but the smile they had offered each other had said more than any words.

Polly felt an unusual pull towards Tommy, and it wasn't just his good looks, or the fact his job seemed so incredibly romantic and different to anything else she had known. No, it was more than that. It was as if she already knew him, although she knew for certain she had never met him before in her life. She would certainly have remembered if she had. It was more as if she just wanted to *be* with him. Be in his company.

Be by his side.

She'd had a few crushes when she was young and had dated a few local lads over the years, but she'd never been really serious with anyone, and certainly had never experienced falling in love.

She hadn't spoken a word to Tommy yet, but Polly had a slightly strange but exciting premonition that they somehow belonged together.

Chapter Fourteen

Arthur heard the familiar roar of his grandson's BSA 500 motorbike, then silence as the engine was turned off, before heavy footsteps approached the house.

'It's only me,' Tommy announced as he walked through the front door, which had, as usual, been left wide open, 'and not some thief,' he added, clomping down the hallway and into the little living room. He found his granddad sitting in his armchair next to the open fire, which had been stacked up with newspaper, kindling and coal ready to be sparked up.

'Haddaway, lad, no one's ganna rob me. There's nowt here to take, anyway. They'd walk in, take a look around and do an about-turn and go out again,' Arthur chuckled, pushing himself out of his much loved but time-worn chair and shuffling towards the little kitchen.

'We're not living in the good old days now, you know,' Tommy replied, putting his helmet on the floor by the side of the table and joining in their usual banter.

'Aye, I know, Tom,' said Arthur, 'but I'm not ganna keep myself all cooped up and shut up through fear of some bad 'un trying to steal from us. And it's nice to feel a breeze through the house. Anyways, what've you got stashed in your top? It smells like supper.' He pointed a knobbly finger at the parcel wrapped in newspaper and peeking out from the top of his grandson's leather motorbike jacket.

'Friday-night treat, Granda – a nice bit of fresh haddock.'

'My favourite. Let's stick the pan on and get it fried up. I've got some fresh bread today from the bakers, and I might have a jar of pickled onions somewhere.' Arthur started to clatter around and chatted at the same time.

Tommy took off his heavy jacket then sat down to pull off his large steel-capped motorbike boots. As he did so, he started to gently whistle the popular Bing Crosby song, 'Sing a Song of Sunbeams'.

'Someone's chipper this evening?' Arthur said with a curious smile on his face. 'What's been happening today down the yards?'

Arthur was eager to hear some, or rather *any*, news of Tommy's day. His frail body may have been starting to fail him but his mind was still as sharp as a tack and he relished any kind of conversation. Arthur religiously read the *Sunderland Echo* from back to front for his local news, and the *Daily Mirror* to learn what was happening in the rest of the world, and he loved his little wireless, but nothing compared to human contact and conversation. This he missed, especially as it had become quite a rarity now he'd hit his seventieth year. He'd outlived most of his friends and had come to realise that longevity wasn't always what it was cracked up to be.

Not that Arthur had particularly aspired to live a long life; he was just glad he was still here for his grandson. And this evening he was particularly pleased to see a lightness in Tommy's being. This told the old man that all was well with the world. At least for today. And at least for Tommy. If truth be told, Tommy was his world. If he wasn't about, Arthur knew that he too wouldn't be about either. He loved that boy more than he loved life itself. He was always relieved to have Tommy safely back home every night. Being a dock diver was a risky occupation, and he should know. Arthur just thanked whatever god was up there that Tommy's skill was needed here and not fighting Hitler's Nazi army on some godforsaken bloody battlefield.

Lately, though, Arthur had felt a sense of unease. Tommy had heard that the navy were starting to use divers to clear mines that had either been dropped into the Atlantic or were being stuck to the hulls of Allied ships. The thought of just the possibility of Tommy going out there and carrying out what he felt amounted to a suicide mission made the old man shudder.

But it was his grandson's mind he worried about as much as his physical well-being. Over the past few months he'd kept a particularly sharp eye out for any change in Tommy's general mood.

Several months before, Tommy had been doing some repair work to the dock close to the fishing quay when he had frantically started to pull on his signal line, demanding to be brought back up. When one of the diving assistants had unscrewed his helmet and lifted it off, Tommy's face had been as white as a ghost's.

Tangled up on the riverbed, Tommy had discovered the bodies of two local children who'd gone missing a few days previously. When he had got his breath back, he'd gone back down to free the tiny corpses from their watery grave and had brought them back to dry land to be given a proper burial. It was believed the boy and girl had been close friends, and when one had fallen into the river after playing too near the edge of the quayside, the other had jumped in to help. Both had drowned. What had been truly heartbreaking was that the two youngsters had been holding hands when they'd been found.

For a good while afterwards, Tommy had spoken to no one, preferring to be on his own. Those who knew him said his tragic find had filled his whole being with the most terrible sadness, which had stayed with him for a long while.

It was at times like this that Arthur not only worried the lad took after his mother, but also cursed her for not being there. Tommy might now be a grown man but he still needed a mother's love, and words of reassurance and calm. Arthur's wife, Flo, had tried to compensate, but nothing compared to the real thing. Arthur hated to admit it, but his anger towards his only daughter had not abated over the years. He'd never been able to forgive her for choosing, in his mind, to take the easy way out. She'd selfishly opted out of life, with no regard for anyone else. Arthur could perhaps have found it in his bruised and deeply damaged heart to forgive her had she not left her only son alone in this world. But she had, and in Arthur's mind that was unforgivable.

'Why haven't I got a mam and dad?' Tommy had asked repeatedly when he was younger.

Arthur had explained that his dad had died bravely in the First World War, but had skirted over his mother's death by saying that the angels had taken her to be with his dad. That had only worked for so long. The older the lad had got, the less convinced he'd been of his granddad's explanation, and Arthur had had to admit that even he had thought it sounded false and pithy. If *he* wasn't convinced, how could he expect Tommy to believe him? Not surprisingly, the little lad had persisted and as he'd got older he had demanded real answers.

Finally Arthur had had to take the bull by the horns and tell the boy the truth when he'd come in one day after being out playing with his friends. Arthur would never forget the look of thunder behind his grandson's hurt and angry eyes when he'd asked, 'Why did my mam top herself?'

Arthur had known then that it was time for him to come clean and explain to Tommy that his mother had in fact taken her own life. Everyone round the doors knew about it, and Arthur had known that one day the story of Tommy's mum's death would eventually filter down to the young ones and, therefore, to Tommy.

'Now, that's a hard question to answer,' Arthur had said, and in the end he'd decided to just tell the boy the truth. He'd always found that was the best way in the end with most things. 'She was very sad when your da died.' Arthur took care choosing his words. 'She just never got over the fact that he didn't come back from the war. She missed him so much. Loved him so much.' Arthur had struggled to keep any of his own anger towards his daughter out of his voice.

'Didn't she love *me*?' Tommy had asked, his young, innocent eyes looking desolate.

Arthur had wanted to say that his daughter had been selfish, thinking only about herself, and not the child she'd made – a child she'd had a duty to stay around and care for. But instead he said, 'Of course she loved you. But sometimes a person's mind can become confused and she decided she didn't want to be here – in this life – any more.'

Tears had welled up in Tommy's sad eyes, but he'd rubbed them away angrily.

'If she loved me she would have stayed,' he'd shouted, stomping out of the house.

Arthur had gone after the boy and found him where he had known he'd be, right at the top end of the quayside, at the very tip of the mouth of the river, breathing in the calm of the fresh, salty air and being soothed by the sound of gently lapping water. The river and the docks had always drawn Tommy like a magnet.

He hadn't tried to explain any more about why his daughter had done what she'd done in leaving them all, but had just sat down next to the boy and looked out to sea.

Tommy had never mentioned his mum after that day, and neither had Arthur. There was nothing more to say. Tommy had been a strong, beefy child, and although his nature had been gentle, after that he had put paid to any more comments about his mum with his fists, and it hadn't been long before his peers knew never to mention 'Tommy's mam' – not unless they'd wanted a good hiding.

'Let's get the tea on then,' Arthur said, lighting up the gas ring on the cooker. As he stooped to get the heavy metal pan out of the cupboard, Tommy unwrapped the haddock and within a matter of minutes had cleaned and gutted it ready to fry up. The perks of working and living on the docks was that fish was never in short supply.

'I saw Jack today,' Tommy said as he watched Arthur lost momentarily in his own world, sprinkling their fish supper with flour to create a thin batter. 'He was asking after you and said to say hello. Not often you see him out in the yards these days.'

Arthur laughed. 'He's gone soft since he moved up the ranks.'

Arthur had been the yard's deep-sea diver when Jack had been a young plater, and despite the age gap the two had become good friends. Jack had always looked up to Arthur, as his own dad had been a total waster, drinking away every penny the family had and leaving Jack's mum to bring her brood up the best she could on next to nothing.

But life for Jack had changed when he'd caught the eye of Miriam Havelock, the wealthy daughter of one of the area's top industrialists who had close connections with all the Sunderland yards. The two had married after a short courtship, and it hadn't been long before Jack had been promoted to head foreman. Twenty years on and Jack was now yard manager and inhabited a very different world to the one he'd lived in when he'd been a lowly plater.

'He might have gone up in the world, but he's never forgotten his roots,' Arthur mused as he carefully placed the fish in the hot frying pan and watched it starting to sizzle and spit.

'Aye,' said Tommy, 'but he never has much of a smile on his face these days.' Tommy remembered when he himself was a child, hanging around the yards and seeing Jack and his granddad have a good old belly laugh about something or other.

'That's what marriage does to you,' Arthur chortled.

Tommy knew his granddad didn't really think that about marriage. Arthur had been heartbroken when Flo had died of pneumonia. He had tried to disguise his raw grief when Tommy was about, but underneath he'd been totally devastated. Arthur would happily have followed his wife, whom he had been with since they were both just fourteen, had it not been for Tommy and the fact he would have been left entirely on his own. Arthur had been determined that he would live as long as possible, or at least until Tommy was a grown man and hopefully had found someone to share his life with.

Which brought Arthur's meandering thoughts back to Tommy's cheery demeanour. And it hadn't just been today – the past week he'd seemed more jocular. Happier.

'So, what's put the spring in your step today?' Arthur ventured, serving up the fish on to two plates, as Tommy buttered the bread and put the jar of pickled onions out on the table. 'There's not a girl on the scene, is there?' he asked casually. The old man would have given anything in the world to find a lovely woman for his grandson.

When Tommy didn't respond, Arthur turned to look at him. He was a strapping lad and seemed to fill their small kitchen.

A shy, boyish look spread unwittingly across Tommy's manly face. 'I haven't met anyone, but I have *seen* someone,' he admitted reluctantly, getting their knives and forks out of the cutlery drawer and sitting down at the table.

Trying desperately to keep his enthusiasm under wraps, Arthur attempted to subtly eke more information out of his grandson. Again he cursed the lack of women in their household. This was their domain. 'Well, there's a turn-up for the books.' He tried to sound casual. 'What's she like? Have you a name for her?'

'I don't know why I've even mentioned her,' Tommy muttered, immediately regretting having said anything. 'I've not even talked to her. She just seems nice . . . looks nice,' he said, feeling more idiotic by the minute.

'Well, you'd better speak to her and see if she *is* nice,' Arthur chuckled and forked an onion out of the jar. 'What's she doing in the yards, anyway? Is she working there?'

Arthur knew they'd started taking on women in the shipyards, and that it had been met with a mixed reaction. There'd even been an official meeting to try to stop the women from infiltrating the yards, with many of the older workers arguing the case that the women would end up taking the men's jobs from them permanently and there would be none left when the men returned from the war – *if* the men returned from the war. Thankfully common sense had overcome their unabashed sexism and the vote had gone in favour of allowing the town's womenfolk to work in the yards, but it had only done so because it was a necessity. The war needed its battleships and cargo vessels and they weren't going to build and repair themselves. The yards needed workers – regardless of gender.

As the two men tucked into their food, Tommy began to tell Arthur about the odd handful of women who had started as trainee welders. Arthur was interested to hear how the women were doing, and if they were being accepted by the other men. He was particularly intrigued as welding was known to be one of the hardest jobs in the yard, and he was surprised any woman would want to do such dirty and gruelling work. But more than anything, Arthur wanted to hear about this woman welder who had caught his grandson's eye, and perhaps was also capturing his heart.

'Well, I know her name is Polly,' Tommy told him.

Jack's daughter, Helen, who worked in the administration offices, was always popping across to see Tommy about something or other. He hoped he had managed to sound as nonchalant as possible when he'd asked her, by the by, about the new welders. Helen had made some bitchy comment about them all, but had also let slip Polly's name, saying she was a like a 'streak of bacon' and wouldn't last two minutes there. Tommy didn't think Polly looked anything like a streak of bacon. From what he could make out, despite the baggy overalls, her body looked pretty perfect to him and she had the loveliest of faces. He'd caught a glimpse of her long, thick mane of light brown hair when she'd taken off her headscarf one lunchtime and let it loose. She'd taken his breath away.

Tommy wouldn't have been surprised if she didn't already have a few men after her. Saying that, she didn't look as if she was interested in anything other than learning to weld. He'd caught her blaspheming a few times when she'd mucked up, and the look of anger and frustration on her face had made him laugh inwardly.

He wanted to tell Arthur all of this, but couldn't. They were men and he'd sound like he'd gone soft in the head.

As there wasn't much Tommy could actually tell Arthur about Polly, he related what he knew about the other odd assortment of women welders who had defied tradition and were now helping to build ships. Tommy may not have talked to any of them, but like most of the workers there, he'd watched them from afar, slightly in awe of these women with welding rods in their hands and massive masks covering their faces, doing what they considered to be a man's job.

'Funnily enough, I think Jack knows one of the older women who's started,' Tommy added as an afterthought.

'Really? Do you know her name?' Arthur was intrigued.

Tommy hesitated. 'Ah, you know I'm terrible with names. One of the linesmen knows her husband, Vinnie, who's a nasty piece of work by the sounds of it. I think her name begins with G.'

'It's not Gloria, is it?' Arthur's attention was now totally grabbed by what his grandson was telling him.

'Yes, that's it. Gloria.'

Tommy started to sop up the last bits of fish and vinegar with his buttered bread.

'Well, that's somebody I've not heard about for a long while,' Arthur said, more to himself than to Tommy.

Gloria was someone Arthur and Flo had known when they'd lived in their first house in Hendon, before they'd been housed on the docks in the Divers' House. Gloria had been a lovely young girl, but, more than that, she'd been *Jack's* lovely young girl. The two had been inseparable. But something had happened. Flo had said that 'something' was Miriam. Whether that was true or not Arthur didn't know, but what he did know was that Gloria and Jack had broken up and he'd become engaged to Miriam.

'I bet you Jack got a shock seeing Gloria,' Arthur ruminated.

But Tommy was only half listening. His mind had been pulled back to Polly. She consumed his every waking thought. If he wasn't sleeping or working, he was thinking about Polly.

As he started to clear away the dishes, he reran the few minutes this afternoon when they had looked at each other for what felt like an eternity, and his mind's eye rested on the smile which had started to play on her lips.

Tommy knew he wasn't going to be able to get this woman out of his head, and he didn't want to either. He just had to figure out how to get talking to her. Words weren't exactly his strong point, and certainly didn't come naturally to him, unless it was something to do with diving or work. The very idea of going up to her and trying to start up a conversation, or being bold enough to ask her out on a date, made him feel more than a little nervous.

But he knew he had to overcome his fear and his insecurities. He needed to be with this woman – that much he knew for certain.

Later that night, lying in his narrow bed, Arthur's mind mulled over everything Tommy had told him. He missed working on the river and in the yards. Thompson's had been his second home, just like it was now Tommy's. Arthur had passed on his trade and his love of diving to Tommy, but not for any altruistic reasons, only because the boy had followed him around like a second shadow from the moment he could walk. Sometimes Tommy would run off during breaks at school and head straight for the river, where he knew he'd find his granddad. Arthur never had the heart to send him back to the stuffy classroom, but had always let him stay by the dockside, watching, learning and helping out when he could.

Arthur and Flo had become Tommy's mam and dad, and they had been a happy unit, but sadly that semblance of a normal family life, and the security it afforded the young lad, had not lasted long, for Flo had died when Tommy was just a nipper.

As Arthur's mind started to slip further into the past and into sleep, he said a silent prayer to his lovely Flo, whom he spoke to more and more often of late, and asked her to work her magic on Tommy and this woman welder called Polly.

'I miss you so much, Flo,' he whispered into the darkness.

Chapter Fifteen

Thursday, 5 September

Tommy had struggled to concentrate all day. It had been a relief every time he'd been lowered back down beneath the river's surface to carry out an inspection of the battered underbelly of a large cargo vessel that had limped into the dock the previous day. Being immersed into the grimy darkness of the Wear was the only let-up he'd had from seeing Polly working alongside a group of platers just a stone's throw away from the quayside.

He didn't know what was irking him the most, the fact that Polly had now been employed at the yards for more than a fortnight and he *still* hadn't plucked up the courage to speak to her, let alone ask her out on a date, or that she was now working shoulder to shoulder with the men. He was pleased Polly and the rest of the women welders were starting to fit in, and that the men seemed to be treating them as fellow workers and not like a group of pin-ups solely there for their own visual gratification, but he couldn't stop himself feeling a swell of jealousy that there was now also the occasional flurry of banter between them all.

When the horn finally sounded the end of the day's shift, Tommy was glad to be free from his torment, but again cursed himself for letting another day slip by without striking up a conversation with Polly. To be fair to himself, though, that was easier said than done, for Polly was always with the rest of the women welders. He'd never seen her on her own. And there was no way he had the confidence to approach her in front of an audience – and a female one at that.

Tommy saw that Polly and a few of the women were still hard at work and were obviously set to do a few hours' overtime. He wished he had something else to do which would give him an excuse to stay even later, but everyone from the diving team had now gone home. Even Helen had left for the day and not kept him chatting as she often did at the end of the shift.

As he walked past the women he raised a hand to Rosie, who returned the gesture.

'Night, Tommy,' she shouted over the buzz of the welding machines.

'Night, all,' he shouted back, his eyes seeking out Polly, who glanced up momentarily from the weld she was earnestly working on. He couldn't see her face behind her grey metal mask, but the glimpse he caught of her greeny-blue eyes showed she had seen him.

Instead of going straight back home, Tommy decided to take a ride on his treasured BSA. He knew he should save on fuel as even this was now being rationed, but if it meant he had to walk to work for a few days, it was worth the trade-off for the feeling of solitude and the freedom his bike gifted him.

He blasted along the seafront, past Roker and then Seaburn, enjoying the thrill of speed and the invigorating sensation of being exposed to the elements. But as he took in the physical changes to this once pretty coastal road – the barbed wire paralleling the promenade, the ugly cement pillboxes and the damage caused by the recent spate of bombings – he cursed what he felt was his impotence at not being able to do more to stop this barbarism that was changing the country he loved. He knew he was helping the war effort with his work in the shipyards, but it just didn't feel enough.

As he reached the Souter Lighthouse on the outskirts of Whitburn village, now an Observer Corps monitoring post, Tommy pulled over to look out to sea. Once again his mind turned to the talk he'd heard about units of clearance divers being formed to rid ports and harbours in the Mediterranean and the Atlantic of unexploded bombs and booby traps laid by the enemy. Tommy knew he would be perfect for the job. He was a strong, competent swimmer, as well as an experienced diver. During his life he had probably spent as much time in the water as he had on land. His job as a dock diver had instilled in him the ability to keep a cool head and to stay calm under pressure. He just couldn't shake the feeling that these skills he possessed would be better used in foreign seas rather than on the home front.

Tommy fired up his bike again and started to ride back along the seafront, his thoughts, as always of late, turning to Polly. He wondered how late she would be working this evening, and what she would do when she got home. He knew next to nothing about her, but something told him there wasn't a man in her life. He'd certainly not heard anything about her seeing anyone. As he rode over the Wearmouth Bridge and dropped back down to the south docks it was just starting to get dark. When he walked through his front door and called out to Arthur, his mind was still whirring, refusing to slow down and stand still.

'Fancy some fish 'n' chips tonight as a treat, Granda?' he asked Arthur as he pulled off his helmet and shrugged off his heavy leather jacket. Arthur was sitting in his favourite chair in front of the fire, which was gently crackling and letting out the occasional spit. He was nodding off, listening to the wireless, a newspaper spread out on his lap and a cup of tea going cold on the side table next to him.

'Never say no to a fish lot,' Arthur said, stirring from his half-slumber.

Tommy took a few bob out of the old teapot they used for keeping their money in. 'I won't be long. And don't worry about setting the table,' he said, seeing his grandfather starting to stir from the comfort of his chair. 'Let's just eat it out of the newspaper in front of the fire tonight.'

'Sounds good to me, lad,' Arthur agreed, nestling back into his chair.

Tommy walked up from Low Street to High Street East, but as he approached their local chippy he could see it was closed. He didn't mind walking further into town as it wasn't often he got to be out when it was so quiet and the streets so empty.

As Tommy continued walking, he spotted a tall, slim woman in dark blue overalls walking on the other side of the street. It took him a few seconds before realising it was Polly. He couldn't quite believe his eyes – or his luck. Without thinking, he shouted out her name.

Polly stopped in her tracks, and squinted across to the man who had called out to her.

Tommy waited for a car to pass and then ran across the road. 'Hello, Polly,' he said as he reached her.

'Tommy . . . hello,' Polly stuttered, clearly surprised.

'Have you just come from the yard?' he asked. It was the first thing which came to mind, but he was just thankful he'd managed to get some words out and not simply stood there like a lemon.

'Yes, they needed a few of us to work late so I volunteered—'

Polly had been about to ask where he was off to when the loud rising and falling wail of the air raid siren started to fill the air.

'How far away from home are you?' Tommy moved closer to Polly so as to be heard.

'Not far, just a few streets away. Tatham Street.' Tommy could just about make out what she was saying.

'I'll take you there!' he shouted.

But just as she was about to tell him she'd be fine, the sound of a massive explosion resonated like thunder. The Jerries had taken the town by surprise and were upon them before anyone had realised.

Without thinking, Tommy grabbed Polly's hand and the two ran as fast as they could along the street. His big paw-like hand enveloped hers, grasping it so tightly that he almost crushed it, so fearful was he that he would lose her. He was determined there was no way they would be parted.

In a split second the streets had gone from being relatively peaceful to noisy and panicky. People were spilling out of their homes and on to the street, running to the nearest shelters. Solid bands of white light swung across the sky, urgently searching the darkness for Hitler's harbingers of death. The ominous drone coming from the engines of the approaching aircraft was punctuated with the short, sharp rat-a-tat-tat of the ack-ack guns as they desperately fought off the approaching bombers, which were chaperoned on either side by the Luftwaffe's fighter planes.

Polly felt a mixture of fear and adrenaline well up and flood her body as they both anxiously looked for the nearest air raid shelter.

'There!' Tommy pointed towards a couple of people hurrying to an Anderson shelter in the grounds of a large house.

Polly's legs had felt like lead when she'd left the yard that evening, but now they were light and quick. She and Tommy ran side by side towards the house, before Tommy dropped back to let her slip through the small gateway first. They both came to an abrupt stop outside their hastily found refuge as they waited for an elderly man in front of them to find his way into the darkness of the makeshift corrugated-iron shelter.

Tommy immediately placed both his hands around Polly's slender shoulders so as to manoeuvre her through the shelter's narrow entrance. As she ducked her head to go in, there was another mighty explosion and the earth shook. Tommy stumbled in behind her, before quickly finding his feet again in the darkness.

It took a few seconds for their eyes to become accustomed to the musty gloom into which they had suddenly been propelled. Half a dozen terrified faces automatically looked up as Polly and Tommy stood there, heads bent against the arched metal panelling which formed the ceiling of the oversized foxhole they had found themselves in.

'Come here . . . sit here.' The offer came from the old man who had been in front of them.

They both sat down, squashed next to each other on one of the two long wooden benches that ran down each side of the shelter. Tommy was next to the kindly old man and Polly was shoulder to shoulder with a young woman with a small baby swaddled across her chest, who was, incredibly, fast asleep.

Tommy turned his head to Polly. 'Are you all right?' he demanded, his face the epitome of worry and concern, his hazel eyes searching Polly's face.

'Yes, I'm fine, thank you,' Polly told him, although she felt anything but fine. Her lungs felt as if they were burning up, her head was pounding, and she felt their world had just been shaken up and turned upside down, like one of those fancy cocktails she'd once seen made.

No one spoke as they listened to the muffled sound of more exploding bombs.

Then, 'Sounds near,' came a woman's voice from the far end of the shelter. There was a mumble of agreement. It was what they were all thinking. A myriad of thoughts pinged around Polly's mind. Worry about little Lucille and Bel and of course Agnes, as well as her new workmates, who were fast becoming her good friends. Where were they all now? Hopefully safe.

As if reading her thoughts, Tommy said, 'Who are you most worried about?'

Polly was taken aback by her sudden need to cry. Those few words of understanding, of empathy, had opened the floodgates of her emotions. She bit hard on her lip, forcing herself to be strong. She could feel her eyes well up with tears and hoped that Tommy couldn't see them in the murkiness they were encased in.

'My little niece, Lucille,' she said, trying to keep the tremor out of her voice. 'She's just turned two. If anything happens to her . . .' Her voice trailed off as she was hit by a huge bolt of anger against Hitler, Jerry, this war – every and any war that caused such heartache, such senseless death. 'My sister-in-law, Bel,' she continued. 'My mam.'

Tommy looked at this beautiful woman next to him, her ashen face smeared with soot from the yards, her eyes glistening with tears, and he wanted more than anything to hold her hand, to hold her whole body in his arms, and tell her everything would be just fine. But of course he couldn't. Over the past few weeks he may have had the strangest feeling that he knew her well, had known her for some time, but in reality he hadn't. They'd exchanged a smile. That was all. And yet he felt a familiarity that made him want to hold her, protect her, talk to her as if they'd been together for years.

'They'll be all right, I'm sure of it,' he said.

Polly forced a smile, knowing there was no way he could tell if they were safe, but feeling comforted by his words of reassurance. 'And you,' she said in return, 'who are you thinking of?'

'Ah, my granda,' Tommy said, 'but he'll be fine. I know he will. He's as tough as old boots. He's lived this long, I'm sure he won't let the Jerries take him before his time.'

Tommy tried to sound upbeat, but inwardly he wasn't at all sure about Arthur. He was such a stubborn old mule at times, he was probably still sitting in his armchair, refusing to let Hitler's bombs disturb his evening. The last air raid ten days ago had been the longest yet, lasting five and a half hours. Both he and Arthur had been stuck in a shelter until after three in the morning, and on finally being allowed out, a disgruntled and agitated Arthur had vowed never to go in another shelter again. For a man who had spent most of his life submerged in water and enveloped in a restrictive body suit with a helmet bolted on to his head, it didn't make sense that Arthur was so fearful of being trapped in a small building.

'No mam or dad then?' Polly asked.

Tommy hesitated. He wasn't used to people asking him personal questions. And there was no way he wanted to tell this woman who had been filling his head with all sorts of thoughts since he'd first clapped eyes on her the depressing story of his mother, even though a part of him felt as if he could tell her anything and everything.

'No, my dad was killed in the Great War,' he began. 'He served in the Twentieth Service Battalion, Wearside . . . And my mam died soon afterwards.'

Tommy didn't say how his mum had died, and Polly was sensitive enough to realise he didn't want to go into detail. Instead she told Tommy about her dad, how he too had served with the Durham Light Infantry and how he'd died just as the war had been coming to an end.

For the next hour the two chatted, both finding relief from thinking about what was happening outside and about the welfare of their loved ones. The other people in the air raid shelter were also chatting quietly amongst themselves, and one of the older women lit a miner's gas lamp which cast a soft light across all their faces. Polly smiled as she told Tommy a little about her life, her twin brothers now fighting in the desert in North Africa, and the father she'd never met.

Tommy soaked up every word and noticed every nuance of her face, her captivating smile when she talked about her little niece, her look of worry when she mentioned her older brothers, and how proud she was when she talked about the dad she'd never met but obviously idolised. And, in turn, he found the words tumbling out of his own mouth, something they'd never done before, telling her about his life with Arthur, and his grandma Flo, who had died when he was young.

As they sat squashed up on the hard bench, Polly took in every word Tommy said, and as she did so she studied his chiselled face and the slight crookedness of his teeth, which only seemed to add to his attractiveness. She was constantly aware of the closeness of his body next to her. She could feel the outline of his thick, muscular arm pressing against her own. It had been hot during the day and she'd rolled up her sleeves as far as she could to her shoulders and had kept them like that, enjoying the slight evening chill. Now her whole body felt sweaty and dirty. She could feel where the material of Tommy's short-sleeved top ended and his flesh began. Everyone in the shelter was so tightly packed together she could hardly move her body, so that whichever way she turned, or moved, her side was pressed against Tommy.

When the all-clear siren sounded out, it was a harsh awakening from the magical world they had slipped into unawares over the past hour or so since they had stumbled in from the chaos. Someone opened the door to the shelter and a gust of acrid, dusty air entered their little refuge.

Polly and Tommy remained seated, both politely letting the others out first. As the last two people left, Tommy put his hand out to allow Polly to go before him. She stepped out into the cool night air, feeling immediately light-headed. She hadn't eaten much and she saw specks of glitter in front of her eyes. Her footing felt unstable on the uneven ground outside the shelter and she stumbled backwards.

Tommy grabbed her, stopping her from falling back into the shelter. The pair were suddenly caught in an unexpected embrace. Polly's body was pressed against his as he held her, his arms wrapped around her body, their faces just inches apart. Tommy felt an overwhelming urge to kiss the lips he'd been looking at for the past hour. Polly's eyes looked straight into his own, telling him she too felt the same. Neither pulled away, not wanting to break free, both feeling an incredible oneness as she was wrapped up in his arms.

Polly wanted so much to stay in the warmth of his body, wanted too much to feel his mouth on hers. But she stopped herself. Brought herself to her senses.

'I'm all right, thanks,' she stuttered. 'I just lost my balance for a moment.'

As she stepped back, Tommy felt bereft, but asked, 'Are you sure you're okay?'

'Yes, yes, honestly, I'm fine, really,' she said, now feeling embarrassed at letting him hold her for longer than necessary.

For the first time, Polly heard the sounds of ambulance sirens and shouts and running feet, which had somehow been inaudible for the short spell of time she'd been in Tommy's arms. As the clanging of a passing fire engine added to the din that now surrounded them, reality hit home, as did all her worries about Lucille, Bel and Agnes.

Tommy immediately noticed the look of worry reappear on her face.

'I'll take you home,' he said, desperately wanting to stay with this woman whom he felt so drawn to, so reluctant to part from.

'No, no, don't worry,' Polly said, starting to walk away. 'I'll see you tomorrow at work. And I hope Arthur's all right,' she added as she broke into a jog and disappeared into the surrounding melee.

Tommy stood there, desolate. His urge was to run after her, but he didn't.

As he made his own way home, he couldn't stop thinking about her. He replayed every word uttered, and every movement she'd made. He too had felt her body pressing against his in their tightly packed shelter, and more than anything wanted her there with him now. He had never felt this kind of intensity for a woman before. It was almost like a madness. It elated him, but his craving for her also perturbed him. He didn't understand this peculiar kind of insanity – all he knew was that he had to make Polly his.

Chapter Sixteen

Friday, 6 September

After Tommy left for work the following morning, Arthur settled down to read the local paper. There was very little about the previous night's attack. It was like an upside-down version of 'The Emperor's New Clothes': in this case, there was plenty to see, but nothing much being said. The Ministry of Information censors had passed for publication a black-and-white photograph of a mound of crushed and charred metal lying at the back of a row of houses. The description read: 'The remains of the German bomber which crashed into a back lane after being disabled by anti-aircraft fire on the north-east coast.' There was no mention that the town was Sunderland, nor that the aircraft had come down in Suffolk Street in the east end not far from where Arthur was now sitting – and had sat throughout the whole of last night's raid.

Arthur's eyesight was starting to fail him, like the rest of his ageing body, and he had to hold the paper at arm's length to focus on another photograph that showed half a dozen soldiers inspecting what looked like two huge metal snails, the bomber's underbelly, lying on a bed of concrete and brick rubble. Curious onlookers peered at the spectacle from afar, and in the background there was a line of red-brick terraced houses which had escaped the fallout from the skies unscathed.

The ministry had also vetoed the facts that a woman had been killed, several people had been injured, and the bodies of the four German airmen had been found at the scene of the crash.

As Arthur was reading his paper, he said a silent prayer of thanks that his grandson had returned safe and sound last night.

Across the river from Arthur, the J. L. Thompson & Sons shipbuilding yard, like just about everywhere else in the town, was starting the day shrouded in an air of bewilderment. But the people of Sunderland were refusing to show just how badly the rain of blows they'd received during the night's ferocious attack had knocked them for six.

As Polly arrived at work she looked around her at the faces of her fellow shipyard workers and saw a look of quiet but determined resolution, a doggedness that they were not going to be defeated. The town had taken a hammering the previous night, and it had shaken everyone to the core. Their vulnerability was inescapable, but there was also an unspoken understanding amongst them all that they would not be crushed. Come hell or high water, they would not stop doing what they knew needed to be done. They would not be beaten.

'Right. We've got our work cut out today, so we're just going to have to crack on and pick up where you left off with the platers.' Rosie forced herself to sound energetic and upbeat in an attempt to break through the sombre mood of the day. 'Everyone but Hannah,' she added. 'You're coming with me to the outfitting dock. The plumbers there need someone with nimble hands and a neat weave weld.'

The real reason, however, why Hannah was being taken across to the dry dock was because she simply didn't have the strength to cope with the kind of back-breaking flat welding the women were doing at the moment. Rosie had been determined not to lose Hannah, so she'd had a quiet word with Jack and asked if she could move her to wherever there was a need for more detailed and intricate welding. Jack had happily agreed, making a point of asking how the other women were getting on.

'I hope she's ganna be all right, and no one takes the lend of her.' Gloria's voice was full of genuine concern. As the eldest of the group, she had assumed the protective role of mother hen.

Martha huffed loudly, expressing her own apprehension. She seemed to have especially taken to Hannah and liked to be by her side, which made for quite a comical sight as Martha must have been twice Hannah's size in height as well as width.

'She's more hardy than she looks,' Dorothy chipped in. 'She's like one of those little birds which migrate to the other side of the world. You'd never believe they'd have the strength, but they do, and then they do it all again and come back.'

The women all agreed as they watched their dark-haired friend disappear into a crowd of workers, before making their own way over to where the platers and their young helpers had gathered.

'Morning, ladies,' exclaimed Bernie, one of the veteran platers, as the women approached. 'Hope Jerry didn't keep you all from your beauty sleep last night?'

The words were barely out of his mouth before Gloria retorted, 'Nah, but it obviously did you lot, by the looks of your ugly mugs this morning.'

Bernie and the men let out loud guffaws of laughter.

Polly wished she had Gloria's gift of the gab, but was just thankful that one of them, at least, was quick-witted enough this morning to give back as good as they got. She herself felt as though she were on another planet today, and it wasn't last night's bombings that had sent her there, but the time she'd spent in the air raid shelter with Tommy. Her mind kept replaying every moment they had spent together, every word they'd exchanged, and every precious second that Tommy had held her when she'd stumbled into his arms.

Bel had noticed the slightly intoxicated demeanour of her sister-in-law the night before and, after prodding Polly for an explanation, had listened misty-eyed as she had told her how she'd first spotted Tommy coming out of the water in his diver's suit, how they had caught each other's eye and exchanged a smile, and how that evening they had been crammed together in the little Anderson shelter in which they'd sought refuge.

Bel had sighed when Polly finished her tale with how she had stumbled and been caught in Tommy's arms. As an incurable romantic, she wanted nothing more than for her sister-in-law to fall in love.

As Polly sat on the ground, one leg stretched out in front of her and the other stuck out at a right angle, a position she now felt was second nature to her, she forced herself to stop thinking about Tommy and concentrate on the job in hand. But just as soon as she had pushed the image of Tommy's face out of her mind, he appeared in the flesh in front of her. The look he wore was all seriousness and concern.

'Was everyone all right when you got back?' he asked, totally oblivious to the open-mouthed stares coming from the women welders.

'Yes, thank goodness, they were all fine.' Polly felt herself go instantly red. 'And Arthur? Was he well when you got back?' The slight warble in Polly's voice betrayed how nervous she was talking to Tommy in front of an audience.

'Yes, thanks. He's still in one piece.'

What Tommy wanted to tell Polly, had she been on her own, was that Arthur had stayed at home, glued to his chair in front of the fire, in defiance of the Luftwaffe's bombers. He'd known from the moment he'd got back home after he'd left Polly that his granddad hadn't moved since the sirens had sounded out. Part of him had been livid, but another part had just been relieved Arthur was all right. And he had to admit, his ire had been somewhat subdued as he was so full of joy about the time he'd spent with Polly. So he'd let his granddad off with a scolding look before making them both a sandwich to compensate for the fish-and-chip supper they were meant to have been having.

'Say hello to the old man from us,' one of the platers shouted over. Just about every one of the older workers knew and liked Arthur, who, although he didn't make it down the yard much these days, was still held in high regard by those who had worked with him.

Tommy smiled and nodded over at the men, before turning his attention back to Polly.

'Good . . . good . . . as long as everyone's all right . . .' he said, running out of words and turning to walk away.

When Tommy was out of earshot, Dorothy piped up, 'Polly, I believe there's a lot you need to be telling us.'

'Come on,' Rosie ordered the women, sensing Polly's discomfort and embarrassment. She had just got back from taking Hannah to her new work area, and had caught the end of Polly and Tommy's short conversation. 'There's work to be done.'

Apart from Hannah, Rosie was pleased with the progress of the women, who were adapting remarkably well to their demanding workload. They were also getting on well with the platers, but were still pretty isolated from the rest of the workforce. If Rosie let them carry on as they were, and didn't give them a nudge, they'd never integrate. So when the women stopped for their mid-morning break, Rosie asked them if they fancied having lunch in the canteen.

On hearing the suggestion, Dorothy couldn't get her words out quickly enough. 'All of us? Together? You as well?'

Rosie nodded, thinking to herself that their luncheon date would also have the added bonus of giving them all some respite from Dorothy's constant pleas to go to the canteen. The girl had become obsessed.

'Yeah!' Dorothy exclaimed.

Gloria rolled her eyes heavenward. 'Calm down. It's not as if she's taking us to the Ritz, you know,' she said, trying to clamp down on Dorothy's excitement, but not succeeding.

The rest of the morning there was a noticeable, slightly nervous adrenaline buzz about the women, and when the lunchtime horn sounded out Dorothy practically ripped off her mask and fished out her small compact from her bag. She must have been the only shipyard worker in the whole of the north-east to take a mirror to work. She wet her finger and shaped her eyebrows and then got her hankie out to wipe away the smears of sweat and dirt from her face.

'Get a move on,' Rosie commanded as the women all stood up and grabbed their holdalls for the walk over to the canteen.

She had to hide her amusement as she looked behind her at her flock, following her across the expanse of the yard towards the cafeteria. It didn't escape her notice that Gloria was leading the other women, like her second in command, with Martha's huge protective presence guarding the rear.

'Come on! Rosie's taking us out to lunch,' Dorothy shouted overexcitedly to Hannah, who was walking away from the outfitting dock and was looking around her like a lost soul. As soon as she saw her workmates she hurried over and fell in behind Gloria.

As they approached the main entrance of the prefabricated dining room, Rosie had to suppress a smile. Her fledgling welders were looking as if she were making them walk the gangplank and not off to get some warm food in their bellies. All apart from Dorothy, who was indeed acting as though she were off to the Ritz, minus the make-up and party dress.

The women entered the building and were hit by the smell of stewed meat and sweaty cabbage and the sound of chatter competing against the clashing of cutlery and plates. As they lined up behind the queue of fellow workers, a quietness descended across the room. What felt like hundreds of dishevelled faces turned from their food to stare at the sight of the strange medley of women who were nervously looking around, trying to act as if this were the most natural thing in the world for them to be doing. Even Dorothy had gone quiet and appeared terribly self-conscious.

Within a minute or so, though, the low hum of eating and talking started up once again, the men's food taking precedence over the midday sideshow.

After the women had ordered their lunch and carried it on thin metal trays over to an empty table at the side of the canteen, Rosie tried to put them at ease by asking about the night before, and if any of them had been affected by the bombings.

Polly shook her head and secretly breathed a sigh of relief that their unexpected visit to the canteen had made the women forget to quiz her about Tommy.

Martha followed suit with a single shake of her head, and, as was usual whenever it was time to eat, started tucking into her food as if it was her last supper. Hannah looked up briefly, smiled and said, 'We fine, thank you, Rosie,' before focusing back on her plate, seemingly more interested in dissecting her meat pie and inspecting what was inside rather than eating it.

Dorothy was too busy looking about her to reply to Rosie's question, and after surveying the territory for a short while, her attention was soon caught by a young man sitting a few tables away from where the women were. There was no denying he had a handsome face, and a thick mop of jet-black hair which he had slicked back, but it was also obvious that he was more than aware of his good looks. He made no secret of the fact that he was giving Dorothy the once-over.

'For goodness' sake, can he not keep his eyes to himself?' Gloria threw a warning glance over at the shipyard Romeo, who was managing to shovel food into his mouth without taking his eyes off Dorothy.

Dorothy was loving the attention, and was obviously not surprised to be the focus of the young man's stares. In fact, there seemed to be a familiarity between the two of them.

'Do you know him?' Polly asked.

At that moment Hannah dared to look up, only to catch the shipyard Casanova winking across at Dorothy. 'Urgh! He wink at you,' she whispered to Dorothy, who was daintily eating her lunch as though it were a cordon bleu meal.

'His name's Eddie,' Dorothy said under her breath, but loud enough for the women to hear. 'He's one of the riveters,' she added conspiratorially.

'How do you know him?' Gloria demanded, not at all happy with this visual dalliance she was witnessing.

'Oh, from when I was at Binns. I used to work with a girl he was dating,' Dorothy said, but it was clear she was holding something back.

As the workers finished their lunches, chairs were scraped back and gradually the dining room started to empty. The women had finished eating, but had put off standing up for fear of being stared at again. Now the canteen was thinning out they felt more comfortable putting their dirty trays to the side and leaving. They walked back to join the platers at their workstation.

Jack was walking across the yard towards the drawing office, where the ship's blueprints and designs were mapped out. When he saw the group of women he stopped to let them pass.

'Hello, Gloria,' he said with a smile.

'Hello, Jack,' Gloria said politely, but there was no smile.

Their salutation was over within seconds, but the question over how the pair knew each other hovered as the women settled back to work. Even Rosie looked a little curious. No one, however, asked how the two were acquainted. Without saying anything, they all felt intuitively this would be crossing a boundary which Gloria intended to keep firmly in place.

The platers, who were all pulling on their thick, oversized gloves ready for the afternoon's work, had also seen Jack, which wasn't surprising as his suit made him stick out like a sore thumb amongst the hundreds of grease-smeared overalls and flat caps.

'I've never seen the gaffer in the yards so much lately,' one of them said.

'I know. I've seen him about a lot. Maybe he's missing his old job,' another added sarcastically.

'Well, I'd swap him any day,' the young apprentice added.

As the men carried a large sheet of steel that had just been emitted from the huge roller in the platers' shed, Bernie said, 'There's talk he may be going over to the Yanks with the big boss.'

'Really? Why?' one of the older men asked.

Polly noticed Rosie had started to pay heed to their conversation.

'Something about a design for a new type of cargo vessel. I've heard they're going to be called Liberty ships. Been designed by Cyril Thompson himself.'

Their talk was soon drowned out by the build-up of noise as drilling, riveting, and the hammering and chiselling of the caulkers joined together to blot out all other sounds. Before long the platers and the women welders were left to their own thoughts.

Chapter Seventeen

When Polly arrived home that evening, all the children from what was now known as Aggie's Nursery had been returned to their parents and there was an unusual quietness and calm in the house.

'Hello, love,' said Agnes. 'I've taken a chance and done cottage pie. Here's hoping we get to sit at the table and eat tonight without that awful siren going off.'

'Sounds lovely, Ma,' Polly said, but Agnes could tell that her daughter was miles away.

'And I think we'll have come caviar and a little tipple of champagne for our hors d'oeuvres,' Agnes added, looking at Polly as she went to sit with Lucille and help her with a particularly messy charcoal sketch which had left her looking as though she'd been welding alongside her aunty Polly all day.

'Sounds great . . .' Polly said, oblivious.

'Right, that's enough. What's going on in that head of yours?' Agnes demanded. 'You've been in fairyland since last night and when I asked Bel this morning if you were all right, she sounded evasive, to say the least.'

'Ma, I'm fine. Just tired. Really. Nothing to worry about – trust me.' Polly got up and gave her mum a big hug.

'Now I know there's something up,' Agnes said, enjoying her daughter's spontaneous show of love but suspicious about the motivation. 'There's not a man on the scene, is there?' Agnes had taken a wild stab in the dark and got a jolt of surprise on seeing her daughter's face and realising that she may well have unwittingly hit her target. 'Is there?' she asked again, now all concern.

'Of course not, Ma,' Polly retorted.

But Agnes knew her daughter was lying. She had never been one for deceit, even if it was just a fib.

Looking at her daughter, so young and vibrant, there was no denying that despite her tomboyish nature Polly had turned out a very feminine and attractive young woman. It was something, however, that her daughter was totally unaware of. She was still naive to the ways of men. Being a pretty young woman and working in a male-dominated place like the shipyards, Agnes knew Polly was going to have to wise up – and fast.

'Just because a man shows you some attention, doesn't mean owt, you know,' Agnes said testily.

Polly felt her love bubble slowly deflate, and although she knew her mum was just being protective, she couldn't stop herself reacting. 'I'm not a child, Ma, so stop treating me like I'm one.'

'Pol, you may be a grown woman, but you've still got a lot of growing up to do,' Agnes warned.

'You'll have me an old maid if you had your way,' Polly shot back.

Before Agnes had time to bat a retort back, Bel could be heard bustling through the front door and down the hall-way. She appeared in the kitchen, took one look at both women and knew instantly that words had been said. She made a beeline for her daughter.

Agnes opened her mouth to speak but then shut it again. Polly seemed well and happy, which was the main thing. And besides, she didn't have the energy or the want for an argument.

'All right then, Mrs I'm All Grown Up, shell us some peas to go with the cottage pie and I'll get the table set,' she said, trundling into the scullery.

Later on that evening, when Agnes had taken herself off to bed, Bel asked Polly if Agnes had picked up on what she called Polly's 'aura of love'.

'Yes,' Polly said, exasperated.

'So, tell me, did you see him today?' Bel demanded.

Polly didn't need prompting. She told her sister-in-law how Tommy had come over and asked her about them all, and how she had asked about Arthur in return.

Bel gave Tommy a mental nod of approval. She liked his concern for how Polly was feeling and for those Polly loved.

'Sooo . . . now we just need him to ask you out on a proper date,' Bel concluded as she heard Lucille wake up and cry out for her.

The thought of going out with Tommy made Polly's heart race.

Bel took one look at Polly's face and laughed as she headed off to bed. 'I don't think I need to tell you to have *sweet dreams* tonight.'

As Bel soothed Lucille back to sleep, her thoughts drifted back to her own first date with Teddy. How it had been different because they'd known each other most of their lives, but how it had still been equally exciting and nerve-racking. It felt like a lifetime since her Teddy had held her in his arms, and it scared her how quickly her memories of his looks, his feel and his smell seemed to be fading. But more than anything, it worried her that she had not heard from him for over two months now. Every day she willed the postwoman to bring her good news, but for weeks there'd been nothing. She knew Agnes was also worried sick about both her sons, but neither woman had voiced her concerns, scared perhaps that if they formed their fears into words it would somehow make them more real.

Chapter Eighteen

Sunday, 8 September

It had been almost three weeks since Raymond had arrived back in his hometown, and he had been enjoying biding his time, reacquainting himself with some old friends, and going to a few of the alehouses he had used to frequent before his incarceration. He was certainly enjoying his new-found freedom, but more than anything he was revelling in researching and formulating his long-held and well-thought-out plan.

He was particularly pleased with himself as he had managed to find out some very interesting information, which he knew would help him get exactly what he wanted. 'I love this war,' he had said to himself on more than one occasion. Raymond couldn't believe how many advantages it had for someone like himself. For starters, everyone was so concerned about what Hitler and the SS were doing, no one was paying much attention to what was happening on their own doorstep. Everyone's focus was on keeping the home fires burning and at the same time keeping Jerry at bay. The whole of Sunderland had been thrown into disarray by the recent bombing, then a couple of days later London had been blitzed, leaving thousands dead and injured. It had caused a tidal wave of anger across the whole of the country.

For Raymond, however, the sound of the air raid sirens was something he positively welcomed, and even looked forward to. Like the other night. As soon as he had heard the familiar electronic wailing sound out across the town, he'd felt a rush of excitement and adrenaline. As was the case every time there was an air raid warning, he knew most people would be in such a panic to get to a shelter that they wouldn't even bother to shut their doors, never mind lock them. It had meant rich pickings for Raymond, and he'd returned that night with a dapper three-piece suit he'd pilfered from a lovely Georgian terrace near Backhouse Park. His only regret was that he hadn't been able to take more, as he simply hadn't been able to carry it. He had, though, stashed a handful of jewellery in his pockets, but would have to wait a while before he tried to flog it for some ready cash.

As well as the welcome sound of the sirens, the black-outs were an extra bonus. They meant that every night, when darkness fell, he could move about as he pleased, without worrying that some nosey parker or do-gooder was watching him and realising he was up to no good.

Raymond had managed to find himself a small but adequate bedsit on the Ryhope Road. With so many men away at war, he knew the landlady had just been relieved to have someone rent a room and so hadn't quizzed him about his past, or where he'd come from. So far he'd managed to keep his ex-con status well and truly under wraps. He had chosen the bedsit as it wasn't far from where Rosie lived, which meant it was easy to keep tabs on her. He had to be careful, though, not to accidentally bump into her, as he was determined that was going to be a well-orchestrated meeting, and one which would have Rosie dancing to his tune and giving him exactly what he wanted.

Over the past week he had been watching and following her, and he had found out that his niece was a stickler for routine. She worked five days a week at the yard and occasionally weekends. She rarely socialised, and she worked alternate nights at the place he now knew to be called Lily's. Rosie was always punctual for both her jobs, arriving fifteen minutes before the half seven start at Thompson's, and by seven in the evening at Lily's.

As Raymond accepted a glass of whisky from his hostess, he looked at his stolen gold fob watch and knew that his niece would now be making her way along the affluent avenues of Ashbrooke – and walking straight into his trap.

Chapter Nineteen

As Rosie put the finishing touches to her make-up and quickly slipped into her evening attire, which she always kept perfectly pressed and pristine, a voice in her head was telling her not to go to Lily's tonight. She didn't know why, as there was no real reason for her not to. Perhaps it was simply because she was physically shattered. Today had been tougher than normal at the yards. There had been a real rush to get one of the merchant vessels back out to sea. It had been a case of all hands on deck, literally. But there was no way she could skip work tonight, even if she wanted to. Rosie needed the money, and Lily ran a tight ship. She expected and relied on her girls to be dependable and punctual, and, in return, she made sure they received their fair share of the takings. If nothing else, Lily was an astute businesswoman. She knew if she treated her staff properly, and paid them well, she would in turn also benefit.

Rosie left her top-floor room and quietly snuck down the three flights of stairs, managing to slip out the front door without anyone seeing her, including the ever-vigilant Mrs T. As she hurried to work, she felt the nip of autumn for the first time and realised that the nights were tapering off. She thought about Charlotte, who had just started a new term, and felt relieved the boarding school was set in acres of remote Yorkshire countryside and was miles away from any town or city, and therefore was protected from the brutality of this soul-destroying war.

The streets became quieter and the traffic practically non-existent as Rosie turned into Mowbray Road, just a few minutes' walk away from Lily's on West Lawn. She smiled to herself as she thought about the burgeoning romance between Polly and Tommy. As far as she knew, they hadn't even been out on a date yet, but it was clear to anyone who saw them chatting, or watched them in the yard, that they were totally smitten with each other. And what made the two of them even more endearing was that they seemed entirely oblivious to the fact that everyone around them could see how they felt about each other. They were like beacons shining out in a darkened sea, unaware of the bright light they were emitting.

Rosie wished she had a love in her life. When she was young her mum had often quoted the words of one of the characters in *Alice's Adventures in Wonderland* – a book both Rosie and Charlotte had loved having read to them over and over again. The story had seemed even more magical as their mother would tell them that Lewis Carroll had walked on the beach just outside of their little cottage and been inspired as he'd strolled by the water's edge.

'"Oh, 'tis love, 'tis love, that makes the world go round!"' Rosie could almost hear her mum's gentle voice recite the words to them. Words which now seemed so ironic as Rosie realised her life was pretty much devoid of any love. She knew she would never have the kind of traditional courtship and romance that awaited Polly and Tommy, but that didn't stop her from longing for love. She was no fool, though. What man would fall in love with her? And if he did, he'd soon fall straight back out again when he learnt about her employment at Lily's.

But, Rosie told herself, they were thoughts for another day. For now she was just taking every day as it came. It was the only way she could survive. She'd save all thoughts of the future for another time.

As Rosie walked down the uneven cobbled street in her heels, going through her usual routine of checking behind her as she turned into the back lane, she dragged her thoughts back to the here and now.

She took no pleasure in the work she was about to do, but she did enjoy Lily's company. Perhaps it was because there was no pretence between them. They were who they were, and they liked each other in spite of it.

'Hello, *ma petite*,' Lily gushed when she saw Rosie arrive. 'We have a new client this evening. He's told me he's been away for a while, but is enjoying being back in his *maison natale*.'

Rosie raised an eyebrow at Lily's attempt at speaking French.

'*Birthplace*, darling, *birthplace*,' Lily explained. 'He's just come back home after a spell away, but is being very mysterious about exactly where he's been. And he's asked for you specifically,' she added.

Rosie was still smiling at Lily's determination to conquer the French language when she walked into the large, smoky drawing room, already full of girls and clients chatting away. But the look of amusement on her face immediately disappeared as soon as she clapped eyes on the new client.

Never one to miss a trick, Lily saw in an instant Rosie's sudden change in demeanour. Not only had Rosie's smile been replaced by a look of complete and utter shock, but she had turned as white as a ghost.

The client, however, who had earlier introduced himself as Mr Gallagher, looked positively elated at seeing his escort for the evening. 'Rosie! What a surprise to see yer bonny face here,' he said with gusto.

Raymond, who was smartly dressed in his new dark grey suit, was standing next to the fireplace with an almost empty whisky glass in his hand. When he had looked in the mirror before leaving this evening, he had complimented himself on how well he'd scrubbed up, and mused on what a difference money and some good-quality tailoring made to a man's appearance. When he had arrived here a short while ago, he'd easily passed as someone who had the money to spend at a place like Lily's. He'd just dampened down his accent a little and had fitted in perfectly.

Raymond put his drink down on the marble mantel-piece, rested his carved walking stick against it and opened his arms to embrace Rosie. A look of pure glee spread across his face on seeing Rosie's mounting horror at simply being in the same room as him, never mind being taken into his arms.

'Well, well. It's been at least five years, hasn't it, pet? And look how yer've grown,' he said, reverting to his native accent.

As Lily looked at her new client and then back at Rosie, she instinctively knew that she had a situation on her hands, and that this man was a charlatan. She had been conned. This bullish man was an imposter, who hadn't come here for the services she offered.

Keeping her composure, Lily asked, 'Monsieur Gallagher, you didn't tell me you knew Rosie personally?' She took a sidelong glance at Rosie, who seemed to have lost the power of speech.

A few of the other girls near enough to overhear the exchange between Lily and this new client sensed the awkwardness of the meeting between their boss and the wiry, well-dressed man with the polished, ornate walking stick. When he'd entered the room earlier, they'd all been

139

secretly glad they had already been introduced to their escorts for the evening and would not be asked to entertain this slightly sinister-looking older man.

'Perhaps we should all retire to the parlour so I can hear more about your former acquaintance,' Lily suggested.

'Whatever *Madame* wishes,' Raymond replied, a smirk sliding across his face.

Lily's regular patron George had been quietly observing Raymond from afar, and didn't like what he was seeing. He knew Lily well enough to know she was far from happy about something, and he'd never seen Rosie look so grim. He watched as Lily gently took Rosie's arm and guided her out of the room and away from her other guests.

As he started to follow them out of the drawing room, Lily spotted him. 'Yes, George, please join us,' she said, giving him a grave look.

George tried his hardest to hide his limp as he walked next to Raymond and they both followed the two women into the back kitchen. George may have been getting on a bit in years, but his mind was still as sharp as a pin and it didn't escape his notice that Lily had positioned herself strategically near the knife stand.

Despite George's show of support, Lily knew she might need a bit of extra help. She had been in this game long enough now to know when there was trouble afoot. She only cursed herself that she hadn't read this man sooner, when he'd first entered her establishment.

As soon as the door swung shut behind them, Lily put both her hands on the end of the large kitchen table, leaning ever so slightly forward, and demanded, 'What's all this about then?' Her voice had now completely lost its melodic French lilt and been replaced by a well-worn cockney twang.

'*Madame*,' Raymond said in a sneering voice, 'I've simply come to call in – how shall I put it? – an outstanding debt.'

They all waited for this shrewish, sneering man, who was obviously enjoying being the centre of attention, to continue.

Rosie, meanwhile, was feeling as though she were in some kind of fog. Even her eyes felt blurred, and she kept getting snatches of remembrances of her recent dreams, or rather the nightmares she'd started to have again in which this man's face played a large part. As she stood there, mind racing, she felt her legs lose their strength and she pulled out one of the chairs from the kitchen table and slumped into it.

Every time she tried to look at Raymond she felt sick to the pit of her stomach. She felt she had been transported back to the darkest and most horrendous moment of her life. The sudden memory of that time had caught her un-awares and had ripped down her defences and left her feeling totally powerless. For the first time in many years she was not in control of what was happening to her, or her life.

'Let me explain,' Raymond said. 'Yer see, Rosie here is the daughter of my sister Eloise, who very tragically died in a road accident, along with her husband, William – Rosie's father. But,' he continued, 'before they died, Eloise owed me quite a substantial amount of money. Money which has grown with interest ower the past five years. And yer see' – Raymond was enjoying the suspense – 'I'm afraid that debt has now fallen to Rosie, who is the oldest remaining relative. *Only* remaining relative, not countin' lovely little Charlotte, of course.'

Rosie sat bolt upright when she heard Charlotte's name come out of this vile man's mouth. His mention of her little sister snapped her back to reality.

She finally found her voice. 'Don't you dare even mention my sister. She's got nothing to do with anything. If it's money you're after, you're out of luck, because I haven't got any.' She practically spat the words out at her uncle.

'Ah, now then, pet, I think yer telling great big porkies. You and me both know you've got money and plenty of it. What, with yer job here at this fancy whorehouse and the money yer making as head welder at Thompson's? But dinnit look upset, pet. If yer ganna be upset at anyone, it should be at that lovely mam of yours. If she hadn't gone and died like that, I would be asking *her* for what's owed – not you.'

Rosie felt her anger bubble to the surface. 'How dare you! You sick, twisted, evil man. My mam didn't owe you a penny. She didn't even mention you *once* in all the time she was alive. And by God, I can see why. How ashamed she must have felt having a brother like you. My mother never owed anyone anything, never mind someone she clearly despised that much that she denied your very existence.' Rosie felt herself run out of breath.

'One day,' Raymond said calmly, 'we'll sit down, when there's just the two of us, and I can explain it all in detail to yer, but for now, yer just ganna have to take my word for it. Yer mam owed me – big time.'

Rosie felt her skin crawl.

Raymond smiled, showing his nicotine-yellow teeth, enjoying seeing the effect he was having on Rosie. He loved nothing more than putting someone in a cage, real or imaginary, and watching them clawing out at the powerlessness of their situation. At their impotence. And Rosie was about to understand just how cornered she now was.

He had waited a long time, but now he would not only reap his financial reward for his patience and planning, but, best of all, he would have the revenge he craved. Had craved for so long. His sister might not be alive, but he was certain she would now be turning in her grave.

'Well,' Lily butted in, incredulous that this rat-like man was making these threats, 'I think I can speak for my girl here and tell you that you won't be getting a penny from her.'

'Do I need to explain it to yer, *madame*?' Raymond asked, smirking over to Rosie, his hand now firmly over the rounded ram's head of his walking stick. Not waiting for an answer, he continued, 'Ya see, *Madame* Lily, if Rosie doesn't give me what I'm owed, I will make sure that every shipyard worker in the town knows exactly where she gans every other evening. She'll never be able to show that pretty face of hers in any of the shipyards from here to kingdom come. And I'll also make sure that the headmistress of that very prestigious boarding school that lovely little lass gans to knows exactly how yer managing to pay their fees. Not that you'll be able to afford to keep her there for much longer. Oh, and Rosie, I must say that Charlotte is looking like yer double these days. She's growing up fast, isn't she?'

That was all Rosie could take. 'If you've been anywhere near my sister,' she sprang out of her chair and flung herself across at Raymond, 'I'll bloody kill you!'

George, who had been standing silently in shock at all he was hearing and seeing, quickly stepped in front of Rosie before she had the opportunity to carry out her threat. The wild look in her eye when Raymond had taunted her about her sister told him that she was more than capable. And much as he would have happily watched Rosie tear this abomination of a man limb from limb, he knew it would be Rosie and Lily who would suffer at the end of the day.

As he held Rosie back, he craned his neck back to Raymond, who was holding his grotesque-looking walking stick across his body with both hands in a defensive stance.

'Get out. Now!' George shouted at him. 'You are a man without a conscience and as such are no man at all,' he said, unable to contain his disgust any more.

Raymond knew he was outnumbered. But he was happy to leave. He had achieved what he had come here to do.

'I'll be seeing yer, Rosie. And soon,' he sneered, tipping an imaginary hat in mock respect and disappearing through the kitchen door.

Seconds later they heard the sound of the back door slam shut.

Chapter Twenty

Lily, George and Rosie stood rooted to the spot in shocked silence for a moment.

It was Lily who spoke first. 'Well, I don't know about you two,' she said, 'but I'm going to have a shot of brandy.' She walked into her large pantry and came out again with a bottle of Rémy Martin she'd acquired from the black market. As she put the bottle on the kitchen table she pulled out the cork, before turning to pick out three cut-crystal liquor glasses from her French armoire. 'And I'm guessing by the silence that you two are going to join me?'

'Yes, yes, thank you, Lily,' George blustered, before adding pensively, 'It just shows you that it's not just Deutschland which has the monopoly on evil – we've got our share here too.' He downed his brandy in one.

Rosie's hand was trembling as she took a sip from her glass and grimaced as the fiery golden nectar burnt the back of her throat.

'I'm so sorry to bring my troubles to your doorstep, Lily,' she said, her voice now trembling as much as her hands. 'And for getting you involved too, George.'

'Nonsense, my dear,' George reassured her, as Lily topped up his glass as well as her own. 'I'm just glad we were here to help you stand your ground against that nauseating excuse of a man.' George took another slug of the Rémy Martin before asking tentatively, 'What I'm curious about, my dear, is how on earth is – or rather, how *can* that man possibly be related to you?'

Lily leant over to take Rosie's trembling hand in her own and squeezed it reassuringly. 'Go on, *ma chérie*, you can tell us,' she said, recovering her French accent.

Rosie took a deep breath. Once she started talking, the words just tumbled out of her mouth. She'd been so shut off for so long it was like opening up a Pandora's box of all her thoughts, memories and feelings. With tears gently falling down her cheeks she told Lily and George how she'd first met Raymond just days after her mum and dad had been killed.

'He repulsed me from the off. I don't know how he got to know about Mum and Dad's accident; there'd never been any mention of him in all the time I was growing up. As far as I knew, my mum was an only child. But then again, she didn't really talk much about her life before she met Dad and had us.'

'And what did he want, when he turned up?' George asked. 'A man like him always wants something.'

Rosie recoiled at the memory.

She explained to George and Lily that because Raymond was a relative, social services had allowed him to stay overnight at their home. 'He made out he wanted to help and stay for the funeral,' Rosie recalled, her mind slowly edging back in time, 'but in hindsight I think he was sniffing about to see if there was any money to be had. Luckily Dad had made a will which left what little there was to me.' She paused before adding, 'I think he was angry at not getting what he wanted. I honestly think he believed he'd get some kind of inheritance because he was Mum's brother and we were both still young, but he didn't, not a bean. Anyway,' she continued, 'he decided to stay on for another night, said it was to look after me and Charlotte as we had no other family . . .' Rosie's voice trailed off as images of that night flashed across her mind's eye. She hesitated, then said, 'But really he had decided to take something else that he wanted.'

Lily felt the bile rise in the back of her throat and her anger boil instantly to the surface. She squeezed Rosie's hand once again and asked quietly, 'And did he manage to take what he wanted?'

Tears poured down Rosie's face and her whole body erupted into uncontrollable sobs. No answer was needed. Lily understood and held Rosie's hand tightly until the tears abated.

Finally Rosie said, 'It was either me or Charlotte.'

Lily and George exchanged a look which was a mixture of pure fury and deep sorrow. Rosie had been forced to cut a deal with the devil. She had been in a no-win situation. She had saved her sister that night, but it had been a truly horrific sacrifice on her behalf. It was one Lily knew from experience would stay with her for her entire time on this earth, and probably beyond. And here Rosie was now; this evil man had once again penned her in. And once again he was using Charlotte as his pawn.

As her mind processed everything that had just happened, Rosie's gravest worries started to gain momentum. 'If that man goes anywhere near my little sister,' she said, 'I will happily go to prison for what I will do to him.' Her voice was no longer shaking but hard as steel.

Rosie wasn't quite sure if Raymond had really seen Charlotte at her boarding school. She knew the school would have informed her had anyone turned up to see her. She had given them strict instructions not to allow anyone to see her sister other than herself and Mr and Mrs Rainer. If Raymond had seen her for real, that meant he'd been spying on her. But even if he hadn't, and he had been lying and hadn't actually seen her in the flesh, he still knew too much. He knew she was at a boarding school and it wouldn't take long for him to find out which one if he put his mind to it.

Not only had he put Rosie in a situation of which there seemed to be no way out, but, she realised as she reran everything that had seeped out of his repugnant mouth, he had played his trump card by indirectly threatening Charlotte. And Rosie knew from bitter experience that Raymond did not make empty threats – and that this was one which he would positively enjoy carrying out.

Chapter Twenty-One

That night, Bel had reluctantly agreed to do the evening shift on the buses, even though she hated being away from Lucille in case of an air raid. But at least she'd been able to spend half the day with her daughter, as well as help Agnes look after the neighbours' children. They were an energetic lot and every day another sibling, or a friend of a friend, would turn up and another child was squeezed into their home-cum-nursery.

Work had been quiet this evening and this was to be the last run from Houghton-le-Spring into the centre of town. The only people out were those in the pubs, and most of them lived within stumbling distance of their homes. As the bus pulled up outside Ashbrooke Sports Ground, Bel looked out and, despite the blackout, she could see what a lovely area this was. She felt a stab of envy as she imagined how wonderful it must be to live somewhere like this.

Just as the driver was about to pull away, Bel spotted a blonde-haired woman hurrying towards the bus. Her face looked dark and distressed, although she forced a smile as she stepped on board and found her seat.

Bel signalled to the driver to get going, and then walked up the aisle to take the woman's fare. As she approached the bus's solitary passenger, Bel was taken aback by how stunning the woman was. She had a perfect profile and her hair was naturally blonde, not dyed. The woman's beauty, however, could not hide the fact she had been terribly upset as her mascara had run and there were still smudges where she'd tried unsuccessfully to wipe her face clean.

Bel asked the woman where she wanted to go when the bus suddenly juddered after hitting a pothole, and Bel and the woman passenger both reached out to grab the pole. As they steadied themselves, Bel noticed the woman's mackintosh had fallen open, revealing a red, low-cut blouse and a skin-tight skirt. It was a uniform of sorts, but certainly not one which was seen out in the light of day.

'Park Lane, please,' the woman said, hurriedly pulling her coat back around her.

Bel was taken aback, even though she considered herself to be pretty broad-minded on the whole. 'That's just tuppence, please,' she said.

The woman handed over her change, again forcing another smile. Bel thanked her but as she looked at the woman's face she thought that she not only looked upset and exhausted, but deeply troubled.

Bel felt truly sorry for her. Who knew what had caused this woman to be doing what she was doing, she mused. Working on the buses certainly gave her an insight into other people's very varied lives. These were peculiar times they were living in, and everyone got by whichever way they could.

When Bel got home that night and walked back through the front door at Tatham Street, the warmth of the fire, which was still glowing, and the smell of a home-made mince and onion pie keeping warm for her in the oven, made her count her blessings. She wouldn't swap this for the world. Or for a fancy house in Ashbrooke.

All she needed to make her life truly happy and complete was for this war to end and for her Teddy to come home.

Chapter Twenty-Two

Monday, 9 September

'Blimey, looks like Rosie had a good night last night,' Dorothy whispered across to the other women during their mid-morning break. Today they were again working alongside the platers, welding together huge metal sheets which had been hung on the ship's hull.

Dorothy was right. There was no denying that Rosie was looking more than a little jaded and tired out. Dark circles encased her eyes, which were also puffy and swollen. She looked tired and gaunt and her skin had an ashen pallor to it. Polly, Gloria and Martha all silently nodded. None of them would ever admit it, but they all secretly hero-worshipped Rosie. Aspired to be like her. Martha because she was an expert welder, Gloria because she was a strong, independent woman, and Polly because Rosie had achieved something she desperately wanted – respect and equality.

'Those eyes aren't the sign of a good night out, that's for sure.' Gloria spoke quietly so only her fellow workers could hear. 'Something's happened to that woman to give her grief, and my guess is it's something bad because I don't think she's the kind of person who upsets easily.'

There was another silent nod of agreement.

Polly looked at Rosie, who was standing on her own, her welding mask dangling by her side, looking out at the river and beyond. She looked as if she were in another world, and not a particularly happy one either.

'It makes you wonder about her life outside the yards, doesn't it?' Polly spoke her thoughts aloud.

Gloria agreed. 'I know. We've been working with her for nearly a month now and we know next to nothing about her.' Even Gloria had talked a little about her own life, and she was someone who kept her guard up most of the time. Working the kinds of hours they all worked, and as closely as they worked, it was hard for the women *not* to get to know each other.

'Shall we see if she wants to come to the canteen with us to cheer her up?' Dorothy suggested.

Gloria and Polly gave each other a slightly despairing look, as they both knew why Dorothy wanted to go to the cafeteria, and it wasn't just to lift Rosie's mood.

Martha said a loud and enthusiastic 'Yes'. She had started to speak the odd word, which had initially shocked the women, but they'd been astute enough not to react. They hadn't wanted Martha to clam up just as she was beginning to open up.

When the midday horn sounded out, though, Rosie left before the women had a chance to ask if she'd like to join them. Still, it was agreed they'd all head over to the canteen regardless. As well as it giving them all a reprieve from Dorothy's continued and persistent pleas to mingle with the men, the women were glad to have a change from their daily diet of sandwiches. So after they had switched off their machines and Dorothy had given herself a quick spruce-up, the women grabbed their purses out of their small canvas work bags and walked over to the fitting-out dock to fetch Hannah.

When they all walked through the canteen doors, they breathed a collective sigh of relief as this time there was only a very brief lapse in the men's eating while they noted the women's presence. The women welders weren't exactly part of the furniture yet, but they were no longer viewed as aliens from outer space, and for this the women were grateful.

After they had paid for their lunch, they made a beeline for the same table they had sat at the first time, finding comfort and confidence in familiarity. As they ate and chatted, Dorothy's eyes flitted across the room before finding Eddie, who was holding court with a group of other riveters two tables along from the women.

Gloria had spotted him before they'd sat down and had noted how he'd inspected Dorothy from top to bottom. She'd also observed how he then pretended not to notice her and how he became louder as he regaled his workmates with a tale the women couldn't hear, but which was captivating the men next to him.

He continued to ignore Dorothy, who had been batting her long and naturally dark eyelashes over at him to no avail, and who looked crestfallen as he cold-shouldered her during the course of their time in the canteen. Then, just as he and the rest of the small group of riveters got up to leave, he threw Dorothy a look, followed by a brief flash of a smile. A look of unadulterated glee immediately appeared on Dorothy's face, having finally been acknowledged by the man with whom she was clearly infatuated.

'How long's he been working here?' Gloria asked Dorothy as they walked back across the yard. There was no need to say who she was talking about.

'Eddie? Not long. I think he got a job here shortly after war was declared.'

'And what was he doing before then?' Gloria probed.

'I don't think he had a job as such.' Dorothy hesitated.

'Funny, that,' Gloria mused.

'What do you mean?' Dorothy asked in all innocence.

'Well,' Gloria said, 'he wouldn't be the first man averse to a bit of hard graft to suddenly find himself a job in the yards or down the mines to dodge conscription. Beats risking life and limb fighting the Jerries, I suppose,' she added with more than a hint of sarcasm.

Dorothy looked at her and for once didn't come back with a retort.

'All right, ladies, that's enough chatter. Back to work.' Rosie was waiting for her flock by the ship's half-built hull. She didn't seem as weary now, but her face still hadn't shaken the look of a woman who had much on her mind.

She had spent her lunch hour walking along to Roker, dropping down to have a stroll along Marine Walk, which ran parallel to the cordoned-off beach. The sea was unusually calm and in complete contrast to her own mental turmoil. Her mind had worked through every possible scenario of her problem, but each time she'd hit a dead end.

For starters there was no way she could go to the police, as Raymond would just deny outright that he was blackmailing her, and worse still, Rosie knew he would be certain to tell the local constabulary all about her evening job and about Lily's illicit establishment.

If Rosie gave in to Raymond's demands and handed over the money he wanted every week, she'd be able to keep working and just about survive, but she wouldn't be able to afford to pay Charlotte's boarding school fees.

Likewise, if she refused her uncle's demands and he carried out his threat and made it known what she did at Lily's, she wouldn't be able to work again anywhere in the north-east, let alone as a welder. But most importantly, she would again be in a position whereby she'd be unable to afford to keep Charlotte in school.

Even if Rosie decided to simply run away and move to another part of the country to work, there was still a chance Raymond would track her down. Even if he didn't, though, he would definitely be able to find Charlotte. There weren't that many all-girl boarding schools in the country, and he would know her sister was probably in the north, somewhere near enough for Rosie to visit regularly.

Whatever way she looked at it, even if Rosie somehow managed to find a way to free herself from Raymond's clutches, he would always be able to claw her back in by threatening Charlotte's well-being.

As Rosie had walked back to work for the afternoon shift, in desperation she had started to think about how she could make this evil, soulless man disappear from her life for good. She thought of the ways and means of doing away with him, and in doing so rid the world of someone who only caused hurt, harm and destruction. Who would miss him? Rosie asked herself. No one. And more importantly, who would care? No one was again the answer. But much as she saw it as a credible possibility – a solution to her problem – she knew deep down that she could never take another person's life, no matter how sick and twisted they were.

Throughout the afternoon shift, all Rosie could think of was getting back to her bedsit and writing a letter to her sister to tell her to be vigilant, and warn her about Raymond in such a way that it wouldn't worry or scare her. Then she wanted to simply put her head down and sleep to give herself a few hours' escape from this living nightmare she'd been plunged into. Perhaps, she hoped, after she had caught up on some sleep, she would have a clearer head and would think of something. Anything.

There had to be a way out of this.

At the end of the shift, Rosie said a quick goodbye to the women and for once was the first to leave. As she hurried through the dense crowd of fellow workers, she was impatient to get out. She felt trapped by so many people. She just needed to breathe and be on her own.

As she walked up the embankment to the main road, Rosie realised Raymond had her exactly where he wanted her. Just like he had when she'd been a grieving fifteen-year-old. After that sickening night, when he had so brutally taken her innocence, she had thought, or rather hoped, that she would never clap eyes on him again. Deep down, though, she'd known she hadn't seen the last of him, and she knew now, without a doubt, that as long as her uncle was drawing breath, he would continue to haunt her for the rest of her life.

Chapter Twenty-Three

'Polly . . . I was wondering . . . are you finishing on time tonight?'

Polly felt her whole body jump to life despite being shattered after a hard day's graft. It was Tommy. Polly knew his voice well enough now to know who it was before she saw him. As she turned around, though, she was still taken aback when she looked at him. His tall, thickset body and worn face gave him a formidable presence, but he never came across as intimidating. Quite the reverse. When you looked into his eyes, there was a vulnerability there which could not be disguised. Polly wondered if Tommy himself was aware of it. Like at this very moment, as he stood there, separated from her by the expanse of a large metal sheet, he looked uncertain of himself, and more than a little awkward.

'Yes, it looks like it. Rosie left on the dot tonight.' Polly managed to sound much more energetic than she felt.

'I know. I think that's the first time I've ever seen her leave work on time,' Tommy said, a wide smile appearing on his face as it always seemed to do whenever he was in Polly's company.

'See ya, Pol,' Gloria interrupted, slinging her boxed-up gas mask and holdall over her shoulder. Martha followed with a big grin, a salutary wave, and a loud 'Bye'. Dorothy and Hannah had already said their cheerios and left a few minutes earlier.

'Bye, Gloria. See ya, Martha,' Polly shouted across to her friends as they left, before turning her attention back to Tommy.

'I was wondering . . .' Tommy hesitated, 'if . . . if you'd like some company on your way home.'

Polly's face lit up. 'That'd be nice. Yes, I'd like that,' she said, gathering up her belongings and hoping the warm glow she felt spreading across her face wasn't making her blush. 'You're not on your bike today then?' Polly had seen Tommy arrive and leave work numerous times on his noisy black BSA.

'No, I thought I'd give her a rest,' Tommy said, quickly making his way round the metal sheet as Polly picked up her holdall. He offered to carry Polly's bag but she declined, and the pair ambled off towards the main gates.

They were just getting their clocking-off cards out when Polly heard someone running up behind them.

'Tommy,' a gentle, sultry voice called out.

Polly turned to see the voluptuous, raven-haired beauty that was Helen Crawford approaching them both. A wolf whistle sounded out across the yard, and Helen smiled. She clearly enjoyed the attention.

As Helen slowed to a walk, Polly felt totally entranced by the vision of this incredible-looking woman. She had seen her from afar many times over the past few weeks and knew she was Jack's daughter and worked in some kind of managerial role in the administration offices, but she had never come face to face with her, or spoken to her before. Her heart sank as she realised this woman was even more stunning up close than when viewed from afar. Her green eyes were startling, and her hourglass figure, with her tiny waist, full hips and a bust she was quite obviously proud of, just screamed sex goddess.

'Tommy,' Helen said breathlessly, 'my mother wanted to give you this for Arthur and to tell him we were all asking after him.' She handed Tommy a cardboard cake box, which had been tied with a pretty yellow ribbon. 'It's his favourite – fruit cake,' she said, gently touching Tommy on the arm. Polly noticed her nails had been French manicured to perfection.

'Oh, thanks, Helen,' said Tommy. 'Arthur'll be chuffed to pieces. Say thanks to Miriam. That's very kind.'

Helen didn't once take her eyes off Tommy. Polly could have been invisible for all Helen cared. Polly had never felt quite so insignificant in someone's company in her entire life. But what was worse was that this stunning woman undoubtedly had the glad eye for Tommy. And the realisation that Helen had her sights set on the man Polly knew she herself was falling for, *had* fallen for already, made her heart sink.

Alongside Helen's vibrant good looks, Polly felt like a faded-out sepia photograph, her mousey hair limp and boring next to Helen's glossy black mane. Envy filled Polly, but not just because of Helen's breathtaking good looks: it was her natural inbred confidence which really prodded the green-eyed monster within Polly.

'See you tomorrow, Tommy.' Helen said her farewells, before turning and sashaying her way back across the yard.

As Polly glanced down at her own baggy overalls and mannish boots, she felt like the biggest frump walking the earth.

'Helen seems nice,' she said, lying through her teeth and immediately regretting saying anything remotely positive about this woman, this seductress, who was clearly trying to put a spell on the man whom Polly had been thinking about almost constantly since first setting eyes on him.

'Oh, Helen is . . .' Tommy hesitated, trying to find an appropriate word to describe the woman who had just poured a great big vat of cold water on his long-awaited attempt at asking Polly out. '. . . is Helen' was all he could muster.

Polly and Tommy handed over their time boards and walked on down to the ferry in silence. They both seemed at a loss for words. Tommy was no fool, and he could see how Helen had made Polly feel. How Helen made most people feel: inferior. And to add to it all, he now had to carry this boxed-up fruit cake on his much-awaited walk home with Polly. It was as if Helen's presence was stuck there between the two of them.

As if reading his thoughts, Polly looked down at the box in Tommy's big hands and said, 'Fruit cake? How lovely.' What she was really thinking was how much Agnes would love more than anything to have the ingredients to make what she would call a 'proper' cake.

'Yes, Miriam – that's Helen's mum – she does like to bake.' Tommy desperately tried to think of something else to say, to change the subject away from Helen and this blasted cake. 'Helen's dad is Jack, the yard's manager. Jack and my granda were good mates when they worked together years ago. I've known Helen for years. Since we were both bairns, really.'

Tommy couldn't believe he had just brought the subject back to the woman who was the last person he wanted to talk about. Why was he so bad at making conversation?

Determined to steer the talk away from Helen, he started to tell Polly about the new Liberty ship design. 'It's a real feather in the yard's cap,' he said proudly. 'Mr Thompson sailed to New York just the other week with a few other big shots, and Jack's been asked to join them.' Tommy was now on familiar territory and chatted on about the need for more ships, as so many were being torpedoed by German U-boats, and how the American yards could mass-produce this new cargo vessel because the design meant they were easier and cheaper to build.

Polly tried desperately to concentrate on what Tommy was saying, but her mind kept swinging back to Helen, wondering how on earth she stood a chance with this man if Helen was on the scene.

Tommy and Polly got off the ferry and walked up the cobbled street away from the docks and towards the east end. Their talk turned to what was happening in Europe and North Africa, and then to life closer to home – the yard, the people they both worked with, and those they loved. Before long all talk and thoughts of Helen had been washed away.

As they chatted, Tommy realised why Polly was so driven and determined to work in the shipyards. She not only wanted to become part of the long line of shipbuilders in her family, but she was also desperate to honour her father's memory by becoming an important part of the war effort. Even though the man wasn't alive, it was as though she still wanted his approval.

Perhaps it was the passion with which Polly talked and described her yearning to do good which made Tommy open up about his own overriding desire to play a more active role in the war. Polly was intrigued as Tommy told her about a group of highly trained Italian divers called 'frogmen' who were clamping mines on to the sides of Allied ships. 'The explosives aren't that powerful, but they can cause enough damage to create a large hole and put the ship out of action.' She listened intently as he talked about the special units that were being formed, and how divers were needed to remove these mines. 'The diving suit I wear and the equipment I use as a deep-sea diver is different to what these frogmen have, but I could easily adapt,' Tommy explained.

'Would they take you?' Polly asked, immediately feeling guilty that her first reaction was that she hoped they wouldn't.

'I've tried but they told me I'm in a "reserved occupation" and because there are so few divers I have to stay here and work on the ships.' Polly caught a hint of bitterness in his voice. She understood that all-consuming urge and knew it would not go away.

The more Polly and Tommy talked, the slower they walked. When they finally arrived at the top end of Tatham Street, she stopped to say goodbye, not wanting Tommy to walk her right up to her front door.

'Thanks for the company,' she said, turning to walk away.

Tommy panicked. 'Perhaps we could do it again? Soon?'

'I'd love that,' Polly said, stepping away from him, even though it was the last thing she wanted to do. 'Oh, and I hope Arthur enjoys his cake,' she added, looking at the box which was now partly crushed, since Tommy had got tired of carrying it and had shoved it under his arm like a rolled-up newspaper.

Tommy watched Polly walk away before turning and making his own way back home. Straightening out the box and its yellow bow, he felt the happiest he had been in a very, very long time.

Polly felt light-headed, almost tipsy, as she breezed the hundred yards down the street to her front door. But as soon as she neared her home she was brought thudding back down to earth when she saw Agnes, arms folded, face like thunder, standing on her clean front doorstep.

'So, I was right,' Agnes said in a scarily low, calm voice. 'There is a man on the scene.'

'Ma, he's just a friend. He just asked to walk me home and I said he could. He's a really nice chap, honestly.'

'*Friend* my foot,' Agnes said, turning and stomping back into the house and down the hallway.

As Polly trailed after her mum, she felt like a little girl again, preparing herself for a good old telling-off. On seeing Bel come in from the washhouse in the backyard, Polly's heart lifted. She had back-up.

'So, come on, spit it out. Who is he?' Agnes stood arms akimbo, staring at Polly.

Looking at the stand-off between Polly and Agnes, it took Bel all of two seconds to realise what had happened. 'His name's Tommy, Agnes,' she butted in, 'and from what Pol's told me he seems a nice man.'

Agnes stared daggers at Bel, as if she had found a traitor in their midst.

'I see. As always, I'm the last to know anything in this house.' Agnes's face was like stone.

'You're her mother,' Bel laughed. 'You're meant to be the last to know.'

Agnes exhaled dramatically. 'Wait until little Lucille isn't so little, then you'll know what it's like – and when that happens I will remind you of this day, make no mistake I will.'

Bel had no doubt that Agnes would do just as she said.

Agnes turned to Polly. 'Well, you just watch yourself, and keep this lad at arm's length. And if he wants to be walking you home and chatting to you, he can ask you out properly. I don't like all this half-baked "friends" nonsense. If you like each other, you can court properly.' There was a brief pause before she added, 'And there's to be no hanky-panky. Little Lucille is quite enough for this household, thank you very much.'

Bel couldn't contain herself any long and erupted into laughter. 'Eee, Agnes, I think you got stuck back in the last century.'

'Enough,' said Agnes. 'I've said my piece. You two can sort your own tea out tonight. I'm going round to see Beryl,' and then she marched out of the room.

Polly flung her arms round Bel. 'What would I do without you?' she said to her sister-in-law, giving her a big hug.

'Heavens knows,' Bel laughed, before demanding, 'Now tell me everything!'

Chapter Twenty-Four

Despite Agnes's disapproval, nothing could burst Polly's love bubble as the week wore on. Even though everyone in the yard had to work overtime and Polly and Tommy hadn't been able to enjoy another walk home together, Polly still felt afloat with a wonderful kind of joyousness and inner contentedness she had never experienced before. And it wasn't as if she didn't see Tommy at all. They worked within a few hundred yards of each other most of the time, and both had started to come into work that bit earlier to enable them to snatch just a few minutes together at the start of the long working day.

The women enjoyed ribbing Polly about her blossoming romance with one of the 'monster men', as they still occasionally called the dock divers. They had seen the way the two of them looked at each other, and they knew the real reason why Tommy now made a point of saying 'Morning' to them all at the start of every shift, and a cheery 'Night all' when they finished. 'Mooorniiing, Tommy!' they all greeted him in unison if they saw him approach their work area.

At first Tommy had been terribly uncomfortable at being the focus of their attention, especially as they revelled in his obvious embarrassment, but he was slowly getting used to it. They meant no harm, and he realised it gave them the chance to have a little fun before the start of a gruelling day of hard work.

'You lot are getting as bad as the men,' he'd joked one morning when they were particularly verbose with their greeting.

They'd all whooped with laughter, with Martha's particularly loud chortle attracting attention from the burners and catchers working nearby. Rosie had smiled at their antics, but the women had all noted that she still didn't seem herself and had continued to appear preoccupied since the day she'd turned up to work with dark circles under her eyes. There was something in her manner that seemed terribly troubled.

Most days the women collected Hannah from the fitting-out dock, their arrival heralded by Martha's loud but perfectly in-tune whistle, and from there they would all hurry over to the canteen, which not only gave them a breather from the yard, but also from the weather, which was starting to get cold and windy.

Hannah's English was coming on in leaps and bounds and in the cafeteria her soft, quiet voice could just about make itself heard, unlike when she was working outdoors and had to compete with the deafening background noise of the shipyard. She'd even begun to regale them with tales of her former life in Czechoslovakia before her parents had had the foresight to pack her off to stay with her aunty Rina, who worked as a credit draper in the town's Jewish quarters selling clothes and goods on tick. Gloria seemed to particularly enjoy listening to Hannah's stories, and she would sit captivated as Hannah described the beauty of the country's capital, Prague, with its fairy-tale castles, towers and ancient stone bridges.

It had been clear, though, that Hannah was worried about her parents, who were now themselves trying to flee their homeland and seek refuge in England. The women had tried to reassure their workmate that her parents would be fine, that they might even be on a ship now on their way over to this country. But Hannah wasn't so sure. It had now been a year and a half since Hitler had invaded and occupied her homeland and she had heard the rumours about the German concentration camps which were now growing in number.

Throughout the week Dorothy had continued her peacock-like flirtations with Eddie and they had even started leaving the canteen together and chatting for a short while before they had to go back to their own work-places at opposite ends of the yard. Today, after such a chat, Dorothy had run to catch up with the women with a particularly big grin on her face.

'Someone looks like cat that got cream,' Hannah giggled, before hurrying back to the fitting-out basin.

'He's going to meet me after work!' Dorothy couldn't contain her excitement as the women picked up their stingers and rods.

Both Gloria and Martha looked up at Dorothy, but didn't say anything. Their lack of words spoke volumes.

Polly forced a smile. She felt a little sorry for Dorothy, although she didn't know why. Probably because Dorothy seemed oblivious to the fact that none of the women liked this Eddie. Not that they really knew him, or had even spoken to him; it was just female intuition, something Dorothy seemed to lack.

As the women worked solidly through the afternoon, the sweat started to drip off them, in spite of the cold weather. Lifting her mask up from a particularly long weld, Rosie could tell by the women's drooping postures that they were all in need of a rest.

'Time for a quick break!' she hollered out over the sound of their machines and the unrelenting clashing and banging around them.

They all switched their machines off and pushed their masks off their faces so their helmets lay flat across their heads. They gathered near the platers' fire, which was being kept alight and refuelled by the men's new apprentice. As the women pulled out their flasks, Rosie shouted across to the tea boy for a refill. He scampered over, his long metal pole like a seesaw across his shoulders, gathered the women's empty cans and jangled off to get them topped up.

As they awaited his return, one by one the women looked at Gloria before quickly looking away. Rosie caught the stares of the other women and cast a glance over to Gloria to see what they had noticed. She felt a stab of shocking realisation, followed by a flurry of anger, as she spotted bruising round Gloria's neck. The bluish-purple blobs were quite obviously the leftover imprints of a man's hands, and it didn't take a genius to work out that the grotesque necklace had been put there by her husband Vinnie.

A shocked silence gradually descended on the group. Dorothy started to rummage around in her bag, pretending to look for something. Polly tried to looked anywhere other than at Gloria, and when she saw Martha gawping at her workmate's neck, she quickly tried to distract her, asking if she'd given the tea boy her flask. It did the trick as Martha shifted her gaze to Polly and nodded that she had.

Gloria had sensed an unease, but was unaware of its cause.

When the tea boy returned with the women's cans full to the brim of steaming-hot tea, Rosie said, 'I know you're no longer novices, but don't forget the importance of keeping your skin well covered. It's easy to forget. And my nagging is better than any nasty burn.'

Gloria's hand immediately went to her neck as she realised her own scarf had come loose. She quickly tightened it so that her terrible contusions were no longer visible. As the women drank their tea, Rosie tried to cover Gloria's embarrassment with talk about the yard's next launch, even though it was several weeks away.

They were all relieved when their break was over and their faces were covered once again by their masks. Each one of the women had found it difficult not to show their outrage that someone had hurt their friend, but more than anything they couldn't believe that Gloria had allowed someone to do this to her. Out of all the women welders, she was the last person they would expect to put up with any kind of violence or abusive behaviour.

At the end of the shift Gloria was the first to leave. No one said anything, but their sad looks as they bade each other goodnight said it all.

Polly so wanted to go and see Tommy, to confide in him what she'd seen, and ask him how a man could do this to his wife, to a woman – to *anyone*, for that matter. Poor Gloria must have been throttled to within an inch of her life to have been left with those bruises. How come they all hadn't noticed this was happening before? Polly now wondered. Or perhaps, she hoped, this was just a one-off.

Dorothy too was horrified that the woman she loved to hate had had this happen to her, and probably had been having this happen to her for a long time. Unlike Polly, Dorothy knew that this was not a solitary incident. As a child she'd seen similar bruises on her mum's arms and wrists, usually places that could easily be covered up. She'd heard the screams and shouts, the smashing of furniture and plates, and the silences which followed, and she knew exactly where her mother's bruises had come from. Her father, now a blur in her memory, or perhaps purposefully erased from her mind, had left one day and not come back, much to her relief. When she and her mum had moved to the other side of town, to where they now lived, her mum had told people her husband was dead, which, to all intents and purposes, he was.

A short while later her mother had quietly got divorced and remarried and gone on to have three more girls. Dorothy's stepfather wasn't her favourite person in the world, but when people presumed he was her real father, she never corrected them. Dorothy never openly talked about her dad, even with her mum, but that wasn't to say he'd been forgotten. The fear he had instilled in both mother and daughter had, like Gloria's bruises, left its mark.

As Dorothy went through her daily after-work routine of cleaning up her face and letting her wavy, chestnut hair loose from her headscarf, a dark wave of depression started to invade her mind as she tried not to think about what Gloria was going home to. But Dorothy was adamant she would not let the looming dark cloud of misery settle. Life was too short. She just wanted to be happy.

She pinched her cheeks to give herself some colour and got out her lipstick, of which there was only a small stub left. She then dusted herself down and walked over to the gates where Eddie was waiting for her.

Tonight she was going to have some fun.

Chapter Twenty-Five

Gloria left the yard as soon as the shift ended, which was unusual for her as she was normally one of the last to leave. She was never in any great rush to get home, but today her desire to run away from the looks of shock and pity which her fellow welders had not been able to hide on seeing her neck was overwhelming.

Gloria herself felt mortified. And deeply ashamed. She felt a fraud, a woman with no backbone. She was weak. Pathetic.

But then, as these self-deprecating thoughts rushed through her head, something inside of her also rebelled against the accusations she was flinging at herself. *I'm not weak or pathetic!* her whole being wanted to scream out. *This is not me! This is not the real me!* But the evidence was there for all to see. And she herself couldn't deny it any more. She couldn't pretend that she didn't have these bruises because now others had seen them. She couldn't bury her head in the sand any more.

Today, rather than get the bus home, Gloria decided to walk the three miles to the newly built council house that she and Vinnie had been lucky enough to get on the Fordham Road in the middle of the Ford Estate. Despite her legs feeling shaky after being crouched down on her haunches most of the day welding panel after panel of steel, she needed time to think. She also felt the need to exhaust herself even more and rid herself of the anger that was boiling up inside of her, anger which stemmed from the humiliation she'd felt when she realised the women had seen her closely kept secret, or rather her deeply buried shame.

Gloria's walk turned into a march as she made her way along the long stretch of Hylton Road, and as she pounded the pavement her mind raced with a myriad of conflicting thoughts and feelings.

How had her life come to this? Why did Vinnie do this? There were reasons he lost control and she had to understand that and try to help him.

He wasn't really a bad person. It was the drink. He had experienced terrible things in the last world war, things which she could not – would not want to – imagine. No wonder he drank and got angry. He wasn't an evil, or bad, person. And after lashing out and losing control, he was always sorry. Always remorseful.

Sometimes Gloria wished he wasn't. Then her situation would be black and white, and not a fuzzy shade of grey. If he was simply a nasty person who saw no wrong in what he did, then she could leave. Leave him. Leave his drinking and his temper to their own devices. But it wasn't so clear-cut. He begged and cried and promised he would sort himself out, that it wouldn't happen again. He said he wanted to change, which gave her hope that their life together could be different. She knew some women on the estate were bashed black and blue on a regular basis and the men believed it was their right to use their wives as some sort of punchbag.

How ironic, she thought as she passed Ford Hall, after which the estate had been named, that she had felt superior to those women, but, in truth, she only hid it better than they did. She had tried to paper over the cracks in her marriage for too long, but it was now clear that no matter how much pasting and covering up she did, the cracks kept showing through. Like her bruises, they could no longer be camouflaged.

As the pitying looks of the women at work flashed across Gloria's mind, feelings of pure humiliation and embarrassment rose again within her, and another voice entered the discussion in her head: Vinnie may be sorry, but he keeps on doing it. And, if anything, the violence was getting progressively worse. It had certainly got worse since their boys had enlisted and gone off to war.

Yes, he'd seen things which no one should ever have to see when he was fighting for King and country, but so had other men she knew. Most of her other friends' husbands had also fought in the First World War, but they didn't hurt their wives like Vinnie hurt her.

Yes, he said sorry afterwards, cried tears of guilt and regret, but did he *really* mean it? And even if he did, his remorse wasn't so great as to stop what he was doing.

Gloria had got this job at the yards to get away from Vinnie. She'd said it was because they needed the money. Vinnie's wages working in Speeding's rope factory were barely enough to live off, but Gloria could have got an easier job, one nearer to home, and one with shorter hours and less overtime. But she had wanted to escape and the yard had given her that opportunity. It had been a real bonus that she had taken to welding so quickly and she felt empowered by learning a proper trade, a real skill.

Of course, to the outside world she was also doing her bit to beat the Germans, but her real reason for working at Thompson's was that it provided her with a break from Vinnie and the increasingly embittered atmosphere of their neat little semi. The shipyard might be a chaotic, grey world made up of metal and steel, cranes and concrete, drowning daily in its own self-perpetuating noise, but it was a different and a better world than the one she inhabited at home.

Gloria loved the sense of camaraderie and the new friends she'd made there. She loved the vibrancy and the laughter, the jokes and the relentless banter. Over the past month she had revelled in getting up and going to work, had been the first to volunteer for overtime, and had been buoyed up by Rosie's encouragement and praise that she was a good welder.

But now she felt that had been ruined. Spoilt. Her bruises had brought her home life into her working life and contaminated it. Now the two worlds had meshed together, and in so doing had doused her little bit of joy in this hard life.

And it was all Vinnie's fault. Or was it? Was it really Vinnie's fault? As Gloria put the key into her front door she realised that it was also *her* fault, because she was allowing this to happen, and had been letting this happen for too long.

As she walked into the little hallway and through to the lounge, Gloria realised for the first time that she had a choice.

She stood in her living room and, as was her habit when she got in from work, she looked at the framed photograph of her two sons which adorned her mantelpiece. She'd been so happy and relieved the other day when she had received a letter from them both. They were stationed together and would always jointly write their letters.

Her joy had been short-lived, though, when Vinnie had decided the letter and the reassurance that they were alive and well was call for a celebration. Any good news always called for a drink, which, of course, would be followed by another, and another, and another. His mood had soared and then soured, as it always did in line with the amount of booze he consumed. And, as was now a regular pattern, when his mood plunged, his temper gained momentum and erupted into violence.

This time Gloria had not been able to stop the words coming out of her mouth and had shouted back at him, defending herself from his hurtful and unfair words. She had immediately regretted it when he'd turned on her, ranting and raving, white spittle forming at the edges of his mouth as he had gone for her, grabbing her round the neck and squeezing the living daylights out of her. She had blacked out for a second or two before Vinnie had come to his senses and released his grip.

Gloria now walked out of the lounge and into the small kitchen at the back of the house. She was greeted by a shamefaced Vinnie, sitting at the table with a wrapped-up bundle of fish and chips in front of him.

'All right, pet?' he said. 'I got us a fish lot to save you cooking tonight.'

Gloria took one look at him and breathed a sigh of relief that he was sober, or at least relatively sober. Tonight she didn't have to be on tenterhooks, adrenaline pumping around her body, waiting to see which way his mood would go, and how much he would drink, and whether he would kick off. Tonight would be a peaceful one. And with that knowledge a fugue of worn-out weariness overcame her.

'I'm sorry about the other night,' he said, tears starting to well up in his bloodshot eyes. Eyes that used to be so bright and sparkling. Eyes which Gloria had once lovingly looked into. Eyes which had made her feel happy and excited by life.

But time had changed so much. She no longer felt loved by Vinnie. It had been a long time since she had felt his gentle touch, or heard any words which told her he loved her, or that he was still in love with her.

'I'm really going to try and knock the drink on the head,' Vinnie said, seeing Gloria's jaded face.

For once Gloria didn't go over to her husband and hold him in her arms, allow his tears to spill and reassure him that he was forgiven. She just couldn't physically bring herself to do it. Something had finally gone inside of her. The desperate hope that Vinnie would change and that her life would be different had evaporated. She knew what she had known deep down for a long time now: Vinnie would *never* change. She was finally facing up to the reality that her husband of nineteen years would never be able to break this cycle of behaviour. It broke her heart that the man she'd married and who'd helped mend her broken heart after Jack had traded her in for a shinier and more expensive model was not the man who sat in front of her now. She had been happy with Vinnie at one time, but that now seemed like a lifetime ago.

Now, she realised, it was time for her to break her own cycle of behaviour. She had to face up to the fact that Vinnie did not want to change. His drinking and his violence would never end. She knew that now. So why did it feel so hard to leave, to walk away, to free herself? It was as though she had finally picked up the key to her prison door but for some reason could not bring herself to unlock it.

As Gloria got the plates out for their supper she forced a smile. She then forced down her fish and chips.

'I'm going to get to bed early tonight,' she told Vinnie as he cracked open a bottle of beer.

'I'm just going to have the one, pet,' he said, a little sheepishly, 'then I'll come and join you.'

Chapter Twenty-Six

Friday, 13 September

Gloria always liked to be out of the house before Vinnie surfaced and this morning she was particularly keen to leave early. She had slept with her back to him the entire night, recoiling from any kind of touch, intentional or otherwise. As soon as she'd woken, she had got up and got dressed, not even looking at her husband's sleeping outline under the bedcovers. She had been as quiet as a mouse so as not to wake him, as she didn't trust herself, didn't feel she could force out any kind of civil morning greeting to him, or pull her mouth into a smile. She felt her face was like an open book and on it was written all the hatred she felt towards Vinnie for what he had put her through.

She was more than aware that work today was going to be awkward and she felt a little nervous about seeing the women this morning after they'd clocked her bruises yesterday. But now they had seen the worst. She had nothing more to hide. In an odd way she felt liberated. There was no more covering up, no more pretence.

As Gloria stepped out of her front door and walked to the nearby bus stop she breathed in the fresh autumnal morning air and was glad she was out in time to beat the main thrust of workers. She needed space. Space to move, and to think her own thoughts.

She got to work sooner than anticipated and for once didn't have to squash up next to a horde of other

177

shipbuilders at the main gates. When she took her white board from Mick, the timekeeper, she was surprised to see he wasn't alone in his little box cabin. Sat in the back corner and partly shaded by the darkness of the office's windowless interior, Gloria caught a glimpse of a wiry-looking older man perched on a stool, his legs crossed, with both his hands resting on the top of an expensive-looking walking stick. Neither Mick nor his visitor spoke a word and Gloria couldn't help but feel an uneasiness about the pair.

She carried on through the main entrance and across the yard, taking in the sights, sounds and smells of the yard – the relative quietness before the start of the day's shift, the occasional blast of heat from fires being stoked up in five-gallon drums, and the overhanging smell of cigarette smoke coming from small huddles of workers. Gloria loved this place and felt a determination that neither Vinnie nor his bruises were going to take it away from her.

As she neared the welders' work area, though, Gloria's heart sank when she saw Jack standing deep in conversation with Rosie. 'Great. That's all I need,' she muttered to herself as she slowed down her pace in the hope their talk would end and Jack would go before she got there. But as Gloria approached, she realised Jack didn't look as if he was going anywhere. Just her luck.

'Morning, Gloria,' Jack said when she reached their work area.

She really wanted to ignore him, didn't want to wish him, of all people, a good morning. What she really wanted to tell him was to go away and not come back. It was over two decades since he'd dropped her like a ton of bricks, hurt her more than any of Vinnie's punches had. She'd tried to forgive and forget, had argued with herself that their relationship was a long time ago, but still there existed deep within her a great stagnant well of resentment towards her former love.

'Morning, Jack.' She forced the words out, but they came out too loud and with a hint of aggression.

Rosie gave Gloria a slightly puzzled look, while Jack returned her 'Morning' with a genuine smile, in spite of Gloria's dark look.

'I've just been telling Rosie here that it looks like the Yanks are going to mass-produce the new Liberty ship. It's a real boost for the yard,' he said with pride. 'And for the war,' he added, looking at Gloria, who seemed unable to offer him eye contact, or say anything in response.

Sensing a slight tension, Rosie filled the awkward silence. 'Jack's going to join Mr Thompson in America to go through various aspects of the production process, as they want to weld rather than rivet.'

Gloria tried to drum up some enthusiasm, but could only manage, 'That's great.'

When Gloria had first got this job at Thompson's she'd known she stood the risk of seeing Jack, but had believed, as he was yard manager, that he wouldn't be about much. But she'd been proved wrong, and every time they'd bumped into each other she had felt very self-conscious. But worse still, she had felt subservient to him, which she hated. Jack and Gloria had once been equals. Now they were poles apart.

It had always amazed her that she had got Jack so wrong, that he had chosen Miriam and her money over Gloria. At the time she'd thought she had known every inch of him, and had driven herself mad asking herself how, in all their time together, she hadn't once picked up that money had meant so much to him – so much so that he'd forsaken her and the love they'd had.

There was no denying that Miriam had been a stunner; you just needed to take one look at her daughter, Helen, to see what Miriam had been like as a young woman. And just like her daughter, Miriam had had all the men falling at her feet. But Jack had never shown any interest. Perhaps that was why Miriam had made such a play for the man Gloria had been courting. The thrill of the chase? Because she'd wanted what someone else had?

'So, I'll chat to you before I go over there about some of the welding issues,' Jack was saying to Rosie as he started to leave. 'Bye then,' he said to Rosie, but his eyes were fixed on Gloria, who had now moved away and was busying herself sorting out the welding rods.

A look of hurt crossed his face as he walked away.

'Morning, all!' Dorothy called out as she approached Rosie and Gloria. Her voice was excited and high-pitched and even caused Jack to look back over his shoulder to see who the shrill voice belonged to.

'Morning, Dorothy,' Rosie replied in the most matronly voice she could muster. Rosie sighed inwardly. It was like having to constantly keep a jack-in-the-box from springing about willy-nilly. She knew Dorothy had been out with Eddie the riveter last night and would be bursting at the seams to tell them all about it. Much to Rosie's relief, though, Dorothy didn't get a chance as Martha arrived, followed seconds later by Polly, who looked harried.

'I thought I was going to be late,' she said, breathlessly. 'Lucille's got chickenpox. And what's worse, she's been up all night crying. I love that little girl to pieces but I felt like putting her in the coal bunker by four o'clock this morning.'

The women chuckled.

Gloria remembered when her two had been covered in pink spots and had driven her mad with their incessant scratching and howls of anger, screaming for the itchiness to go away. 'The joys of being a mother,' she said more to herself than anyone in particular.

The women all turned in unison to look at their work-mate. The vision of Gloria's bruised neck was still very much in all their minds. It was the elephant in the room. They were all staring at it, but no one would mention it.

'And that's why I, for one, have no intention of becoming a mother,' Dorothy declared loudly, saying the first thing that came into her head to smooth over the women's embarrassed silence.

Gloria was visibly relieved. 'Well, at least that's one poor bairn saved,' she retorted, quick as a flash.

All the women chuckled, dispelling the feeling of unease which had fallen over them.

As the hooter went for the start of the shift and the women all turned to their welding machines, Dorothy looked across at Gloria and gave her a smile, which was etched with both compassion and sadness. Gloria looked back at her workmate and returned her smile with one of thanks.

The women worked solidly until noon. Then they downed tools and trooped to the canteen, where they were met by Hannah, who now felt brave enough to go there on her own. Today there had been a new influx of workers, which included a number of women who'd been taken on as painters and crane operators. All the women smiled over at the new recruits, who smiled back, although a few stared longer than was polite at Martha. One of them, a brassy-looking bottle blonde, even gave a cheery wave.

'Am glad we not the new ones any more,' Hannah said.

'I know,' Polly agreed, stifling a yawn. 'It seems an age ago that we started.'

'They not so nervous as us,' Hannah observed, looking at them from under her thick fringe. 'They here in canteen on first day.'

'Or perhaps they're just better at hiding it,' Dorothy mused. 'Anyway,' she said, demanding the women's attention, 'enough about them. Who wants to hear about my wonderfully romantic date last night?'

Martha put her head down and continued to feast on her plate of food, which was piled high. Whether consciously or not, the canteen staff always gave Martha a larger than normal helping.

'No one does, but I guess we're going to hear about it anyway,' Gloria said with a deadpan face.

Dorothy took a dramatic deep breath before regaling them all with every second of her evening with Eddie: how he had met her after work and they had gone for a drink in the Admiral Inn, just a stone's throw away from the shipyard's entrance, and how they had chatted all night and she had been introduced to his friends. Dorothy had watched Eddie play darts before he'd walked her into town, where she'd got her bus home.

'Well, I hope he paid for everything,' Gloria said. 'Never trust a man who doesn't like putting his hand in his pocket.'

Dorothy shifted uncomfortably. Eddie had paid for their first round of drinks, but had told Dorothy that he had lent most of his wages to his mate, who'd needed the cash as one of his children was very poorly. She had thought how kind Eddie was and had insisted on paying for their drinks the rest of the night.

'Of course he paid,' she lied to Gloria. Eddie had asked her not to say anything as his mate didn't want to be seen as a charity case.

As the canteen was now emptying, the women all got up to go.

'And Polly,' Hannah ventured, 'how is the lovely Tommy?'

Hannah was the only one who could get away with asking Polly about her love life, probably because she was such a delicate soul it would have been impossible to be remotely angry at her, and also because she reminded Polly of Bel, as the two were out-and-out romantics.

Polly blushed as they walked towards the door.

'Well, like us, he's working lots of overtime . . .' Polly's voice trailed off. What she really wanted to say was that she was gutted they hadn't been able to enjoy another walk home together, and that she was now wondering if Tommy had perhaps had a change of heart.

Hannah headed off, and Polly and the rest of the women sauntered back to their workstation, where Rosie was fixing one of the welding machines, which had spluttered and died just before their lunch break.

'Does that woman never stop?' Gloria asked.

'I know. I wish I had her energy,' Polly said, yawning for what felt like the hundredth time that morning.

While she put her hand to her mouth, she spotted Helen trotting over to see Tommy, who'd just been brought back up from the river. He was working on the underside of a ship that had been moored by the quayside. He'd been in and out of the river like a yoyo this past week. Typical, she thought when she spotted Helen, who, as always, was looking as though she'd just stepped out of a beauty parlour, which she probably had. Polly had heard through the yard gossip that Helen spent whatever money she had on manicures, make-up and clothes. That woman has a sixth sense when it comes to Tommy, she thought bitterly. She always seems to know exactly the right time to catch him. As Polly put her helmet on the last image she saw was Helen, looking stunning in a tight black skirt and an expensive grey cashmere jumper, chatting animatedly to Tommy, who was smiling back at her and looking as rugged and as handsome as ever.

Polly attacked the metal she was welding, enjoying the feeling of burning steel into submission. She kept seeing the image of Helen and Tommy together. They'd looked the perfect couple. Her love bubble was now totally deflated. How on earth did she think someone like Tommy would fall for someone like her? She was poor and plain; Helen was rich and gorgeous. How had she managed to fool herself that Tommy had feelings for her? This woman was in a different league. She was educated, attractive and sexy – even her voice was lovely.

Polly didn't think she'd hated someone as much in her entire life.

Chapter Twenty-Seven

Polly spent the afternoon convincing herself that Tommy's heart was really with Helen and that she herself had just been a passing fancy. She couldn't wait for the horn to sound the end of the shift so she could take her wounded heart and tired body back home and straight to bed. She had been so engrossed in her own thoughts of rejection and unrequited love that she jumped with shock when she switched off her welder and pushed up her helmet to see Tommy standing a few yards in front of her. He had obviously finished work a little early and stood holding his motorbike jacket in one hand, his helmet in the other.

She pulled off her leather gloves and rubbed one of her eyes, which had got some dirt in it. Her face was streaked with soot and she now had one big panda eye. Tommy had to suppress a smile. It was what he loved most about Polly. She could be dressed in rags and looking as if she'd just been up a chimney and still look gorgeous. And, most of all, she didn't care what she looked like. She was who she was.

'Are you still on for that walk home?' Tommy asked, suddenly nervous that she might have changed her mind.

Polly looked confused. 'Erm, yes . . .'

'I wondered if you'd like to go for a ride on the bike first, and then I can drop you off home?'

Polly's spirit immediately soared. The lead weight suddenly lifted. Tommy *did* like her. Didn't he? If he didn't, he wouldn't be stood here now, wanting to take her out after work.

'Oh, I've never been on a motorbike before.' Polly felt a little uncertain, and more than a little nervous.

'You'll love it,' Tommy enthused. 'You can have my jacket and helmet, but I won't go fast. It'll just be nice to go for a little ride along the coast, if you like.'

Polly felt the thrill of excitement, all tiredness now pushed aside. 'Yes, that sounds nice,' she said, standing up. She quickly put away her tools, took off her headscarf and stuffed her belongings into her holdall.

The rest of the women were also getting ready to leave and were trying not to show that they were earwigging in on Tommy and Polly's conversation. Dorothy forced down a squeal of excitement at the day's surprising turn of events and instead grabbed a clean hankie and marched purposefully up to Polly.

'Let me just do this,' she said, gently taking hold of Polly's face and quickly erasing the panda eye and a few other streaks of dirt from her friend's face. She was done before Polly had time to object.

'Have a nice time, you two,' Rosie said.

'Thanks,' said Polly and Tommy in unison as they turned to walk away.

'Finally,' Hannah said with a sigh. Martha grinned, showing off the gap between her two big front teeth.

'Looks like they're finally going out on a date,' Gloria said.

Watching Polly and Tommy chatting and laughing as they became lost in the bottleneck of fellow shipbuilders gathering at the gates, Gloria was transported back to when she would meet Jack after work when he'd been a plater in this very yard. But it wasn't that particular memory which caused the physical constriction she now felt in her heart, but the remembrance of being in love. That rush of love and happiness and frivolity she'd had when she was with him. Those feelings seemed like such a distant memory. She mourned them and felt an incredible sadness that her life now held no real joy. It was as though she had suddenly just realised how unhappy she really was, had slowly become over the years, and at that moment it seemed her heart had never felt so heavy.

'I want you to wear this jacket and helmet,' Tommy said, holding out the sides of the jacket wide with his two hands so that Polly could easily put her arms into it. When he let it drop on to her shoulders, she felt her body sag under its weight.

'Blimey, it's heavy, isn't it?' she said as Tommy turned her around and zipped up the front.

'It's the metal plating sown into it. It'll protect you if you come off. Not that you're going to come off,' he added quickly.

He then picked up his helmet and pulled the two bottom chinstraps wide, ready to put it on Polly's head. 'Legally, you don't have to wear this,' he said, raising it above her head and gently pulling it down, 'but I think it's best to.'

Polly felt like a child dressing up in grown-up clothing. The jacket swamped her and the arms almost covered her hands. She could just see the tips of her fingers poking out the ends. The helmet had partially deafened her, and it felt a little loose, but it was Tommy's closeness that Polly was most aware of. When he moved towards her to fasten the straps, their faces were just inches apart and Polly again felt that wondrous intimacy she'd experienced the night she had stumbled and been caught in his arms.

'I feel a little nervous,' she admitted as Tommy stood up straight.

'Don't worry, you'll be fine. I won't go fast. Just hold on to me and if you want me to stop just tap my shoulder and I'll pull over.'

He went over to the shiny black BSA and swung his leg over the seat, kicking back the bike stand with his left foot so that the bike was standing upright. He motioned Polly to get on the back.

Polly felt clumsy in all her heavy gear, but was glad she had her overalls on as she copied what Tommy had done and swung her leg over the back of the seat. Both of her feet just about touched the ground.

'Put your arms around me,' Tommy said, 'and your feet on those two rubber pegs jutting out the side.'

Polly did as he'd said and felt her body slide naturally into place behind him. Every part of their bodies was now touching.

'Here goes,' he said, kick starting the engine. It roared to life and Polly immediately was hit by a boost of adrenaline.

Tommy slowly steered the bike on to the main road and then gently accelerated.

Polly clung on for dear life. She was just able to peek over Tommy's broad shoulder and see the road ahead. As they rode steadily along the coastal road, the feeling was like nothing she had felt before. It was exhilarating and seemed to fill her whole body with energy and life. She looked about her at the passing sights and at the cars on the other side of the road. She could see the faces of the drivers and their passengers and into the gardens of the big houses that lined the seafront. And beyond the barbed wire, she could see the sea, which today looked angry and grey.

'You all right there?' Tommy turned his head slightly to shout back to Polly.

'Yes! Great!' She felt unable to contain her feeling of elation.

She could feel the salty wind in her face as they reached Whitburn and Tommy slowly rode the BSA around the village's small roundabout. As he did so, Polly followed his movements and leant to the side when he did.

They were now riding back down the same road they'd just come along and Tommy twisted the throttle ever so slightly to go a bit faster. Polly could feel her hair flicking around the bottom of the helmet and across her face. Now she wasn't looking at the scenery, just revelling in the feeling of speed and abandoning herself to the elements.

They came to the end of the coastal road and headed into town. Polly heard the changing sound of the gears as they slowed down and Tommy pulled the bike over and on to the pavement in front of the Bungalow Cafe at the tip of Roker's upper promenade. It was a well-known landmark and was frequented mainly for its views straight out to the North Sea. The bike came to a standstill next to the famous three signposts which read 'To Beach', 'To Village' and 'To Germany'.

As Tommy brought the bike to a halt and flicked the bike stand forward with the tip of his boot, Polly dismounted.

She fiddled with her helmet straps, at the same time watching Tommy get off the bike and grab the handlebars. With one big heave, he pulled the bike backwards so that it stood upright, balancing on the stand of its own accord.

'Let me give you a hand,' he said, coming towards her and helping her undo the chinstraps. 'Now,' he said once he'd untied them, 'just put your head forward and pull the helmet off gently.'

As Polly did so her thick brown hair tumbled forward. She lifted her head to find Tommy standing just looking at her. Once again she felt an urge to lean up and kiss him.

'That was wonderful,' she gushed, still a little breathless from the thrill of it all. 'I can see why you love riding a bike so much.'

Tommy broke into a big smile. At that moment he felt he had finally found his perfect woman. Or rather, a woman who was perfect for him.

The pair walked into the warm cafe and were hit by the aromas of coffee and freshly baked cakes and bread. 'Would you like something to eat?' Tommy asked.

'Just a cup of tea, please.' Polly was far too excited and nervous to eat.

She sat down at a table next to the window where they could see the north and south piers that curved in such a way as to create the illusion of a giant horseshoe. There was an older couple sitting at the next table who weren't saying anything to each other, but it was a comfortable silence. On the other side of the small cafe there was a young mum with her two young children. This was obviously a treat for them all as her sons were on their best behaviour and happily slurping down lemonade through a straw and making a mess eating iced buns.

When Tommy came back he was carrying a tray on which there was a pot of tea for two and a big wedge of cake. 'I thought we could share the cake,' he said. Polly picked up a hint of nervousness in his voice. It felt strange, just the two of them, away from the yards and the other workers. On their own.

Polly took the knife and divided the piece of cake in two before pouring their tea. As she did so, she was reminded of her former life working in the cafeteria just a mile down the road on the seafront in Seaburn. It was only a month or so since she'd handed her notice in to Mrs Hoggart, but it felt a lifetime away. So much had changed since then. She almost felt like a different woman. She was no longer a waitress but a welder, working in a place she had never imagined she could. At first she'd had her doubts that she would be able to do the job, but now welding had become almost second nature to her. The strange mix of women she had started work with had now become her friends, but most of all, something had happened to her which she'd never imagined in her wildest dreams – she had fallen in love.

'Look at the sun,' Tommy said, staring out the window.

Polly looked at the fiery, golden sun which was just starting to drop down towards the horizon. It seemed as though you could see to the end of the world.

'No wonder people used to think the earth was flat,' she said as she took a sip of her hot tea.

For a short while they sat, both enjoying the beautiful view and looking down to Marina Way which stretched alongside the beach, and where, before the war, people had flocked for a day out by the sea.

As they shared the cake they started to chat. Before long they were the only people left in the cafe and the waitress was clearing away their tray and their pot of tea, which was now stone cold.

'We'd better get going,' Polly said. 'I think it's closing time.' As they got up to leave, Polly noticed Tommy left a little tip on the table.

They rode back along Dame Dorothy Street and across the Wearmouth Bridge. Polly looked about her, enjoying the alternative perspective on a place she knew like the back of her hand.

When they pulled up outside Polly's home in Tatham Street daylight was fading fast. Polly got off the bike and took off the jacket and helmet, ready to hand back to Tommy.

'Thanks, Tommy, I really enjoyed that,' she said.

Tommy had quickly put the bike on its stand so he could walk Polly the few yards to her door. He didn't want this evening to come to an end, and he desperately wanted to kiss this woman whom he was head over heels in love with.

But just as Polly and Tommy were saying their goodbyes to each other, Agnes was leaving Dennis's general store, halfway down the street. She had bought some bruised fruit and was thinking how she could turn it into something more appetising when she spotted Polly and Tommy and his glossy black BSA.

It was clear her daughter had been out on a date. 'And,' Agnes mumbled to herself, 'she's been out on the back of a bloody motorbike.' Agnes's instinct was to inflict holy war on the pair of them. 'Is that girl trying to put me in an early grave?' she said out loud as she marched as fast as she could towards the two lovebirds. The very least she could do was stop them having a goodnight kiss. As she got nearer she scrutinised the man who had captured her daughter's heart.

'Is that my errant daughter?' Agnes said as she approached the pair.

'Oh, Ma,' Polly said, surprised to see her mum in the street and not indoors at this time. 'This is Tommy. We've just been to the Bungalow Cafe for some tea and cake after work.'

Tommy stepped forward and put his hand out. 'Pleased to meet you, Mrs Elliot,' he said with great formality.

'Call me Agnes, Tommy,' she said, taking his hand and giving it a firm shake.

Agnes realised she had two choices: she could either rant and rave like a protective mother hen and send Tommy away with a flea in his ear, or she could get to know him and see if he was good enough to be courting her daughter. Agnes's sensible head told her that all she would succeed in doing if she tried to tear Polly and Tommy apart was to push them together.

'Well, with all that gallivanting about on that bike you'll both be hungry. Tommy, would you like to join us for a bit of mutton stew? I was just about to dish up.'

Tommy looked at Polly, who gave him an encouraging smile. 'I'd love to, Mrs— I mean Agnes. That's really kind of you, thank you.'

And so Agnes followed by Polly and then Tommy all trooped into the house. When Tommy walked into Agnes's kitchen, he was immediately struck by the warmth of the stove and the mouth-watering smell of the stew.

'Tommy, this is Bel and her daughter, Lucille. Bel, Tommy,' Agnes added as Bel turned round from feeding Lucille her tea.

On seeing Tommy, Bel's face broke into a wide smile, and her eyes shone with a gleeful mischievousness. 'Tommy!' she declared, putting out her free hand. 'It's lovely to meet you. Are you staying for tea?'

'Yes, he is,' Agnes answered for Tommy before marching into the back scullery to fetch a loaf of home-made bread to go with their supper. 'You can get the plates and cutlery out, Pol,' she shouted back through to the kitchen – a demand more than a request.

'Here, sit down,' Bel said to Tommy, moving one of the kitchen chairs back and patting the seat. 'Welcome to the Elliot household.'

Bel had to try really hard to contain her excitement at this unexpected visitor. Tommy was just as Polly had described him: handsome but not in a traditional way. He was what she imaged a Roman warrior would look like – tall and broad, with a strong jawline, but a little battered around the edges.

As Polly put the plates out, she told Bel where they'd been.

'Oh, that sounds lovely,' said Bel. 'I used to love walking along the promenade with Teddy and stopping there for a cuppa.'

Tommy asked about Teddy and was formally introduced to Lucille, who gave Tommy her soft little hand to shake.

Tommy gently took the toddler's tiny hand between his thumb and finger and moved it up and down.

Bel put Lucille to bed and as she sat down with Polly, Tommy and Agnes around the kitchen table, she said, 'It feels strange to have a man in the house.'

Tommy laughed. 'It feels strange to be eating with three women.' After that, the chatter started and didn't really stop.

Agnes gradually dropped her harsh exterior. She asked Tommy about his home life and on hearing that Tommy's granddad was presently alone at home, awaiting his grandson's arrival, she was mortified.

'Oh, that's terrible. Next time Arthur comes as well,' she commanded.

Bel and Polly smiled. Agnes's fretting over Tommy's granddad meant that her daughter's new beau had met with her approval.

'Arthur would be in seventh heaven here, that's for sure,' Tommy said, finishing off the last drop of his stew. 'Neither of us are the best cooks in the world. And I think Arthur misses being with other people.'

Agnes so wanted to ask about Tommy's own mum, but knew that had to come from Tommy himself. He seemed like a nice lad, and even though he was easy to laugh, she could see a deeply buried sadness in his eyes. Perhaps that had to do with his mother. Time would tell.

For now, Agnes stuck to the present day and asked Tommy about his work. 'I don't think I've ever met a deep-sea diver, or know anyone who even knows a diver,' she said. 'Tell me exactly what it is you do.'

Tommy explained his role in the yards and his work along the river, but then drifted into telling Agnes about what he really wanted to do. Both Agnes and Bel were all ears.

When Polly nipped out the back to the wash house, Bel asked tentatively, 'So there's a possibility you might end up as one of these clearance divers out in the Atlantic?'

Agnes knew what Bel was thinking. Both women could understand Tommy's eagerness to join these specialist teams of navy divers, but they worried about how that would affect their Pol.

Polly came back into the kitchen and Agnes changed the subject and told Tommy a little about her two 'Desert Rat' boys who were stationed with the 7th Armoured Division of the British Army, presently fighting in Egypt. She proudly told Tommy how her boys had told them in a letter that their nickname had come about after the commander's wife had visited the zoo in Cairo and drawn a sketch of a jerboa. 'A jerboa is like a rat which hops and has big ears,' Agnes explained, adding, 'But they're fast and their huge lugs mean they can hear when there's danger about.' As was usual when Agnes had company, she then got out her husband's treasured medal to show Tommy.

When it was time to go, Tommy thanked Agnes several times over for the lovely meal.

'Just you take care of my daughter,' Agnes said, as she bade him goodnight and headed off to bed.

Bel also got up to turn in for the night, but gently squeezed Tommy's arm affectionately as she left, telling him that she hoped to see him again soon.

Polly walked Tommy to the front door, leaving it ajar and stepping out into the cold night air. Tommy shrugged on his jacket before going to his bike and putting his blackout cover over the headlight. He put his helmet down on the ground and walked quickly back to Polly, who he saw was shivering as she stood on the doorstep.

When he reached her, without thinking he instantly took her into his arms. His whole body seemed to envelop Polly and he felt her shaking stop. She raised her face to his, and there was no hesitation. He had waited what seemed like a lifetime for this moment.

He kissed the lips he felt he knew so well. And those lips kissed him back.

Chapter Twenty-Eight

Saturday, 14 September

When Polly got up the next morning, she was greeted by Bel's very impressive rendition of 'Cheek to Cheek'. Polly just laughed and Agnes told them both to get a move on otherwise they'd be late for work.

'Honestly, Ma, I remember a time not so long ago you forbade me to work in the yards. Now you cannot wait for me to get there.'

'Well, I've given up trying to tell you what to do – it just falls on deaf ears,' Agnes retorted.

As Polly headed to the front door, her mother came bustling along the hallway after her. 'Ask that Tommy of yours when's a good night to invite him and his granda round for a bit of supper,' she commanded, drying her hands on her pinny.

Polly knew the image of the old man sitting on his own, waiting for his grandson to come home last night, had unsettled her.

'Thanks, Ma, I will do,' she said.

'And say hi to lover boy,' Bel teased as she watched her sister-in-law walk out the door.

Polly turned and scowled, but her expression belied the happiness she felt inside.

A few minutes later Bel gave Lucille her goodbye kiss, and said her usual 'Be good for Grandma' before she hurried out the door.

It was cold today so Bel had her coat on over her conductress's uniform. She was glad of the warmth it afforded her as she made her way to work, although it did nothing to shield her from her worries about Teddy, which came to the fore, as they always did, when she was on her own. Bel was fine when there was company about, or she was working, but as soon as she had a minute on her own her heart started to beat a bit faster and her breathing got shallower as she thought about Teddy – and Joe too, whom she loved like a brother. Her concern for them both was escalating by the day as they hadn't heard anything from the twins for months now. Bel listened to every news report and during her lunch break read every newspaper she could get her hands on in the depot's canteen. There had been news that Mussolini had sent troops into Egypt and the Allied forces had held them off and even taken a substantial number of Italian prisoners, but there had been no information about any British casualties, and Bel knew there was never a victory without a number of lost lives – on both sides.

'Oh, Bear, please be all right,' she pleaded aloud. 'I really don't know what I'll do if you're not.' Just the thought of spending a life without her cherished soulmate filled Bel's whole being with a terrible darkness.

As she passed the town's magnificent museum and glass-fronted Winter Gardens, which had been designed to emulate London's famous Crystal Palace, Bel waited until the road was clear before hurrying across, hopping over the thick metal tramlines. As she did so she was hit by one of her earliest memories of Teddy, when they had both just been youngsters, no more than six or seven years old, and as usual Bel had been out playing on her own in Tatham Street. The tramlines had been her imaginary tightrope and she'd loved to pretend she was one of those circus performers she'd seen on posters advertising the arrival of the annual big top, walking along a narrow rope with their long poles helping them to balance. Bel would wait for a tram to go past, and before the next one would arrive she would step carefully on to one of the tramlines, place an imaginary pole across her chest and carefully put one foot in front of the other as if she was the tightrope walker being applauded by the crowd below. She had even mastered a pretend wobble as if she were just about to fall into the net.

One Sunday when there were only a few trams running, she had been re-enacting her performance, jumping off and doing a theatrical bow to her enrapt audience. As she'd stepped back on to her tightrope and started the careful walk back to the other side of the big top, she had been shocked out of her imaginary circus daredevilry by a sudden thump right in the middle of her stomach. It was so forceful it had totally knocked the wind out of her and she had been left gasping for air in the middle of the tramlines.

She'd looked up to see one of the local lads standing over her with a big grin on his face.

'What did yer do that for?' she'd rasped, creased up in agony.

It was then she'd heard Teddy bellowing across the street, 'Oi!'

The grinning bully boy had looked up, seen Teddy, and scarpered. Teddy had run over to Bel and escorted her doubled-up body back on to the pavement.

'You all right?'

She'd squinted up at her friend, but had still been too breathless to say anything.

Teddy had taken her back to see Agnes, who'd made her a milky cup of tea with a big heaped teaspoon of sugar in it, and had let her sit in front of the range while she'd prepared the dinner.

Teddy had gone back out and returned a little while later. The next time Bel had seen the bully boy he'd given her a wide berth. After that he'd never laid a finger on her again. It wasn't until she was older that Bel understood what Teddy had done for her, and she loved him all the more for it. He had always been there for her, even when she hadn't known it, and she couldn't bear to think of the prospect of a life without him.

'Be safe, Bear. For me. And for Lucille,' she said to the darkening skies above that were just starting to spit down fine droplets of rain.

As Polly hurried through the drizzle, dodging the other workers, she spotted her workmates chatting to each other as they got their welding gear together. She took a deep breath, knowing she was about to walk into the spotlight of their scrutiny and face the inevitable questions they would surely fire at her about last night.

A few moments later, as predicted, as soon as the women saw Polly they started up a loud ruckus, led naturally by Dorothy. 'We want every detail. Tell us *everything*,' she demanded.

'Oh yes,' Hannah said, excitedly. 'Was it romantic?' she asked imploringly, while Martha stood by her side, stock-still, gawping at Polly and eagerly awaiting her response.

The buzz coming from the little group of women didn't go unnoticed elsewhere in the yard. A thunderous-looking Helen watched the women's excitement at Polly's arrival from the window of the accounts office. She didn't need to hear what they were saying, for she too had seen Polly's departure last night with Tommy. Watching Polly and Tommy walk off together, chatting and laughing, Helen had been livid, beside herself with jealousy. Tommy was hers. She had known him most of her life. He knew her, liked her. Spent time with her and her family. She was in the process of reeling him in. She had just about everything she wanted in life. Tommy was to be the cherry on her perfectly baked cake. She only needed a little more time for him to realise that he wanted her, and that he could have her – and everything which came with her: money, a lovely house, the best of everything.

But now this scrawny, boring, brown-haired church mouse had scuttled into the yard and had, unbelievably, caught Tommy's eye.

'What does she have that I don't?' she'd almost screamed in frustration at her mother the previous night. Helen had been so angry, so frustrated, that she'd had to vent to her mother of all people. Not that her mum really gave two hoots about her. She was probably secretly glad – Helen knew deep down that her mother wanted her to marry someone of what she called 'equal standing'.

Well, Helen didn't need that. She was standing up fine on her own. She didn't need another man to prop her up. She wanted Tommy and no one else. And by hook or by crook she was going to get exactly what she wanted.

When the women broke off for lunch they practically begged Rosie to join them. It was the last thing she really wanted to do – her mind still felt confused and disturbed, as if it were a million miles away – but seeing the women's pleading faces and being aware for the first time of their merry mood today, she surrendered and agreed.

When they had all got their lunch and were sitting down at their usual table to the side of the canteen,

Dorothy took centre stage as she always did, filling them all in on the yard's latest gossip: 'You wouldn't guess what I heard!'

The women knew that Dorothy must have been seeing her fella Eddie last night, as she always had some titbit to impart to them the next day. They all shook their heads between mouthfuls of food.

'Well, apparently there's a rumour going round that some of the women working in the yard are earning a little extra on the side, by *being* a bit of extra on the side, if you know what I mean.' She lowered her voice to a loud whisper.

Martha looked at her as if she was speaking a different language. Even Polly and Hannah seemed a little thrown.

'She means *selling their bodies*,' Gloria said bluntly.

Rosie froze.

'Like Prague, where there are . . . how do you say it, brothels?' Hannah asked, genuinely intrigued.

'Well, I don't know *where* they are *doing it*, as such,' Dorothy said, wishing now she'd quizzed Eddie more after she had overheard the men chatting, 'just that they're *doing it* for money.'

'Oh, that's awful,' Polly said, shocked. 'Why would any woman do *that* – for money?'

'I know. I'd rather starve,' Dorothy exclaimed, before adding, 'Ugh, can you imagine having to do it with some horrible, crinkly old man?'

'That's enough,' Gloria said. 'You're all putting me off my food. If a woman wants to do that with her body, then that's up to her. It's no different than someone who marries for money.'

The women all thought about it for a moment before Rosie spoke up. 'Where did you hear this, Dorothy?'

'It was Eddie's lot that were talking about it. I think they'd heard it from that old bloke Mick who does our time cards.'

'He's a weird one, he is,' Gloria said. 'He had a strange-looking man in there with him the other day. Right creepy he was, sat in the dark in the corner. Gave me the willies.'

As the women continued their chatter, none of them noticed Rosie blanch, or the look of panic which had spread across her face.

To the innocent onlooker the afternoon shift passed pretty much as normal, but under the veneer of business as usual there was a lot more happening other than the building and repairing of ships.

In the account's office Helen made some feeble excuse and snuck out for a mid-afternoon break. None of the other comptometer operators tapping away on their steel green mechanical calculators complained as Helen was, after all, the boss's daughter, and no one wanted to rock the boat or, worse still, get on the bad side of Helen. Her unsanctioned break, though, was not to have a sneaky cigarette but to go and see her friend Norman, who worked in the boiler room. He was the only homosexual Helen knew, and she was the only one in the shipyards who knew he was what the men in the yard would call a 'willy woofter'. It was not something Norman wanted to broadcast. His fellow workers would more than likely rip him apart and eat him alive if they thought they had a 'pansy' in their midst. Helen had reassured him that his secret was safe with her, but in return it meant that he was pretty much firmly under her thumb. And if she wanted him to do something, then he had to jump to it, and quickly.

*

Helen wasn't the only one to sneak off for an afternoon break. Dorothy's Eddie had also given his boss a wink and a nod and been allowed to go and chat to one of the new girls, a pretty, blonde crane operator, about some bogus job they would possibly need help with next week. He'd been given just enough time to work his charm on the young, naive girl. But it was also long enough for him to be spotted by Gloria, who was answering nature's call and was walking over to the women's lavatories. When she spotted Eddie leaning into the young girl and touching her arm as he made a joke, she felt like clocking him one there and then, but stopped herself. She had her own problems to deal with and Dorothy was just going to have to learn about men like Eddie the hard way.

After work the women all went their separate ways. Polly went over to see Tommy to invite him and Arthur round for tea. The look on his face spoke a thousand words. Martha was met by her elderly parents, just a few hundred yards up from the shipyard gates, as they were off to see some relatives in town. And Hannah left the yard on her newly acquired second-hand bike, which she was delighted about as it reminded her of her life before the war, when she would cycle round the cobbled streets of her homeland without a care in the world.

Dorothy left with a heavy heart, as she had been meant to be going out with Eddie but he had made some excuse and called off their date. Gloria, meanwhile, regretted leaving the yards at all as the moment she walked through her front door she saw that Vinnie was drunk. He was in the happy phase of inebriation, but Gloria knew from bitter experience that this would most certainly change as the night wore on.

Rosie was the last to leave work, and had done so feeling as though she was carrying the weight of the world on her shoulders. Hearing Dorothy's gossip and the women's ensuing comments at lunchtime had been like a stab in the heart. But worst of all, it was proof that Raymond was ready to put his threats into action. Rosie knew time was now running out for her.

As she trudged home, she didn't think she had ever felt more lonely or more isolated. Or so desperate. Over the past week she had spent every waking minute trying to work out a solution to her problem, but she still had no idea what to do.

Rosie walked along Dame Dorothy Street. She knew she should get a move on as she was working at Lily's tonight, but as she passed St Peter's Church she was hit by a wall of tiredness and when she saw a double-decker waiting at the bus stop, she jumped on.

When the bus stopped for a short while in Fawcett Street in the town centre, Rosie spotted a woman who was down and out, sitting huddled in a doorway. She had a half-empty bottle of spirits next to her. As an aged couple passed her, she raised her hand to beg a few pennies from them. Rosie looked at the woman's face and realised she recognised her. It was her old friend from school who had been orphaned and sent to Nazareth House and into the care of the nuns. When Rosie had seen her as a young girl all those years ago, she had been shocked at the change in her friend, and had felt, rightly so, that she'd had the life beaten out of her. Now here she was again – the fallout of a brutal childhood clear for all to see.

Rosie didn't think her day could possibly get any worse. Here was a future which she had always dreaded might befall her little sister, and if Raymond had his way, it still easily could.

It was then that Rosie knew what she had to do.

As she got off at the Park Lane depot and walked back to her bedsit, she knew she somehow had to find the money to pay Raymond *and* keep Charlotte at her boarding school. She had to earn enough to feed Raymond's evil and keep her sister safe. There was no other option. And there was only one way of doing it. She would have to work every minute of every day, every second of overtime, and every night at Lily's to make ends meet.

She *would* do it. She *had* to do it. There was no other choice.

Chapter Twenty-Nine

'Be careful what you wish for,' Miriam warned her petulant, spoilt daughter, who had started in on her favourite subject: Tommy. The large gin and tonic Miriam had poured herself a little earlier on was already making her more loquacious than normal. She had an evening free of social engagements and was at home with just Helen for company. Jack – as usual, she thought bitterly – was working late at the yards. Probably on this new ship design he was obsessed with. It was the only thing he seemed to think about these days. Or care about. He certainly didn't give two hoots about his wife. Not that he had for a long time now.

'Well, you *wanted* Dad,' Helen shot back at her mother, who she could see was already well oiled, 'and you *got* him. And you don't seem to have fared too badly.'

One evening years ago a very tipsy Miriam had told Helen how, if you really wanted something, you had to go out and get it, no matter what, and that this was exactly what Miriam had done when she'd decided she wanted to marry Helen's father.

'I *want* Tommy, and I'm going to *get* Tommy, whatever it takes,' Helen declared adamantly.

Helen had no real friends she could confide in, so whenever her mother was about, and still sober enough to hold a coherent conversation, Miriam would often end up being a stand-in confidante of sorts.

Miriam sat down on the large leather Chesterfield sofa in her immaculate living room and placed her gin and

207

tonic on the mahogany coffee table. She looked at her daughter and saw a reflection of her younger self and felt a stab of jealousy. What she would give to be young again and beautiful. She knew it was wrong to feel envious of your own offspring, but Miriam did. It was as simple as that. She yearned for her daughter's soft, smooth skin, and her vibrancy and energy. Miriam had just turned forty and despite her trim figure and her beauty treatments, there was no denying the unstoppable ravages of age. It was as though all of a sudden she had aged, developed wrinkles and lost her vitality. It probably didn't help that she enjoyed a drink or two every night, but her evening tipple was now her only comfort and enjoyment. Helen was a grown woman and lived her own life. And Jack rarely spent any time with Miriam unless he had to. He no longer even joined her in their marital bed any more, preferring to sleep in the spare room.

'All I'm saying, darling, is think about what you really want, and be patient. You know the expression. Good things come to those who wait.' Miriam knew her words would wind her daughter up.

'Urgh! Mother! I'm being patient. If I wait any longer I'll be an old spinster. And if I don't act now Tommy's going to be sailing off into the sunset with his little welder. How on earth he can like someone who walks around in scruffy overalls and big clumpy boots all day is beyond me. She looks more like a man than a woman.'

Helen knew this was not true. When she had seen Polly up close she had been taken aback by how pretty she was, and that had been without a smidgen of make-up.

'Perhaps Tommy likes her because she is more like a man than a woman,' Miriam prodded. The gin was just starting to hit the spot and kick-start that lovely couldn't-care-less feeling.

Helen looked at her mum and felt like slapping some sense into her. Sometimes she felt that her mother enjoyed seeing her suffer.

'Don't be stupid, Mother. Tommy knows which side he bats for. Any fool can see that,' Helen said dismissively.

But Miriam's puerile comments had turned Helen's devious mind to Norman. Now there was a man who did bat for the other side. It amazed Helen that none of the other workers realised they had a homosexual in their midst. Norman tried his hardest to reign in his effeminate mannerisms, but occasionally they broke free and it was so obvious he was what the men would call a 'fairy' – either that or one of those blokes she had read about who really wanted to become a woman.

'Anyway, I've got a strategy,' Helen told Miriam. She hadn't wanted to tell her mother about what she had asked Norman to do, but she really needed to share her plan to ensnare the man she had wanted since she'd been a little girl. Men went out and grabbed what they wanted, so why couldn't a woman? Besides, she knew time was now of the essence and she had to act quickly, as it was clear to all and sundry that pretty Polly had turned Tommy's head. It was up to Helen to wrench it back in her direction. And if she had to be manipulative and devious to make that happen, then so be it. All's fair in love and war was Helen's often-repeated philosophy.

'A *strategy*?' Miriam was now more than a little interested. 'Tell me more.' Miriam was enjoying her evening's entertainment. Not for the first time did it occur to her just how much her daughter really did take after her.

As Helen sat down next to her mum she took a sip of her mother's drink, and then began to set out her plan.

Miriam listened to her daughter's excited monologue, about how Helen had already made it her mission over the past few weeks to be seen talking to Tommy whenever she knew Polly was nearby, knowing that Polly could not fail to notice Helen who, of course, was always looking glam and gorgeous. She nodded sagely, knowing how much it would wind this woman welder up to see her chap being chatted up by a beauty like Helen. Women were experts at knowing which buttons to press to get a desired reaction, or at least women like herself and Helen. They had the art of manipulation down to a tee. And Miriam knew how seeing Tommy and Helen chatting and laughing would, in turn, inevitably cause friction between Tommy and his new girl.

Miriam knew there was nothing more off-putting to a man, nor anything more unattractive, than a woman's open display of jealousy or neediness. Miriam herself had used similar tactics with Jack. But it was her daughter's subterfuge of using Norman to spread a rumour that Polly had started to see one of the platers, who also happened to be good-looking and around the same age as Polly, which really impressed Miriam. She thought this specific rod in her daughter's fire of deceit was particularly beguiling. And her timing, by the sounds of it, was perfect. Everyone was working flat out at the yards, which meant lots of overtime, which in turn meant little time or energy for dates or any other kind of courtship. Her daughter was wise enough to know that she had to act now, before Tommy and this Polly became too attached.

'And that's when I gently draw Tommy into my womanly web and work my feminine wiles on him,' Helen said, before adding, 'And as soon as I do, I will make damn sure that Polly is the first to know that Tommy is mine!' On that victorious note, Helen stood up, gave her mum a peck on the cheek and said her goodnights.

After her daughter had flounced out of the room, Miriam got up to mix herself a little nightcap. She had to hand it to her daughter – her self-belief was unshakeable. She certainly did not lack confidence in the least. But, she guessed, that was what you paid for when you sent your child to an expensive private school.

As Miriam stared into the fire, she couldn't help but ponder the eventual outcome of her daughter's unscrupulous plans, and the long-term consequences. Miriam had to admit it had been fun listening to her daughter but now that the high she got from the gin was dropping to a more melancholic and pensive low, she began to reflect on her own life and the ramifications of her own youthful manipulations.

Like Helen, she had been ruthless in her determination to capture Jack's heart when they had been just teenagers. It had been no easy feat as Jack and Gloria had been courting seriously for some time, and it was only a matter of time before they got engaged. And like Helen, Miriam had also used her looks to draw Jack away from Gloria, but after a while she had realised that she was never going to really win him over. Despite showing him an enviable life of wealth and good fortune, a life someone like Jack could never have imagined possible, she knew he was going to go back to Gloria. He was going to choose his childhood sweetheart and a life of drudgery and poverty over everything that she was offering him.

That was when she had played one of the oldest tricks in the book, but a trick no one ever dared to admit engaging in. She had played a dangerous game, especially back in those days of enforced virtue, when women were meant to be pure as the driven snow and walk down the aisle in virginal white. Not like nowadays when women were falling pregnant at the drop of a hat simply because their men were going to war and might never come back again.

As she finished off her drink Miriam congratulated herself on her daring back then. She had seduced Jack one night after coaxing him back to her parents' house when she'd known they would be out. Their evening of passion hadn't been enough to make her pregnant, but it had been enough to make Jack *believe* she had fallen. It had hurt her to see the look of disbelief, shock and hopelessness on his face when she'd lied to him and told him she was carrying his child. But she'd known Jack well enough to be certain he would do what was right and expected in decent society. And she had been proved right. Jack had broken off his relationship with Gloria and done the gentlemanly thing and made Miriam his wife. Miriam had got exactly what she'd wanted.

Before the physical signs of her phoney pregnancy were due to become visible, she had put on the performance of a lifetime and orchestrated it so that Jack had found her hysterical. As he had comforted her and begged her to tell him what was wrong, she had told him in gut-wrenching sobs that she had lost their baby. Of course, by this time it was too late for Jack. He had committed himself to Miriam. He'd married her. There was no going back. It hadn't taken Miriam long to fall pregnant for real after her faked miscarriage, and with the arrival of baby Helen, she had successfully tied Jack to her for a lifetime. But, Miriam reflected, she hadn't succeeded in giving Jack any more children, and she wondered if this had been some sort of punishment for her duplicitous behaviour.

Miriam swayed a little as she got up from the comfort of the sofa, having consumed more gin than she had intended. As she walked a little unsteadily over to the fire, she felt a deep sorrow. She may have got what she wanted, ensnared the man she thought she loved, but she had learnt as the years had gone on that their love was always going to be one way. It didn't matter how much she had plotted and planned, just like Helen was doing now – Jack would never love her like he had loved Gloria. Like Miriam loved Jack. In fact, sometimes she saw pure hatred in his eyes and at times like this she had to ask herself if she had done the right thing.

With a sadness she rarely allowed herself to feel, and in a moment of rare maternal concern, Miriam worried that Helen was about to repeat exactly the same mistake that she had made all those years ago.

'Be careful what you wish for, because you might just get it,' Miriam said aloud to the empty room.

Chapter Thirty

Saturday, 28 September

'I think we could fly back home, never mind walk,' Polly joked as she and Tommy prepared to leave the shelter of the stone-pillared entrance of the town's museum, where they'd been enjoying a pot of tea together and some biscuits. It was teatime and after finishing their shift at the yard they had hurried into town to snatch a precious few hours together.

Over the past few weeks the town had breathed a tentative sigh of relief as there had been a lull in the number of air strikes, but the need for ships had never been greater and all the yards on the north-east coast were working at full pelt. Neither Tommy nor Polly resented the long, hard hours required of them as it filled them both with a sense of purpose that they were doing everything they could for the war effort, but it didn't stop their intense longing to simply be with each other.

Since meeting Tommy, Polly had been the happiest she'd been in her life, despite the war and all the worries which went with it. Tommy made her feel so happy, so loved and desired. The way she felt for him had been bewildering at first as she had never experienced this intensity of love before. Every moment she and Tommy snatched to be together was magical. When there were just the two of them she was in seventh heaven, and the way she felt for him hadn't waned in the least, only grown with each passing day. And she could tell he felt the same.

And it was a great relief that both Agnes and Bel had taken to Tommy, and that Arthur had also made it quite clear that he had a real soft spot for Polly. He often talked about Flo, and how Polly reminded him of his treasured wife in younger days.

Following Arthur's initial invite to tea at the Elliots', he had become a regular visitor at the house, generally around teatime, when he would knock on the front door, even though it was usually wide open. Agnes would bustle down the hallway to find the old man standing there, often with a bit of fish wrapped up in newspaper, or armed with a few crabs he'd bought from the old woman who was well known around town for selling her freshly cooked crustaceans from an old pram.

Today Polly and Tommy had stayed chatting in the little tearoom on the first floor of the museum, so wrapped up in each other's company they'd been totally unaware that the weather outside had turned, and the wind had whipped itself up into a frenzy. As they stepped into what was fast becoming a gale, it was so powerful they both struggled to battle their way forward against the fierce scooping gusts bellowing in from the North Sea.

Polly's coat flew open and whipped up behind her like a magician's cloak. She felt Tommy's hand squeeze her own tightly before pulling her over to the side of the pavement. Clutching his hand, Polly was happy to follow Tommy's lead, his thickset body forming a partial barrier against the wind. As she turned her head she could just about make out his beckoning face as her long hair lashed around her own face, partly obscuring her vision. The wind was howling and blotting out any other noise but she could see Tommy's mouth move in speech and his head jerk over towards the side of the museum's Winter Garden. Polly followed after him, the change in direction causing them both to be pushed forward into a half-jog.

'This way.' Polly could now just about make out Tommy's words as he continued to gently tug at her arm and guide her away from the pavement and towards the side entrance to Mowbray Park at the rear of the museum.

They both stumbled as they turned off the main street and down a narrow footpath to the side of the large oval-shaped park that was said to be one of the oldest and prettiest in the whole of the north-east. It was like stepping out of a wind tunnel and into relative calm – the battle against the elements leaving them breathless but also adrenaline-filled.

Tommy walked quickly, still clutching Polly's hand, stepping across the grass verge and into the shelter of an imposing oak tree, its trunk expansive and solid and a natural barrier against the harsh weather. It also afforded them a private space, the oak's huge drooping branches weighed down and creating a modest screen from any passers-by.

Tommy pulled Polly towards him and pressed himself against her, kissing her gently but with growing fervour. She could feel his longing for her and she kissed him back with equal passion, showing him that she too longed for him. His broad frame dwarfed her as they kissed and caressed each other. Polly had never wanted a man as much as she desired Tommy and, like the wind, it took her breath away.

He was also taken aback by the strength and passion of his feelings for Polly. He had experienced the physical love of a woman before, but nothing compared to the ardour he felt for the woman now wrapped in his arms, responding to his touch.

They both knew, though, that they could not give in to their desires for each other. Polly had been raised with the understanding, like most young women her age, that she would keep her virtue until she had walked down the aisle, and she knew she would not rebel against the morals she had been brought up with. But it was hard. Especially when her love for Tommy felt so natural. So right. And so true.

Chapter Thirty-One

Three weeks later

Lily had been keeping an eye out for Rosie, waiting for her to come back downstairs after she had finished with her last client of the evening. She was determined to catch her before she left for the evening. When she saw Rosie walk down the thick-carpeted staircase, her coltish legs looking slightly unsteady as she held the wide wooden handrail to aid her descent, Lily decided just to come out with it. 'You can't keep going like this, *ma chérie*,' she told Rosie, trying not to sound too maternal or as if she was angry with her.

Lily had fought with herself these past few weeks. On the one hand, she knew it wasn't really any of her business, that she was, to all intents and purposes, Rosie's boss and that she should keep that professional distance. But on the other hand, she couldn't stop herself from caring. She knew it wasn't her place to meddle in the lives of her girls, but it had now got to a stage where she just couldn't hold her tongue any longer. She couldn't watch someone drown right in front of her very eyes and just stand there, without even sticking a hand out to help.

She followed Rosie into the kitchen as she waited for a reply.

'I'm fine, Lily! Honestly,' Rosie said, a little sharply, 'but what I could do with is a glass of brandy to see me home.'

Lily looked at Rosie and thought she seemed anything but fine. The dark circles under her eyes were becoming more prominent. Rosie was wearing more make-up these days than she ever had, but it didn't matter how much she slapped on, it was getting harder to hide just how drained she really was.

Ever since the day six weeks ago when that odious, repugnant man had conned his way into Lily's establishment, Rosie had gone downhill quickly. Which wasn't surprising: the girl was working every hour of overtime she could at the yard, and she was at Lily's every night. Rosie was her main girl and very popular with her clients, so there was certainly the work for her. Really Lily shouldn't have cared less about Rosie's life outside of her work here, but she did. She might be a hard-nosed madam, and, make no mistake about it, she was as tough as old boots, probably tougher, but she still had a heart. And her heart went out to Rosie.

'That girl's working herself into the ground,' Lily had said to George the other night. Neither of them had breathed a word to anyone else about Raymond. It was none of anyone's business, but they had both been shocked by the man's pure evil, and Lily and George were fairly unshockable, having seen just about the worst sides of human nature in the lives they had lived.

Now it was obvious that Raymond's poison had infected Rosie and was slowly dragging her down, sapping away her energy and her spirit. Lily had seen it before and didn't like the way it normally ended. It reminded her of some of her girls who'd come to her after being sucked dry by their purported 'minders'. These procurers would take every last bean from the women they put out to work and then dump them when there was nothing left.

Lily knew that Rosie was now making weekly payments to Raymond, enough to keep him happy, *and* she was somehow managing to cover Charlotte's boarding school fees. But you didn't have to be a mathematician to work out this left Rosie with barely enough to feed herself as well as keep a roof over her head.

She knew that Rosie had been terrified Raymond would leak her name to that meddling timekeeper Mick, and she'd be exposed in the yard as a working girl. So Rosie had forced herself to go to a bedsit on the town's Ryhope Road, the address Raymond had left with the young cloak-room girl on the night he'd duped his way into Lily's. There she'd agreed to start paying him a set weekly amount – her uncle's way of collecting the debt he claimed was owed to him by Rosie's mother. And since the money had now been owing for over five years, and had therefore accumulated interest, the debt would take for ever to pay off.

What Lily didn't know was how nauseous it made Rosie just to think about her visits to Raymond's horrible little bedsit, how the place stank of stale smoke, sweat and unwashed bedlinen, how the room was so small Rosie couldn't help but breathe in his body odour, which was as foul as his very being.

When Rosie had first gone to see Raymond, she had tried to lie about how much she earned, but her uncle wasn't stupid and had known how much her wages were, almost to the penny. Rosie guessed he had given Mick a backhander to show him her time cards, and had been able to work out how much she was being paid from the hours she put in at the yard. She was also pretty certain that Raymond would have a fair idea how much she earned at Lily's. He mixed in the type of circles that knew such things. Rosie was praying he wouldn't find out she was now working every night at Lily's and that she'd doubled up on her overtime.

A concerned Lily poured them both a glass of brandy. It pained her to see how drawn and washed-out Rosie looked. Her cheekbones were more prominent than was natural due to the amount of weight she'd lost. She was also drinking most nights – something she'd rarely done before, usually preferring a hot cup of tea before her walk home.

Lily was the first to admit that she herself liked her Rémy Martin and her French wine whenever she could get hold of it, but she knew the nature of addiction and could see Rosie slowly going down its slippery slope.

She decided just to come out with it: 'You're doing too much.'

'I haven't got a choice.' Rosie glared back at Lily, before taking a large glug of brandy, almost emptying her glass in one go.

'You're going to make yourself ill if you keep going like this,' Lily said, before adding, 'And that stuff needs to be sipped, not downed like it's a glass of pop.'

Rosie's head shot up to look at her employer. 'What? You my mother now?' she snapped, immediately regretting her short, angry retort. 'Oh, I'm sorry, Lily.' Rosie was flooded with guilt. 'I'm just at my wits' end. It's not your fault. I just seem to be on such a short fuse at the moment.'

Lily walked over to Rosie, who looked totally dejected and desolate.

'I know, I know.' Lily put her hand on Rosie's head. She wanted to give her a big cuddle, tell her everything would be just fine, and then go out and hunt down that demonic man. But she couldn't, no matter how much she wanted to.

'After he started that rumour in the yards,' Rosie said, anger creeping back into her voice, 'he then wrote to Charlotte's school, asking if he could come and visit her as he was her uncle. Thank goodness they wrote to me to get my permission and I was able to put a stop to it.' Rosie carried on talking, more to herself than Lily. 'The thing is, he knew he wouldn't get away with it, but he was proving a point, tightening another screw, reminding me of what he could do if he put his mind to it.'

Lily felt a shiver go down her spine. Rosie really was well and truly cornered. Who was this man? What could she do to stop him? She could offer to help Rosie out with money, but she knew this wasn't only about money. It went deeper than that. This man wasn't out to rob Rosie of just her livelihood but also her life. He was a sadist in the true sense of the word. He wanted to destroy Rosie. And what was even more perverse was that he wanted to do it slowly, like catching a rabbit in a trap and keeping it there for the pure enjoyment of seeing it struggle. He sought to hold Rosie to ransom, to keep her hostage, to watch her suffer. He wanted to slowly drain every drop of life out of her. But the most disturbing thing of all, Lily thought as she looked at Rosie now, finishing her glass of brandy, was that he was succeeding.

'Get yourself home and get some sleep,' Lily said. 'There's got to be a way out of this.' She tried to sound as convincing as possible, but in her heart Lily couldn't see any way out of this impenetrable cage in which Rosie was now well and truly trapped.

Rosie made her way home, feeling a little light-headed from knocking the brandy back so quickly. She realised Lily was right, but she had no choice.

As she walked back to her bedsit along the dark streets, she didn't bother to get out her little torch. A solitary car, barely visible in the blackout, drove past her as she crossed the road. It occurred to Rosie that a part of her wouldn't have cared if she was run over. At least if she became another blackout fatality, she thought morbidly, it would give her a permanent escape from this hellish existence she was now living, and from the constraints in which Raymond now held her and would continue to hold her for as long as she lived. The thought of death no longer seemed something to be fearful of. In her increasingly distorted world, Rosie felt it would truly be a welcome release. If it hadn't been for Charlotte, it would most certainly be an option, but Rosie knew she could never leave Charlotte on her own in this hard, cruel world. Charlotte had lost her mother and father and Rosie was her only family. She needed her.

Rosie trudged back home, thoughts of death continuing to swim around in her head, reflecting the pool of darkness surrounding her. She opened her front door and climbed the stairs, her despair and despondency feeling never-ending.

Chapter Thirty-Two

Monday, 21 October

'Will that woman not leave that poor man alone?' Gloria said under her breath, but loud enough for the others to hear.

The women welders now had their own makeshift outdoor fire that they were all presently standing around. They had acquired a five-gallon barrel from one of the storerooms and copied the male welders by creating a hearty fire to warm themselves next to, much needed now that the bitter cold autumnal weather was taking a real hold. Martha had more or less single-handedly hauled it over to the little area of the yard that they had claimed as their own, just like the other pockets of caulkers, riveters, and platers dotted around the flat expanse of the shipyard.

As they stood warming their hands, Polly didn't need to look to know whom Gloria was talking about. Lately it seemed that Helen was seeing more of Tommy than Polly was. They'd barely been able to have a quick chat with each other this past week or so, never mind snatch a few hours together – unlike Helen, who was now chatting to Tommy as though she had all the time in the world to spare. Polly hated herself for it, but every time Helen swanned across the yard to chat to Tommy, she felt immediately plunged into a state of anger, paranoia and jealousy.

Gloria was right, Polly seethed to herself. Why couldn't Helen just leave Tommy alone? Why couldn't she find her own man? And why couldn't Tommy just tell her to go away, get lost, leave and not come back? It was so annoying. No, actually, it was torturous.

It had been hard but Polly had forced herself during their snatched moments together not to question Tommy about Helen for fear she would seem needy and jealous. Polly wasn't the most experienced woman in the world when it came to men, but she knew well enough that any show of clinginess or possessiveness could easily cause a man's interest to cool off. She had, however, chewed off Bel's ears with her insecurities, which she had to admit had plagued her ever since she had fallen for Tommy almost two months ago.

Every time Polly saw Helen in the yard, inevitably heading over to see Tommy, it fired up her deep-seated jealously and ate into her confidence. And she hated it, hated being like this. She had never been jealous like this before in her life.

'If only I could stop myself feeling like this,' she'd confessed to Bel, who'd smiled at her overwrought and very-much-in-love sister-in-law and tried to tell her that, unfortunately, this was the flip side of the love coin. She had listened as Polly, who had never been keen on putting on make-up, or dressing up in a skirt and heels, had told her how she wanted to make herself look 'totally fabulous' for Tommy.

'I don't think he's ever seen me in anything but these dirty overalls,' Polly had said, pulling at her loose denim work clothes which, as Rosie had predicted on that first day, had become her second skin. 'Then again,' Polly had despaired, 'am I ever going to be able to compete with a woman who's made it her life's mission to look drop-dead gorgeous every minute of the day?'

Bel had laughed and told Polly that if Tommy wanted to be with Helen then he would be taking *her* out and not Polly. But Bel's reassurances went over Polly's head as the very thought of dressing up made Polly inwardly despair. She and Tommy could barely snatch the odd few hours together after work – and only then if they both finished at the same time – never mind have the luxury of dressing up in their glad rags for an entire evening out.

As Polly now looked up from the fire, she tried not to stare at Tommy and Helen, still chatting. She tried not to scrutinise every inch of this horribly perfect woman, with her coiffured hair and polished nails, but she just couldn't drag her eyes away whenever Helen flaunted herself at Tommy.

'Time's up,' Rosie shouted out as she walked over to the women.

They all reluctantly dragged themselves away from their mini inferno. Polly stole a glance in Tommy's direction and felt a slight relief that the yard's goddess had floated back up to her cloud on the first floor of the administration block.

As they all returned to the sheets of metal they were welding, Dorothy sidled up to Polly. 'Don't you think the boss is looking dreadful lately?'

Polly glanced over to Rosie, and for the first time she realised just how much Rosie had changed over the past month.

'She is, isn't she?' Polly agreed.

'She probably just needs a nice man to cheer her up,' Dorothy said, looking at Polly and thinking how vibrant she looked and had looked since getting together with the hunky Tommy.

'It's probably a man who's making her look so wretched,' Polly retorted, without realising just how true her words were.

'Are we all going to the canteen today?' Dorothy shouted over the usual racket orchestrated by the yard's machinery.

'Anywhere warm,' piped up a shivering Hannah, who'd been brought back to help out with the women's hefty workload.

'Yes,' Martha's voice boomed, her enthusiasm stirred by the return of her little friend to the welders' fold.

Gloria added, 'Just as long as we don't have to watch you moon over that randy riveter of yours.'

'He's not randy, and his name's Eddie,' Dorothy said, offended. 'And I don't *moon*.'

Rosie commanded, 'Machines on now,' pushing down her own helmet as they all switched on their welders.

As Dorothy started to melt metal, she thought about Gloria. Since that shocking day they had all seen her bruised neck, she hadn't been able to stop carefully checking her workmate out each day for any other signs of bruising, or any other telltale signs that Vinnie had hurt her. The women hadn't ever talked about what they'd seen that day, but that was not to say it hadn't affected them, or had been forgotten.

Dorothy knew for a fact that Gloria's husband was still being violent to her. She hid it well, just like Dorothy's own mother had. And like Dorothy's father, Vinnie mightn't be able to control his temper, but he was savvy enough to make sure he didn't cause any injuries that could be obviously seen. Dorothy, however, knew where to look, and the other day when Gloria had pulled off her welder's gloves Dorothy had caught a glimpse of her wrists and the telltale faded yellow marks of old bruising. Last week it had been a particularly windy day on the docks and Dorothy had recoiled when she'd seen a patch of Gloria's bare, pink scalp where a clump of her hair had been ripped out.

Dorothy wished she could stop thinking about it, that she didn't care so much for Gloria. Although why she cared so much about this woman who only had harsh words and jibes for her, she didn't know. But even though the two of them were like chalk and cheese in all ways – their age, their background, their looks, their personalities – there was some kind of strange connection there.

In a funny way, Dorothy felt that Gloria cared about her too. Even if she had made it obvious she thought Eddie was a waste of space, she had at least shown an interest in Dorothy's life, more than her own mother had done over these past few years. Nowadays her mum never had two minutes to turn around, let alone ask her daughter anything about what was happening in her life. Her mum's time and energy were completely given over to Dorothy's stepfather and her three younger sisters. And now, to make matters even worse, there was a fourth sibling on the way. If Dorothy got little attention at the moment, she would become totally invisible by the time this next child arrived.

An hour or so later, when the women were all walking over to the canteen, shielding themselves from the bitter cold that was starting to really pierce through their multiple layers of liberty bodices, thick cotton shirts, jumpers and overalls, Jack hurried past. Dorothy noticed him looking over to Gloria, who pretended not to see him.

What was it with those two? Why was Gloria ignoring Jack, who seemed like a decent enough chap by all accounts? And why be so rude to someone she knew and had appeared to be friends with? What was also intriguing was that Gloria clearly did not like his daughter Helen. Not that many people did, come to think of it.

What Dorothy would give to know what was really going on there.

As the women filed into the canteen, they collectively breathed a sigh of relief at being somewhere warm. Dorothy, as usual, began her surreptitious scouting for Eddie. He had promised to take her out tonight and make up for the fact she'd once again had to pay for all of their drinks the other evening. He'd said he would pay her back by taking her to the cinema to see *Gone with the Wind*. Dorothy was desperate to see the film as she thought Eddie looked like a younger version of Clark Gable, and in her overactive imagination she saw herself as a British Vivien Scarlett O'Hara struggling to survive a war – albeit the Second World War in the north-east of England, rather than a civil war in America's Deep South.

Chapter Thirty-Three

Tommy waited for the head foreman to come back to chat to him about a problem he was having with a particularly tricky repair. He started to think about Polly and how little they'd been able to see each other of late. It had become the norm to be working over seventy hours a week. Although they didn't like to see each other during their lunch breaks, as they would only have to endure cajoling and jokey jibes – Polly from the women welders and he from his diving team – Tommy decided it had got to the stage where they'd just have to suffer the ribbing and verbal banter if they were to stand a cat in hell's chance of being with each other any time soon.

As Tommy stood waiting, his thoughts were interrupted by a small group of caulkers talking very loudly about 'that bonny welder'. At first Tommy thought they were talking about Dorothy, but as the idle chatter continued about the 'quiet, stuck-up one', Tommy knew it had to be Polly. Not that she was stuck-up in the least. He knew she still felt a little intimidated by the yard, but what the men perceived to be snobbishness was really a lack of confidence.

Tommy felt his heart pound as he moved a little closer to the workers, and listened with an overwhelming sense of disbelief as they gossiped about how 'the one with the long brown hair' and legs which 'went up to her neck' was seeing one of the young platers called Ned.

'Lucky bugger,' one of the lads said through a mouthful of Stottie cake. He stood with his workmates, all eating and chatting round their blazing drum fire.

Tommy's first reaction was to stomp over to the gaggle of old fishwives, haul the gossipmonger up by the lapels of his shabby black work jacket and demand to know every minuscule detail of this soul-destroying tittle-tattle.

But he didn't. He wouldn't let anyone, let alone any of the other workers, know anything about his business, or what he was feeling. He knew that the only people in the yard to really know about him and Polly were the women welders. They didn't have to say anything but they knew how he felt about Polly and that the two had started to court, or were *trying* to court, even though the past week or so they'd barely exchanged a few words, never mind gone out on a date due to the amount of overtime they were all doing.

Could Polly have lost interest in him? The welders had been working alongside the platers for some time now – had Polly and Ned become close?

Tommy couldn't bear to be near the caulkers and wandered back in a daze to the diving team.

His mind felt in turmoil. If Tommy had been told Polly was seeing this Ned a few weeks ago, he would have dismissed it without a second thought because they'd been spending every spare minute they could together. But lately the two of them had hardly seen each other. It was becoming increasingly difficult for them to have anything resembling a normal courtship as the hours at the yard had increased, and it seemed whenever one of them managed to get some time off, the other had had to work.

It hadn't bothered them, though, or so Tommy had thought, because they were both passionate about doing what they could to bring an end to this godawful war. He had felt there was an understanding that they could wait, knowing they were doing an invaluable job which had to take precedence over their blossoming love affair, and had felt safe in the knowledge that their love would last well beyond this war.

Tommy had believed this was how they both felt, but more than anything he had been convinced that there was a loyalty between the two of them. A trust. Now he wondered if he'd been living in cloud cuckoo land. Had he been kidding himself about Polly? Had he been living an illusion? Had he presumed she felt the same about him, when, in fact, she hadn't?

He cast his mind back and remembered seeing how the women welders had first begun working with the platers.

Had Polly liked this Ned from the start?

Chapter Thirty-Four

Tuesday, 22 October

'Tommy,' Helen called out, wrapping her red woollen shawl tightly around herself so that it accentuated her hourglass figure as she tottered across the yard.

Tommy had just resurfaced from the river in time for his lunch break. He was determined to grab Polly before she headed off to the canteen with the rest of the women. He needed to confront her and ask her outright if she was seeing Ned. He had been in bits since he'd overheard the caulkers' idle chatter yesterday afternoon, and was totally frustrated he hadn't been able to catch Polly after work as he had finished later than anticipated, by which time the women welders had packed up and gone home.

He'd begun to wonder if perhaps the gossiping caulkers had made a mistake or had been misinformed. Perhaps the Chinese whispers going round the yard had distorted the whole sorry saga and it was some other woman, not Polly, who was seeing this Ned. Tommy knew he was snatching at straws but was desperately clinging to the hope that there was still a remote possibility that Polly was his and his alone.

'All right, Helen,' Tommy mumbled. He looked over her shoulder to see that the women welders were all packing up for lunch.

'I just wanted a quick word,' Helen said, holding her thick black hair back in one hand to stop it being blown into a tangled mess by the blustering sea winds.

'Can it wait?' Tommy said. 'I was just going to try and catch Polly.' He bent down to unstrap his feet from his large lead-weighted boots.

'Actually,' Helen said, trying to sound as serious and as sympathetic as possible, 'it's Polly I wanted to chat to you about.'

Tommy gave her a questioning look.

'I didn't really want to tell you this, but I know if it was me, I would want to know. And besides, we've known each other for a long time. It's what friends are for.'

A feeling of dread started to rise within Tommy at what she was about to say.

'You see, I've known for a few days now, and, obviously, I know you are keen on Polly . . .' Tommy stared at Helen as she continued, 'But, well, it would seem she's had her head turned by one of the platers.'

'What do you mean, "head turned"?' Tommy demanded, his face like thunder as he practically tossed his diver's boots aside.

'Well,' Helen continued, trying her hardest to appear concerned, 'I think it's more than that. One of the girls in the office told me she'd seen Polly out with Ned the other night and they looked very cosy together.'

Helen watched Tommy for his reaction and caught a murderous look on his face before he pulled on his normal leather boots, stood up and stomped off towards the far end of the docks. As she watched him march away, she felt a nervous thrill – an excited anticipation of what she hoped was to come. She had already started the ball rolling weeks back, but it wasn't going as quickly as she'd hoped so now it was time to give it an extra push.

She hurried back to the main office and into the accounts department, where she had a word with one of the juniors. The junior nodded as Helen informed her that two of the workers, a Polly Elliot and a Ned Pike, needed to come into the office at the end of the shift because some of their personal details has been misplaced and were needed to process the week's wages. The girl listened carefully before nipping out into the yard to carry out her orders.

At exactly five thirty, as the horn sounded out the end of the day's shift, Polly grabbed her bag and headed over to the admin office, just as Ned was also making his way there.

'You going where I'm going?' Ned asked as the two of them walked together.

'Accounts?' Polly said.

Ned nodded, adding, 'Any idea why we've been summoned?'

'No idea. You?' she asked.

'Nah, me neither. Perhaps they've decided to give us a pay rise as we've been working so hard,' he joked.

Polly laughed. 'I wish.' She smiled at her workmate as they walked side by side across the yard.

Polly and Ned's brief exchange wasn't heard by Tommy, but he saw the pair together and watched as Polly smiled and laughed with Ned.

He had just spent the afternoon in hell as his thoughts of them had hurtled around his head, driving him to distraction. It had been hard to stop himself going straight over to Polly while she'd been in the middle of her afternoon shift, but he'd somehow managed to hold back. But as soon as the hooter had sounded out he'd hurried over to welders' area to confront her, only to see her walking off with Ned.

Tommy felt the rage rising inside him. He wanted to go and knock seven bells out of this man Polly was now with, this man who was making her laugh and smile.

Somehow Tommy managed to contain himself. Somehow he managed to push his feelings of anger and hurt back down. It was something he was very good at doing, and had been doing all his life.

It was now as clear as day that Polly was seeing another man. They weren't even trying to hide it. It seemed as though everyone but Tommy had known about it: the caulkers, the office workers, Helen. Tommy felt his heart harden. How had he got Polly so wrong?

Chapter Thirty-Five

Thursday, 24 October

Over the next week the weather on the north-east coast seemed to be deteriorating with each shift. The winds howling in from the North Sea were getting more vicious, whipping round the workers and creating wind tunnels in some parts of the yards. And the air was icy cold. There had been a forecast that the whole of the area was to be hit by one of the harshest winters in years, and the workers' stinging faces and numb fingers and toes were testimony to that prediction.

Like the dire weather, Tommy's mood had also worsened as the week had progressed. The dock's diving team had never seen their workmate in such a raging temper, and most of them had known Tommy for years, ever since he'd started at the yards when he was a teenager.

'Who's got your goat?' Ralph, one of the older divers, asked a stony-faced Tommy. Ralph was past retirement age, but had stayed on after war broke out, determined to do his bit to beat what he called 'the bleedin' Nazis'. As a hardened dock veteran, and a respected one at that, he was the only one in their small team who dared ask Tommy what the matter was. The two younger lads in the team were wisely keeping a safe distance. 'You're like a bear with a sore head,' Ralph continued to prod Tommy. 'It's either a woman . . . or a woman.'

The four other workers – the two young divers and the two assistants responsible for the men's safety – stifled their chuckles, knowing if Tommy caught them he'd flare up. And no one wanted to get into a fracas with Tommy. Not just because of his size, but because they all got on well with him. They were all aware that he did suffer occasionally from dark moods, but had accepted that was just the way he was, it was part of his make-up. But they'd never seen him really angry before. And at the moment he was like a bit of tinder, ready to flame up at the slightest breeze.

Tommy looked at Ralph, whom he liked and respected, and gave him a nod and a grunt, confirming that it was, in fact, a woman causing him to feel this fury. It had been seething inside of him and gradually building up over the past few days since he'd found out about Polly and Ned.

He hadn't told anyone about Polly simply because he never really told anyone anything, especially about his personal life. He'd never been one to talk much anyway, never mind open up about his feelings – let alone reveal what he thought about a woman. Besides, the men he knew and worked with didn't have serious conversations. In their opinion that was for soft sods. Sissies. They had to prove they were 'real' men, which meant being hard and unsentimental. They didn't get upset, least of all about a bit of skirt. Their chat was all jokey banter and a bit of carry-on.

'Aye,' Ralph nodded knowingly, 'it's always the way. Can't live with them, can't live without them. Come out for a few jars tonight and we'll put the world to rights,' he offered.

Ralph was the unofficial head of the diving team, mainly due to his age and experience, and he hated seeing any of the divers in such a spiky frame of mind. Once that copper helmet was bolted on and a diver had been dropped down into the water, a calm, level head was essential. This was a dangerous job which required a clear focus on the job in hand.

Tommy knew Ralph didn't really want to know about his woman woes, and that he had made the offer of a few pints and a sympathetic ear as a means for Tommy to vent and release any pent-up feelings. He wanted his number-one diver safe when he descended into the murky waters of the Wear. Tommy knew Ralph's unspoken concerns were legitimate, that he needed to get rid of these feelings. He'd never fallen for anyone like he had for Polly. He'd been convinced that she was the one for him, and he'd firmly believed Polly had also felt that he was the one for her.

That was, until now.

'Are you ready?' Ralph shouted over, interrupting Tommy's dejected musings. The team were getting ready to fix a particularly large gap that had been blown through the hull of a cargo vessel.

One of the men came over, carrying Tommy's cumbersome twelve-bolt helmet which was to be sealed on to the brass corselet Tommy was now wearing over his diving suit. Tommy's whole body was soon to be weighed down by copper and metal – even his feet were encased in lead-soled boots – but this was feather light in comparison to the heavy burden of despair he felt pressing down on his heart.

Chapter Thirty-Six

'You look ready to drop, Pol,' Bel said as soon as she saw her exhausted sister-in-law trail into the kitchen and slump into the armchair next to the range.

'Oh Bel, I am,' Pol said wearily. 'But it's not the work or the long hours that's dragging me down.'

Bel looked puzzled.

'I don't know if it's me, whether I'm just tired and not seeing things for how they are, but I swear Tommy is being a bit strange with me. Not his normal self.'

'Really?' Bel said, surprised. 'What do you mean?'

'Well, he usually manages to get away, even if it's just for a few minutes, to come and say hello and have a quick chat.'

Polly stared at the gentle orange glow coming from the coal fire. Her mind was back at the yard, seeing Tommy's pale, serious face. She had caught him looking over at her a few times over the past few days, but as soon as she'd looked back at him he'd turned away – and the look she had momentarily glimpsed had been alien to her. She had never seen him stare at her that way before. Overwork might be making her insecure, but his eyes seemed distant, cold, unfeeling. Almost as if he was looking at something – someone – he really didn't like.

'That doesn't seem like Tommy.' Bel was troubled at what she was hearing. Any fool could see that Tommy was head over heels with Polly. On top of which he was a straight-up, no-nonsense bloke, and he was quite obviously completely committed to Polly. Bel had even joked with Agnes that they might need to buy themselves new hats in the not-too-distant future. So why this change?

As if reading Bel's thoughts, Polly said, 'I just can't understand it. What's caused this change in him?'

Bel really had no clue whatsoever, but she was concerned about Polly. For the first time in her life Bel had seen Polly truly in love and so happy. And it was infectious. Even Agnes had got over her initial worries and motherly protectiveness and welcomed Tommy into the fold. And Tommy's granddad was fast becoming part of their family. Bel knew they would all be devastated if Polly and Tommy were to fall out and their relationship end before it had even had a chance to really get started. The seedling of romance had brought them all a little frivolity and joy in these dark, uncertain times. If their love were to wither and die so soon, it would sadden the whole household.

Polly said, 'I do wonder . . .' but then stopped.

'What?' Bel asked, hungry for an answer, a solution, herself.

'I wonder whether his heart has always really been with Helen. Whether he hasn't realised that until now . . .' Polly's voice trailed off as a vision appeared in her head of Helen, the epitome of gorgeousness and femininity, chatting and laughing with Tommy. Perhaps the two of them had always been destined to be together, but Tommy had never realised it until now. After all, they had more or less grown up together, even if they were from different ends of the social spectrum. Polly could see the familiarity between the pair of them.

As Polly stood up to pour herself a cup of the tea stewing on the kitchen table, she caught her reflection in the bevelled mirror hanging on the wall and felt her heart sink to even greater depths. She looked terrible. Her hair was matted after being twisted up and shoved into a headscarf all day long. Her face looked wan and dirty, as though she hadn't had a wash for weeks. Polly loved being a welder, wouldn't swap it for the world, but there was no denying it was a dirty, sweaty, hard and totally unglamorous job.

She felt like a street urchin next to Helen, with her raven hair so smooth and glossy, her bright emerald-green eyes and perfect, rosy complexion. And that body which just oozed sex appeal. Even Polly, as a woman, couldn't fail but be struck by it. Who wouldn't choose her over me? she wondered to herself.

Her heart felt as if it was experiencing real physical pain at the thought of losing Tommy. She knew the love she had for this man was a one-off. It could never be replicated, or repeated. It was a rarity, something she had been lucky to find at all. And it was her belief that in this life, love, like lightning, rarely strikes twice.

Chapter Thirty-Seven

Saturday, 26 October

'Happy birthday *to me!*' Dorothy announced as soon as she reached her workmates. It was the start of their Saturday 'half-shift', which wasn't really half a shift as such, as it was just one hour short of a full one, but as they'd been working from 7.30 a.m. to 9 p.m. most weekdays, it really did feel like half a day.

'Happy birthday, Dorothy.' Rosie forced the words out through a clenched jaw.

The weather today really was bitterly cold, but it wasn't just the icy winds that were causing Rosie to suffer sporadic bursts of uncontrollable shaking. Every now and again she felt her body start to tremble and, try as she might, she couldn't stop it.

Her tremors had not gone unnoticed by the women, who'd begun to openly comment to each other, whenever Rosie was out of earshot, on how ill she was looking of late. They had been puzzled by their instructor's increasingly ragged demeanour. They'd tried to rationalise that they all looked pretty washed-out these days – everyone was looking far from their best thanks to being blasted by the elements on a daily basis – but even Martha had felt compelled to speak up when the women were voicing their concern a few days earlier about how terrible Rosie looked. She'd moved her big spade-like hand from the top to the bottom of her own face and said gravely, 'Grey.'

The women had agreed. Rosie's pallor did have a sallow greyness to it, but, more worryingly, it seemed that it was coming from deep within.

'*Všechno nejlepší,*' Hannah declared excitedly, before seeing the women's confused faces and explaining, 'That's "All the best in" Czech.'

'*Všechno . . . ne . . . jlepší.*' Martha carefully repeated Hannah's words quite perfectly.

The women all turned to look at Martha and gawped at her in total disbelief. Martha still rarely spoke and when she did her words were, on the whole, monosyllabic.

Gloria dragged her astonished gaze away from Martha, who seemed completely unaware of the effect she'd had, and asked, 'How old?'

'Eighteen,' Dorothy immediately replied. This really was a much better reaction than she could ever have expected. She was particularly heartened by the women's response as she'd felt really down in the dumps this past week or so. She was used to her family's lack of interest in her and her life in general, but it was Eddie's ebbing fervour for her which had really caused her mood to plummet.

She had been trying to convince herself that she was being oversensitive in thinking that the man she was totally batty about was no longer quite so keen on her as he had been at the off. But the logical part of her brain told her she couldn't keep making excuses for Eddie. He hadn't followed through on his promise to take her to the cinema to see *Gone with the Wind*, and each time they'd rearranged their date he had made some excuse or other, usually that he had to work, or that he didn't have any money, which was something else Dorothy could no longer ignore. There always seemed to be some excuse for Eddie not having any cash. And, worse still, Dorothy now had next to no money herself. Since she'd started seeing

Eddie, just about every penny of her wages had been blown when they went out on dates, which were usually spent drinking in the local pubs near the yard or those in the town centre. It was a good job she was living at home, and although her parents weren't exactly rich, they were comfortably off and, thankfully, didn't demand she pay board and lodgings.

'Is that Eddie taking you out tonight to celebrate?' Gloria tried to keep her voice sounding impartial. She knew Eddie would not have stopped at chatting up the blonde crane operator. In fact, she wouldn't have been surprised if Eddie had been seeing other women behind Dorothy's back. Gloria had lived long enough, and seen enough of life, to know the sort of bloke Eddie was. She'd also noticed that Dorothy hadn't been quite as loquacious of late as she usually was about her philanderer of a boyfriend. Something was amiss.

'Oh, well, no. I think he's working two half-shifts today,' Dorothy said, but she sounded unsure.

Gloria looked at this girl who was easily young enough to be her daughter and felt a stab of sympathy for her. She had to give Dorothy her due, she always managed to brighten up their working day, even though Gloria was sure she didn't always feel like being as chipper as she made out. More than anything, though, Gloria hated seeing a man take advantage of a woman, especially when she was young and naive.

'Your mam and dad got owt planned?' Gloria's broad north-east accent always became more defined when she was trying to be kindly.

'Mmmm . . . well, I don't think my mum's feeling up to much at the moment,' Dorothy said hesitantly. 'She's now six months gone and I think she's been struggling with this one. She's blown up like a barrel.'

Gloria had always made a fuss over every one of her sons' birthdays – and had really pushed the boat out when they'd turned eighteen. Wasn't that what every mother did, or wanted to do? 'Well, you've gotta celebrate yer eighteenth,' she declared.

All the women were now looking at the group's elder, surprised at how amiable she was being to Dorothy. They were more used to the two of them having verbal sparring matches than actually being nice to one another.

'Oh, I have idea,' Hannah trilled. 'We all go to pub for a drink after shift . . . to – how do you say it? – *toast* Dorothy's birthday?'

'Oh, yes. That sounds like a great idea!' Dorothy could hardly get the words out quickly enough. 'I'd love to *toast* my birthday with you all,' she added with undisguised glee.

'Everyone come?' Hannah was enjoying being the women's social organiser.

There was a resounding yes and an enthusiastic nod from Martha. Even Rosie mumbled that she too would go for a quick one.

By the time the women had finished their half-shift they were all frozen to the bone. As soon as the last welding machine was switched off, Rosie assumed her role as leader. 'Right, let's get to that pub,' she said. 'It's far too cold to stand around here for a second longer than necessary.'

The women grunted in agreement. None of them spoke as they walked briskly across the yard. After they all handed in their time cards, they hurried the hundred yards to the pub's entrance.

Hannah dropped behind so as not to be the first person to walk through the door of the Admiral. Dorothy happily took the lead. This was her domain, especially as, over the past month or so, she had become quite a regular on her dates with Eddie.

As soon as they walked through the door they were hit by a fug of cigarette smoke and a blanket of toasty warmth.

'Ah, that's better,' Gloria said, rubbing her hands together and unbuttoning her thick work coat. 'Come on, Rosie,' she said, 'we'll get the drinks. You lot, find us somewhere to sit. I think there's a free table over there.' She pointed over to the corner of the pub.

A few minutes later the women were happily ensconced around their table. Their all-female group had caused just a little wave of interest amongst the men, with only a few glances being cast over in their direction, but that was it. It had taken them a while, but their presence in the yard, coupled with their work attire, seemed to have given them a pass to go into the yard's prime watering hole without being on a man's arm, or being forced to have their drinks in the snug. There seemed to be an unspoken code amongst the workers that if you did the same work as a man – and dressed like a man – then you could drink like a man.

'Okay – a toast!' Hannah announced when they all had their glasses of stout, gin and tonic, or port in their hands.

'A toast,' the women all chimed.

'Happy birthday, Dorothy,' Polly said. She tried her hardest to sound upbeat despite the terrible low she had slowly sunk into following Tommy's evident change of heart.

Hannah looked at Martha and then they both said, in perfect unison, '*Šťastné narozeniny*.'

All the women stared at Martha for the second time that day and burst out laughing. '*Staaastneee narozenineee!*' they tried to repeat.

Dorothy was beside herself with excitement. 'This is the best birthday *ever*,' she declared, taking a dainty sip of her gin and tonic and feeling extremely grown-up and sophisticated.

Revelling in the warmth and their impromptu get-together, the women chatted about past birthdays, work and any titbits of gossip they had heard on the yard's grapevine. The pub started to fill up as more and more workers came in from the cold.

Polly and Hannah went to the bar to get another round in, but as they were both squeezing their way back to their corner table they stopped in their tracks. 'Oh *my*,' Hannah said to Polly. 'It's Eddie.'

Polly had also seen him, shouting out greetings to his mates, playing the big man. But it was the fact that he had his arm around a very pretty blonde woman which was causing Hannah and Polly so much consternation.

'Oh dear,' she said, dismayed.

As they approached their table they looked at Dorothy, laughing and in such high spirits. But as they put the drinks down on the table Polly saw the change in Dorothy's demeanour. Her laughter seemed to stop dead in its tracks as she spotted Eddie and the woman he was now introducing to his friends. All the women welders followed Dorothy's stare and fell silent.

Unaware of the six pairs of eyes glaring at him, Eddie continued to hold court at his table of fellow riveters.

The women turned back to look at Dorothy, who seemed totally stunned at the tableau unfolding in front of her.

'It's one of the new women,' she mumbled.

Gloria felt her own heart sink and a twinge of guilt as she wondered if perhaps she should have told Dorothy about what she had seen the other week. But, then again, it wasn't a crime to chat to another woman at work, and if she'd told Dorothy she might well not have believed her, or thought she was trying to cause trouble. Either way, it looked as if Dorothy was going to have to deal with the inevitable hurt and heartache of becoming attached to such a no-good waster.

'It's the crane operator. Angie, I think her name is,' Dorothy added, unable to take her eyes off Eddie, who was now giving the pretty young Angie a very public kiss and show of affection. The two certainly couldn't be misconstrued as merely friends.

The five other women watched Dorothy and waited with bated breath.

A myriad of thoughts gushed through Dorothy's head as she realised that all those suspicions she'd kept pushing aside these past few weeks had been right. She had been used. It was now plain as day: Eddie had used her for a bit of fun, but worse still, he had also used her financially, draining her of the little money she had. Money she had worked damned hard for. She had been his free ticket to a good time and copious amounts of complimentary beer.

Dorothy rose slowly from her seat and the other women watched as she purposefully walked over to the bar. None of them said anything as she bought a pint of beer and steered her way round a few men who were standing with their drinks in their hands, chatting happily. Eddie was unaware of Dorothy as she approached the gaggle of riveters all smoking and gobbing off loudly.

She stood looking down at them all, shoulder to shoulder, crushed around the small pub table. The men gradually fell silent as they became aware of Dorothy's looming figure. Angie innocently smiled up at Dorothy with a slightly puzzled expression on her face. Eddie turned and looked up to see who, or what, had captured everyone's attention.

'Hello, Eddie.' Dorothy seethed fury, and as she held out the glass of beer she said, 'This one's for free, like all the others you've had out of me,' then poured the pint of frothy pale brown liquid on to her former lover's head.

Eddie automatically jumped up out of his seat, shocked by the feel of the cold ale shower he'd just been given, and by the unexpected actions of his jilted girlfriend. The gang of riveters he'd been sitting with burst into braying laughter. Eddie was gasping for air and shaking his arms out in a vain attempt to get rid of the rivulets of beer trickling down his body.

With great show, Dorothy carefully placed the empty pint glass on the round wooden table and turned to Eddie's latest conquest. 'And if I were you,' she said, 'I'd keep my legs and purse shut with this one. Trust me. No good will come of it.'

Dorothy turned on her heel and walked back to her workmates, who were all agog at their friend's behaviour.

As Dorothy pulled out her stool and picked up her gin and tonic, Gloria was the first to find her tongue. 'Good girl,' she said. 'He's had that coming for a while.'

'Blimey, Dorothy. Well done,' Polly said, totally taken aback by her dramatic performance.

They all agreed and raised their glasses.

No one had to say anything else, but Dorothy realised then that they'd all had Eddie sussed from the start. She just wished she'd seen it before now, or admitted it to herself sooner. Deep down she had always known there was something up with Eddie. Something had pricked her antennae even when he'd started to make a play for her, when she'd been working at Binns and he'd been seeing one of the other sales assistants there. But she had chosen to ignore it. She had been thrilled by his attention and compliments, and ignored the fact that he was courting someone else, a woman she knew and liked. Dorothy understood now that the truth had been staring her in the face all along, but it was as if she hadn't been able to stop herself. As if she had seen the fire and walked straight into it. If only she had listened to her inner voice, she might have saved herself this heartache. This humiliation.

'Another toast,' Hannah said.

'Another toast,' they all agreed, clinking their glasses.

'And to think he was the only reason I got this job at the yard,' Dorothy half laughed, half cried. 'I left a perfectly good job at Binns – an easy, clean and *warm* job – for this. I think I need my head examining.'

The women turned to Dorothy in shock. Had she really just got this job to be near a man she liked?

Much as it pained Dorothy to admit it, it was true: she had in fact followed Eddie like a lost puppy to Thompson's and signed up for a job she would never normally have even considered doing. Common sense had been overridden by her desire, her obsession, her need for love at any cost. In a moment of clarity she realised she had been so desperate for love, any kind of love and attention, she had resorted to giving herself over to someone like Eddie, who wasn't worth a light. Dorothy's big blue eyes filled with tears.

'Well, yer know what they say,' Gloria tried to reassure her, 'every cloud has a silver lining and all that.'

'And that silver lining would be?' Dorothy asked, a big tear now running freely down her face.

'Us, yer daft bugger. Your mates,' Gloria said.

Martha reached over the table and slapped a big hand on top of Dorothy's, giving her a wide grin which spread across the width of her round face.

'Yes,' Hannah added. 'I know another English expression: more fish in sea?' she asked, uncertain whether she had made any sense.

'Yes, Hannah, more fish in the sea,' Rosie told her, before looking at Dorothy and saying quietly, 'You might be hopeless at catching a decent fella, Dorothy, but you're a natural when it comes to welding.'

Dorothy's face immediately brightened up. 'Do you think so?' she mumbled through her tears.

'And what's more, you're fast,' Rosie said. 'That idiot Eddie's done you a favour. You're helping the war effort – *and* you've now got yourself a trade for life.'

Everyone looked at Rosie. None of them had heard her speak so personally before – and to Dorothy, of all people.

This birthday celebration was really turning into so much more than they had all anticipated. Not only had they heard Martha speak a foreign language, and witnessed Dorothy wreak wonderful revenge on her two-timing beau, but they had also, for the first time, felt that Rosie had become a part of their little group.

As the women left the warmth of the Admiral and faced the wind and rain, Polly heard the familiar growl of a motorbike starting up before it took off up the road. It was Tommy. He must have seen the women leave the pub, must have known Polly was part of the group, yet he hadn't stopped to chat to her.

What was wrong? Why had he changed towards her? Polly wanted desperately to speak with him and ask him what the matter was. Had he gone off her? Found someone else? Someone called Helen Crawford?

As the women made their way up the embankment to get the bus into town, Polly tried unsuccessfully to push away her feelings of hurt and anger. Was she too going to have to go through this torment – the same demeaning and very public rejection Dorothy had just suffered this evening?

Chapter Thirty-Eight

When Tommy saw Polly and the rest of the women welders spill out of the Admiral, he felt his mood plummet further. When he had seen the women from afar, linking arms, all leaning into the strong winds and the lashing sheets of rain, their coats pulled tight around them to keep out the cold, he could still make out Polly. Tommy felt as though he could pick her out of a blizzard.

He had immediately breathed a sigh of relief that she wasn't with Ned, and that she was just with the other women. He knew Polly had spotted him as he had seen her head turn towards him when he'd started up his bike. But there had been no smile on her lips. Lips he'd touched with his own, and which he'd enjoyed tracing with his fingers when they had been alone together. They were lips he'd felt he could have kissed for ever and a day.

When he had seen Polly this evening he knew he should have turned off his engine, walked over to her and asked to talk to her. He needed to talk to her. He wanted to ask her so many questions, and more than anything he wanted to ask about this Ned. But he hadn't. He had done what he'd always done in his life: he'd turned his back on what mattered.

As Tommy rode home he didn't thrash the bike and release his pent-up emotions by opening up his throttle, like he often did. His mood was too low even for that. He just wanted more than anything to be on his own, to stew in his own misery. But when he pulled up outside his home and walked through the front door, as soon as he saw Arthur sitting in his armchair, bending forward and giving the fire an enthusiastic poke, it was clear the old man was full of beans and after a bit of chat.

It hadn't escaped Tommy's notice that his granddad seemed to have a new lease of life since he'd started to go round to Agnes's for his tea on a regular basis. Nowadays he seemed to be out and about more, going to the market from some offcuts of meat, or to the fish quay to get a choice bit of haddock or cod. There had even been a number of nights when Tommy had come home and Arthur hadn't been in, which Tommy didn't mind in the least. If anything, it put his mind at rest that if there was an air raid, he would be forced to go to a shelter with Agnes, Bel and Lucille and not stubbornly sit in his armchair, daring the Jerries to bomb him. The two families had become close and he knew Arthur felt the same way about Agnes's as Tommy did – that it was the kind of home they had both yearned for over the years.

'How yer been today, lad?' Arthur asked.

Tommy felt that his granddad was scrutinising his face, trying to read his troubled thoughts.

'Busy,' he answered. What else could he say? That his heart was breaking? That his mood felt as dark and as murky as the river he spent so much of his time in?

'No time to see that lovely lass of yours?' Arthur prodded, knowing he was venturing into dangerous waters, but determined all the same.

He had never interfered in his grandson's business before, especially when it came to women, but this, he felt, was different. This was important. Arthur couldn't keep quiet, especially after what he'd learnt the other day when he had been round at Agnes's. Bel had moved her chair a little closer to him and in a conspiratorial but concerned tone had started to ask Arthur a few questions. She hadn't had to quiz him for long, for as soon as Arthur heard the name 'Helen' he knew in an instant what was up.

'Yes, pet, I know Helen. Jack and Miriam's daughter,' Arthur had told her.

'That's her,' Bel'd said, checking Agnes was out of earshot. 'Polly told me that you and Tommy know the family quite well, from way back, and that Helen and your Tommy are quite close?'

Arthur had looked straight into Bel's big, blue, inquisitive eyes. He had never beaten about the bush, and so he'd asked straight off, 'What's been going on?'

'Oh, nothing . . . I hope,' Bel had said. 'It just seems that this Helen, well, to put it bluntly, is all over Tommy, and that the two seem to spend a lot of time together. Or at least Helen always seems to be about when Tommy's on his breaks.'

Arthur might have been an old man, and not exactly up to date with the younger generation, but he knew exactly what was going on. Knew how this would make Polly feel. How she was a lovely lass but lacked confidence. He'd then done something he probably wouldn't have done before and had told Bel the story of Jack, Miriam and Gloria, which Bel had listened to thoughtfully.

Tommy opened a bottle of beer and asked Arthur if he wanted one.

'Go on then,' Arthur said, 'let's live dangerously.'

Tommy went into the kitchen and opened another bottle, grabbing a half-pint glass and handing it to Arthur, who carefully poured himself his drink.

'Ta, lad,' Arthur said, before taking a deep breath. He was annoyed at himself that he actually felt a little nervous. 'Now, about this Helen . . .'

Tommy looked at Arthur as if he were going senile. Why on earth was his granda asking about Helen? It was Polly he really needed to talk about. Tommy wanted to know what was going through *Polly's* mind, not Helen's. Once again Tommy's mind went off at a tangent and the same old thoughts thrashed around in his head. His heart told him Polly loved him, but if she was seeing another bloke his head told him this most certainly wasn't the case, far from it.

'Well, you know what Helen's like, don't you?' Arthur asked.

'Aye,' Tommy answered without much thought.

'Yer know she's just like her mam, don't you?' Arthur persevered.

'Aye,' Tommy repeated. He really had no interest in talking about Miriam or Helen. Why was the old man obsessing about the Crawfords?

Arthur looked at Tommy and was stuck for words. Why was this so hard? He again felt that familiar anger and resentment towards his daughter, who'd left him to fulfil the role of both a father and a mother – never mind that of a grandparent.

He tried to find the words to ask Tommy if he was interested in Helen, or if he had considered that Helen was interested in him. He wanted to warn him that, like her mother, Helen had the capacity to be very devious in order to get what she wanted. Arthur had seen Helen grow up from a little girl – if she wanted something, she had always got it. Now she was a young woman and, from what Bel had told him, Helen wanted Tommy. Arthur tried but he just couldn't find the words to articulate these concerns. He kept opening his mouth to speak, but no words found their way out. By the time he had finished his drink, still nothing was forthcoming and Arthur resolved to try again another night.

Tommy, who had taken a chair from the kitchen table and was now sitting next to his granddad directly in front of the fire, was also stuck for words. He too had given up on speech and was lost in his own thoughts, drinking his ale straight from the bottle and gazing at the small mound of hissing coals.

Both men sat and stared, their frustrations pushed down but, like the fire, still burning hot.

Chapter Thirty-Nine

'And the rest is history, as they say.' Bel repeated Arthur's exact words to end her telling of the Jack, Miriam and Gloria love-triangle story.

The other night Bel been captivated as Arthur had sat and told her all about Jack, his wealthy wife, Miriam, and his first love, Gloria, who'd recently started as a welder with Polly. Bel had listened intently while Arthur had explained how Jack and Gloria had been all set to marry and settle down when Miriam had suddenly come on the scene. Choosing his words carefully, he had described Miriam as a shrewd woman who also had the benefit of a wealthy family behind her, and how out of the blue Jack had suddenly started seeing Miriam – and that within a matter of months they'd got hitched. Word had gone round the yard that Miriam had been pregnant but had lost the baby shortly after she and Jack had tied the knot.

Just like Bel had done that night, Polly listened intently to the story. Afterwards they agreed it seemed likely that Miriam's pregnancy had not exactly been unplanned, and it had had the desired result and landed her the man she'd made up her mind she wanted.

'Blimey,' Polly said when Bel had finished. 'It's like a story in one of those women's magazines you sometimes bring home. Poor Gloria.'

'And poor Jack too,' Bel said.

'What do you mean, "poor Jack"?' Polly blustered. 'He should have stayed true to Gloria and then none of this would have happened.'

The women both sat thinking about the story.

'And *then*,' Polly added, 'they wouldn't have had Helen – and she wouldn't now be the bane of my life.'

As the two sipped from their cups of tea – which was now their nightly ritual after Agnes had gone to bed – they talked and talked. Polly confided in Bel about the awful marks and bruises she had seen on Gloria's neck all those weeks ago. 'That's what makes this story so much more tragic,' she said sadly.

Bel didn't know Gloria, but she'd seen the aftermath of a man's beating on her own mother's face, and on the faces of many other women during her lifetime. It made her rage inwardly.

'But I still don't know if Tommy has feelings for Helen,' Polly said despondently. 'From what you've told me, Arthur didn't say whether he does or not – only that Helen is a chip off the old block when it comes to getting what she wants.'

Bel didn't reply. She too had thought the same. That night after Arthur had left, she had rerun his story in her head several times over, and realised that not once had Arthur reassured her that Tommy didn't harbour any amorous feelings towards Helen. After all, the families were still very close. Jack thought the world of Arthur – and Helen and Tommy had known each other for many, many years. And, Bel thought, if Helen had loved Tommy since they'd been young and was as calculating as her mother, then Polly really did have something to worry about.

'I'm so shattered I can barely even think now,' Polly said, rubbing her tired eyes.

Bel looked at the clock. It was now nearing midnight. 'Whatever happens with this Helen, I think you should tell Tommy how you feel,' she said in earnest.

Polly nodded before sloping off to bed. She knew Bel was right, but she also knew that her pride wouldn't let her. It was up to Tommy now. If he wanted her as much as he said he did, he would come to see her and talk to her. Polly might be doing a man's job, but she still wanted to be treated like a woman. Tommy was the man, and in her mind he had to do all the running. That was just the way it was.

Besides, at this point in time she was simply too exhausted by work and the endless hours of overtime they were all doing to have the energy to do any kind of running herself.

Chapter Forty

Monday, 28 October

Tommy couldn't sleep despite being physically exhausted. His body had managed to get some rest as he had lain awake all night on his narrow bed, but his mind had been active, whirring around with endless theories. He kept thinking about Polly and the way they had been with each other these past few months: their time together, their chats, their passionate kisses and their gentle caresses. Their happiness at just being in each other's company. Which made it all the harder for Tommy to understand how Polly could be the way she'd been with him, then simply flip like a switch to another man. Unless Tommy really had been blinded by love, had totally misread the woman he'd fallen head over heels in love with. Tommy knew he often saw the world differently from others, but he really didn't think he'd got Polly so wrong. And why hadn't she had the decency to tell him she was with someone else, that – as Helen had put it – her head had been turned by someone else?

He had believed Polly didn't have a ruthless bone in her body, yet it would appear she had several. Since he'd seen her with Ned, she had been so cold towards him, as though *he* had done something wrong. She had actually scowled at him the other day, after Helen had been down to the quayside to tell the diving team about a ship that was due in. When he had scowled back at her she'd already pulled her helmet back down over her face and he had lost sight of her behind a shower of sparks and molten metal.

As the night's darkness gave way to the early-morning light, Tommy's obsessions about Polly were gradually nudged aside by other thoughts that had nothing to do with love and everything to do with war. Tommy had tried to take on board the movements of every political pawn being played in this all-too-real game of human chess. He had scoured every newspaper and listened to the late-night news bulletins on the wireless about any and every bombing, battle, victory and defeat. He and Polly had even been to watch newsreels playing at their local cinema. During their last visit his eyes had been glued to the speckled black-and-white images showing snapshots of the battle presently raging in the Atlantic. Yet again his need to be there, in the thick of it, had flared right back up inside of him.

Tommy got up out of bed and drew back the tatty blackout curtain across his small bedroom window. As he looked out across the Wear and beyond to the North Sea he realised he could no longer ignore this inherent need he had to go to war. He knew in his heart that his skills could be utilised more fully and more effectively outside the confines of the shipyard. He could easily attach or remove mines and explosives from the sides of ships. And he could use his underwater welding and masonry skills to quickly repair vessels that had managed to limp into Allied ports and harbours.

When war had first been declared he had gone to sign up straight away, but had been told in no uncertain terms that he was needed here, to do essential work in the shipyards. He had actually been forbidden from enlisting in military service. But a year had now passed and during that time the River Wear Commissioners, which employed the town's divers, had taken on another lad, whom Tommy had helped teach and who'd taken to the job well.

During his time with Polly, Tommy had pushed back his deep-rooted desire to go to war, and had argued with himself, like the recruitment officer had done with him that day in September last year, that he was fighting the enemy by the crucial work he was doing here. Tommy now realised he'd let his desire for Polly override his need to undertake a more active part in this brutal war. But now that it seemed Polly no longer wanted him, the mist had lifted, his mind had cleared, and he now needed to do what he'd always known he had to do, for the sake of his country, and for his own sake.

After Tommy got up and got dressed, instead of heading straight to work he took a detour into the town centre. He walked quickly and within twenty minutes had arrived at his destination. A resolute Tommy took a deep breath before walking into a small, musty office, the signpost above the door of which read 'Recruiting Office'.

Chapter Forty-One

Thursday, 31 October

As Rosie sat in the warmth of the canteen with the women, she felt one step removed from reality. It was as if her body was acting in a way that it was supposed to behave, but her mind was a completely different entity. Perhaps, she thought as she smiled at Dorothy's chatter, even though she hadn't taken in a word she'd said, this was what happened when you lost your mind, although Rosie didn't feel as if her mind was really *lost*, more that it had become disjointed, cut off from the rest of her being. Like her weekly visits to Raymond, which were now passing in a haze. It was as if she was not really there, as if she was not really in physical proximity to the man she despised more than words could ever describe. Like how, at this very moment in time, she could see that her hand was holding a spoon, and that she was putting food into her mouth, but it was as if she was watching someone else do it.

Strangely enough, though, this displaced reality didn't bother her. What did bother her were the stomach pains and headaches she seemed to be suffering from of late. She realised they were probably due to overwork. She knew she was driving herself to exhaustion, but there was no other option.

'Sooo,' Hannah's sing-song, bird-like voice weaved its way into Rosie's consciousness, 'are we agreed? *Gone to the Wind* on Saturday?'

'*Gone with the Wind*, Hannah. *With* the wind,' Dorothy corrected. She had become Hannah's self-appointed language teacher, something Hannah seemed happy enough with, which was just as well as Dorothy had never really asked her workmate if she minded. Dorothy had even brought a few of her own books into work and told Hannah to read them. 'To improve your vocabulary,' she'd told her. The novels were all romances or, judging by the pictures on the front, swashbuckling sagas set in another time in far-flung lands, which Hannah had been forced to hide from her aunty for fear she'd think her work at the yard was leading her astray.

Gloria laughed. 'Well, we will all be gone *with* the wind if it gets any worse out there.' Gloria was in a particularly good mood because Vinnie had gone to stay with his aged mother in Gateshead for a week, as she was unwell and it looked as though she might not see the year out.

'So, we all going?' Hannah persevered. 'Saturday. Cinema. *Gone* with *the Wind*?'

'Why not?' Gloria said. 'Just as long as they have some sort of heating there.'

Martha nodded in reply to Hannah's head count and grinned enthusiastically, repeating the words '*Gone with the Wind*'. The women were now getting used to Martha's growing habit of repeating an occasional word or phrase that she heard.

Polly agreed that she too was up for their girls' night out. In fact, she was up for anything to take her mind off Tommy, whom she still hadn't spoken to. She knew she was being stubborn, but so was he, and she was damned if she was going to give in. Besides, she had done nothing wrong. He was the one who'd cooled off and seemed more interested in Helen than anything, or anyone, else.

'And you, Rosie?' Dorothy asked, tentatively. 'Pleeease, say you're coming.'

Rosie looked around the women's expectant faces and nodded. 'All right, count me in.'

'Hurrah!' Dorothy gave a little jump of joy.

The rest of them smiled. They were pleased Rosie had agreed to come as she had not seemed at all herself for a good while now.

'It's like she's not really here,' Polly had mused to Gloria one day.

'Mmm, like she's going through the motions,' Gloria had conceded.

Hannah had overheard their conversation and chipped in, 'And she not look good either. Like – how you say it? – a ghost?'

'Yes,' Polly told her, 'like a ghost. White as a sheet.'

The idea to go to the cinema had, of course, been Dorothy's. After her split from Eddie she'd become a little quieter and more thoughtful than normal, but she was gradually getting back to her old self. She had opened up more about Eddie and how he had drained her of money and how he'd promised to take her to see *Gone with the Wind* but never had, which, Dorothy now realised, was because he had been secretly seeing Angie.

The women knew this was Dorothy's way of standing tall after the humiliation she'd suffered at Eddie's infidelity, so when she'd suggested they all had a 'work jaunt' they had agreed.

'The last film I saw was *The Wizard of Oz*,' Rosie said a little distractedly as they all prepared themselves for another harsh shift. It had been a film Rosie had seen with Charlotte and she knew it would feel strange going to the cinema without her little sister in tow.

'Oh, I looove that film,' Dorothy said, 'but I could never quite work out if she dreamt the whole thing or not.'

There was no time for an answer or a discussion about the film as the women filed out with the rest of the workers, all busy buttoning up their coats and making sure their scarves and hats were firmly in place so as to keep out as much cold as possible.

As Rosie walked with the women, she pondered Dorothy's question. Was it all a dream or not? Was life a dream or reality? The lines were becoming blurred. She no longer knew if her life was real or imagined.

Chapter Forty-Two

This really is the life, Raymond thought, his walking stick stabbing the pavement as he marched down Ryhope Road. He had been totally spoilt during all the air raids the town had been subjected to recently and had a fortune stashed away in his bedsit – women's jewellery, men's watches, expensive gold and silver trinkets. He'd even acquired a whole new wardrobe of expensive suits and shirts. Now every time he stepped out the front door he looked the epitome of an aged but wealthy gentleman. He had even stolen a few military medals and enjoyed making up stories to strangers he got chatting to about his escapades in the First World War. It was amazing the effect this had on people, how easily they believed him, how amiable they were towards him. Some had even invited him into their homes for some tea.

Raymond was particularly pleased with himself at this moment in time as he had a few what he liked to call 'projects' on the go, and they were all coming along nicely. Since his tenancy with His Majesty's Prison Service had come to an end and he'd returned to his old stomping ground, he'd had plenty of time to have a good scout about. This typical northern weather that was presently battering the town was also perfect for checking out potential projects. The wet and windy conditions had everyone hurrying about, not taking much notice of anything around them, their main concern being to get home as quickly as they could and to stay as dry as possible.

Those presently of interest were al'
development, but this dark, misty
easier for Raymond to carry out
'prep work'. He had considere
conductress he'd met on his initia
but he could see underneath the cu
polite manners that she was a tough co
had been plenty to choose from in the mean
was a bonny lass who worked in the men's dep
at Joplings who was particularly ripe for the pick
Young, naive and vulnerable, no father at home and an
overwrought mother who was too busy juggling a family
of eight to know, or care, about what was happening in
her daughter's life. They were always the best ones, the
lonely and the innocent, looking for the attention and love
they'd been starved of most of their lives for one reason or
another.

But out of all his projects, Rosie, of course, was his main
one, and brought him the most pleasure. Just seeing her
disintegration in front of his very eyes each week was
worth all the work he'd put in. And of course the money
she was handing over to him was his due. He was a kind
of human artist in its most literal sense, he mused as he
strutted along, looking about him as if he owned the place.
He was an artist who could create, manipulate and change
an actual live being into whatever he wanted. But best of
all, he could destroy his works of art when he was done.
And it was that which brought him the ultimate satisfaction. It would seem that Rosie was now turning into quite
a masterpiece, and one which he had created in a relatively
short period of time.

He really hoped there was an afterlife, and that his sister Eloise could witness the revenge he was wreaking on
her beyond the grave, that she was now looking down in

what he was doing to her treasured daughter,
 her become a shadow of her former self. He'd
ed it for himself, seen the empty look in Rosie's
 as she walked to and from work. He had spied on her
ork and followed her as she walked to and from Lily's.
e was just about burnt out – spent.

It wouldn't be long before that cow Lily let Rosie go. Raymond had scrutinised Rosie from afar. He'd seen her well-made-up face, but she couldn't hide the fact that she had all but lost her once lovely figure and was now practically skin and bone. Raymond was sure her clients wanted someone who had at least a little bit of meat on them and not some undernourished waif. Raymond had known a few madams in his time. They might appear all charming and ever so genteel on the outside, but once their prime racehorses were past their best, they were soon slung on the scrapheap.

It only took Raymond about ten minutes to reach Park Lane. The bus depot was busy as usual, and the air full of engine fumes. Today he had made sure he was looking smart and well groomed. He might just need that clean-cut, old war veteran veneer to get him what he had ventured out for today.

As he came to the large wooden door just a few minutes away from the hustle and bustle of the bus station, he cleared his throat and walked up the steps. He didn't knock on the door, but simply stood and listened so that he could hear if there was any movement inside. It sounded quiet, so Raymond tried the round brass knob. He smiled when it turned all the way round and he heard a click and the door opened. People were so trusting. He dreaded the day when they actually started to lock their doors.

Raymond walked into the tiled hallway, taking care not to let his walking stick strike the floor with its metal tip. Again he stood still and listened, before quietly making his way up the frayed carpeted stairs, hoping that the wooden floorboards underneath did not creak as he trod carefully up to the first floor. So far so good. When he reached the second floor, though, he heard a door swing open and an old woman shuffled out.

Sod it, Raymond thought, there was always one busy-body about in these bedsit places. Raymond could see instantly that she was partially blind, if not totally, by the light blue colouring of her eyes and indiscernible pupils. The old woman had very bad cataracts.

'Hello, there,' she said, pleasant enough but with an edge of caution in her voice.

'Hello, madam.' Raymond used his best speaking voice as he knew his clothes wouldn't carry much weight with this one. She was looking at a space over his shoulder and was obviously blind as a bat.

'Can I help you?' she asked.

'You most certainly can,' he replied, all charm. He started into his prepared preamble about how he was looking for Rosie Thornton, that he was an old relative who had come to visit.

'Oh, how lovely,' said the old woman. 'Rosie doesn't get many visitors. In fact, I don't think I've ever known her to have any. She does go out a lot, and she works a lot too.'

Raymond feigned interest, saying he would knock on her door and if she wasn't in he would come back. 'But it would mean a lot if we could keep this a secret,' he said. 'I'd love to see her face when she sees me. It will make an old man very happy.'

'Of course, I understand,' said the old woman as she heard the kettle she'd left on her hob start to screech. 'All the best.' She went back indoors and left Raymond free to walk up the third flight of stairs.

When Raymond reached Rosie's room he turned her front door handle but found it locked, which was no surprise. He'd guessed that his niece, unlike most, would be very security conscious. Raymond, however, had come prepared. He quickly slid his hand into his coat pocket and pulled out two short lengths of tarnished metal. In a matter of seconds he'd inserted them into the keyhole and gained access to Rosie's room.

Chapter Forty-Three

Saturday, 2 November

'You lot get yourselves off to the Admiral,' Rosie told her group of shivering but excited welders. 'Let me just finish off here. I'll be over for a quick one before it's time for us to leave.'

The much-anticipated night out to see *Gone with the Wind* had finally arrived. A freezing fog had rolled in mid-morning and stayed put, pervading the whole yard and making the workers feel that they were shrouded in a veil of frost.

'Don't be long,' Dorothy commanded, teeth chattering, as she grabbed her work bag.

'Shall we get you a brandy in?' Gloria's breath created a mist as she spoke.

'Yes, please,' Rosie shouted back. As she went to check the main generator was switched off, the thought of a large cognac spurred her on, even though she knew she was drinking too much lately. Every night she poured herself a good measure after coming back from Lily's. It was something she would never have dreamt of doing before, but which she had quickly become accustomed to. Needed now. Not just to get to sleep, but as her reward for getting through another day.

Rosie swiftly tidied up the work area. She glanced up to see Polly and Gloria, deep in conversation, followed by Dorothy, Hannah and Martha, all making their way to the main gates, and she felt a real sadness that she could never really become their friend. Of course, Rosie doubted very much whether they would want to be her friend if they really knew her – knew what she did every evening. When Dorothy had shocked them all with the gossip about the women in the yard who were supposedly on the game, their disgust had been more than apparent. Of course, their reaction had been expected, normal, she knew that, but it had still cut deep. At least this way, by keeping her distance, she would be spared that humiliation. She would make sure they never found out.

As Rosie gathered up the odd discarded welding rod, an involuntary shiver went down her spine that had nothing to do with the incoming arctic weather. For the first time ever Rosie felt the yard had a slightly eerie feel about it, and as she looked around for her holdall she realised just how quiet it had become. Even the seagulls had stopped their incessant squawking. Through the thickening fog, Rosie could see a few stragglers in the distance making their way over to the shipyard's main gates. Today it felt as though the whole workforce had downed tools in one fell swoop and left the yard in record speed, heading for either the warmth of their homes or, like the women welders, to their local alehouse.

When Gloria gave her card over to the sour-faced time-keeper, she did a double take as she caught the glint of shiny metal coming from behind Mick's stooped figure. It wasn't until she was walking away that she realised she had glimpsed the tip of a walking stick. She was sure it was the same intricately carved cane she'd spotted all those weeks ago when she had arrived at the yard early, the day after the women had spotted the bruising around her neck.

As Gloria and the women squeezed themselves into the Admiral, now heaving at the seams with workers, Gloria felt Martha staring at her. 'What is it?' she asked, looking up at her sizeable workmate.

'She wants a drink,' Dorothy butted in, 'like we all do. Now come on, let's fight our way to the bar, and me and you'll get the first round in.'

Gloria forced herself to shake off her uneasy feeling and followed Dorothy into the melee of rowdy drinkers.

'Thanks, Mick, I owe you one.' Raymond slipped the old timekeeper a ten-bob note as the two shook hands.

Mick took a quick look at the money and nodded in appreciation. 'I'll leave you to it, then,' he said, turning his back on his unofficial visitor while he pulled down the counter's shutter. Mick had known Raymond for many years, but he never liked to be in the man's company for long. And he didn't like to think too much about what his former work colleague was up to.

By the time he swivelled back round again, the office was empty. Raymond had gone. Mick shook his head. For someone who looked as aged and decrepit as Raymond, he couldn't half move quickly, and quietly at that.

As Mick stepped out into the cold and pulled the door shut behind him, he heard a blast of coughing and knew that Raymond was already within the confines of the yard. Mick quickly pulled the bolt across and clicked the padlock shut. It was time for him to go home. His work for today was done.

Leaning his back against one of the prefabricated outbuildings, Raymond cleared his rattling chest and spat out the phlegm in one go. He wanted a fag but knew that would have to wait. He didn't have the time and he didn't want to draw attention to his whereabouts. Not that he could hear anyone else about, and he certainly couldn't see anyone, not in this fog.

Luckily he knew this expanse of flat concrete well enough to get to anywhere he wanted, even if he was blindfolded, which was just as well as the smog was now so dense he could barely see two yards ahead. Using his walking stick as a guide, he stealthily made his way across the breadth of the yard to where he knew the welders' area to be. He had to make haste though. The weather might be on his side, but time wasn't. Rosie would be packing up and getting ready to go now, and she wouldn't be hanging about, not in this weather. Raymond gently tapped the ground with his stick, making sure he didn't trip over any of the piles of thick iron chains that made up the metal jungle terrain of the shipyard, or any tools left lying about in the rush to leave work.

After a hundred yards or so the faint outline of a woman started to take shape through the grey mist. She was bending down, as if she was looking for something. Raymond needed to make sure it was Rosie. He didn't want to make any mistakes, especially as there were now more and more women working – not only in this yard, but just about every other shipyard in the north-east.

Raymond quietly snuck forward. He saw the woman's figure suddenly straighten up and sling a bag over her shoulder. As she half turned, her face became visible. Raymond sucked in air and stopped in his tracks. For the briefest moment he was caught off guard. Like a ghostly apparition rising out of the smog, for a split second he could have sworn blind he was looking at his sister, Eloise, that she was right there in front of him, within touching distance.

The moment of astonishment and fear passed as quickly as it had come upon him and he laughed inwardly at the jab of panic he'd just felt, something he rarely experienced. The fog was playing tricks with his mind.

'Eee, Rosie, pet, you really are the spit of yer mother,' Raymond said in an unnervingly soft voice.

'Jesus!' Rosie jumped out of her skin, the look on her face one of sheer shock.

A wide smirk spread across Raymond's sunken, lined face. 'Now, now, no need to blaspheme, pet.' He couldn't have been more condescending. He was pleased: his surprise visit was going to plan. He had succeeded in catching her totally unawares.

Rosie stood rooted to the spot. Raymond was the last person she expected to see here at work. In her disjointed head, this loathsome man now only existed within the confines of his slovenly bedsit, and, of course, in her past. Over time her brain had successfully compartmentalised her life and the people in it. Seeing Raymond here in a place where she'd always felt safe had thrown her – scared the living daylights out of her.

'What are you doing here?' Her words came out in a whisper. She felt she had literally had the breath drawn out of her.

'I think yer know why, pet,' Raymond said in his mock-gentle voice. 'You underestimate yer uncle Ray.'

Rosie's mind immediately leapt to the overtime she had been putting in. He had realised she was earning more than he thought. He'd come for his cut.

'Money.' Rosie tried her hardest to inject some volume into her voice, desperately trying to calm herself down. To be brave. She watched as her uncle's face contorted itself into a look of mock puzzlement.

'Money? What money, pet? Ah, now, let's think. Do yer mean the money you've been earnin' with all that over-time you've been deein'?' With each word his face became more vindictive, more angry, more hateful. 'Yer *have* been a busy girl, haven't yer, pet? Did yer think I wouldn't get to know about it?' Raymond laughed. 'I've got eyes and ears everywhere round this town. Everywhere.' His voice was now a harsh growl. 'And I've watched you myself, clip-clopping in your high heels to that whorehouse every night, and then back to that little bedsit of yours.'

Rosie felt nauseous at the thought of this abhorrent man spying on her, watching her in secret. The bag on her shoulder suddenly felt heavy and she let it drop to the ground. A feeling of complete exhaustion overcame her, as though she'd finally spent the last drop of energy she possessed.

'Yer guessed right, pet. I'm here about the money you've been pilfering away like a little beaver.' Raymond's hand delved into his inside jacket pocket. 'Hours and hours of overtime. I'm surprised you've had the time to write to that pretty little sister of yours.' His voice dripped with venom as he pulled out half a dozen wage slips along with a couple of Charlotte's carefully penned letters. He waved them in front of Rosie's waxen face.

A tidal wave of despair washed over Rosie as she realised what Raymond had in his hand.

Enjoying the moment, Raymond carefully stuck his walking stick under his arm, and with both hands held out the papers in front of him, as if he were standing in a pulpit ready to read the lesson of the day.

'"Sunday, half-shift, a pound,"' Raymond read aloud slowly and deliberately. He then pulled out a larger sheet of paper. 'Ah, and what do we have here? "Runcorn Girls' School, Harrogate, Yorkshire. Dear Rosie, how are you?"' Raymond looked up from his recitation and stared at Rosie, enjoying seeing every nuance of emotion skitter across her face.

Rosie's mind was racing. He must have broken into her bedsit when she wasn't there. And it must have been within the past day or two, otherwise she would have noticed. She had got in late last night, had a nightcap and fallen straight asleep. She had seen her box was still there in the back of the wardrobe, but she hadn't looked inside it like she normally did.

As if reading her thoughts, Raymond said, 'I really mustn't forget to go and see that lovely old woman who lives on the second floor. Tell her thanks for keeping shtum. That it was worth seein' the look on yer face.'

Rosie imagined Mrs T standing talking to Raymond, being taken in by his lies and his false courtesy.

'Fancy my surprise when I found all this, as well as all of those lovely pound notes you've been squirrelling away in yer secret box. I kept asking myself, "Now why would Rosie be keeping her hard-earned cash a secret from her uncle Ray?" It wouldn't be to pay for little Charlotte's school fees, would it? Or are yer planning on leaving? Runnin' away? Or perhaps yer leaving a stash for your sister in case something happens to yer, pet? Like what happened to yer mam and dad? God rest their souls,' he added with a derisive look on his face.

Rosie's head jolted round and for the first time she looked at him straight in the eye. There was something in his tone of voice, something he wanted her to know.

'Shame *they* didn't have any more savings, isn't it? Otherwise you might have been spared having to lay on yer back every night in that brothel of yours.'

Rosie visibly flinched.

'And yer wouldn't have to work yourself to the bone here, in this godforsaken place,' he said, sweeping his walking stick around like a circus master. 'All that relentless hard work just to keep little Charlotte safe and sound in that boarding school of hers.'

Rosie's mind started to spin. She was hit by an image of Raymond turning up the day after she and Charlotte had been told their parents were dead, the day their old life ended and the new one had begun. She remembered thinking that there had always been something odd about his timing, and she'd wondered how he had heard about the accident so quickly.

Raymond tilted his head at Rosie a little. 'They never did find the – what did the police call him? – the "hit-and-run driver" who killed yer mam and dad, did they?' A sinister smile was now cutting across his face.

Rosie stared at him in disbelief.

Then the penny dropped. Her parents' deaths had been no accident. This man, who had stolen her innocence from her, had also ruthlessly taken the lives of her parents.

The shock of comprehension made Rosie step back, away from this evil, insidious man. This rapist. This murderer. Why? Why had he done this to her? To her mum and dad?

'The money yer mam owed me,' Raymond hissed, 'the money you've been paying me back. Well, pet, that was *my* inheritance. Money *I* should have rightfully had from the start. I was the eldest, the firstborn, but my mam and dad decided to ignore their son, like they always did, and leave it all to their golden girl. I told yer mam that the money was mine. Legally it was mine. But she wasn't havin' any of it. I didn't get a penny, not a bean, so I had to make her pay.'

A well of hatred rose up, instantly consuming Rosie and propelling her body at the monster in front of her. With clenched fists she swung at him, but Rosie was no fighter and Raymond was too quick. He niftily sidestepped her, at the same time sweeping his walking stick back and then whacking it with all his might down on Rosie's arm.

The blow felt as if it had shattered her wrist, and Rosie instinctually crumpled over, clenching her arm in agony. A second later she felt another crack. This time pain seared through her skull and the fog around her was replaced by darkness.

Chapter Forty-Four

'Where's Rosie?' Dorothy asked. 'Surely, it doesn't take her this long to pack up?' The women had all nearly finished their drinks and Rosie's brandy was sitting untouched.

'Perhaps she talk to someone?' Hannah suggested.

'*Talking*. Perhaps she *is talking*,' Dorothy corrected.

'I doubt there's anyone left in the yard now – I think they're all in here,' Polly said as she was pushed forward by one of the fitters making his way over to his mates with a triangle of pints he was trying not to spill.

'You don't think she's had a change of heart, do you?' Dorothy worried.

'Nah,' Gloria said, 'she wouldn't have got us to get her a drink in if she wasn't coming.'

Gloria looked across at Martha, sipping her beer shandy, and the troubled feeling she had felt earlier returned. As if reading her thoughts, Martha suddenly stood up, making the table wobble as she did so.

'Hold your horses, Martha,' Dorothy said, putting her hands out to steady the glasses on the table. 'We're not ready to go just yet.'

Martha stared hard at Gloria, before saying simply and loudly, 'Rosie.'

The other three looked up at Martha and then at Gloria.

'We're really going to have to teach Martha to speak in whole sentences,' Dorothy said, exasperated.

'What is it?' Hannah asked Martha. But Martha didn't look at Hannah; she just kept staring at Gloria.

'Blimey,' Dorothy said, 'are you two having some kind of telepathic conversation you want to let us all in on?'

A feeling of concern and worry now spread rapidly around their little group. 'I wonder if we should go and find Rosie,' Polly volunteered. 'She should have been here by now, don't you think?'

Martha turned her burly body around and began to bulldoze her way through the crowd of tightly packed workers. 'Come on,' Gloria said and followed Martha, who was successfully beating a clear pathway to the pub door.

When they all tumbled out into the lane, it was dark and foggy. 'Bloody blackout,' Dorothy cursed, rummaging around in her bag to get her little torch. 'Not that this thing's much help, but it's better than nothing.' As she switched it on a weak beam of light appeared, but it was enough for the women to see where they were going.

Arriving at the main gates they found them shut, but the little entrance to the side had been left open.

'If we miss the start of the film I'm going to be so annoyed,' Dorothy said, trying to break through the seriousness that had permeated the group. The women all kept close to each other as they slowly made their way through the thick fog and across the yard.

When Rosie came to she could see the most amazing light. For a moment she thought she was dead and she felt a fleeting sense of relief that now everything was over. Finished. No more struggling. No more fear, or worry, or work. No more life. She could finally let go.

But then she felt a searing pain in her wrist and her head started to throb. She was alive.

The wonderful light, she realised, was the naked sparks of a weld. She wasn't used to seeing the effects of burning metal and ultraviolet light without her mask or goggles on. It was beautiful, but blinding. She forced her eyes shut and tried to turn her face away from the fluorescent light and the burning heat she now felt on the side of her face. But as she tried to move away she felt Raymond's fingers entwined in her hair, twisting, pulling, pushing her head forward, forcing it towards the spluttering fireworks.

Rosie jerked involuntarily as she felt the painful bite of metal on her face and realised she was being burnt. Raymond yanked Rosie's head back. She breathed in the odour of his rancid breath as his lips practically touched her ear, and he snarled, 'Did you really think you could beat me? Get out of our little agreement?' She could feel speckles of his spit hit her face.

All of Raymond's pent-up fury was now being allowed to run riot. He had been storing it up since his discovery of Rosie's deception, had reined it in, until now. Now he could finally set it free and, by God, he was going to enjoy every second of it, every moment of what he was about to do.

Rosie's eyes struggled to make out what was in front of her. She could see what looked like a smoky grey fog. Her vision cleared enough to make out the top of the wooden workbench and the scrap metal in front of her, still glowing with the after-effects of a messy weld. Her body was crushed against the edge of the bench, pressed there by the force of Raymond's body weight behind her. She felt weak, weaker than she'd ever felt in her life. And her head continued to throb. Her wrist felt limp and hurt like hell. Her nose was streaming and she was starting to feel pinpricks behind her eyes, which she knew only meant one thing.

'You stupid bitch,' Raymond hissed, 'to think you actually thought you could get away with it.'

Rosie coughed and tried to swallow. The heat had burnt the back of her throat and was making her swallow involuntarily. She saw her wage slips and her sister's letters flutter down in front of her. As she strained to look to her side she caught a glimpse of Raymond's hand clutching a lighter. She heard a click and her eyes fluttered as a small flame was ignited.

'No more bits of tittle-tattle from your little sister. No more savings,' Raymond snarled, as Rosie watched the faltering flame draw towards the loose papers. She heard the sound of gentle crackling, before a sudden whoosh and the pile turned into one large yellow glow. It took just seconds for it to burn, elevating slightly from the top of the table, before metamorphosing into blackened, charred ashes. 'No more overtime. No more anything.' Her uncle's words continued to spew forth.

Rosie knew she was defeated.

She now understood everything. It was clear as day. From the age of fifteen her life had been shaped by Raymond's greed, as well as by his sexual perversions. Her uncle's bitterness over being left out of his parents' will had burnt into his vindictive and cruel mind. His sense of rejection by his own flesh and blood had fuelled his hatred towards his younger sister, Eloise. And that smouldering fire had turned into an inferno when Rosie's mother had refused to share with her brother the small legacy she'd been left.

Of course, he must have expected to recoup that money when he'd caused his sister's and brother-in-law's untimely deaths, but again, much to his sheer frustration, he had been thwarted. The little which remained had been left to Rosie and had been immediately spent on Charlotte's school fees.

It had taken over five years, but her uncle had finally won. He had succeeded in gaining his long-sought revenge, over the living and over the dead.

With this realisation Rosie gave up. She had nothing more left. No more fight. Part of her was happy for Raymond to take her life there and then and be done with it. Since her parents' deaths, and the rape she'd suffered at Raymond's hands, her life had been one long struggle.

Rosie watched Raymond push his lighter back into his pocket before picking up the welding rod from the top of the wooden workbench. She could hear the gentle murmur of the welding machine as he held the rod slightly away from the scrap metal. Once again he pressed himself against her back, pushing his face next to hers and whispering into her ear, 'I could take yer here. Now. Just like I did before. But you've gotten too old, too used. Like a bit of tough old mutton, and yer know me, Rosie, don't you? I like a nice bit of lamb. Much more tender. Much more tasty.'

Rosie could hear him draw a long wheezy breath before offering his *pièce de résistance*.

'But before we say our final farewells, I want you to leave this world with the knowledge that very soon I'll be gannin' to pay yer little sister a visit. I want you to breathe yer last with the image in yer head of me havin' my fill . . . feasting upon some succulent tender meat. Just like I did with you all those years ago.'

Now he struck the welding rod on to the scrap metal and once again ignited a sparkling cascade of white light.

'No!' Rosie screamed, but she couldn't hear her own voice. All she could see was a dazzling fountain, and all she could feel was the stinging sensation of burning flesh. Her last desperate thought was for her little sister, her lovely innocent Charlotte. She closed her eyes and prayed. Please save Charlotte, she begged. Please.

As if in answer to her prayers, a woman's voice boomed out across the quiet of the yard and over the buzzing of the welding machine. 'Ger off her!' Despite being on the edge of consciousness, Rosie recognised the harsh woman's voice, with its hard northern accent. She had been around that voice every day for months now. It was Gloria.

Raymond automatically stopped welding and quickly turned his head around to look in the direction of the voice. He spotted the small circular glow of a torch bobbing through the fog, before seeing five figures walk through the mist. He threw the rod holder aside and grabbed his walking stick, which he had propped up by the workbench.

He wrenched Rosie's head up and pulled her in front of him, creating a human shield. Her body was now like a rag doll, barely able to stand on her own two feet.

Gloria, Dorothy, Polly, Hannah and Martha stopped in their tracks.

'Let her alone!' Polly spluttered in disbelief at what she was seeing.

The women stared, each shocked to the core by the sight of their instructor, their workmate, their friend, her head bowed, her body limp. She looked half dead. Hannah let out a sob.

Rosie managed to lift her face and Dorothy drew a sharp intake of breath. Rosie's face was blackened and spotted with small circular welts where she had been burnt. Part of her blonde hair was frazzled and burnt to the roots. Her eyes and nose were streaming and she was coughing, choking, unable to catch her breath.

'Give her here!' Dorothy demanded, but her voice came out childlike and high-pitched.

Raymond laughed. 'What you all ganna do, *squeak* me into submission?' As he spoke his hand moved around the top of his walking stick.

With a spark of recognition Gloria spotted the cane. She opened her mouth to say something, but stopped as she heard a click and saw the bottom part of the walking stick fall away, revealing a thick, glistening knife. In the blink of an eye, Raymond had pressed the knife close against Rosie's blackened cheek, the sharp point of the blade just piercing the skin so as to draw blood.

'Are you really going to bother yourselves with this whore?' he asked.

All five women were still rooted to the spot, not daring to move forward in case more harm was done to their friend. The mention of the word 'whore', though, threw them all – except Gloria. In a flash, little bits and pieces of information slotted together and formed a complete picture. The gossip in the shipyards. The rumours spread by this foul man through his mouthpiece, the surly time-keeper. The change they'd all noticed in Rosie.

They stood stunned, as if in some kind of physical stale-mate, not daring to move.

'Ah, you all look so surprised. Yes, Rosie here, your instructor, Miss Butter Wouldn't Melt in Her Mouth. Well, newsflash, girls: she's nothing more than a common whore, a prostitute, a slag, a slut—'

These last words were barely out of his sneering mouth when, like a bat out of hell, Martha barrelled forward and knocked Raymond flying. She had been partially obscured from his vision as she'd been standing behind the women. But on hearing his derisive words she had hurled her-self forward and with both her enormous hands had pushed Raymond with such force she'd catapulted him backwards.

Raymond instinctively waved the knife away from Rosie's face and at this colossal woman now bearing down on him. The blade glanced off Martha's thick winter coat, slashing through to her overalls but no further. Raymond staggered backwards, still clutching his knife.

Dorothy and Hannah ran forward to grab Rosie, who had collapsed to her knees, while Gloria swiftly moved to Martha's side.

Raymond's face was twisted with rage. 'You stupid bitches!' he hissed. 'You've no idea who yer messing with,' but the confidence in his voice was contradicted by his movements as, with each word he spoke, he took a step back.

Martha and Gloria watched his retreat. He opened his mouth to utter more threats, but before he could he took one more step backwards. His foot landed perfectly on a thick metal rod that had been left lying on the ground, hidden by the low-lying mist. Raymond's footing faltered and his arms flailed backwards as he tried not to fall flat on his back. He managed to just about stay on his feet, but he hadn't realised how close he'd got to the edge of the quayside.

Gloria and Martha stood mouths agape. It was as if they were watching in slow motion as Raymond's foot lifted up into the air, his arms swung back, and he desperately tried to catch hold of something to keep him upright.

But there was nothing there. Just wisps of fog. Raymond let out a strangled cry as he disappeared over the side of the dock.

A second later there was the sound of a heavy weight hitting the water's surface. And then nothing but silence.

Gloria dragged her eyes away from the spectacle she had just witnessed and looked behind to check on the other women. Four faces, all white as a sheet, stared back at her.

The stillness was broken by the sudden sound of Rosie dry retching.

'Are you all right?' Polly asked her between gasps of air.

Rosie nodded her head as she put her hands on the ground and slowly lifted her body back into a standing position. Dorothy took one arm and helped to steady her. For once words seemed to have escaped her.

Hannah stood in front of Rosie and pushed burnt strands of hair away to get a clear look at her face. 'Looks bad,' she said, knowledgeably, 'but will heal. You still beautiful,' she added with tears rolling down her delicate face. What she didn't say was that Rosie's eyes looked badly bloodshot, her pupils were like pinholes, and Rosie didn't seem to be focusing on what was in front of her.

Rosie knew her eyes were damaged. Everything was a blur, although she had still been able to just about see what had happened to Raymond. Now, though, she desperately needed to find out if her abuser had surfaced. She leant heavily into Polly and pointed to the quayside. With Polly and Dorothy on both sides and Hannah fluttering around them, they staggered the short distance to where Gloria and Martha were now standing.

All six women peered over the edge. Dorothy, who was still clutching her torch, shone it down into the river's choppy, black water.

There was no sign of Raymond. Nor was there any sound of life below them, other than the slapping of water against the sides of the dock's stone walls, and the sound of a couple of small wooden boats moored nearby, rhythmically knocking together. The women stood and stared in silence.

'Is he all right?' The group, their nerves frazzled, jumped at the sound of Jack's voice.

'Who?' Gloria asked, as if she had absolutely no idea what he meant.

'That bloke! The one I've just seen go over the side!' Jack looked panic-stricken as he stepped between the women and crouched by the dock's edge, staring down into the darkness.

The women all looked at each other.

'Jack,' Gloria said, her voice sounding softer and more gentle than any of the women had ever heard her sound. 'Come here. Come away from the side,' she cajoled him. 'There's no one there now.'

Jack turned to look at Gloria and his face relaxed. 'What's going on? Why are you all here? Who the hell was that bloke?'

'I'll explain everything later,' she said, walking over to him and steering him away from Rosie and the women. 'Are you here with anyone else?' She looked straight into his eyes, demanding an honest answer.

'No, no. I've just come from Frank's wake, in the east end.'

Gloria could smell whisky on Jack's breath and realised he was a little tipsy. 'Of course,' she said, 'Frank – the old-timer, the one in the welder's office, the one you kept on.' She hoped the effects of the booze would make it easier for her to distract him away from the women and from what had just taken place.

'Gloria, I know I'm a few sheets to the wind, but I still know what I saw. I'm not blind. Tell me what's going on.' Jack touched her arm. 'You're shaking. Are you all right?' He knew something had happened, and that it was serious.

'It's not good,' Gloria admitted. 'I think we need to chat, but we can't do it here. Let me quickly have a word with the girls and then . . . Is there anywhere we can go where it's quiet and warm?'

'Yes, of course, we can go to my office. There's a heater there, and I've got a bottle of whisky stashed away. You look like you need it.'

Gloria walked over to the women, who all looked expectantly at their workmate. 'Right, first of all,' she said, 'Rosie, are you all right? Or as well as can be?'

Rosie nodded by way of reply. She couldn't speak because her jaw was chattering and she had clearly gone into shock, although she was managing to just about stand up.

Gloria looked at Polly, Dorothy and Hannah. 'Can you three take care of Rosie tonight?'

The trio nodded.

'Yes,' Polly said, 'I can take her back to mine. She can stay with us for the night. My ma'll patch her up.'

'Good. Now, Martha, are *you* all right?'

Martha nodded, although her big bulbous eyes looked confused and perturbed.

'Listen to me, Martha,' Gloria said. 'You did well there. You did well, you hear me?'

Martha nodded again, the worried look leaving her face.

'I need to chat to Jack now. Not a word to anyone, all right?'

They all agreed.

'Dorothy, that means you too. Not a word!'

'Of course,' Dorothy said. There was a second's silence before she added, 'On condition you all promise to come to see *Gone with the Wind* with me.'

Gloria looked incredulously at Dorothy. 'They really did break the mould when it came to you, didn't they?' She shook her head before heading back over to Jack.

Chapter Forty-Five

After Gloria and Jack disappeared through the smog in the direction of the administration offices, Polly suggested they wait just a few more minutes in case Raymond's body surfaced – dead or alive. The women agreed and stood stock-still, listening intently for any sound of a floundering body splashing about in the water, while Dorothy directed the faint beam of her little torch across the water.

After a while they decided that if Raymond had survived his fall into the freezing-cold river, they couldn't hear or see him, and if his drowned corpse had floated back up they couldn't spot it.

They were just getting ready to leave when Polly suddenly glimpsed a flash of shiny steel on the ground in front of them. 'Oh my goodness. The knife!' she panicked.

Dorothy immediately hurried over to the discarded dagger and carefully picked it up between her thumb and forefinger. 'Urgh, how hideous,' she said, holding it up with one hand and shining her torch at it with the other. The intricately carved ram's head seemed to stare back at them all.

'Just get rid of it.' Polly's voice was now trembling with nerves and cold.

Dorothy put her torch down, pulled her arm back, and like a professional javelin thrower hurled the knife out into the river. It disappeared into the darkness before the sound of a gentle splash could be heard in the distance. Dorothy then bent down and picked up her torch, before scouring

the ground nearby. Within seconds the light had illumin-
ated the rest of the walking stick. She grabbed it and
tossed it into the women's five-gallon barrel heater which
was still glowing with the dying embers of the day's fire.
The wooden cane soon caught alight, creating a vibrant
flame.

'Come on then, Rosie,' Polly said. 'Let's get you back to
mine.'

But it was clear Rosie hardly had the strength to stand,
never mind walk anywhere. Martha stepped forward and
ever so gently took hold of Rosie's arm and slowly positioned it around her own neck. She then wrapped her
thick, muscular arm around her instructor's waist so that
she was able to more or less single-handedly carry Rosie
back across the yard. By the time they all reached the ferry
landing, Rosie barely had the strength to even move her
legs, and her feet were practically dragging along the
ground.

A few workers, obviously the worse for wear, were leaving the pub and making their way home.

'Pretend we're drunk,' Dorothy commanded them all.
Playing the role of a gaggle of intoxicated women was not
hard – they all felt as though they were not quite of this
world anyway after the evening's surreal events.

'Make sure that one doesn't throw up on deck!' the ferryman ordered the women during the crossing. Rosie's head
bobbed about as she coasted in and out of consciousness.

'Thank goodness it's Saturday night,' Hannah muttered
to Polly as a group of merry workers broke into song. The
attention was off the women.

Within twenty minutes they had made it back to Agnes's.
When Polly opened the front door and shouted out, 'Ma!'
Agnes came hurrying down the hallway, alerted by the
seriousness in her daughter's voice.

'Why, you're back earlier than expected . . .' Her voice trailed off when she came face to face with the women and saw the state of Rosie, whose legs had now totally buckled, giving the impression she was a puppet hanging from Martha's large frame. 'Oh my Lord. Come on. Bring her in here.' Agnes directed Martha and the rest of the women into her bedroom, just off the hallway at the front of the house.

Polly was thankful for her mother's practical and matter-of-fact approach to the drama she had brought into their home.

'Put her on the bed and let's have a look,' Agnes commanded as they all crammed into the front bedroom. She quickly checked the blackout curtains were tightly shut before switching on her bedside light.

Martha gently laid Rosie down on the bed, and Agnes told Dorothy and Hannah to take themselves and Martha into the kitchen and for one of them to bring her a bowl of boiling water and her first-aid box from the scullery. 'And make a big pot of tea for everyone,' she added.

The women did what they were told while Polly stayed with her mum. While Agnes inspected Rosie's injuries, Polly briefly ran through the events of that evening: how they had gone back to the yard to look for Rosie when she hadn't turned up at the pub and had found her looking as if she'd been battered and tortured within an inch of her life, with her attacker forcing her head over a live weld.

'That explains the burns,' Agnes mumbled as she inspected the welts on Rosie's face.

Rosie was now only semi-conscious and kept calling out 'Charlotte'.

'Charlotte will be fine, love,' Agnes reassured her, even though she had no idea who Charlotte was. Her gently spoken words seemed to do the trick, and Rosie's body finally relaxed into the comfort of the bed.

As Agnes trimmed the black, frazzled ends of Rosie's singed blonde hair, she noticed an egg-shaped lump had erupted on her head where she'd been smashed with Raymond's walking stick. Agnes grimaced and asked Polly to find a small pot of arnica she had in the back of one of her cupboards. She then put Rosie's badly swollen wrist into a splint in case there were any broken or fractured bones, before tending her facial burns. 'She's going to have quite a few little scars,' Agnes thought out loud.

When Bel arrived back home from her late shift, Martha, Dorothy and Hannah were just coming out the front door. 'Have I missed the party?' she joked, before seeing the women's tired and worried faces.

Dorothy managed to keep up appearances, jesting that there was some of the 'hard stuff' left in the kitchen in the form of a strong pot of stewed tea. She knew Bel would find out soon enough what had happened, but it wasn't their place to tell her.

Standing outside on the pavement, before heading off to their own homes, Dorothy, Martha and Hannah gave each other a big hug.

'Now, listen,' Dorothy said, trying not to get too emotional, 'we should all get home around the time we would've done if we *had* actually gone to the flicks. There's no reason for anyone to wonder where we've been. So,' she stressed, 'remember – not a word about what's happened tonight. Say the film was "fantastic", and that you're shattered and need to go to bed. Okay?' Dorothy looked down at Hannah and up at Martha.

'Okay,' the pair agreed in unison.

*

Fifteen minutes later, when Martha walked into her parents' neat little terraced cottage in Cairo Street, she did just as she'd been told. When her mum asked her if she'd had a good night, Martha nodded and smiled as instructed. She even said the word 'Fantastic', much to her mother's surprise.

When Martha's mum spotted the tear in her daughter's coat, caused by Raymond's flailing knife, she sighed. 'What've yer done here, you clumsy clot?' But her words were spoken with a smile as she lovingly touched the side of her daughter's big childlike face.

Hannah escaped any awkward questions as her aunty Rina had fallen asleep in her rocking chair in front of the dwindling open fire. Hannah smiled when she noticed one of Dorothy's books open on her aunt's lap.

And Dorothy herself didn't have to worry about being quizzed about her night. As usual, her return home went unnoticed. For once, though, she was glad. After the night they'd all had, she just wanted to eat a sandwich and be alone with her own thoughts.

Back in Tatham Street, Polly fell into an exhausted sleep after relaying a sanitised version of their traumatic evening to Bel. When they had both gone in to see Rosie and ask if Agnes needed any help, Polly thought she'd seen a fleeting look of recognition on her sister-in-law's face, but when she'd asked Bel later if the two had met previously, Bel had shaken her head and told her they hadn't.

Agnes stayed up all night with Rosie, who was delirious with a serious case of arc eye and was thrashing about in agony. Tears silently spilled down Agnes's face as she watched this wreck of a girl cry out, her eyes and nose streaming constantly, while she clutched her banging head in agony. No amount of cold compresses on her eyes or her forehead eased her pain. She knew Rosie just had to ride it out. She just hoped and prayed the poor girl was left with her sight intact.

Agnes wasn't the only one not to sleep a wink that night.

Gloria spent the entire time with Jack in his small, warm office, talking and sipping whisky. The hours passed like minutes as they discussed the events of the evening, and then they started to chat about their own lives and the many years they had spent apart. Neither of them said anything about it, but it was clear they still shared a very natural bond. An outsider listening in would never have guessed they'd spent two decades apart with hardly a word spoken between them.

For once Gloria didn't have to worry about Vinnie, as he was still away visiting his ailing mother. Jack also knew he wouldn't be missed. Miriam wouldn't notice that the bed in the spare room hadn't been slept in, and in the morning she would presume he'd left early for the yard. He wouldn't have cared, though, if Miriam did know he'd stayed out all night. The reason he had ended up back at the yard after Frank's wake was that he hadn't been able to face going home, had needed somewhere to be on his own and just think. And he had a lot of thinking to do – had been doing a lot of thinking since the day he'd first spotted Gloria standing in the queue for her wages back in August. He had seen her working in the yards just about every day thereafter and hadn't been able to push away thoughts of their past love – and nor did he want to.

Gloria's reappearance in his life had brought all his old feelings back, feelings which, he realised, had never really gone away. He'd argued with himself that over twenty years had passed and life had moved on for them both, but then the other day he had seen the bruises on Gloria's wrists and had felt the most violent rage towards Vinnie. He'd heard rumours in the past, but had dismissed them because Vinnie was Gloria's husband, they had two boys together and, besides, no one really knew what went on in a marriage behind closed doors. These well-worn excuses for not getting involved had been his argument to let well alone, but after he himself had seen evidence of Vinnie's brutality, and had it confirmed after a quiet chat with Rosie, Jack hadn't been able to rest. When he had seen the dark form of a man falling backwards into the river, with Gloria standing watching by the quayside, he had thought that the man was Vinnie. And, if truth be told, he'd actually wished it was.

When Jack and Gloria parted in the early hours of the morning, with the yards bathed in a frosty sunlight, all traces of the previous day's thick fog gone, they did so as lovers. The yard was empty, and no one witnessed their tender farewell, or saw the way their hands stayed clasped for a time before Gloria finally forced herself to pull away and leave her old love standing alone, watching her disappear from his sight.

Over the next week, and much to the women's relief, Rosie recovered remarkably well, thanks to Agnes's nursing and Rosie's own steely determination to get better.

Neither Agnes nor Bel prodded Polly for any more details about what had happened that night, with Agnes saying sagely, 'Ask no questions, hear no lies.' She knew the truth would eventually out, but she trusted her daughter and was just glad Polly and the rest of the women had survived their ordeal relatively unscathed.

There was no denying that Rosie had been incredibly lucky, although the after-effects of the arc eye she suffered were severe, and there was no way she could be near any kind of bright light, never mind do any welding herself. Her wrist was also weak and was still too painful to even hold a cup of tea; no way could she spend hours clutching a rod holder.

Rosie was given sick leave by Jack, who had agreed with the women that there was no reason to tell anyone about what had happened that night. They had done no wrong. Raymond had stumbled and fallen back into the river. It had been an accident. 'Besides,' he'd rationalised to Gloria, 'the yard's behind as it is, we're late with a launch, and there's ships waiting in line to be repaired. There's no way we need any more hold-ups.'

Rosie took her sick leave and used it to go and visit Charlotte, who was a little shocked at the state of her sister's scabbed face but overjoyed at her surprise visit. Mr and Mrs Rainer, however, were nobody's fools and knew something very bad had happened to their charge's sister, but they said nothing. Instead they did what they thought best, and for the two days of her stay they simply fed Rosie lots of hot dinners and gave her a big home-made apple pie to take back, which, on her return to her bedsit, Rosie had shared with Mrs T.

She also went to see Lily after she got back. It was a relief to tell her everything that had occurred that night, although it had taken Lily a few moments to regain her composure after she'd seen the state of Rosie's face. She had ushered Rosie into the kitchen, grabbed two glasses and her bottle of Rémy Martin and demanded to know every detail. Later, the two women had been joined by a concerned-looking George, and Rosie had left there feeling lighter after finally being able to talk about the whole nightmare.

She decided to return to work after just a week off, not because she had to, but because she hated sitting around doing nothing.

'Hurrah! She's back!' Dorothy yelled. She couldn't contain her excitement when Rosie arrived back in the yard.

Gloria cast her a warning look, as they had all agreed to try to behave as normally as possible, and not to make too much of a fuss over Rosie in case any of the other workers suspected her injuries were more than simply a weld gone wrong.

Rosie was not able to do any welding – there was still a question mark over whether or not her eyesight would recover enough to go back to the job she loved – so Jack asked her to help him with the managerial side of the shipyard, and to prepare for his trip to America to talk the Yanks through the building of the new Liberty ships.

As Rosie recovered from her near-death experience, the most wonderful feeling of relief started to infuse her being. It really was as though she had stumbled, battered and bruised, out of a living hell and back into some semblance of normality. And she was under no illusion who she had to thank for that. The women welders she had taught and tried to help integrate into shipyard life had ended up repaying her in a way she would never have imagined was possible. They had saved her life. Not only that, but they had also saved her sister, Charlotte. One day Rosie would tell Charlotte the whole story. It was important that she knew.

Rosie herself felt an immense release now that the tremendous weight of worry and the awful threats she'd had to live with over these past few months had been lifted from her. They had been taken from her that night and had disappeared over the quayside along with her abuser.

And today, when she had gone back to work and seen the joy on the women's faces when they'd welcomed her back, she had seen there was no judgement. They knew what she did for money, and they still liked her, regardless. What's more, they'd made it clear that her secret was safe with them.

With that came the most wonderful feeling ever. For the first time in her life she had friends. She no longer felt alone. When Rosie got home that evening, she made a silent vow to herself that she would always be there for her women welders, each and every one of them. They would have her love and her loyalty for life.

Chapter Forty-Six

Monday, 11 November

Tommy caught the stout middle-aged postwoman cycling into the docks as he was walking to the ferry landing. He had started to get the ferry to and from work in the vain hope he might accidentally bump into Polly, who he knew used it daily. It was Sod's Law, though, that he hadn't once spotted her this past week and he had only caught glimpses of her at work.

Much to his mental torment, the women were back working with the platers, which included Ned. Tommy had tried not to become obsessed with trying to catch Ned and Polly talking to each other, or having any kind of interaction. Every time he had the chance, he would look over to see if he could catch the two of them together. He'd thought he might have seen them having a chat round the platers' fire during a tea break, but so far he hadn't. He couldn't help but feel relief every time he saw Polly had her helmet down and was hunched over a weld. Mind you, the weather had been so bad everyone in the yard had their head down and were just ploughing through the work they had to do.

'Mornin', Tommy,' the postwoman said, frowning against the morning drizzle. She rummaged in her bag, which was full to overflowing. 'Let me see if there's owt here for you.'

Tommy immediately felt his heart beat faster. It had now been two weeks since his visit to the recruiting office, when it had taken some time to explain to the elderly man sitting behind the large wooden desk exactly why he should be considered for military service. The old man had said about him being in a reserved occupation, but a determined Tommy had argued his case, stressing the fact there were now more divers working for the River Wear Commissioners, and that if the navy accepted him, he would need next to no training as he was physically fit, an experienced diver and knew just about everything there was to know about ships.

In the end the old man, who was a war veteran himself, had nodded knowingly and got out his pen and an official-looking form and started writing. He'd asked Tommy a few health-related questions, given him a cursory medical, and asked him to take a general knowledge test. Tommy had struggled with that as he rarely picked up a pen in his line of work, but he had completed it, or at least most of it. The recruiting officer had then asked Tommy to sign his name on a form and told him to expect a response in the post in the next few weeks.

'Ah, here we are,' the postwoman said, handing Tommy an official-looking brown envelope.

'Ta.' Tommy took the letter before adding, 'Take care down the dock, there's been some flooding with last night's heavy rain.'

As soon as he turned to walk on he ripped open the envelope. It was, as he'd suspected from the official-looking stamp, from the recruitment department of the Royal Navy. As he scanned it, he felt his body come to life. They wanted him. He'd been accepted; he was finally going to go to war.

A rush of emotions hit him. Excitement, a sense of pride, trepidation, nervousness and then more excitement.

As the drizzle turned to thick dollops of rain, Tommy shoved the letter into his jacket pocket and ran to catch the ferry, which was just blowing out steam and preparing to make its way across the choppy river. The ferryman nodded at Tommy, whom he'd known from a nipper, and let him jump aboard without taking a fare, just as he'd done for as long as he could remember.

While the ferry groaned into action, Tommy's mind churned around. He would have to tell Jack as soon as possible about leaving the yard. Tommy knew Jack would understand, as he himself was going halfway round the world to help with the war effort with the new ship design.

Arthur, however, would be a different kettle of fish. Tommy knew that he would be angry. He would feel that Tommy had denied him the chance of talking him round, but Tommy also knew the old man would realise that even if he'd told him beforehand, Tommy would have gone ahead and signed up regardless.

Finally, and most importantly, he needed to tell Polly. Thoughts of the woman he still loved, whether or not she loved him back, were never far away. As Tommy contemplated talking to Polly and telling her his news, he felt himself fire up inside, a feeling she'd always managed to stoke up in him even though she was not aware of doing so. He couldn't wait to tell her his dream had come true, to talk to her and be near her once again, even if it was for the last time.

Chapter Forty-Seven

'Get the boss!' bellowed out one of the linesmen who worked with Tommy and the other divers. 'And quickly!'

The only reason the women heard him was because the hooter had just sounded for the lunch break and the yard had descended into relative quiet. They could hear the panic in the man's voice. Polly's head swung round to look at her workmates, who returned her look of grave concern.

No words were needed. They were all thinking the same thing: Tommy.

'Oh God, no . . .' Polly said. She flung her bag down and ran towards the side of the dock.

She knew she would never forgive herself if something happened to the man she still loved, still thought of every hour of every day. At that moment she hated herself for her stubbornness, for not talking to Tommy before now.

As she reached the edge of the quayside she looked across at the divers' pontoon just a few feet away, bobbing in the river. The diving crew were clearly alarmed at whatever they were hauling up and Polly felt a sick foreboding in the pit of her stomach. Everyone knew diving was a dangerous job, and there had been fatalities in the past when a diver's body had been dragged up limp and lifeless out of the river.

'What's wrong?' Polly shouted across to the workers. 'Is Tommy all right?' She tried not to sound hysterical, but the fear that something terrible had happened to Tommy was overwhelming, and she didn't give a damn what anyone thought of her.

'Aye, pet, Tommy's all right,' Ralph, the head diver, who knew Polly and knew of her closeness with Tommy, reassured her. 'It's the other bloke who's not looking too good,' he added. He gave one last pull of the ropes, bringing Tommy's huge copper helmet into view by the side of the boat.

Polly had now been joined by the other women, who were all waiting with bated breath to see what was happening. As Tommy was pulled up out of the water they all stared in horror to see, lying limp in Tommy's arms, a man's corpse. There was no doubt as to who it was: the dead man Tommy was carrying was Raymond.

'Oh no,' Polly whispered quietly to the women, all standing together.

'Why couldn't the bugger have been washed out to sea, like every other bit of rubbish?' Gloria mumbled under her breath.

Martha grunted her agreement, and Hannah grasped her friend's giant arm as they both stared down at Raymond's dripping, grotesque body.

Over this past week the river had done its own work on Raymond. His body had blown up like an inflated balloon, distorting his physique out of all proportion. He still wore his suit but it now looked two sizes too small for him. But it was his face that had undergone the greatest transformation; it was puffed out and had turned a ghastly white colour, tinged with green.

As the men took the body from Tommy's outstretched arms and laid it out on the decking, Raymond's head fell to the side. The women all jumped back in unison at the monstrous sight of his oversized, bulging eyes. What was truly hideous, though, was that one of the eyes had come out of its socket, but was still attached by a thin, veiny membrane.

'I think I'm going to chuck up.' For once Dorothy wasn't exaggerating and she gagged.

By now dozens of other workers had forsaken the warmth of the canteen, or their blazing outdoor fires, to see what was causing the disturbance by the quayside. A few of them took off their cloth caps on seeing the dead body splayed out in the boat. 'Beer in, wits out,' one commented. It wasn't unheard of for a drinker frequenting one of the many riverside taverns to stagger outside after one too many and plunge straight into the Wear, especially during these times of blackouts.

One of the divers' assistants unbolted Tommy's helmet and carefully lifted it off his head. Polly's stare penetrated the man she loved, whom she'd feared had come to harm. The relief that he was alive and well was etched across her face. As if feeling the heat of her gaze, Tommy looked up and found Polly's face. Her heart leapt when a broad smile immediately spread across his face. If she could have got to him there and then she would have grabbed hold of him and not let go.

But just then Polly heard an all-too-familiar voice. 'Tommy, Tommy!' Helen was calling out from behind her. A few seconds later Polly felt a firm nudge as Helen squeezed past her to get to the front of the quayside audience. 'Tommy, are you all right? What's happened?' Helen seemed genuinely worried. When she saw the abhorrent-looking corpse laid out by Tommy's lead-booted feet, she squealed out her disgust. 'Oh my goodness!'

Gloria took hold of Polly's hand, partly to reassure her, and partly to stop the urge she knew her friend would be having to push this annoying woman into the river. Polly looked at Gloria, glad of her friend's understanding.

Just then another voice sounded out from behind the swell of onlookers: 'Make some space. The show's over.' It was Jack. There was a brief moment when he caught Gloria's eye and they looked at each other. Jack seemed about to say something but stopped himself, and instead turned quickly to the mass of onlookers and commanded, 'Go and have your lunches.'

The workers dispersed back across the yard, chatting loudly about who it could be and what could have happened. Cigarettes were lit and the clanging of the tea boys busying about could be heard.

'You lot too,' Jack said, staring hard at the women welders, who still seemed to be rooted to the spot.

The women didn't need telling twice. As they walked away, Jack caught Gloria's arm and they stopped to chat for a few moments.

Dorothy looked back at her workmate and saw the change in her. There was now a slight softness to the group's mother hen, and it was very apparent at this moment as she talked to Jack. They stood close together – closer than necessary, Dorothy thought. Over the past week, whenever Jack and Gloria had had any kind of contact, there had not been even a trace of animosity between the pair of them. In fact, the more Dorothy thought about it, the more she realised how comfortable they both seemed in each other's company, and had been ever since what Dorothy called in her head 'that evening'. Gloria and Jack had quite obviously more than resolved their differences.

When all the women got to the canteen only Martha felt able to eat. The rest sat and quietly chatted while they drank their tea.

At the end of the lunch break, they headed back over to their work area. Polly tried not to stare daggers at Helen as she fussed over Tommy, relishing the unfolding drama and enjoying being in the thick of the action.

Gloria reprimanded Dorothy quietly for gawking over at the coroner's black van when it arrived to take Raymond's body away.

'Quick drink after work, everyone?' Gloria asked the women during a tea break.

They all nodded silent agreement.

At the end of the shift, Polly went to the main admin block to see if Rosie wished to join them. It was odd to see her there amongst all the suited men, and the women who were dressed like women, rather than clad in men's overalls and hunched over a weld.

Polly could completely understand if Rosie never wanted to go back to work in the yard, or be near another rod holder in her life, but she still hadn't come to terms with Rosie's second job, and no one had talked about it since that night. There was an unspoken understanding amongst Polly and the women that what Rosie did of an evening was her business.

'Yes, I'd love to,' Rosie said, smiling back at Polly.

As they left the office Polly was glad she didn't bump into Helen, although her heart sank as she realised this was probably because she was somewhere else in the yard with Tommy.

When Rosie and Polly caught up with Gloria, Dorothy, Hannah and Martha they were hurrying towards the pub, eager to get a seat before the place filled up.

When they had all settled with their drinks, Hannah asked quietly, 'What everyone thinking? Police find out?' She took a large gulp of her half-pint of stout and grimaced. She had taken to drinking the black stuff after hearing it would build up her strength, but the women hadn't had the heart to tell her that the bitter-tasting liquid was no miracle cure and was unlikely to put muscles on her skinny arms.

'Police?' Martha said, looking more than a little confused as she searched the other women's faces for an answer.

'Well, there's nothing for the police to find out,' Gloria said. 'It was an accident – even Jack saw that it was an accident.'

The women looked at Gloria. It hadn't only been Dorothy who'd noticed a change in their workmate. Despite the dramatic and fatal events of that night, Gloria had seemed so much happier this week. The women were more than a little curious about the mystery surrounding Gloria's relationship with Jack. She had told them that they'd known each other when they'd been growing up in the east end, but hadn't elaborated.

Polly, of course, knew the real story, and she wondered how Gloria felt now after all these years. Had time mended her broken heart? And did Jack have regrets? She knew not to say anything to the other women, though. That would be up to Gloria.

'I agree with Gloria,' she chipped in. 'There's nothing to worry about because we've not done anything wrong.'

'Of course we haven't done anything wrong,' Rosie said in a steely voice. 'There was only one person responsible for what happened that night, and he bore the consequences of his own actions.' She looked round at her women welders and saw they had been reassured. She knew, though, that soon she would have to tell them the whole story, but not tonight.

Hannah took another gulp of stout before looking at Polly and cautiously asking, 'And Polly, you mind me asking, what happening with the lovely Tommy?'

The other women practically froze. This was something they had all been desperate to find out, but had understood Polly's need to keep her love life private.

'Oh,' Polly said, somewhat wearily. 'It seems so irrelevant after all that's happened.' The women were hanging on her every word. 'After what's happened to you, Rosie, I feel like I've no reason to moan about anything in my life.'

Rosie just shook her head, showing Polly that she wanted her to go on.

'What went wrong?' Dorothy couldn't help herself asking. She'd been itching to find out what on earth had happened between the pair. 'You both seemed so together . . . in love,' she pushed.

Polly took a deep breath. 'So I thought, but then Tommy just seemed to change. Like he just went off me. I have a feeling he might have decided he prefers Helen's company to my own,' she speculated, feeling a great heaviness in her heart. 'The way they both are around each other . . .'

There was a moment's silence. None of the women wanted to agree, even though they too had all come to the same conclusion. They hadn't said anything, but they had eyes, and they'd all seen the way Helen talked with Tommy.

'Well, I heard something today in the office,' Rosie ventured. Everyone was all ears. Even Martha looked rapt. 'It really is a different world up there,' Rosie said, touching a scab on her cheek. She had felt incredibly self-conscious today amongst all the office women and their perfectly made-up faces and lipstick. She still couldn't bring herself to look at her face in the mirror and there was no getting away from people's shock when they saw her for the first time.

'Tell us more,' Dorothy demanded.

'I probably shouldn't really fuel the gossip, but one of the secretaries was asking me today if it was true that Polly was seeing Ned.'

'Who? The plater?' Dorothy asked.

'Yes,' Rosie answered, looking across at Polly's puzzled face.

'How odd,' Polly said. 'I don't think I've ever spoken more than a few words to him. I wonder why they think that.' Her words hung in the air. Everyone was as perplexed as Polly.

'It might explain why Tommy seems off with you,' Gloria thought aloud. What she didn't say, though, was that she would bet her weekly wage that Helen had had something to do with this. She had seen the way Jack's daughter behaved around Tommy and it didn't take a genius to see she had more than her eye on Tommy.

When the women finished their drinks they all admitted to feeling shattered. Rosie in particular looked tired out. But at least now she was able to sleep. In fact, she seemed to be making up for all the hours she'd missed out on over the past two months, and every night she was out like a light the moment her head hit the pillow.

As they squeezed their way through the growing crowd of drinkers and stepped out of the pub and into the fresh night air, Dorothy perked up and turned to Polly. 'Well, like you all told me not so long ago, there's plenty other fish.'

But as she spoke the women all fell quiet as they spotted a familiar figure in the distance. It was Tommy, standing next to his bike, his helmet dangling from his hand.

Chapter Forty-Eight

'Polly?' Tommy's voice sounded out across the quietness of the dark, wintery-cold evening.

Polly stood stock-still, staring over at this man who had won and broken her heart in a matter of months, but whom she missed desperately. Despite the drama of the last week, her head had still been wrapped up in thoughts of Tommy, her mind full of questions about what had happened between the two of them, asking herself why it had all gone so wrong over the past few weeks, and, worse still, wondering what he was up to – and more importantly, with whom.

'Can I have a quick word?' He walked purposefully over to Polly, who seemed fixed to the spot. Her face, pale in the light of the full moon, was unreadable as he moved towards her.

Polly finally found her tongue. 'Yes, of course.' She looked across at the other women, who were slowly inching away, wanting to give their friend and the man they knew she was still very much in love with some space.

'See you!' Gloria said, putting her hand in the air to wave farewell.

'Yes, see you tomorrow,' Dorothy added excitedly.

'See you all tomorrow . . .' Polly replied distractedly as her eyes flitted back to Tommy, whose presence she felt as much as saw.

The others disappeared into the surrounding darkness, the sound of their booted footsteps quickly fading. Tommy bent his neck down slightly to look straight into Polly's eyes, trying desperately to read what she was thinking and what she was feeling.

'Can we go somewhere to chat?' He tried hard to keep any kind of emotion out of his voice.

'Yes, of course.' Polly too tried to sound as if she was just talking to a colleague or an acquaintance, but – and she hated herself for it – her whole being cried out to put her arms around his broad neck, touch his weather-beaten face, press her body close to his and cover his lips with her own. The terrible shock of believing something fatal had happened to him today still played strongly on her mind, and it had brought with it an overwhelming desire to see him, talk to him, and to touch him.

Tommy offered Polly his helmet. 'There's patchy fog tonight and the odd bit of ice on the roads. Not the best weather to be on a bike, so I'll ride extra carefully.'

Polly swung her work bag and boxed gas mask across her body and took the helmet, their hands touching for the briefest moment. As she pulled on the helmet and tucked her muffler around her neck, she could feel her body start to shiver, partly because of the cold, but mainly through a nervous apprehension. But as soon as Tommy sat on the bike and she slid in behind him and felt their bodies close together and the immediacy of his warmth, the shaking stopped.

They rode across the Wearmouth Bridge and dropped down to the south docks. Polly's mind ran through all the possible reasons why Tommy wanted to talk to her. He must have watched them all leave work, seen where they were all headed, and waited until they'd surfaced from the Admiral. Why would he do this if he was courting Helen? Perhaps things had become serious with her and he felt that Polly, finally, deserved an explanation for being dumped so suddenly and without any kind of explanation. But something in his eyes just now, and the way he had stared at her earlier on today at work, suggested otherwise. Polly felt the look in his doleful, sad eyes reflected what she herself felt – a longing, a deep yearning.

As they rode down the bumpy surface of the cobbled road that ran parallel with the river, Tommy changed down a gear before stopping outside the home he shared with Arthur. Once they'd both dismounted, Polly freed herself from the oversized helmet and gave it back to Tommy.

'I know it's bitter, but do you fancy a walk along the river?' Tommy put the helmet down next to his bike, taking off his leather gloves and handing them to Polly.

'Yes, that'd be nice,' she said, glad of the offer of his gloves as her hands were now frozen to the bone. Seeing how cold she was, Tommy started to take off his leather jacket, but Polly stopped him. 'No, really. My coat's fine, warm enough.' She lightly touched his arm and, for the first time, he smiled.

The night was icy, but the sky was clear and the moon made up for the lack of street lamps.

'I love this town, these docks,' Tommy said. He stared out at the expanse of dark, glinting sea ahead of them, then gently took Polly's arms and guided her to the part of the quayside where there were bulky stone steps leading down to the river. 'I used to sit here for hours as a child, just looking out to sea and imagining what was out there.'

He turned to look at Polly, who also seemed entranced by the water's dark, moving landscape. He had to ask. After all, this was why he'd brought her here, had waited for an hour in the freezing cold outside the pub, determined not to miss her. 'I wanted to talk to you . . . to ask you if you are seeing someone else.'

Polly was snapped out of the lull she'd fallen into, listening to the sound of the water softly lapping against the quayside's solid stone wall.

'Seeing someone else? Why would I be seeing someone else?' The thought of being with another man seemed so preposterous. How could she be with someone else when he had her heart? Polly turned her puzzled face to look at Tommy. 'Why would you think I was with someone else?'

Tommy decided just to spit it out. 'I heard you were seeing one of the platers, a bloke called Ned.'

Polly looked up at him with a frown on her face. 'That's odd – Rosie's just said when we were having a drink back there that someone in the office had said I was seeing Ned.'

'I heard you had been out with him, had been cosying up with him on a night out.' Tommy couldn't keep the jealousy out of his voice. 'Why would someone say that if it wasn't true?'

'Tommy, I think I'd know if I was going out with someone – and "cosying up" with them. Who said they'd seen me and Ned together?' She was now mystified herself.

'Helen told me one of the girls from the office had seen the two of you together,' he said, now uncertain of himself.

'Well, that's a downright lie,' Polly said, growing upset. 'Why would anyone make something like that up?'

Tommy felt his hopes rise. 'Most of the yard seem to think you are seeing Ned,' he persevered. 'And I saw you walking with him myself – across the yard.'

'Tommy, I don't know who's been making up this gossip, but it's just not true. And the only time I've been anywhere near Ned was when we both had to go to the main office because of some problem with our wages.'

Tommy felt a growing sense of elation well up inside of him. He could tell by Polly's reaction, her words, by the slightly confused look on her face, that she was telling the truth. The most wonderful feeling of relief started to pass over him – and with it the beginnings of an understanding as to what had happened.

Helen.

He'd known Helen had always been keen on him, but not that she would try to wreck his chances of happiness with another woman by spreading an outright lie. It was complete madness, but at this point Tommy didn't care. All that mattered was that Polly wasn't seeing Ned, or anyone else. She was still his.

Polly thought for a moment before letting out a short laugh of disbelief. The thought of her courting another bloke was actually quite ridiculous. 'Work's been mad. We haven't had a minute to ourselves, never mind to go out on any dates,' she said.

More than anything, though, she wanted to tell Tommy that even if she'd had all the time in the world there would never be another man whom she wanted to go out with, or to be with, other than the one standing in front of her now. But she didn't. First she needed her own answers. 'And what about you? What about you and Helen?' Polly felt nervous all of a sudden.

'What *about* me and Helen?'

More pieces of the jigsaw puzzle started to fall into place for Tommy. Helen's constant presence whenever he was out of the river. The peculiar conversation he'd had with his granddad the other day. People thought he and Helen were an item. Of course, to an outsider Helen might seem desirable. Most men would happily throw themselves at her feet, in lust and adoration. She was most men's dream woman. But Tommy had never been in the least bit interested in her.

'I'm not interested in Helen. Never have been.' Tommy took hold of Polly's hands. 'Helen's like a sister to me. I care for her, but I find her quite annoying most of the time. Even more so now.'

Polly had to say what was on her mind – had been on her mind for too long now. 'You two are always together. Whenever you have a break, she's there, chatting, by your side. Everyone in the yard thinks you're a couple.' That wasn't strictly true. No one had ever said that to Polly, but she knew it was what people thought. She knew it was what her workmates thought, although they'd had the sensitivity not to say anything to her directly.

Tommy opened his mouth to speak, but shut it again. Instead he gently took hold of the lapels on her thick work coat and pulled her close.

'There is only you. I have only ever wanted you, ever since the day I first saw you in the yard.' His deep eyes searched Polly's face. 'You must know that, surely?'

In that moment Polly saw it. She saw the love which had always been there, which had got obscured from her vision, just like her love for Tommy had been hidden from him by the lies spread about this Ned bloke. Her eyes pooled with emotion, and leaning her body forward so there was not a breath of air between them, her mouth found his and they kissed, and kissed some more, trying to make up for all the kisses, caresses and love they had been denied these past weeks.

When they finally broke free, Polly looked at Tommy but was taken aback by the deep sadness she saw etched across his face. 'What?' she asked. 'What is it?' She felt a dread at what was to come next. Her heart didn't feel able to withstand any more hurt.

'There's something I have to tell you,' Tommy said.

Polly looked askance at him.

319

'It's cold. You're shivering. Let's get warm at mine. Arthur'll be in bed now and I can stoke up the fire . . . and I can explain everything.'

She nodded and Tommy put his arm tightly around the woman he loved but knew he was going to lose. He held her close as they walked back along the quiet, moonlit dockside.

Chapter Forty-Nine

Rosie had enjoyed a brief chat and a cup of tea with Mrs T before heading off to her own room. She was just about to get ready for bed, and was thinking about Polly and Tommy, and how she and the other women were all hoping that the pair of them would just sort themselves out and kiss and make up. The rest of the women were a little worried that Tommy might have been seduced by Helen, although they would never admit that to Polly, but Rosie didn't think for one moment that Tommy would be interested in Helen. Any fool could see the woman was an idiot and from what she knew of Tommy, Rosie didn't think he would be the kind of bloke to go with someone as vacuous as Jack's daughter, even if she was rich.

Rosie was pottering about her room, putting Charlotte's latest letter away in her little storage box, when there came a loud knock on the door. She nearly jumped out of her skin – her nerves still felt pretty frazzled.

'Who is it?' she demanded, in a voice that she tried to make as loud and as authoritative as possible. Part of her still felt extremely vulnerable, something she hoped would go with time.

'DS Peter Miller from Sunderland Constabulary, ma'am,' said a voice through the door.

Rosie felt fear course through her. Get a grip, she told herself. You haven't done anything wrong. She took a deep breath and walked over to unbolt and open her door.

'I'm sorry to disturb you,' DS Miller said, showing his identification. 'If this isn't convenient I can come back another time.' The detective, Rosie noticed, was immaculately turned out in a smart black suit, starched white shirt and blue tie. He appeared the epitome of professionalism.

'No, no, come in.' She directed him to a chair next to her dressing table.

Seeing Rosie's injured face, DS Miller tried to keep his expression impassive. 'I'm sorry to see you've had some sort of accident.' He touched his own face by means of explanation.

'Oh, I'm a welder at Thompson's,' Rosie said. 'Bit of an accident. Looks worse than it is, though.'

DS Miller looked at this young woman in front of him and could see that underneath the scabs that had formed over her burns there was a very attractive face.

'Tough job,' he said, 'and much needed in these times. I know there's a few out there who wouldn't agree, but I think it's a good job we've got you women doing these jobs while the men are away.'

Rosie smiled and agreed, not wanting to explain that she'd had this job long before war broke out.

'So, DS Miller, can you tell me the reason for your visit?' Rosie tried not to let her anxiety show through, but as she spoke her legs suddenly felt a little shaky and she had to sit down on the chair she had offered her unexpected visitor.

'Yes, I'm so sorry. It's always a bit of a shock having the police knock on your door. I'm afraid I've come with some bad news.'

Rosie sat quietly, looking up at DS Miller's face, which was starting to age, but was by no means an old or an ugly face.

'Your uncle, Raymond Gallagher, has died. His body was pulled from the river today. You might have heard about it at work?'

Rosie nodded. 'Yes, it caused quite a rumpus. But obviously I didn't know it was my uncle . . .' Her voice trailed off. Rosie tried to keep her reaction as unaffected as possible. She had to play this one right, and knew if she pretended she was in any way distressed by her uncle's sudden departure, DS Miller would know she was lying. She had met a few police officers in her time and the older they were, the better they were at reading people. And DS Miller had intelligent eyes. He didn't look as though he would miss a trick.

'I'm guessing by your reaction that you aren't too upset by his demise?' DS Miller watched Rosie, trying to keep his focus on her pretty light blue eyes and not stare at the small halfpenny-sized wounds dotted about her face.

'Well, we weren't close by any stretch of the imagination. I only met him the once, just after my parents died when I was young, and after that I never saw hide nor hair of him. He just disappeared.' Rosie hoped no one had seen her go to Raymond's bedsit when she'd taken him his money. She had always taken care to be discreet.

DS Miller was curious. 'You don't know where your uncle's been these past five years?'

Rosie answered truthfully that she didn't. She had always assumed her uncle had simply taken what he'd wanted from her and moved on. She had wondered over the years whether or not he was still in the north-east, and had dreaded him coming back into her life – which was partly the reason she liked to keep a low profile and had moved around so much.

DS Miller cleared his throat. 'I have to speak plainly and tell you that your uncle was not a good man.'

Rosie looked again at the police sergeant, with his grey-flecked hair and earnest face, and realised he was not testing her. He had believed her when she'd said she had only met Raymond once.

'Please, just move that box off that chair and have a seat,' Rosie said, starting to relax, 'and tell me more.'

The policeman did as he was told, moving Rosie's box of letters on to the bed and sitting up straight in the wooden seat that Rosie normally used as a bedside table. Taking care to choose his words carefully, he said, 'Five years ago your uncle was convicted of raping three girls from the town. He used to leave the yard after work, follow his victims, before sexually assaulting them. At the time the trial was never reported in the press at the request of the victims.'

What he didn't tell Rosie was that there had always been the suspicion that Raymond had raped more women, and that there had also been talk that he was involved in the cases of some missing girls that the police had never got to the bottom of.

'He used an alias, so we never made the connection between him and your family. It wasn't until he'd spent some time in His Majesty's Prison Service that we found out his real name, by which time, sadly, your parents had passed away, and we were not able to locate you or your younger sister. Not,' he added, 'that I think it was deemed to be of great importance. As far as we could tell, he had been pretty much estranged from all of his family for most of his life.'

Rosie tried not to show the myriad of emotions that were skating across her mind.

So he had done this before. At least three times. She desperately wanted to know more details, but didn't trust herself. If she started engaging this policeman in conversation and asking questions, he might see or hear something in her voice or demeanour to make him curious about her. And there was no way she wanted the detective to know what Raymond had done to her – or anything else about her life, for that matter. Her life was her business, and she wanted to keep it that way.

'Well, that is truly awful. Really shocking.' Rosie kept her comments as brief and to the point as possible.

There was a few seconds' silence, and when DS Miller realised there were no more questions forthcoming from Rosie, he stood up.

'Well, I guess my job here is done. You're his next of kin, and you've been informed of his untimely death.' He stretched out his hand to Rosie. Hers felt clammy. 'I'm guessing you won't be wanting to organise his funeral or give him a send-off?'

His hand felt warm in Rosie's. 'No,' she said. But I'll be sure to dance on his grave, she thought.

As Rosie went to open the door, DS Miller turned suddenly. 'Oh, I forgot to mention one thing. We found a number of items in your uncle's accommodation, which we are looking into, but we also found quite a substantial amount of cash. Once we can ascertain that this was legitimately his money, and no one else's, then you, as his only surviving relative, will be legally entitled to that money.'

Rosie fought hard to keep the look of disbelief from her face.

'Well, if it's rightfully mine, in the eyes of the law,' she added quickly, 'then that will be most welcome.'

DS Miller and Rosie said their goodbyes, and Rosie closed and bolted her door. She stood listening to her visitor's muffled footsteps treading down the carpeted staircase and the noise of the heavy front door being closed.

The irony, she thought. Oh, the irony.

Chapter Fifty

As Polly sat in the warmth of Tommy and Arthur's small but cosy living room, staring at the fire that was now blazing, she felt tears prick the backs of her eyes. She kept thinking how all the men in her life whom she loved had been taken away from her. Her father had been taken from her before she'd even had a chance to meet him. Her beloved brothers had left as soon as war had been declared. And now Tommy was leaving her too. She cursed this war. All wars. War had taken her father, her brothers, and now the love of her life.

Polly felt angry. For so many different reasons, but most of all she felt angry at herself for her sheer stubbornness. If she'd only let go of her pride and done as Bel had suggested and talked to Tommy at the start of their falling-out a few weeks ago, then they would have had so much more time together. She would have realised his heart was not with Helen but with her and her alone, and then she could have told Tommy that the gossip about her and this Ned had been a total fabrication. She might even have persuaded Tommy to stay here and keep on doing the invaluable work he was doing at the yard.

Deep down, though, Polly doubted that she would have been able to change Tommy's mind. As she'd looked into his eyes she had seen his staunch determination. She'd seen the way he talked about joining up, heard the passion in his voice. And she knew that even if she had persuaded him to stay, it would have been a decision that would have eaten away at him, that it would have ultimately infected their love for each other and perhaps even destroyed it. There was only one option: she had to let Tommy go, no matter how much it hurt to do so.

When she had listened to Tommy as he'd told her how he had gone to the recruiting office in town and enlisted, she had been so incredibly proud of him, of his selflessness, of his bravery. She had fallen in love with this courageous, strong-minded but extremely sensitive man, and she knew it was these traits that had led to him being taken from her now. And that realisation caused her eyes to fill with tears, which were now spilling over and tumbling down her cheeks.

Seeing her upset, Tommy immediately jumped out of his chair. He wrapped his arms around the woman he loved, who he now knew loved him back, as she quietly wept. 'Don't cry,' he whispered into her ear as she responded to his embrace, putting her own arms around his solid body and holding him as if she never wanted to let go.

'I'll wait for you,' Polly whispered back. Tommy's whole body seemed to be enveloping her, his cheek pressed close to her own, catching and sharing her tears. He lifted his head away from hers and looked straight into her eyes. She could see the depth of his seriousness.

'Please, don't wait for me.' Tommy cupped Polly's head in his hands. 'Please, don't. Don't waste your life. Live it. Live it without me.'

Polly could see, could hear, that he meant every word he said and she loved him even more, if that was possible. But she also still felt angry. 'No, Tommy,' she said. 'You have chosen to go away and fight, to risk your life for what is right, for this country, for those you love, and I am *choosing* to wait for the one I love. That is *my* choice and you are not going to tell me to do different.'

Tommy had to smile. He loved the way her eyes sparked up with defiance when she was determined not to give in. He loved the way that one moment Polly could be radiant and soft, and the next fierce and angry. It was what made him adore this woman so much. He felt his whole body swell with untamed joy. Her words fired his passion. The thought that Polly would wait for him made him feel not only hopeful, but strong. Invincible. There was reason to this life. He *would* return to her.

Without thinking, he took his hands away from her face and dropped down to his knee. Taking Polly's hand in his own, he looked up into her solemn face, now streaked with tear stains, and said, 'Polly, I want you to be mine for ever. I want you to be my wife, for me to be your husband, for us to love each other for all of our days.' He pressed her hand to his face, then kissed it hard. 'When I come back to you, Polly, when this war is won . . . will you marry me?'

Polly's face lit up.

'Oh Tommy! Yes. Yes, I will!'

Feeling the heat of the fire on their faces and the burning passion from inside them both, Polly and Tommy kissed and held each other as if tomorrow might never come.

In the room upstairs Arthur sat on his bed. He had woken when he'd heard Tommy and Polly come in from the cold and his heart had lifted when he'd realised that finally the two of them had worked out their differences and were back in each other's arms.

Wanting to give them their privacy, he had got up to shut his bedroom door when he'd heard Tommy's voice turn serious. Arthur's ears had pricked up as he listened with growing concern about his grandson's trip to the recruiting office. By the time Tommy had explained to Polly that this morning he'd received his letter of acceptance from the

Royal Navy and would be called up in the next few weeks, Arthur had forced a hand over his mouth to stifle the gut-wrenching sobs that had erupted from his aged body.

Deep down he had always known this day was coming – he'd seen it in his grandson's eyes when he read about the battles in the Atlantic. But, despite this intrinsic knowledge of what lay ahead, it hadn't made the pain he now felt any easier to bear.

To calm himself, Arthur talked to Flo. His one-sided chats with his wife always helped him. He had always sought solace in Flo's presence, which he felt was there, and had been there ever since she had been cruelly and too suddenly taken away from him.

It was then that he overheard Tommy's proposal, and at that exact moment the most remarkable thing happened: a fleeting orb of light flashed through his blackout curtains and across his room. He had no idea where it came from, but he did know it was a sign. A message from his Flo.

'Where there's life, there's hope' had been one of her often-repeated sayings. With that thought in his mind, Arthur finally put his head down on his pillow and slept, leaving the young lovers to the little time they had left together.

Chapter Fifty-One

It was late by the time Tommy dropped Polly off, so she wasn't expecting either Agnes or Bel to still be up. As she walked through her front door she felt her whole being was as light as a feather, almost ethereal, heavenly, as though inside she was glowing with a truly joyous happiness. She had never felt like this before in her life. She couldn't believe that the man she loved not only loved her back, but had asked her to marry him.

Polly felt in a dream-like state. She had found her true love – a real love. This was no passing fancy, no here today, gone tomorrow love. It was a forever love. Tommy was hers, and she was to be his wife.

Her dread of Tommy's imminent departure for war was, of course, simmering under her sense of elation, but Polly refused to let it bubble through. For just these few hours she was going to immerse herself in the love she had felt this evening. For now, all thoughts of war would be pushed down below the surface and ignored. She would deal with those fears tomorrow. For the rest of this evening she refused to even think about the reality of Tommy's enlistment.

Polly carefully tiptoed down the hall, trying to be as quiet as possible, not wanting to disturb the sleeping household. But as she reached the end of the long hallway and neared the entrance to the kitchen, she heard the muffled sound of Bel quietly crying. As she pushed open the door, she saw her sister-in-law slumped on the kitchen table, her face buried in her arms. Next to her lay a torn-open envelope and a concertinaed letter.

Polly immediately went to Bel and put her arm round her and squeezed her slender shoulders, asking, 'Hey, what's up?'

She looked at Bel's bowed head and then at the letter: 'To my dearest Bel . . .' The large scrawling writing was unmistakeably that of her brother Teddy.

'What's happened?' she said. 'What's wrong?'

Polly forced Bel to lift her head off the table and face her, to answer her question. They had all been worried sick about Teddy and Joe as they had not heard anything from them for months. The postwoman had reassured them that this wasn't unusual – it was getting increasingly difficult to get correspondence from abroad back to loved ones at home – so their anxieties had been quelled a little.

As Bel looked up, Polly saw that her sister-in-law's eyes were red raw and puffy, her mascara had run down her cheeks, and her hair was uncharacteristically messy, hanging around her face in strands.

'It's from Teddy,' Bel said. 'He's fine. Well, he says he's all right, but Joe's been injured.'

Polly felt her body go rigid as she stared at Bel, not daring to breathe before she told her more.

'Teddy says Joe's got some shrapnel wounds and a leg injury, and that he can't stay out there, so they're bringing him home. He's going to be shipped back soon. May well have been already.'

'Oh God,' Polly said. How could one night bring such exhilaration and then such sorrow in one fell swoop? 'Does Ma know?' she asked Bel.

'Yes, I told her earlier on. She went to bed an hour ago, sick with worry.'

Polly saw in Bel's face that all her deeply buried anxieties and fears had come to the fore and were now running rampant. This, she knew, was what she too would have to go through with Tommy. This was the punishment of love.

Seeing Polly's panic-stricken face, Bel tried desperately to pull herself together. Teddy was her husband, but he and Joe were also Polly's brothers. She was their little sister, and even though they'd all fought like cats and dogs, they were close, and they all loved each other dearly.

'It could be so much worse,' she said, trying to lift her voice and force it to sound hopeful. 'Joe is going to be fine. He's alive, and so is Teddy. Honestly, I don't know why I'm such a mess.' As she spoke, more tears came and she tried to stifle her sobs.

Polly gave Bel a big hug but didn't say anything. Sometimes words seemed so meaningless. She knew Bel needed this time to let all her terrible worries roam free before rounding them up again and locking them away.

She made them both a cup of tea and they convinced themselves that the twins were going to be just fine. Polly didn't tell Bel her news. It could wait until tomorrow.

'You look exhausted,' Polly said. 'Go to bed, and give that gorgeous little daughter of yours a goodnight cuddle from me.'

When she heard Bel's bedroom door shut, she straightened Teddy's letter out on the table and read it. It was only then that she understood just why her sister-in-law had been feeling so desolate.

To my dearest Bel,

I hope you receive this letter and it finds you all well – especially my precious Lucille.

You may have already been informed, but Joe is soon to be home with you all. He has been injured, and has bad shrapnel wounds as well as a leg injury but he will live. He is due to sail very soon, although the journey is likely to take weeks.

I will write to tell you more as soon as I learn more myself, but in the meantime I feel compelled to tell you, my love, that I love you and our daughter more than anything in the world.

But I want to stress to you that should something happen to me out here, it is important that I know you will carry on this life without me, and that you will not waste this life with mourning. Our daughter needs a mother who is happy – not sad. So, I beg of you, if I do not make it back into your arms, you must remain strong and find happiness where you can.

Look after Joe when he gets back. He will not be the same man you remember who left all that time ago.

I must go now, my love, but I always carry you in my heart, and when I close my eyes, it is you I see.

I miss you.

Forever yours,

Teddy x

Polly folded the letter up and stuffed it back into its envelope. There was something in the tone of it which felt dark and despondent. She had a terrible sense of foreboding, which, try as she might, she could not get rid of.

Chapter Fifty-Two

'Gloria, over here,' Jack's voice sounded out from the darkness.

Gloria squinted into the surrounding blackness before she made out the faint outline of the man she now couldn't deny she still loved – in spite of everything that had happened all those years ago. In spite of her broken heart, and the life that could have been.

She quickly looked around her to check no one they knew was about, and then smiled as Jack stepped out from the shadows of a nearby back lane just up from the shipyard's main entrance. He took five quick, long steps before he reached the woman he too loved, had always loved, taking both her hands into his and pulling her towards him and risking a kiss.

Gloria welcomed his embrace and his gentle mouth, but only for a moment. 'I feel terrible,' she confessed as she forced herself to pull away.

'I know. I hate sneaking about like this.' Jack took Gloria's hand again as they left the vicinity of the yard and joined the main road that led to Monkwearmouth. It was cold so he wrapped his arm around her shoulder as they chatted and walked. The irony that their love affair could be conducted, to all intents and purposes, out in the open didn't escape either of them. They must have been two of the few people to actually welcome the stringent blackout regulations.

'I want to tell Miriam.' Jack's face was deadly serious. '*Before* I go to America.'

Gloria stopped and looked at the ageing face of her first love – her only true love. Jack might now be in a managerial position and spend most of his working day in an office, but his impoverished upbringing and the years he'd spent working out in the yard in all weathers had left their mark.

She touched his cheek with her cold hands. 'No, Jack, not yet. Wait . . . wait until you get back. It could cause problems.'

'But we can't go on like this. It feels so wrong to be skulking about. Besides, we've wasted enough time already,' Jack argued. 'I don't want to spend another moment parted from you. We have so much time to make up for.'

'I know,' Gloria said. 'I agree, and we *can* and *will* spend the rest of our lives together, but we need to think rationally. It's only a few weeks before you sail, and if this gets out it might jeopardise the good work you've already done and are going to do over there.'

'But I worry about you.' His face was streaked with genuine concern. 'I worry about what Vinnie might do to you.'

Gloria wanted to tell Jack that she would be fine, that she had coped with Vinnie, his drinking and his violence, for so many years that she felt almost desensitised to it. She wanted to tell him that she had survived all these years and would manage a few months more, but she didn't. She still hated to admit to herself, never mind anyone else, that she had allowed her husband to treat her the way he had.

Instead she said, 'Which is all the more reason to wait until you come back. If Vinnie causes problems, at least you'll be here.'

Gloria knew she had to persuade Jack to hold fire until his return. It was for the best, and she needed more time herself. She felt that everything had happened so fast – was happening so fast. Since the night Rosie's attacker had fallen into the river – the night she and Jack had talked and talked, and their love for each other had been reignited, and they had made love in the true sense of the word – since then it had been as if they'd both been thrown into a whirlwind. After that shared evening in Jack's little office, it was as though neither of them could bear to be away from each other. Despite the twenty years they'd spent apart, it had felt as if they had only just separated, as if they'd never really been away from each other. Perhaps in their hearts they hadn't.

From the moment they had become lovers, the pull they'd felt towards each other was magnetic. Gloria had tried desperately to hide it, but was sure the women at work had picked up on it, seen it, felt it. She knew for certain Dorothy had. But, oddly enough, she trusted Dorothy. Sometimes she seemed to have an understanding which belied her age.

Gloria knew nothing could get in the way of Jack going to America. The country needed him to do this: it could change the course of the war. Their love affair had to take second place, without a doubt.

And she had to admit to herself that she needed time to deal with what was happening, and to work out what they were going to do – and how they were going to do it. Gloria loved Jack. She loved everything about him, but she knew he could be impulsive. And she knew this was not the time to give in to any such rash actions. As a woman she knew only too well the serious consequences of their rekindled love and that they would be severe and far-reaching.

She was a married woman and a mother of two boys. Gloria understood just how big a scandal this would be when it came out. It mightn't be so shocking that a woman had committed adultery, but it was if that woman admitted her indiscretion and then actually left her husband of twenty years to be with her lover. Gloria would be painted

337

a wanton, loose woman, and Jack would more than likely lose his job at the yard – especially if Miriam had anything to do with it. Gloria was also terrified of being sacked. Her job wasn't just a job; it had become her life. Her new life.

'What I would give to be snuggled up with you in front of a roaring fire,' Jack said as they reached the small fourteenth-century church of St Peter's, a total anachronism in the surrounding industrial landscape. They reached the shelter of the church's arched porch, wrapped their arms around each other and kissed. 'Remember when we used to come here as teenagers?' he asked as they cuddled to keep warm.

'Of course. How could I forget?' Gloria had never been able to pass the church without recalling her time with Jack. She would never have thought then that they would be here now, with the world at war, and her and Jack in the situation in which they now found themselves.

It was time for them both to return to their own homes – homes that might have been warmer than where they were now, but which were cold in love and had been for a long time.

'So, we're agreed,' Gloria said as they prepared to leave. 'We wait until you're back.'

Jack nodded gravely. 'I know you're right,' he told her, kissing her cheeks and neck. 'It's just that it feels so very wrong.'

Chapter Fifty-Three

Over the following week Polly existed on a knife edge, just waiting to hear when Tommy had to leave for his Royal Navy training before being sent off to foreign lands, or, more likely, foreign seas. Time away from the concrete-and-steel environment of the yard and spent with each other had become precious. And although any chance of a proper date and dressing up and going out to a Saturday-night dance was pretty remote, it didn't stop them pretending.

One night after they both left work late and the moon afforded them a little light, they took a walk along the river. Polly took Tommy's hand in a theatrical fashion and told him, 'We're going to have a make-do-and-mend date.'

Tommy looked at her, still dressed in her overalls, as she freed her hair from the confines of her headscarf, and thought he had never seen a woman look so lovely and so feminine despite her work gear.

'Listen,' she said with a teasing look on her face, 'can you hear the orchestra? I think it's playing the waltz.'

Tommy had no idea what a waltz sounded like, but he knew enough to know it was a slow, intimate dance. 'I can hear it,' he said with a smile. 'Would the lady care to dance?' he asked in the best King's English he could muster.

Enjoying the role play, Polly stretched out her hand and told him, 'The lady most certainly would.'

The two slowly danced, moving their bodies together in perfect unison to the sound of the imaginary music.

'So much better than the Palladium,' Tommy whispered as he gently kissed the smooth, tender skin of his dancing partner under the pale light of the full moon.

As each day passed, Polly felt her heart burning with so much love, but also with so much fear and torment. How would she get through each day when Tommy was away at war, risking life and limb, not knowing if he would return to her and make her his? For the time being, though, she knew she had to be strong. And at least they were spending every spare minute they could with each other, trying their hardest to make up for lost time. When they heard the news that the whole of Coventry had been more or less destroyed in a prolonged ten-hour air raid, they knew that whatever the future might bring, Tommy had made the right decision.

Agnes and Bel were both as pleased as punch that Polly and Tommy were back together, and engaged at that, although Agnes admitted to Bel that she was more than a little relieved that her daughter and future son-in-law were going to wait until the war ended before they got married. Secretly she worried that Polly might end up on her own with a child to look after, just like Agnes had done. She didn't want history to repeat itself like it seemed to have a habit of doing.

Agnes insisted that Tommy and Arthur come round for dinner every night. Polly felt that this was partly because she was determined to build Tommy up before he went off to war, but also because her mother was on tenterhooks and snatching at any chance to keep herself busy. It was as though she didn't want a moment spare to think about her two sons and what was happening to them both. Every day Agnes would listen intently for the postwoman, and if she didn't push anything through their letter box, Agnes would run out and catch up with her to check she hadn't mislaid any kind of correspondence destined for their house.

She had confessed to Polly that she too had been perturbed by the tone of Teddy's letter, but had put it down to the effects of the war. 'We've no idea what's really happening out there. And Teddy's right to warn us that Joe's changed. Of course he's going to have changed. We're just going to have to brace ourselves for that.'

Polly agreed, but knew her mum was really talking to herself, telling herself to be prepared for what was to come.

Bel, meanwhile, was putting on a brave face – which was her way, but it was also because she had to for the sake of Lucille. Her chirpy demeanour wasn't fooling anyone, though, as they all knew underneath her cheery facade was a woman who was worried to distraction about her husband.

Seeing how her sister-in-law was trying desperately to cope, Polly was given a glimpse of her own destiny. She realised she was going to have to somehow deal with what she knew was to come – the constant anxiety about the mortality of the man she couldn't imagine living without.

Chapter Fifty-Four

Monday, 18 November

'I've got to see my husband!'

The woman making the demands of Alfie, the newly appointed timekeeper, was very clearly expecting a baby – so much so that the young lad let her through the gates without the required dock pass, fearful she might have the baby there and then if she got any more agitated.

Alfie had taken over from Mick, the old timekeeper, who had suddenly left his position after being struck down by some mystery ailment. It hadn't escaped the women's notice that his illness had come about on the same day that Raymond's body had been pulled out of the river.

Alfie asked the expectant woman who her husband was so he could direct her to the correct area of the yard.

'Ned Pike,' she told him in a loud, angry voice.

The young lad pointed her in the direction of the platers, telling her to be careful, especially in her condition, but watched concerned as the woman walked – or rather waddled, her hand on her large belly – over to the main office.

She had timed her arrival perfectly, whether intentionally or not, as it had just gone noon and the yard was relatively quiet. When she reached the area just at the foot of the administration block, she took a deep lungful of air before bellowing at the top of her voice, *'Helen!'*

A mass of flat caps and soot-smeared faces, many with cigarettes hanging out of their mouths or chomping on thick-crusted sandwiches, automatically turned to look at who was causing the commotion and, more interestingly, shouting for the boss's daughter. As they looked from the pregnant woman up to the main office on the first floor of the administration building, they saw Helen's perfectly made-up face tentatively appear at the window.

A crowd had now started to form near the woman as she took another deep breath. 'Open the window,' she commanded.

Much to everyone's surprise, Helen did what she was told, probably relieved that the deranged pregnant woman wasn't demanding she come down to meet with her face to face. Helen looked apprehensive as she stood, leaning forward slightly, with both hands resting on the windowsill.

Satisfied that she now had Helen's attention, and that of the entire yard, the woman said what she had come to say. 'I am Ned's wife. And as you can see, I am expecting Ned's baby.' She took a deep, angry breath. 'Why you would want to spread lies that my Ned is seeing one of your women welders is beyond me. But I want you, and everyone else in this yard, to know that not only is this *not* true, but that you, *Helen Crawford*, are a lying, conniving, sly bitch, who has nothing else to do but cause trouble for others. As if we all haven't enough worries to contend with these days.'

Then Ned's wife did an about-turn and marched, or rather walked as quickly as she could, considering her size, back across the yard, her head held high.

Helen looked dumbstruck as she watched Ned's wife stomp away. Her face flushed red through a mixture of embarrassment and fury. She slammed the office window shut, causing the glass to rattle.

The office workers started to make themselves busy as if nothing out of the ordinary had just happened, although they were bursting with glee that the woman they all thoroughly disliked had been so publicly humiliated. Meanwhile Norman, who'd been watching the whole scene from the doorway of the boiler room with growing horror, cursing himself that he hadn't considered that young Ned could be married, quickly made himself scarce.

The women welders were also surprised and more than a little amused by what they'd just witnessed. As they all headed over to the canteen, one by one they turned to look at Dorothy, who, they'd realised, didn't look the least bit shocked by this piece of midday theatre.

Chapter Fifty-Five

Wednesday, 20 November

'He's going today! He's going today!' Dorothy was running across the yard as though her life depended on it. Her cries were aimed at the women welders who were just returning to work after their lunch break.

She had nipped out to meet up with an old school friend and had been walking through the gates when she'd heard Arthur calling to her. 'Lass! Lass! Had yer horses,' he'd shouted across to her between deep gasps while he tried to catch his breath.

As she was the only woman about, Dorothy had immediately turned round to see a tall but frail-looking old man with a mop of grey hair, waving frantically at her, hurrying up the embankment from the ferry landing towards the yard.

'Do you know a welder called Polly Elliot?' he'd asked.

Dorothy had approached the old man with a slightly wary look on her face. 'Yes. She's my friend – workmate.' She cast her eye over to the new boy in the timekeeper's cabin, as she was cutting it fine to make it back in time for the afternoon shift.

'Tell her that Tommy's going today. Now. His letter arrived late: he's leaving on the one thirty p.m. train . . .' Arthur was now wheezing and struggling to catch his breath.

Dorothy hurried across to the old man, worried that he was going to keel over there and then. 'Are you all right?'

345

'I'm fine.' Arthur flapped his hands at Dorothy to shoo her away. 'Tell Polly . . . she might just make it in time to say goodbye . . . Go!' he commanded her with the last bit of strength he had left.

Dorothy looked at the old man before turning on her heel and sprinting back up the lane and through the gates, ignoring the cries from the timekeeper.

As she ran across the yard, she started shouting as soon as she spotted the women. 'Polly! Tommy's going! One thirty p.m. train!' Now it was Dorothy's turn to be gasping for air.

Polly stared at Dorothy for a second before her words sank in. 'What? Now? How come? . . . Oh no . . .' She turned around, not knowing what to do.

Within seconds Hannah was by her side. 'Take my bike. Behind supply shed . . . by entrance,' she spluttered the words out.

'Hurry,' Dorothy said. 'He can't leave you without saying goodbye.'

Martha grabbed Polly's work bag and gas mask and hurled them over her shoulder.

'Go,' Gloria told her, pushing her in the direction of the gates.

As Polly ran in a panic across the yard, dodging the other workers, she could hear the women's chorus behind her: 'Good luck!' they all shouted. When she reached Hannah's bike, she jumped on it and pedalled through the gates. Her legs felt as if they'd turned to jelly, but she forced them into action. She knew if she didn't get a move on she wouldn't make it.

Arthur watched Polly cycle up the slight incline and on to the main road. He was now bent over, hands on his knees, trying to get his breath back. He'd got the message to her in time. If she hurried she might just make it. He felt as though he could have jumped for joy if only his old limbs would have let him.

By the time Polly reached the train station she was sweating and felt as if she was going to collapse. She practically flung Hannah's bike against the front of the tobacconist shop beside the railway entrance.

Her heart sank when she raced into the station and immediately hit a mass of bodies. The station was crowded, bursting at the seams. Nothing was going to stop her, though, and she pushed her way to the ticket counter amidst shouts of annoyance from disgruntled travellers waiting in line to pay their fare.

'Sorry . . . sorry . . . sorry,' she repeated whilst pushing people aside, desperate to get to the woman behind the glass-fronted counter. 'What platform is the half one train leaving from?' Polly practically begged.

The young woman knew in an instant why Polly was so frantic, had seen the same lovelorn look on many a woman's face since war had broken out. She quickly got up from her seat, leant across the counter and shouted across to the station attendant, 'Let this woman on to platform one!'

Polly immediately fought her way across to the railway official holding up his hand, who had opened up a small wooden gate ready to let her through. She could have hugged both the woman behind the counter and the man letting her through the 'staff only' barrier.

'Thank you!' she shouted as she practically fell through the gate.

As she ran down the steps leading to platform 1, she caught sight of the large round clock hanging from the dome-shaped roof of the station. There were just minutes to go before the train left.

Polly frantically looked down at the platform, already teeming with travellers, porters and loved ones waiting to say goodbye, and could see that the black locomotive waiting by the platform was gearing up to leave. People were getting on; doors were slamming. The steam from the train's funnel was filling the air.

She stood on the last step to give herself some extra height and craned her neck, desperately looking at the crowd but only seeing a sea of flat caps, hats and headscarves.

'Tommy! Tommy!' Polly shouted out as loudly as she could. As she did so she caught a movement in the crowd and saw a head turn and look up.

It was Tommy.

His face immediately lit up when he saw her and he shouted back, 'Polly!'

Polly struggled to squeeze through the tightly packed mass of bodies, hearing the whistle sound out and more steam emerge from the train. She saw Tommy jump into a carriage before quickly pulling the compartment window down and leaning his body out. His hand tried desperately to reach for Polly as she neared the train. Polly felt as though she was swimming against a strong current, as though she would drown if her outstretched hand did not reach Tommy's.

As soon as their hands touched, Tommy grabbed her arm and pulled her up to him. Polly managed to put one foot on the edge of the train's ledge and grab hold of Tommy with her other arm.

He pulled her face to his and the two kissed – a kiss which felt like it was the end of the world, and these were their last moments together.

The whistle sounded again and the train started to slowly move forward. Polly stepped down but walked along the platform, still holding Tommy's hand as the train gained momentum.

'I love you, Tommy Watts,' she said.

'I love you too, Polly Elliot,' he shouted back. 'Look in your po—' Tommy's words were lost in the noise of the train's engine.

'What?' she shouted, her hand now forced to let go of her lover.

'Pocket!' Tommy shouted out as the train gained speed and Polly waved to him. She stood, waving and waving, not taking her eyes off the train until it had disappeared from sight, leaving only a trail of smoke and the smell of burning coal. While she stood there, the crowd dispersed around her.

'Please, God, look after him,' she begged.

As she turned to leave the station she put her hand in her pocket and pulled out a small velvet box. Tommy had obviously dropped it in there during their final embrace. Polly carefully opened it to see a beautiful ruby-and-diamond engagement ring.

She took it out of its box and put it on her finger, while tears broke free and streamed down her face.

Chapter Fifty-Six

Thursday, 19 December

A week after Polly waved a tearful goodbye to Tommy, Gloria had also said her goodbyes to her lover. But her farewells to Jack had had to be done under the cover of darkness and very much in private.

Gloria and Jack had held each other during a snatched hour after work on the evening before he left. They'd said that they each loved the other, and that they always would. Words, though, weren't really needed, as they both knew they could no longer deny their love for each other. Not any more.

For their short time together, standing in their regular meeting place in the entrance of the historic St Peter's Church, Jack had tried to appear strong, saying that it would not be long before they were together again and that time would fly. But his face had been awash with woe.

Gloria too had tried her hardest to appear brave, but inwardly she was also in bits. Her devastation and heartache at her lover's departure, however, had not just been down to losing her true love for the second time in her life, but because Gloria had been harbouring a secret, a wonderful, bittersweet secret, but a secret nonetheless, and one which she knew she had to keep from Jack.

She was pregnant with their baby – their love child. As she'd kissed her lover goodbye that night, it had broken her heart that she could not tell Jack her secret. And she'd so wanted to tell him, more than anything else in the world.

Gloria had known straight away that she was expecting. As soon as she had missed a period, her bust had seemed to swell up practically overnight, and she'd then been hit by the most intense tiredness. In a panic she had gone straight to the doctor, who'd said it was more than likely she was going to have a baby.

And there was no denying whose baby it was. She knew exactly when and where this baby had been conceived. The night Rosie's attacker had fallen into the river and drowned, another life had been created. Gloria hadn't needed to work out the dates; she had only made love to one man in the past two months and that was Jack.

Her physical relationship with her husband was practically non-existent. Most of the time Vinnie was too inebriated to either want or be able to make love to her, which suited Gloria just fine. Her love and her passion for her husband had been beaten out of her a long time ago, and although very occasionally she did what she saw as her duty as a wife, she and Vinnie had not had any kind of intimacy since well before the night Rosie's attacker had fallen into the river and her love for Jack had been resurrected.

Gloria had thought long and hard about what to do since finding out she was expecting. She didn't know how she would deal with a baby. She had thought her child-rearing days were well and truly over. She had, in fact, thought she was now too old to fall pregnant. There weren't many women in their early forties having children. They were more likely to be helping out looking after their grandchildren.

When Gloria had said goodbye to Jack, she had watched him walk away and had nearly called out after him and told him. But she hadn't, even though her heart had yearned to tell him that they were going to have a child together. A child made out of a real love, even if that love was a secret. A love which would be scandalous, looked down upon and judged. But thankfully Gloria had stopped herself calling after Jack that night, and she had let him go. She knew if she told Jack about the baby, he might have refused to go to America, and the war needed him more than she did.

Gloria had known she would miss Jack terribly, and for the first week after his departure she'd felt as if there were an immense void in her life which had left her feeling almost bereaved. But she'd put on her mental armour and soldiered on. She was tough. She'd had to be throughout her life. Her resilience was like a familiar garment that she wore well. And now, more than ever before, she needed to be hard. For now she had another life to look after, to protect.

Although she had realised for a long time that it was not safe to live under the same roof as Vinnie, it was only when he again became abusive and violent that Gloria had found the strength to finally make a stand. She realised now with clarity that it was because her own sense of self-worth was so low that she had never been able to put her own welfare first and leave him. Now all that had changed because it was no longer just about her, but about the safety of the baby growing inside of her.

The other night, as was usual after a skinful, Vinnie had kicked off about nothing in particular, and after working himself up into a frenzy he had released his pent-up frustrations and anger on Gloria. He had ended up punching her so hard in the stomach she had been sick. She had been terrified his brutality would cause her to miscarry – and had felt that her world would surely end then and there if she was to lose her and Jack's baby.

She had been overwhelmed by an incredible primal urge to protect her unborn child at all costs. So the next day she had gone into town and walked into a small, stuffy office, its walls lined with leather-bound books, and had done something she had never done before in her life – she had seen a solicitor. She didn't know anyone who had ever required any kind of legal help, and she had felt totally intimidated. But none of that mattered. The only thing which had mattered to her at that moment, and ever since, was her baby.

The solicitor had advised her well. It had cost her a week's overtime, but she had come out of it with an official-looking letter that she knew would scare Vinnie. It spelt out in no uncertain terms that if he did not leave, she would prosecute him for assault and battery. If he went quietly, she would let the matter drop.

Later on that day, when she had presented the letter to her husband, the look on Vinnie's face had been worth every penny of the solicitor's fee. It was the first time she'd realised how the power of words could be so much more devastating than a blow to the body. Vinnie had stood rooted to the spot as he'd read and reread the letter. His face had gone a bright red and Gloria had braced herself when she had seen his fists clench in anger. But, for the first time, he had held his temper.

She had already packed his bags in anticipation and had pulled them from behind the sofa and pushed them towards him. She hadn't uttered a word. There had been no need. The words printed on her solicitor's correspondence had spoken for her.

Vinnie had run his hand along their mantelpiece, smashing the few ornaments she owned as well as the framed photo of their two sons. He had jabbed his finger in her face, and spat out a load of bile and vitriol. But then he had picked up his bags and left, slamming the door so hard it seemed to shake not only their own house, but their neighbours' as well.

Gloria was so thankful and more than a little surprised at just how easily Vinnie had left the marital home. She put it down to the threat of being exposed and the potential involvement of the police, but she had a niggling feeling something else was afoot.

Her intuition had been proved right when a few days later one of her friends from the estate had popped round and told her that Vinnie had set up home with another woman who lived just ten minutes away in Grindon. It would seem that Vinnie had already had another woman, and had been seeing her for the past year.

Gloria had been bowled over with complete shock, especially when she'd found out Vinnie had not been visiting his ill mother in Gateshead all those weeks ago as he had claimed, but enjoying a break with his lover in a B&B in Seaham. Her first reaction had been a sense of utter disbelief that he had been so deceitful, but, moreover, that he had been able – and sober enough – to carry on such a long-term affair. But afterwards she'd been filled with an immense sense of relief – relief that it was unlikely he would try to come back to her – as well as a reprieve from her own feelings of guilt that she herself had been unfaithful.

As Gloria shut her front door and made her way to work, she looked up at the morning sky. The day's light was just starting to break through the remnants of the night's darkness. She would think of what to do as the weeks and months wore on and her bump grew and could no longer be disguised. When that happened she would let everyone think that the baby was Vinnie's, much as it pained her to do so. But it would at least give her time.

She hurried down the road to catch her bus into town. She thought about the day ahead and how she knew her workmates would be in good cheer, because today was going to be a day of celebration for the women and the whole of the shipyard.

Chapter Fifty-Seven

'Hurry up,' Dorothy shouted as the women all gathered up their belongings. 'We don't want to miss it!'

Today was special to all the women, for today they would see the first launch of a ship they had all worked on. A ship they had all helped to build.

'Calm down,' said Rosie. 'We've got loads of time.' She was now back with the women welders after her spell in the shipyard's management office. She had stayed there until Jack had left for America, after giving him whatever help he needed for the prototype of the new Liberty ship. But now he was gone she was happy to get back to what she knew best. Office life was not for her.

After collecting their things, the women welders all walked across to the quayside where most of the yard workers were headed. The magnificent beast of steel about to be unleashed into the water was a cargo vessel, to be used for the transportation of food and fuel back and forth across the Atlantic. Every worker in the yard had, in some way, contributed to the building of this four-hundred-foot-long ship, commissioned by the Ministry of Shipping.

From where the women were standing they could see the throngs of townsfolk gathering on the other side of the river and that it was now just about jam-packed with men, women and children lining the length of the south dock, all waiting to see this whale of a ship plough into the river before she was towed out for her trial run along the coast.

As the women welders took their place by the long stretch of thick black metal balustrades – which had so far escaped being melted down to boost dwindling stocks of steel and iron – Hannah perked up. 'So, tonight we are going to, how you say it, the flick?'

'The flicks, with an "s",' Dorothy corrected Hannah, adding excitedly, 'And yes, we are, so don't forget, everyone.' Dorothy raised her voice and looked at Gloria, Polly, Rosie and Martha. 'This evening we're all going to the Regal.'

'To see *Gone with the Wind*,' Hannah said, putting great emphasis on the 'with'.

Hannah's understanding of the English language was now very good, although it had taken her quite some time to get to grips with the area's very peculiar dialect and expressions. But she had improved tremendously since she had started at the yard, particularly so after finding her very own personal tutor in Dorothy.

As she tried in vain to spot her aunty Rina in the crowds on the other side of the river, she wished more than anything that her mother and father were here now. They would be so proud of her, amazed that she was doing the job she was doing.

Next to Hannah stood Dorothy, who kept shuffling around, trying to see over the heads of the thick swell of workers gathered around them. And next to Dorothy was Martha, who, seeing her workmate's frustration at not being tall enough to see over the crowd behind her, put her oversized hands around Dorothy's waist and lifted her up so she had a clear view across the expanse of the yard. Dorothy let out a squeal of laughter before she spotted who she was looking for.

'Angie! Over here!' Dorothy shouted out between giggles as Martha put her excited friend down with unusual grace.

Gloria had to smile as she saw Angie's bottle-blonde hair bob through the crowd of workers towards them. Over the past few weeks Dorothy and the crane operator Angie had become good friends, which had surprised them all. But, Gloria mused, they shouldn't have been all that shocked by the girls' burgeoning friendship. They were getting used to Dorothy defying expectations. None of them had thought she would last two minutes in the yards, never mind turn out to be the best and fastest welder in their group. And there was no denying they had all been totally taken aback by her gall when she'd given Eddie an ale shower in the middle of the pub. So when she and Angie had become good friends, it was not so surprising. Admittedly it had been Angie who'd initially approached Dorothy and told her how much she admired her for what she had done to Eddie and that afterwards she'd dumped the two-timing good-for-nothing pronto.

Gloria and the other women all agreed that Dorothy and Angie were frighteningly similar, and, in their own words, were 'double trouble', but they were also a great source of entertainment.

'Hi, Angie,' Gloria said, as Dorothy grabbed Angie and linked her arm so they were standing side by side. 'You not sick of this one yet?' she joked, nodding her head in Dorothy's direction.

'Nah,' Angie said. 'Not yet, but I think she'd do my nut in if I was working with her all day, every day. She's been trying to get me to join you lot, but I think I'll stick to driving cranes. It's easier, and I don't get any earache from anyone.'

Gloria laughed. Looking at Dorothy and Angie, she wondered if she had a daughter what she would be like. As she buttoned up her work coat – which was getting tighter by the day – she felt a sudden flush of nerves. She had already decided she was going to tell the women her news over their pre-cinema drink. She knew they would all be asking why she was drinking lemonade rather than her normal preferred tipple of port, and at the rate she was putting on weight, it wouldn't take them long to guess.

Besides, Gloria really wanted them to know. They were her friends, after all, and she wanted to share her secret with them, although she knew they would be more than a little taken aback. Women of her age just didn't get pregnant. Nor did they throw their husbands out of the marital home.

She had already imagined their individual reactions. Rosie would look determined and offer to help in any way she could. Polly would be shocked, but wouldn't show it. Hannah would take a little while to digest the information, as would Martha, before showing their solidarity, as well as their excitement about the baby.

And Dorothy, of course, would go into overdrive.

She would never have guessed when she first started as a trainee welder just how much her life would change. This yard had become many things to her. It had provided her with a sanctuary away from the brutality of her home life, and it had also given her the joy of friendship. And now it had given her another life growing inside of her.

As she surreptitiously touched her stomach under her work coat, Gloria realised for the first time in many years that she felt free.

Rosie looked about her and caught Gloria looking uncharacteristically pensive, and thought how well she looked. She seemed happy today, which made Rosie happy too as she knew how, out of all the women, Gloria had a particularly harsh home life. She had come to realise just why Gloria had wanted this job so much, and had stuck it out, despite her age and the long hours it demanded.

As her attention was drawn to the familiar shouts and noises which signalled that the ship was about to launch, Rosie looked at this grand vessel, this amazing piece of metal workmanship waiting to make its way down the slipway, and her chest literally lifted with pride. This town might have already taken a battering from Hitler's Luftwaffe, and been scarred with the sorrow of too many senseless deaths, but it was not giving in. This ship was another example of the town's defiance – its steely warrior spirit. It would never give in, and its people would continue building ships and fighting for what was right for as long as it took.

Rosie smelt the sea air and looked up to the flurry of seagulls squawking above them as if they too were excited by the ship's imminent launch. She wished Charlotte could be here too, but contented herself with a letter from her sister which had arrived yesterday, and which was now tucked safely in her coat's inside pocket, close to her heart.

Her eyes squinted in the winter sunlight, and, as they often did these days, they started to water. They would probably always be overly sensitive to light, but at least she was alive. And at least she still had her sight. She had suffered slight damage to her retinas, but she could live with that, just as she could live with the splashes of scars on her face. They were a small price to pay for her life.

Indeed for her *new* life.

When she had been recovering from her injuries Rosie had known deep down it was unlikely she would go back to her evening work. It was hardly surprising that after the night she had been attacked and had nearly died, her perspective on life had changed.

Her need, however, for money and survival hadn't.

Since then she had talked honestly with Lily, who had agreed that her scarred face could be disguised by make-up, but that, in her line of work, it was going to change her earning potential with the kind of clientele Lily's attracted. The men who came through the large oak door in Ashbrooke wanted to walk into a different world from the one they had just left. They wanted escapism. They didn't want to pay good money to see up close the real scars of what life could inflict on a person, of life's pain. They saw enough of that in reality.

But Rosie still needed to survive, and survive she would. She was determined to keep Charlotte in her boarding school, whatever it took. So when Lily had mentioned the possibility that she might be opening up a small, exclusive bordello in London's affluent red-light district, Rosie had got out the cut-crystal glasses from the armoire and fetched Lily's favourite Rémy Martin from the pantry and made her a business proposition.

Her idea had been aided thanks to DS Miller staying true to his word. After ascertaining that her uncle did not, in fact, have any living relatives who might have stood to inherit the money found in his bedsit, he had brought her a substantial wad of cash. Cash which was not just rightfully hers, but *was* actually hers: Rosie's hard-earned wages. Money which had nearly cost her her sanity, never mind her life. And because of that, Rosie was going to make damn sure it was used to the best possible advantage.

As she looked across the River Wear, she caught sight of an orange mop of hair. It could only be Lily, Rosie thought as she smiled to herself. Next to Lily stood George and some of the other girls.

Just at that moment Lily caught sight of Rosie and waved to her with such enthusiasm that she nearly knocked the hat off the woman she was standing next to.

'Oh, Ma's just been clobbered by some woman with the most amazing hair,' Polly laughed to Rosie, who was beside her.

Rosie broke into a big smile. The two women who had shown her such care and kindness had unwittingly ended up standing shoulder to shoulder with each other, and in true fashion Lily had managed to nearly knock poor Agnes's block off. Lily still had a long way to go before she managed to emulate a chic Parisian madam. Her cockney roots would always get in the way, and Rosie hoped they always would. One day she hoped Lily and Agnes would meet. It might be too much of a stretch, but she would love the two to become friends. They might be complete opposites in many ways, but they were also remarkably similar. And, what's more, they had both been there for Rosie when she'd needed it the most.

'Is that Arthur, Tommy's granddad, there as well?' Rosie asked Polly. She could just about make out the outline of a tall, grey-haired old man standing next to Agnes, Bel and Lucille.

'Yes, that's Arthur. He's become part of the furniture since Tommy left,' Polly joked, but Rosie heard a sadness in her friend's voice. She knew Polly's heart yearned for the man she loved.

'He'll come back,' she said quietly to Polly.

Tears started to come into Polly's eyes. She stared straight ahead, forcing them back. 'I'd love him to be here now – even if it was just to see this launch.'

'Where's your ring?' Rosie asked.

She knew Polly couldn't wear her engagement ring to work, but carried it with her all the time.

Polly reached into the top pocket of her overalls and fished out the beautiful ruby engagement ring Tommy had slipped to her when they had said their rushed farewells at

362

the train station. He had written to her when he'd arrived at his training digs in Portsmouth and explained that the ring had been his grandma Flo's engagement ring, and that it had been Arthur's bidding that he give it to Polly.

'Put it on,' Rosie said, 'then at least a part of him will be here with you today.'

Polly slipped the ring on and smiled.

At that moment there was a loud smashing sound as the ship was officially launched by a suited dignitary who performed the long-held tradition of smashing a bottle of champagne against its bow.

There were loud, jubilant shouts of 'There she goes!' and 'God bless all who sail in her!' as the enormous vessel slowly started down the slipway. Gaining momentum, it sliced into the murky river water, causing enormous waves at either side to splash against the walls of the dock, spraying those nearest to the quayside with a shower.

Polly touched her ring while she watched the tugboats gently guide the ship through the mouth of the river and into the North Sea, and made a wish for Tommy's safe return. He had just completed two weeks of intensive training and been shipped out to Gibraltar. That was all Tommy was allowed to tell her in his letters. But even though they were miles apart, Polly still felt that nearness she had always felt from the start with Tommy, from the moment they had caught each other's eye all those months ago, just a few feet away from where she now stood.

Watching the huge cargo ship turn into the expanse of the North Sea, Polly felt as if it signified the end of a part of her life, but also the start of another.

Her work at the yard had brought her such intense highs and lows, such heartfelt happiness and gut-wrenching sadness. And, of course, such terrifying drama. She could never have imagined that her determination to work here would enrich her life so much more than she had ever expected.

She had succeeded in becoming an important cog in the war effort, and she had also become a part of her family's long-standing legacy in the shipyards.

But most of all, her work in the shipyard had also brought her something she had never thought she would find.

Love.

And that wasn't just the love she had been lucky enough to find with Tommy, but also the love of true friendship.

'Come on then, you lot.' Rosie's voice broke through Polly's reverie. Polly looked at Rosie, Gloria, Dorothy, Hannah and Martha and saw them all as a strange family of sorts. A family of friends, who were bonded by so much more than blood. And it was a bond, like their welds, that was steely strong and totally unbreakable.

'Let's go and have a quick toast down the Admiral,' Rosie said, 'and then off to the Regal. We're going to see this *Gone with the Wind* if it *bloody kills us!*'

The women all chuckled as Dorothy let out a loud 'Hurrah!'

Find out more about

Nancy Revell

Read on for an insight into *The Shipyard Girls,*
plus the chance to sign up to find out more about
Nancy and our other saga authors...

Dear Reader,

I hope you've really enjoyed the first instalment of *The Shipyard Girls* and will be joining the women as they continue to ride the ups and downs of love and life both in and outside of J.L. Thompson and Sons shipyard.

For me, what I love most about Polly, Rosie, Gloria, Dorothy, Hannah and Martha is the steely bond they have formed, despite their different personalities and backgrounds, as well as the sense of love, care and loyalty they have for each other. I think we could all benefit in this day and age from having a 'family of friends' in our lives.

During my research for the book, I was heartened to hear that this kind of camaraderie and support in times of need – as well as simply enjoying a good old chinwag – was very real for the shipyard workers during the Second World War – and, indeed, for those employed in the Wearside yards both before and after the conflict.

I was lucky enough to find one woman who was employed at the Austin & Pickersgill shipyard in Sunderland during the war, a lovely lady called Joan Tate, and what struck me when we started chatting about her time there was how her face instantly lit up as she recalled the memories she had. It was also telling that the first words she spoke about her experiences there was to describe the playful banter and the sense of togetherness.

The romantic in me was heartened to hear that just like Polly, Joan also found the love of her life in the shipyards – a man who she went on to marry and have children with.

My research for this new saga series has also taken me on my own personal journey of discovery as my mum comes from a long line of shipbuilders. Both my grandfather, great-grandfather, and great-great-grandfather all worked in the Sunderland shipyards, as did most of their sons and relations.

My own father also served his apprenticeship at North Eastern Marine Engineering on the South Dock in the late fifties early sixties, and shortly after moving back up to my hometown last year he took me for a tour of the now barren area where he had learnt his trade as a tool maker.

Although it's a real shame the shipyards are practically non-existent now, the River Wear still has a magical quality about it and over the years other businesses have flourished, reshaping the river banks where once there were shipyards.

The culturally-acclaimed National Glass Centre, constructed solely from glass and steel, now stands in place of the J.L. Thompson shipyard, next to which is the University of Sunderland, which enjoys enviable views over the river and out to the North Sea.

The historical St Peter's Church, which first introduced glass making into Britain, and where Jack and Gloria seek solitude and rekindle their love for each other, is now a popular tourist attraction as one of the country's first Anglo-Saxon stone churches.

What also remains unchanged is the beautiful stretch of coast along which Tommy takes Polly on the back of his bike. The stunning beaches of Roker and Seaburn have just been given the Blue Flag award 2016 for their high water quality, cleanliness and amenities.

And, the Bungalow Cafe overlooking the harbour, where Polly and Tommy go on their first proper date, is still a thriving little tea shop.

I'm now writing the second book in *The Shipyard Girls* series which follows the women as they stick together and help each other through the highs and lows of the first tumultuous six months of 1941. There is also the return to the Elliot household of Polly's brother Joe, whose arrival back home has a great impact on those around him – as does the unexpected arrival of Bel's mother, Pearl.

I hope you will come with me and join the women – and the men – as they continue to fight adversity on the Home Front.

With love,

Nancy x

History Notes

During World War Two seven hundred women worked in the Sunderland shipyards carrying out dangerous and backbreaking jobs such as welding, riveting, burning and rivet catching, as well as general labouring, operating cranes, and painting.

The work, which had previously only been deemed suitable for men, was not only carried out by unmarried young women, but also by married mothers, many of whom had just waved the men in their family off to war.

These women chose to undertake such difficult and often perilous jobs in the yards, not only because they needed to work – but also because they wanted to be a part of the war effort – often working time and a half, seven days a week in order to repair and build ships desperately needed to win the war.

Many war babies and children were looked after by neighbours and older siblings so that their mother could work long shifts in the shipyards – and sometimes even a second job at night.

The conditions in which the women laboured were harsh and hazardous, with scant regard paid to health and safety. They also had to contend with constant air strikes by Hitler's Luftwaffe, and many of the women workers would do so with the added worry that their children were in another part of the town.

The yards in the 'Biggest Shipbuilding Town in the World' produced a quarter of Britain's merchant shipping at the time, causing it to become one of the most heavily bombed towns during the war.

It is believed that without the shipyards, the country would have been forced to surrender, as the cargo vessels being built were essential for the transportation of vital food, fuel and minerals, as well as taking troops to wherever they were needed in the fight against the Axis alliance of Germany, Italy and Japan.

During the war years, Sunderland's shipbuilding industry won Royal and political praise, and the town was also credited with producing Doxford

Engines, known for their efficiency and reliability, while J.L. Thompson developed the prototype of the American Liberty Ship.

Initially the women's induction into the yards was made even more difficult by the authorities who were opposed to the idea. A lot of men in positions of influence were very keen to protect the traditions of ship-building on the Wear. They wanted to protect the jobs for men returning from service and so were opposed to offering the jobs to women as they did not know what would happen when the men returned.

Women were eventually offered work in the yards, even if some people were reluctant. Many, however, were referred to as 'dilutees'. This title was given to imply that one woman could not offer the same skills as one man and so ensured the women would not be able to continue in the jobs when the men returned.

Interestingly, in a report in the *Sunderland Echo* in 1942 it revealed: 'At keeping the place tidy, sweeping up and so on, the women are, not surprisingly, better than the men. But those in skilled and semi-skilled work have also done well, and I have heard of machinists who have turned out far more work, of as good quality, than the men. Indeed, I have been told of one woman who produced as much work as six men – and she was a married woman who, after her day's work, went home to look after her family.'

It is perhaps a sad omission in our history books that the remarkable women who did some of the most dangerous work in both the First and Second World War, have now died with little recognition or praise for the work they did and the conditions they encountered.

Let us not forget the brave and inspirational women who played such an important role in such a crucial period of our history.

To find out more about Nancy and her books,
you can join our mailing list by sending in your
name and contact details (address and email) to:

Saga books,
Random House,
20 Vauxhall Bridge Road,
London,
SW1V 2SA